Time Stands Still

EMI LOST & FOUND SERIES
BOOK TWO

Photography and Cover Design : Christi Allen Curtis
Photography Assistant : Katrina Boone

Lori L. Otto Publications

Visit our website at: www.loriotto.com
Third Edition: May 2016

Printed in the United States of America

DEDICATION

to the friends who feel like sisters:

clarinda

katie

BOOK TWO
EMI

CHAPTER 1

"Nate?" I say frantically, pushing his shoulder gently in an attempt to wake him. I lean over him, slightly disoriented, looking at the peaceful expression on his face. I hadn't meant to fall asleep, but I couldn't keep my eyes open any longer. "Nate, wake up," I urge him again, my voice louder. He continues to lie there, seemingly comfortable, his breathing slow and deep. His forehead is dotted with perspiration. By looking at him, I can't even tell we were in an accident. There are no visible signs of his injuries, but I know they're there.

"Come on, Nate," I say one more time. I struggle free from the crisp sheets I'm tangled in and climb up to him, placing my lips on his. They're still, make no attempt to match the movement of my own. I can still feel his breath, though, and I'm comforted by that. I straddle one of his legs and kneel over him, careful to avoid the left side of his body.

Suddenly, I feel his hand moving up the back of my leg, up my pearl-colored silk pajama shorts, his fingers tucking under my lace underwear. I grab

1

it forcefully and hold it still. He opens one of his eyes tentatively, a smile spreading across his face, which appears slightly tanned, contrasting against the stark white pillowcase his head lays upon.

"Damn it, Nate!" I laugh. "Have you been awake this whole time?" I slap his chest harder than I intend to.

He breathes in quickly through his teeth, wincing, but letting out a quiet laugh. "Careful," he warns me softly.

"I'm sorry," I tell him. "But you deserve it. I thought something had happened to you!"

"I'm fine, Emi," he says.

"But the doctor said you're not allowed to sleep because of the concussion."

"*I* didn't fall asleep, baby. *You* did. I just watched you," he tells me as I curl up next to him, my leg resting on his thighs. His right arm pulls me in tightly.

"Are you feeling okay? Do you need anything?"

"I'm fine."

"Does your head hurt?"

"Emi, I'm fine," he repeats.

"How does your rib feel?" I ask him, pulling back the sheets and touching the large colorless bandage on his ribcage gently.

"Broken, I guess," he says. "That's fine, too, as long as I don't move or get beat up by my girlfriend... or laugh."

"You'll let me know if you need anything, though..."

"Right now, the drugs are keeping me completely relaxed. The only thing I need is you, Emi," he tells me, attempting to shift his body slightly. He groans, grimacing in pain, and pokes me a few times in the side to get my attention. "Kiss me again."

I assume my position of leaning over him again, careful to put no weight on his body, and oblige him. He holds my head to his with his right hand. He tries to lift his other arm, but it's obvious the strain on his ribs is too much.

"We were lucky," he says.

"Yes, very," I admit.

"I'm glad you weren't hurt, Em," he says sweetly.

"I'm sorry you were," I respond.

"What this?" he says, acting overly-confident. "This is nothing." We both smile at one another, and I'm lost in his stare. For a brief second, it pierces through me, almost scares me, as my heart literally skips a beat.

"What?" he asks.

"Nothing," I smile, looking away. "Is this not the most beautiful day?" I ask him, staring out the large window in his apartment. "Look out there. There is not a cloud in the sky. Everything just looks so clear and vibrant... and happy. Even the sun seems brighter. I can barely look out the window it's so bright."

"Maybe near-death experiences make life look better."

"My life has never looked so good," I tell him, kissing him again. I pull away to look at him once more. His eyes are focused down my ivory nightshirt, hanging open as I hover over him.

"Mine either," he smiles slyly. "*So* good..." He puts his hand down my shirt, touches me, moans quietly.

"Nate," I whisper, a lame attempt to stop him from doing something I desperately want him to do. "The doctor said no vigorous activities, remember?"

"I'll be careful," he says. "I am just so grateful right now, Emi. I want to be close to you. I want to feel you, make sure you're here, that you're real, that you're fine."

"I am," I smile as he unbuttons my shirt.

"That was really scary," he says, serious. He tugs at the sleeve of my shirt, and I take it off for him, saving him the trouble. "Let me look at you."

I sit up and allow his eyes to inspect me. They slowly scan every inch, every millimeter of my torso, his fingers brushing lightly against my stomach, then my breasts.

"Not a scratch," he smiles. "Your skin is still perfect." He sighs. "Emi, I don't know what I would do if I had lost you... or if we had lost the baby. My god, we're lucky," he repeats.

"I don't even want to think about it," I tell him, bringing his hand back down to my abdomen, intertwining our fingers and pressing his palm against it. "We are all fine."

"I just can't believe we walked away from that," he says. "The car was completely totaled. You really didn't see it?"

"No," I tell him. I find it a happy coincidence that I can't remember any details of the accident. I don't try too hard to remember them, either. I just want to focus on how blessed we are to have each other. "I don't want to think about it."

He nods, and again his eyes, this strange, vacant stare startles me, causes me to shiver. I tuck my head into his chest to escape his haunting gaze.

"Are you okay?" he asks, flinching again as he bends slightly to pull the white down comforter up over us. "Lie down, baby."

I tuck my body next to his again, my arm resting comfortably across him. He pushes through the pain and moves his left hand to rest next to mine, takes it into his, rubbing my fingers slowly. I watch the rise and fall of his chest as he breathes, listen to his strong heartbeat pounding against my ear. When I close my eyes, I can still see the bright sun against my eyelids. As soon as I begin to wonder how I'll be able to sleep with all the light in this room, I feel the exhaustion of the night overwhelming me, quickly.

Letting my mind wander to the wonderful time we shared together at the hotel last night, warmth spreads over me, comfort sets in. Nate was in bed with me, his arms wrapped tightly around my naked body, his irrepressible smile lit only by a dim lamp on the hotel room night stand. The smell of his cologne lingered around me, his perspiration mixed with my own. His voice was thick with affection as he whispered the words in my ear, "God, I love you, Emi," before his head collapsed on the pillow next to mine.

I pull the white comforter up a little more, snuggle closer, hold on tighter to him... to everything I know of him. *God, I love you, too, Nate.*

"Love ya, Em." His voice is strained, as if the air has been stolen from his lungs. I smile, recognizing that he has the same effect on me. He draws another deep breath, one last phrase escaping his lips as he succumbs to sleep. "Hold me."

I shouldn't let him sleep, but I can't fight my own exhaustion any longer. I wrap my arms tightly around him, the sound of his pulse fading quickly as I lose consciousness.

~ * ~

It's still terribly bright when I open my eyes again. One of my arms is clutching tightly to a pillow, the other in a cast. *I wonder when that happened?* Nate is no longer next to me, is nowhere to be found. I look around the white room and realize it's not his room. I'm in a hospital. Bouquets of flowers line a shelf next to the window. Then I realize my leg is also wrapped tightly, restricting any movement. I turn my head to the left to see my brother sleeping in a chair in the corner of the room.

"Chris?" I say, the sound scratchy and foreign. I'm very thirsty. "Chris?" I say louder, and he lifts his head, and then quickly runs to my side.

"Emi," he cries, relieved. "My god, you're awake. Emi, how do you feel?"

"I'm thirsty," I tell him. He picks up a small cup and pours water in it from a pitcher. He finds a straw nearby and places it in the cup, holding it to my lips. I drink it all and ask for more.

"Do you hurt? Are you in pain?" he asks.

"A little," I tell him. "What happened? Where's Nate? He was just here." I survey the room again, still a little startled at my unfamiliar surroundings. "Or I was... there?" *We were at his loft... why am I here?*

He stares at me silently, looking confused. "You don't remember?" he asks.

"No," I laugh, the movement of my muscles causing more pain than I expected. "Where exactly am I?"

"At Methodist General Hospital. In the ICU," he says, sitting on the bed with me, taking my non-bandaged hand into his.

"And why exactly am I here? I mean, I see the casts, but... what happened?"

"Emi," he hesitates.

"Did you say ICU?" I interrupt, just now putting meaning to his words.

"You've been in a coma... Emi, what *do* you remember?"

"I remember your engagement party last night... and Nate's band played for you guys... and then he and I left the party for a few minutes..." My brother didn't need to know the details... he didn't need to know that the time Nate and I shared together last night was the most amazing, most satisfying, of my life. That secret was left for me and Nate. I'm sure he wouldn't want to hear about it anyway.

"And then... there's a gap in time. I remember waking up next to him this morning. I know there has been an accident... but I can't remember it. He does, but I don't... but he said it was bad."

"What do you mean, Emi? Who remembers?"

"Nate. He said we were lucky. Where is he, anyway?"

"Emi, the party was on Monday," he tells me.

"Okay... well what day is it now?"

"It's Thursday, sis. You were in a coma for three days."

"How did I fall into a coma? It was Nate that wasn't supposed to sleep, with his concussion. Did something else happen? I mean, where did these casts come from... and where is he?"

My brother shakes his head, the movement so slow and subtle I barely catch it. "Oh, god," he starts, speaking softly, swallowing audibly.

"What?"

"Emi, I don't think you're remembering things... clearly."

"I know. I can't remember an accident at all. But Nate says that's a good thing." I smile, thankful that my brain has apparently shielded me from something pretty horrible... pretty scary.

"When did you talk to him again?" Chris asks, his eyes begging to understand.

"The morning after the accident. Which I thought was this morning... but I guess not. I've apparently slept since then," I joke with him.

"No, Emi, you were already in the hospital then."

"When? When was I admitted to the hospital?"

"The night of the accident," he says.

"No," I laugh. "Nate and I were at his apartment the next morning. I'm guessing something else happened after that? Was there another accident or something? Why isn't he here?" I realize he still hasn't answered that question.

Did he fall asleep after all? Was it the concussion? My breathing becomes shallow.

"Emi, you were brought here directly from the accident scene on New Year's Eve. You've been in a coma ever since. We've been worried sick."

"No," I argue. "I mean, you weren't there. I think you're confused. Nate and I were definitely together."

"Stop, Emi. I'm not confused. I think–" His next intake of air is shaky as his eyes widen and his jaw drops, a look of terror coming over his face. In one quick moment, he grasps the metal railing of the bed tightly with one hand and pushes a button on the wall with the other. "I think we need a nurse," he says hurriedly.

My brows furrow in an effort to understand his demeanor, but he averts his gaze quickly, pacing nervously, his eyes darting around the room in obvious avoidance of mine.

"I'm fine," I argue. "Where is Nate?" I ask, demand. He grabs my hand again, squeezing it tightly, as the speed of my breathing increases immeasurably, along with my pulse.

"Emi, do you remember leaving the party that night?"

"Yes, I told you already, I remember that part. We went upstairs to our room," I tell him, blushing as a flash of our night together fills my vision. "Where is Nate?" I repeat, becoming impatient.

"And do you remember leaving your room? Leaving the hotel, maybe?" A tear falls from his eye. I don't remember the last time I saw my brother cry.

"No." I try harder to fill in the increasingly-obvious blanks brought on by the last three days. I remember making love to Nate. I remember it so clearly, so vividly. I remember waking up in his arms the morning after. He was hurt, but he would be okay. I was fine, too. He said there had been an accident. My days are getting messed up... *when was this?* Whenever that was, I wasn't in plaster casts like I am now. That morning in his bed, that's the last memory I have. "Come on, Chris, where's Nate?" It's impossible for me to hide the building panic in my voice.

Anxious and determined, I try to sit up quickly, but the tubes tethering me to the bed pull against me, and my sudden movements cease immediately, thwarted by a sharp pain in my good arm and a sickeningly dizzy head rush. I feel Chris putting his hands on my shoulders, steadying me, pushing me carefully back toward the hard and lumpy pillow.

"Emi, calm down," he says softly. "Just lie down. I'm trying." He swallows hard. "You both left the hotel, together," he begins. I close my eyes in an effort to see the events of that night as he talks. Instead, I see Nate smiling beneath me the morning after, his face bathed in the bright, warm sunlight. I sigh as I feel his hand on my thigh, a flash of heat spreading over my body. "You went to the store, do you remember that?" my brother's voice snaps me back to the present.

"No," I begin to cry, tears of frustration. "Chris, please, just tell me where Nate is."

"Emi," he squeezes my hand tighter and pauses, obviously searching for the right words but clearly not wanting to say them. "God damn it, where is the fucking nurse?"

"What is it, Chris?"

"Emi, I don't know how to tell you this..."

My chest gets tight.

"I didn't want to be the one to tell you."

"Tell me what?"

"Nate is gone, Em," he blurts quickly. A deafening silence fills the room. His words make no sense to me. I know he's not gone. I was just with him. It was just the two of us. Maybe my brother just didn't know he was okay.

"No," I choke out in disbelief. "No, you're wrong."

"Em..."

"I was just with him..." I mumble. "He's okay." *Why wouldn't Chris know this?*

"No, you weren't," he returns. "And he's not... okay. He's... not with us... anymore. Oh, Emi," my brother breaks down, his head bowed to the floor, his tears dropping on my hospital gown.

"He's at his apartment, Chris, I know he is. Has anyone looked there?"

"He's not there, Emi," he says sternly.

"He *is* there! I was there! I *saw* him!" I struggle to get up, again wrestling with the tubes and wires and really heavy casts. "Help me out of here. I'll take you to him."

"Stop, Emi!" I continue to fight, wishing my *fucking* arm wasn't in this *fucking* cast, keeping me from pulling away from these *fucking* tethers! Chris walks abruptly to the door and yells down the hallway. "Where is the god damn nurse?!"

"Let me up!"

"Emi, just... don't move. I don't know what all those tubes are doing, but if one of those is keeping you alive... fuck," he sighs. "I can't lose you, too." He collapses back on the chair he had been sleeping on, his head in his hands.

"You haven't lost anyone, though," I say to him... attempting to sound positive and upbeat, but the rapidity of my heartbeat is telling me that something isn't quite right.

"We've lost Nate," he sighs, slumped over, sounding annoyed and resigned. "He's... he's dead, Emi."

"No," I say quickly, trying to erase his words. "He said he'd never leave me, Chris," I explain through tears that flow freely out of nowhere. "And I know he meant it. He's not gone. He was just here, with me, in bed."

"Emi, no. He wasn't. And it wasn't his choice to leave you. I'm sure he didn't want to go," he attempts to soothe me by sitting down next to me and holding my good hand tightly.

"No, Chris, you don't understand, he promised he'd never leave!" I sob, loudly, heavily, and he leans over the bed to put his arms around me. "He was just here! He is fine! He has a concussion... some cracked ribs... but he survived!" I try to fill my lungs with air, but the lump in my throat is so big, so painful that I can't even inhale. "Chris, I can't breathe," I cry. "I need Nate."

"Emi, he's not here," he tells me again.

"No, he's not gone. I need him. I need him, Chris. I can't live without him. Please get him. I need him."

Two nurses in scrubs enter the room, and Chris backs away from the bed.

"She said she can't breathe," he tells them. "And I think she's hallucinating or hysterical or something."

"I'm not... why are you lying!?" I yell at him.

"I don't know what to do," he continues to cry, his hands pulling at his hair. One of the nurses ushers him out the door, then returns to my side, restraining me.

He can't be gone, he can't be gone, he can't be gone. I just repeat the words in my head, sure that they will bring him back. Am I dreaming, is this a nightmare? We just made love, we just *fell* in love. I love him and he loves me. He is not gone.

I close my eyes tightly until I see him here with me again. *God, I love you.* I reach out for him, trying to touch him, but he seems so distant even though he's right next to me in his bed. His smile is enough to soothe me, to stop my sobbing... comforted again by my love, I suddenly become very tired and allow myself to sleep, knowing he's with me.

~ * ~

"Emi?" a woman's voice wakes me. I peek over at Nate as we exchange smiles. He touches my cheek and nods before I try to roll over to see who's calling my name.

My head hurts so badly at my efforts, and I decide I don't want to move, much less open my eyes to let any light in. They well up with tears that immediately fall down my cheeks. *Why am I crying?* I struggle to figure out where I am. *Why is a woman saying my name?* Wasn't I with Nate, in his loft? When I open my eyes to survey my surroundings, I recognize the hospital room and remember the conversation that I had with Chris in this very room.

"Nate?" I ask, looking wildly for him. He was just here. Where could he have gone so quickly?

"He's not here," the woman says. I turn my head to finally see who's talking to me.

"Teresa?" I say. "What are you doing here?"

"I came to visit you."

10

"Where did Nate go?" I ask her, not quite awake, feeling his absence immediately.

"Em..."

"He was at his apartment, right? Just like I told Chris he would be... right?"

"No," she whispers.

"Where's Chris?" I ask her, suddenly annoyed that she is here with me and not my brother, the only one I've told of Nate's whereabouts. I can't expect her to know what's going on. "Where's my family?"

"Em, do you remember what happened?"

"Sure, Teresa, I remember a lot, but no one wants to fucking believe me. There was an accident, whatever. Nate and I were together after that."

"But you don't remember the accident..."

"No, Teresa, I don't remember," I snap at her. "I know Chris thinks something horrible happened–" I don't even allow my brain to go there– "but he's wrong." I tell her, my voice becoming louder. "What day is it?" I ask her.

"It's Friday, Emi," she says, shifting uncomfortably on the bed next to me. "Emi, I'm so sorry," she says, starting to cry. "Chris is right."

"He's not," I argue, giving no credence to her statement. "Nate has been here, hasn't he? He's come to see me? He was just here..." *Wasn't he?*

"No, he wasn't. He hasn't. He couldn't–"

"Well, I don't know what's going on, but I know he's okay. He told me so himself." *What the fuck is going on? What is wrong with everyone?*

"Emi, I'm sorry. I don't know what to say. He's gone, sweetie."

"I get that he's gone," I tell her through gritted teeth. "His whereabouts seem to be in question. He's somewhere. I don't know why he hasn't come to see me during the days to show you all he's fine, but he's been sleeping with me at night. I know that.

"I mean, I was just with him," I remind her after a few deep breaths. "I don't understand what's happening."

"They said you two left in his car," she says, recalling the events of that night, not acknowledging my statements. "You went to the store or something... and when the light turned green, he drove out into the intersection, and another car went through a red light and hit his car, on his side."

I hear her words, but have no recollection of this. All I can do is shake my head. Since I can't even focus on anything through the tears, and since my head is pounding, I just close my eyes. My heart jumps as Nate appears again, his body a dark shadow against the brilliant sun. His familiar features come into focus as he comes closer to kiss my forehead and dab my cheeks with a tissue, but a stream of tears continues to move down my face.

I jump at the feel of someone else touching my face and open my eyes abruptly. Teresa takes a tissue, attempts to dry them, tries to stop them from falling. *What the fuck?*

"Where did he go?" I whisper, disoriented.

"He died there, on the scene," she informs me.

"No, just now..." My voice fades quickly, my heart pounding. *He was just here... but I know, deep down, he wasn't...* "What did you say?"

"That he..." She swallows hard. "That he died at the scene."

"It just didn't happen," I tell her. "We woke up together after that. He had some broken ribs... I was fine..."

"Emi," she hesitates, "I'm not sure that really happened..."

"But we were together the next morning," I plead, wanting someone to listen to me, to understand that I saw him. That I was with him. That he *was still alive.*

"No, you weren't," she explains. "You were here, Emi. I was here, with you, with your family and friends. Nate was gone. Maybe you dreamed that you were together..."

"It was too real to be a dream." *I don't understand.* "And if it was, well, then let me go back there. Let me dream forever," I begin to sob. "I need him. You don't understand," I mumble to her. "Where is Chris? Surely he found him." I'm grasping, I know.

"He's at the funeral," she tells me, "with your family."

"No, no, no, no..." I cry. "Nooo..." I moan.

"Oh, Emi, I know," she says, holding my hand.

"My head hurts, Teresa, and I want to sleep." *Get me back to him, God.*

Help me find him. He's here, I know he's here. Take me to him. I don't want to be anywhere but with him. Let me be with him.

"Do you want me to get a nurse?" I nod.

When the nurse arrives, Teresa tells them I'm very upset, that I want to sleep. She acts like I'm not even in the room, like I can't hear her, but I can... But I do want to sleep, and the nurse can make that happen.

"Emi, honey?" the nurse asks. I direct my eyes to hers. She has very kind eyes. "Emi, can I get you something?"

"Just Nate," I tell her, and begin to cry uncontrollably again. "He's the only thing I want."

"I know, baby, I know," she rubs my arm. "Do you want to sleep?" I nod. A few minutes later, my body feels heavy, and the world becomes black again before he comes back into focus. Nate's brown eyes stay with me before he ducks his head into the pillow, disappearing from my field of vision. I cling to him with all the strength I have.

~ * ~

The next time I wake up, it's dark in the room. I immediately know where I am. I immediately know the circumstances that brought me here– or at least I know what people have told me. Still, I see this vivid image of Nate in the hotel room, leaning over me in the bed, his naked body next to mine. He was gazing into my eyes, and the way he looked at me... I knew he loved me, completely. I remember him moving a strand of hair from my eyes. I remember him kissing my forehead, touching my breasts, smiling at me, telling me he loved me. *God, I love you, Emi.* That was what he had said. I remember the words, every inflection, the look on his face when he said it before his head collapsed on the pillow next to mine.

I remember the morning after... when he confirmed that we were okay... that we were lucky.

"I'm sorry," a man's voice whispers through the darkness. "What have I done?" I mistakenly thought I was alone... and I don't recognize the voice.

"Who is that?"

"Emi?" the man asks, surprised.

"Who are you?" I question nervously, wishing I could move to turn on some lights. My body is weak, though, and my stomach is nagging me with dull cramps.

"It's, uh, Jack." I pull the blankets tight against me, uncomfortable. *Who? And why is he here? What is he sorry for?* "I'm Chris's friend. We met briefly at the party," he explains further, likely sensing my fear.

"Where's my brother?"

"He just stepped out a minute ago to get some coffee," he explains. "He hasn't left your side in thirty-six hours."

"What day is it?" I ask, clutching my stomach curiously at this feeling I've never felt before.

"It's early Monday morning, about three o'clock." I slept for two-and-a-half days. Visions of Nate in his sunny loft filter in and out, hazily. Was I dreaming? Was I there? Was he here? I wonder how many more days I'll have to sleep through until I get to be with Nate again. "Emi, can I get you anything? Water?" *You can get out of my room.* I don't even bother to answer.

After a few minutes of silence, the unfamiliar voice cuts through the darkness again. "I just sent Chris a text message. He's on his way back up." I stare at the bouquets of flowers. In the moonlight, they all just look grey. Grey daisies, grey roses, grey lilies... a few grey potted plants. Everything looks ugly, lifeless.

"Thanks, man," I hear Chris enter the room.

"Anytime," his friend says. "Call me if you need anything."

"Thanks."

"Goodnight, Emi." Again, there's no use in talking to him.

"Why hasn't Nate come by?" I step on the end of Chris's friend's goodbye, unable to wait any longer to ask the question.

Chris walks into view, obscuring the seemingly-dead flowers. I tear my eyes away from the bright moon outside and search my brother's face as I wonder quietly where Nate is. Does he see this moon?

"Emi," he begins with a sigh. "Are you hungry, Em? They've been tube-feeding you for days, you have to be hungry." Maybe I am, but his avoidance of my question makes me sick to my stomach. I remember what he told me before, and go back to staring into the vast nothingness in front of me. My life means nothing now if what he had said is true. I don't answer him.

Chris sits down on the bed. "Mom and Dad and Jen, they want to see you, Em. Donna, too. I called them on my way up. They're on their way."

"I don't want to see anyone but him."

"I know," he says. "Mom and Dad have been here all weekend, hoping you'd wake up. They just left the hospital a few hours ago."

"I don't care."

"Sure you do, Em."

"I don't care about anything but Nate. Why hasn't he come?"

"He can't," Chris answers. "Don't you remember?"

"I don't believe it. I was there, with him. I told you."

"I know," he whispers, and I hear his voice waver. "Emi, this is hard on all of us."

"Don't even say that. You have no idea."

"I don't, Emi. I know that. But he meant something to all of us."

"Don't say that like he's not still with us," I warn him. I need proof, hard proof that he's gone. *But what would that be?*

We cry together. He hugs me, and with his help, I find the strength to sit up in the bed, holding on to him for dear life. "I hate to see you like this," he chokes out his words. "I would do anything to take it away, Em. If there was a way."

"I want him back," I whisper, my tears beginning to soak his shirt. "He's out there, somewhere."

"No, Emi. I can't bring him back," he cries.

"Then I want to find him. I want to be where he is."

"Oh, Emi, don't say that..."

"I belong with him. My life is... *his*..."

"We love you, Emi. Your life is yours, live for us."

"I love him so much," I tell him.

"He loves you, too, Emi."

I immediately pick up on the present tense of his verb. "He loves me? So he *is* here..." *I knew he was...*

"Loved you," he corrects himself, his head in his hands. "He said... before he..." Chris stutters, pauses mid-sentence.

"What?"

"You called me from the car, Emi, after the wreck... you didn't say anything to me... just dialed my number, I guess. When I answered, I heard you talking to him, comforting him. I heard you... I listened... the last thing he said, Emi..." He starts to cry again. "The last thing he said was, 'Love ya, Em. Hold me.'"

"No," I whisper, trying hard to decipher what did and did not happen. "No, Chris. Tell me again, what did you say?"

"He said, 'Love ya, Em.' And then he asked you to hold him." *How could Chris know that? How could he know what Nate said to me that morning?* I remember us in bed, how I held him tightly in my arms... my ear on his chest, listening...

"And then what?"

"And then, nothing... just silence... I thought I..."

Listening to his pulse, fading... fading as I fell asleep... my breath races, air straining to get through my tightening throat. My heart stops and I feel nauseous, thoughts of reality and fantasy whirling sickeningly through my muddled mind.

I can't remember the accident... could this... *dream*... somehow be my altered memory of the accident? Could he have said those words to me as he lay dying? Did he die in my arms?

"He's not coming, is he?" I force the words out, forcing the reality in that I had been fighting off for days.

"No, he's not, Em."

"Oh, god, why?" I sob. "Why him? Why me? Why did God take him from me?"

"I don't know, Emi."

"And why didn't He take me, too?"

"Maybe He has something else planned for you, Em." I hear the door creak open and see my mom, stepdad, dad and sister walking into the room. Jen finds the lamp and turns it on, then sits down on the bed, opposite from Chris. She joins in our hug.

"Oh, Emi," she says, crying. My mom and dad sit at the foot of the bed, my stepdad lingers behind Mom, his hands on her shoulders. Mom starts crying as she rubs my leg. I see tears in my dad's eyes.

"I'm so sorry, baby," my father says, and I cry harder. He stands up to kiss me on the forehead. The last person to do that was Nate... in bed... that night... I rub my forehead, as if I could take away the kiss my father had just put there, and bring back the one Nate gave me. All evidence of Nate was gone from this world. He would never kiss me again. Never hold my hand. Never nibble on my ear. Never make love to me. Ever again.

Donna, barely recognizable with her unkempt hair and lack of makeup, enters the room, and everyone just sniffles, cries, everything else is silent. Chris stands up to let Nate's mom come to my side. "I'm sorry," she whispers.

"I am, too," I choke back. We hug tightly.

"Chris?" my mom says. "Why don't you take your father and Don to get some coffee?" I observe Chris giving Mom a sympathetic glance, and he hugs me one last time before standing up.

"I'll be right back," he assures me. It's no secret to anyone in our family that Chris and I have a special bond. They all know that I need him more than anyone else. I almost don't want to let him leave at all, for fear that he, too, may never come back. I know it's unrealistic... but I never expected to lose Nate, either... never expected him to leave me. Chris leads the other men out of the room, leaving Jennifer, Mom, Donna and me. I lie back on the bed, feeling weak without his support, his presence.

My mother moves up to sit next to me as Donna stands behind her. She holds my hand while Jennifer rubs my shoulder.

"How are you, hon?" Mom asks.

"Empty." I tell her. It's the best word I can think of, the only word that describes how I feel. I am just... empty. Something inside of me is missing, just completely gone. My heart is broken.

"I know, Em," she says. "I know this is hard."

"I just don't understand," I tell her. "And what's worse is that I just don't remember..."

"Do you remember *anything* from the night?"

"Yes," I feel the heat rise in my cheeks. "I remember him performing with his band... and then he walked toward me with such intensity, kissed me, and lead me out of the ballroom." Everyone sits, silent.

"We went up to our room," I tell them. "We snuck away. I don't know why, but we just needed to be together. I felt it, this need... I couldn't contain it and couldn't wait to be with him."

Jennifer smiles the saddest of smiles.

"We made love..." I cry, my face becoming hot, holding on desperately to the memories of that night, afraid that they will disappear, and they're all I have left of him. "It was the perfect night."

"And then what happened?" Jennifer says.

"We were debating going back up to the party for the toast at midnight," I explain, confused. "I don't know what happened."

"Chris told you that you went to the store?" my sister asks.

"Yes."

"But you don't know why you went?"

"No."

"Emi, I don't know how to tell you this," my mother says.

"What?"

"Well, there was a bag in the car with you, from the drug store..."

I listen intently, wanting details, hoping something will remind me of the night's events. It makes me sad to think there are memories of him that I have already lost. It doesn't seem fair.

"There were some chocolate bars in the bag..."

I shake my head. None of this sounds familiar. "I don't think they were ours... I hate chocolate and he never snacks... snacked..."

"Emi, they were," Jennifer says. "They were purchased at the store, along with a pregnancy book and a child's toy, just before eleven-thirty on New Year's Eve."

"I don't know," I tell them, confused. All of a sudden, I am optimistic. I remember the morning after the accident, pressing his hand against my abdomen. I was pregnant. The baby was okay. "I'm pregnant!" I announce, hopeful and relieved. How could I not remember this? All my attention had been focused on losing him, but now... to think that a part of him might still be with me...

The women all look at each other, sensing my hope, my desperate need for Nate, or a part of him. My mother shakes her head, a tear falling from her eye.

"You were, Emi..." Nate's mother tells me. "He told me a few days after Christmas... and the EMTs on the scene found the book in the car, and notified the doctors immediately. They did some blood work... confirmed that you were pregnant... and the doctors did everything they could..." Her voice, now weakened with sorrow, wavers. "We were so hopeful." She pauses, bringing her hand to her mouth, shielding me from the words she had to say. "But you lost the baby..." she barely whispers, standing quickly and moving toward the window, touching the bouquet of daisies tenderly.

"Oh, god," I cry. We all do. I grasp my stomach, the emptiness I'm feeling now clearly and cruelly defined. "I want to die, Mom. I can't do this."

"We'll be strong for you, Emi, sweetie," Jennifer says. "You don't have to be... not now... but we need you."

"We love you," Donna adds.

"And Clara, she adores you. She wants to see her Anni-Emi..."

"And Nate-Nate," I cry. She loved Nate, and he was so good with her. He was going to be the perfect father. He would have been. He was going to be. We were pregnant. We were going to have a baby together.

"How did this happen?" I ask. "Who hit us?" I'm angry now. I want to know who stole my perfect family from me. Who took my soul mate, the love of my life, and my tiny... baby? Who took my entire life from me? I suddenly remember that voice from earlier, Chris's friend, apologizing... I feel bile rising in my throat, to think he was in the same room as me...

"It was a 21-year-old kid from Rochester. He had a carful of friends. They were all drinking."

"So he was drunk?"

"Yes."

"But it wasn't Jack?"

"Jack who?" my sister asks.

"Chris's friend. The one who was just in here."

"No," Donna says. "It wasn't Jackson." I briefly wonder why he was apologizing, to whom he was speaking...

"Then why..." I let it go to find out more about the boy who did kill my love, my hopes, my dreams... everything. "Is this kid... is he in jail?"

"No, Emi, he died in the crash. So did two of his friends."

A drunk driver did this to Nate. All of a sudden, I look at Nate's mother. She nods at me and begins crying even harder. Her husband killed himself by driving into a tree after a night of drinking. And now her son was lost in another drunk driving accident.

"It's not fair," I cry.

"No, it's not. And Emi, we were all so hopeful," my mother says. "We prayed so hard for that little baby, we did. The stress and shock were just too much."

"They said it was between six and seven weeks old," Donna tells me, brushing my hair out of my face as her son had done so many times.

"You miscarried two days ago, Emi," Jennifer adds.

"Probably conceived right around Nate's birthday," his mother adds. *His birthday. Of course it was. His birthday. I remember his birthday... and I remember we didn't sleep together again until... no wonder I needed him so badly.*

"Who knows about the baby?"

"Just your family and me," Donna says. I nod. I don't think I want anyone else to know.

Chris, my dad and my stepfather enter the room, handing coffee to my mother and Jennifer. Mom stands up, giving Chris his place back on the bed next to me. One look into his eyes, and I know that he is aware of the conversation my mom and sister just had with me. He cries first, leaning down to embrace me again, and the tears erupt quickly from my own eyes. He kisses me on the cheek, smoothes back my hair.

"It's not fair," I tell him.

"No, it's not." I hear soft cries and sniffles around the room.

"What did I do that was so wrong, to deserve this? Is this bad karma? Did I do something to someone?"

"I don't think it has anything to do with anything you did, Emi."

"Then with him? What did *he* do to deserve this?"

"Emi, I don't think he did anything, either."

"Well, then why?" I ask him.

"I don't know, Em... I just don't know."

"I want him back," I whisper. Is there a way to get him back? What could I give of my life, of myself, to get him back? I would do anything. Anything at all. Volunteer all my time. Donate any money I ever make to charity. I'll never ask for anything else. I'll go to church every week, every day. *Anything in the world, God, what can I do to bring him back?*

CHAPTER 2

After a few more days, I'm released from the hospital. Because both of my left limbs are in casts, they've put me in a wheelchair and I'm reliant on the help of everyone around me. Knowing that I will be unable to maneuver through Manhattan in this state, my brother has invited me to stay with him in New Rochelle until at least one cast comes off– I say he's *invited* me, but I really don't have a choice. My family wants to make sure I will somehow be able to manage life on my own. They're not worried about my temporary loss of mobility, but rather the permanent loss of my entire foundation.

Anna was supposed to move in with Chris this next week, but they have postponed that to accommodate my stay. I feel bad, holding up their life, imposing on their time together, but this decision was made for me, by them, by my family. If I could get up and walk away, I certainly would.

I would walk away from it all. Run from the reality of my life. Find Nate and the child we would never have in this life... wherever they are, that is where

I want to be. I know I am on unofficial "suicide watch" with my brother. He is going to take a few weeks off from his job to stay with me. I know I will never have a moment to myself.

If I have to spend my time with someone on this planet right now, though, he is the only one that I want around. He's not overly chatty, leaves me to my thoughts most of the time, understands my needs. The time I spent with my mother in the hospital just grated on my last nerve. She was constantly hovering, wanting me to talk about my feelings, expressing her sadness for me, constantly reminding me of how scared they were that night, how worried. She just wanted me to know how grateful she was that I survived. I wasn't.

My father was the complete opposite. He never really could find words, so when he was with me, he was mostly silent, watching the television with me or reading the newspaper. He avoided the topic of Nate the whole time. I don't know if it made him too sad to think about it, or if he just didn't know how to comfort me. Either way, it was just strangely awkward. With him, though, there were times when I could escape, allowing myself a minute or two to listen to whatever show was on. They were brief escapes, though. There was always something– some man, some word, some incident, some phrase, some small token– something– that reminded me of Nate, brought me back to my hell.

Jennifer didn't come by after that one night, when they told me I had been pregnant. Her marriage was quickly falling apart. She was in a constant juggling act between Clara and her job and her insensitive, preoccupied, selfish husband. She would call every day, though, to check on me. She promised to bring Clara to see me soon, whenever I told her I was ready. I missed my niece, but in truth, I knew it would be difficult to be around her. They had told me that Clara was having a difficult time understanding what had happened to Nate. The concept of "death" was still foreign to her, too grown-up for her young mind to understand. She was lucky.

Teresa had offered to be my "sitter" once I was released from the hospital. Her job as a writer kept her home most of the time, anyway, and she complained that the apartment was just too quiet without me there. I did voice my opinion about this option, begging my family to not make me go back there yet. Had I been forced back to my apartment, I would have had literally no escape from her sex life. It was bad enough before; it would be a million times worse now, hearing other people enjoy the pleasures that I was sure I never would enjoy again. How could I? Nate was my soulmate. Now that he is gone, I have nothing to look forward to.

"We're home," Chris announces. My dad hops out of the backseat of the car and pulls the wheelchair out of the trunk. Chris walks around to my side of the car and helps to put me in the chair. "Em, the first thing we're going to do is get you to eat something. You've lost a lot of weight... you should not be this easy to pick up," he jokes. Even if the hospital food had actually been good, I had no appetite to eat. I held on to the empty feeling. Wanted to feel it, wanted to live it, wanted to remember it, remember Nate every second. If memories were all I would ever have of him now, I wanted them all the time.

I close my eyes and smile weakly to myself as I remember lying on top of him in his bed the morning after the crash. It's still hard to believe that didn't happen. It was too real. *He* was too real... too Nate. The way he smelled. The soft touch of his hand climbing up my thigh. How he peeked at me with one eye still closed, teasing me, and the quiet laugh that escaped his lips. The desire I could see in his eyes and feel in the air around me. If only I could breathe that air, surround myself with him.

"I'm not hungry," I tell Chris.

"Too bad," he responds. "We have a ton of food and someone has to help me eat it." He pushes me into his first-floor apartment, where I am greeted by my step-mother.

"Hi, Emi," she says.

"Hi, Elaine," my greeting monotone, with no emotion. She visited me once with my dad in the hospital. I like his second wife a lot. I think they're a good match, better than my mom and dad had ever been together. She comes over to hug me.

"I brought some comforts from home," she says. Chris pushes me into his guest room, where the room is made up with my things. My comforter and my pillows are on the bed. Some of my pictures are hung on the walls, though noticeably, none of the paintings Nate had given me over the years are here. As much as I don't know whether or not I'm ready to see them, their absence is undeniable and deliberate. I pull the comforter toward me and sniff it. It smells clean, the sanitary smell of detergent. How I wanted his smell to be on there.

"I washed everything up for you," Elaine tells me, smiling. I start to cry. "Oh, sweetie, I'm sorry, I didn't think..." she trails off, herself beginning to cry, my dad walking over to comfort her. I wonder if there will be a trace of him left anywhere in this world. Did they just destroy all evidence of him while I was in the hospital? They buried him without me there. I didn't even get to say goodbye. The one person who doesn't remember him even leaving this world didn't even get to say goodbye. I guess that's why it's still so hard for me to accept. I'm not entirely sure I want to accept it. A small part of my mind just believes that he's away for awhile, and that this whole death thing is a fabricated lie to hide his actual whereabouts from me. Like a fucking soap opera or something.

I'm not ready to say goodbye. I just want to cling to him, like I did that following morning. Basking in the bright sun, we were together and happy. It felt like forever was encompassed in that singular moment. His bare skin was so warm beneath mine, his kiss soft and gentle. His smile soothed me, his arms protected me from harm. I want Nate back. I want my forever back.

"It's okay, Elaine," Chris says at my lack of response, alerting me of my actual surroundings in his apartment and not Nate's loft. "It's fine." I know she had good intentions, I do. I'm just beginning to fear what else of him might be gone for good. I'd do anything to be able to smell him, touch him, kiss him, just one more time. "Emi, there are clothes in the closet and the dresser. And I brought your computer, some books... your iPod's right here." He smiles, knowing how much I cherish my music.

"Emi, what can I fix you to eat?" my dad says, Elaine wiping the last tears from her eyes.

"I'm not hungry," I remind him.

"Well, a lot of people have brought over food. You know Chris can't cook," he laughs. "You should probably take advantage of it."

We go into the living room and Chris turns on the television before heading into the kitchen. I hobble to my feet and move to the couch, lying down on my side uncomfortably. "Dad, can I have a pillow?" Elaine walks into the bedroom and emerges with both of the pillows. She props them underneath my shoulders.

"Are you cold? Do you want a blanket?" she asks.

"No. I'm fine." I stare blankly at the TV.

"Alright, Em," Chris says, bringing in a plate and setting up a tray in front of me. "Sit up."

"I don't want to, Chris."

"Emi, please do this for me. You have to eat. Just a little. It's macaroni and cheese... Aunt Margie's... your favorite." I glare at him, but reluctantly sit up.

"Okay," I sigh. It *is* macaroni and cheese. My favorite. I pick up the fork and take a bite. Flavorless.

"Thank you," he says.

"Chris? Do you need anything else before we take off?" my dad asks.

"No, I think we'll be okay. Anna's coming by later, so if I think of anything, she'll take care of us."

"Okay," he says. "Well, let us know if you change your mind."

"Alright, Dad, Elaine," he hugs them both. "Thanks for your help." Dad nods before walking over and patting me on the leg.

"You call me anytime, hon," he says. "We love you." He looks at me, his eyes full of sympathy.

"Love you, too." Overcome with emotions, my eyes start to water again.

"Oh, baby," he says, hugging me.

"I'm fine, Dad," I tell him, knowing that the embrace will only make the tears stream faster, harder, longer. "I'll be fine."

"I know you will," he says with confidence. I'm glad he believes it. I was just saying it for his benefit. Elaine hugs me, then they leave together. I find a tissue and wipe my eyes and nose, breathing deeply to calm myself down. Chris goes back to the kitchen, and comes back with a plate full of food. He sits down next to me, putting the plate on the tray next to mine.

"If you want any of this," he says, waving his hand over the food, "just take

27

whatever." I eye his fruit salad and stab my fork into a strawberry.

"Thanks," I mumble to him. I shrug away when he puts his arm around me. "How could you let her do that?" I ask him angrily.

"Do what, Emi?"

"Wash my linens."

"She thought you'd want clean sheets," he scoffs.

"I want *him*. I don't care about anything else."

"We can't give you *him*, Emi... he's gone."

"Well, then I want the next best thing. I want to smell him, Chris. When I lay my head on these pillows, I'm overwhelmed with spring fresh-ness. It used to smell like his soap and his cologne."

"Elaine was only trying to make it more comfortable for you."

"You should have stopped her. For me. And you've gone to the trouble of bringing my fucking decorations over here, but where are his paintings? Where are his things? This doesn't help me. This doesn't make it feel like home. Home is where he is."

"I know you're angry, Emi. But we're only trying to help."

"Well then bring me his t-shirts that I usually sleep in. Hang one of his paintings in my room. Show me a fucking picture of him or something. Prove to me that he lived... that he loved me."

"We didn't think you'd want to be constantly reminded of him."

"Well, I do. He's all I think about anyway. Why wouldn't I want something tangible of his?"

"Alright, truthfully, we didn't think you should be constantly reminded of him. We thought it would be best for you."

"You don't know what's best for me. None of you do. None of you could have any idea what's best for me. What would you want, if you were me?"

"I don't even want to think about that, Emi," he says as he takes our plates into the kitchen.

"You'd want something to hold on to," I tell him with certainty.

"I don't know what I'd want," he calls back to me.

"Well I know what I want. Just... something, Chris... please?"

"Emi..."

"What's happening with his loft?" I ask him, hoping to preserve it exactly how it was when he last left it, hoping his scent will linger on his sheets long enough for me to go over there.

"Donna is taking care of it," he explains.

"What does that mean, exactly?"

"Emi, I don't know what that means. But if you think no one understands what you're going through, you're wrong. She knows."

"Well, then why didn't you consult her and ask her opinion?"

"You know why, Emi? Because she just lost her *son*, that's why. She has her own grieving to do, and we're going to let her do that. You're not the only one affected by his death."

I want nothing more than to storm out of the living room, but in my current condition, I would need his help to do that... and that would be pointless. I stare blankly at the television, unable to focus. Chris laughs at the sitcom. How the fuck can he laugh?

"This show sucks... can we watch something else?" I know I'm being selfish, but why does he get to be happy? Why does he get to find pleasure in anything? *I* don't get to.

"Sure," he mumbles. "Is there anything in particular you wanted to watch? I recorded your shows for you, if you want to catch up on them."

"Whatever," I sigh. Part of me doesn't want to see them, doesn't want to find enjoyment in them... but another part is curious to see if the distraction will actually deter my constant thoughts of Nate and my inability to remember the events of the night– and then my stranger ability to remember the events of something that never even happened. I decide to indulge my curiosity and watch the shows, but I quickly realize that nothing can keep the vision of him out of my mind.

Anna shows up a few hours later as Chris and I are propped up on opposite sides of the couch.

"Emi," she greets me, "it's good to see you out of that drab hospital room!"

"Thanks." She hugs me and then walks over to kiss Chris before sitting down in his lap. I sigh, watching their affectionate exchange. I try to focus again on the television.

"How was your day?" he asks her.

"It was good," she says. "Yours?"

"Fine," he tells her. "We got settled okay."

"Good," she smiles. "Em, is there anything you need?"

"Nope," I answer, quickly tiring of everyone's concern for me.

"Well," she says. "Your brother didn't want to help you bathe, so sister, you got me."

"Fuuuunnn," I say without enthusiasm.

"Let's go figure this out," she suggests. She begins to get the wheelchair.

"Please, no," I tell her, struggling with my immobile limbs to eventually stand up on my own. "I'd rather limp."

"Very well." She takes my bandaged arm and helps me toward my temporary room which has its own bathroom. She closes the door behind us. "I want to talk to you for a minute," she whispers.

"Okay," I sigh.

"First, I want you to know you can come to me whenever for whatever, okay?"

"I know that."

"Now, I don't want to upset you more..." she starts. "but I've been really trying to put myself in your shoes... trying to figure out what I can do for you... like, if I were you, what would I want..."

"Okay..." *Finally... someone...*

"And it's an awful thought, Emi, and my heart aches for you," she says. I look at her, searching for her reason for this line of conversation. "I know there's nothing that can bring him back," she adds. I nod. "But if I were in your shoes– and just tell me you don't want it if you don't, it won't hurt my feelings..."

"What, Anna?" I say impatiently.

"If it was me, I'd want something that felt like Chris, something that made me feel closer to him." I nod again, relieved that someone is actively trying to understand me, how I feel. "So, I brought this for you." She reaches into her purse and pulls out a zippered plastic bag. I recognize immediately what is inside. My face crumples, remembering the last time I saw the black striped silk tie. He wore it to the party. I took it off of him, put it around my neck. Later in the night, he ceremoniously untied it, taking it off of my naked body. I open the bag slightly and inhale deeply. It smells just like him. His scent, mixed with a faint hint of the cologne he often wore. The sobbing overwhelms me.

"Shhh," Anna comforts me. "Jen and I... we found it in your hotel room. Jen said that Nate told her it's your favorite."

"It is," I gasp.

"Listen, Emi, Chris doesn't know I brought this. He didn't think it would be good for you to have it, not this soon. I promised I wouldn't give it to you, but if it was me, Em, I'd want something... something that made me feel like a part of him was still with me."

"Thank you so much, Anna," I whisper, trying to control the crying. The last thing I want is for someone to take this precious article of his clothing away from me. I quickly seal the bag up to contain his smell. "I need this." I hug it tightly to my chest, closing my eyes, remembering that night and keeping close the sacred moments that Nate and I shared between us in the hotel room.

"I thought you might," she says. "Let's put it somewhere safe," she adds, tucking it under the mattress. She hands me a tissue and hugs me as I calm down, as the tears cease. "Alright... shower?"

"Great," I murmur. "Please, humiliate me now."

"You're lucky it's me and not Chris," she tells me. "Get over it and come on."

After the shower that seemed to go on forever, Anna leaves me alone in my bedroom to attempt to dress on my own. I need to be able to do some things on my own. I hate relying on other people.

I open the dresser and pull out some underwear and pajamas. My flannel pants and thermal shirt should be sufficient. I had gotten used to sleeping in Nate's t-shirts, but no matter how far I dig in the drawers, none of them managed to make it to Chris's apartment. Someone was screening my clothing options. I just hoped they were still at my apartment. Or his apartment. I wonder what will happen to his loft. I wonder what Donna has done, if she's already sorted through his things. Would she give me anything to remember him by? Would I ever get the chance to go there again? *Would I want to?* It was my place to escape, my second home. I wonder if it's already emptied out... I wonder if I'll ever get to see it again. I loved his loft. Loved being there with him. I have so many memories of us there, going many years back. The place had become sacred to me even before he... left... I had hoped to move in there with him one day.

His loft appears once more when I close my eyes. This was the last place I was with Nate, only now I understand that it was a dream. In his arms that morning, I had never felt more safe or more complete. In the aftermath of what could have shattered us to pieces, we were whole in those moments together.

But it *did* shatter us to pieces.

I held him that morning, just like he asked me to. I held him tight. I could feel his love move through me in each labored breath. They *were* labored, I remember now. He tried to be strong, to mask his pain, but I could hear it in his voice now, in my vivid memory of what *didn't really happen.*

But it *did* happen, didn't it? I was holding him when he breathed his last breath... when his precious, delicate soul left his body...

It had been so bright in his room. So bright it was almost painful to look, and yet my eyes were drawn to the windows as if they called out to me. Was this the light they talk about when people die? Was it coming to take Nate?

Was it coming to take me? The air around me becomes stagnant and still, making it difficult to breathe.

I was so close, so close to being with him forever. Maybe one less gasp of air, or one more drop of blood, leaving my body. One more second without help. If the impact had been a little stronger. Had I not been wearing a seatbelt. If he had pulled into the intersection a second earlier. Or later.

I could be with him and our baby.

Why couldn't I have gone with him?!

Why didn't he take me with him?

The crying envelops me wholly, so quickly and powerfully that I have a hard time breathing. My head feels tight, throbbing, stars filling the darkness when I squeeze my eyes tightly shut.

Gasping for air, I crawl under the covers and begin to reach for the baggie when someone knocks on the door.

A loud sob is all I can force out. *Go away* is what I wanted to say.

"Em, can I come in?" Chris asks.

Not catching on to my silent message, he enters the room, carrying my pillows. "Thought you might want these." I take them into my arms and fall into them, burying my head into the comforting down, wishing they would suffocate me.

"What is it, Emi?" Chris whispers between breaths, sitting next to me and rubbing his hand up and down my back.

"Why couldn't I have gone with him?" I wail.

"It obviously wasn't your time," he answers plainly as he moves his hand to the back of my neck, rubbing the tense muscles. He can't know this, but I can. I know that Nate and I were soul mates, that we were meant to be together, forever... wherever that forever may have been. I start to take some deep breaths, trying to calm myself under Chris's soothing touch.

"How do you know?" I finally manage to ask him.

"Because you're still with us. And Emi," he pauses, "I'm so grateful you are."

"Thanks," I mumble, anything but grateful. Eventually, I sit up and place the pillows against the headboard and lean back, pulling my one bare knee into my chest. "Where's Anna?"

"She left."

"Why?"

"She was going to stay at her place," he explains.

"Chris, you know I don't care if she stays here. I like her. She's more of a sister to me than my own sister."

"Oh, I know," he says. "She had some things to take care of over there."

"Well, make sure she knows she's welcome. I really don't want to impose."

33

"She knows, and you're not. Stop thinking that."

"Okay," I tell him. He puts his arm around my shoulders and I lay my head on his. We both look into the mirror facing us. "I hate this, Chris. I hate being here. I hate being around people... I just want to be alone."

"I'm sorry, Emi. I don't know what I can do to make it better."

"Nothing," I admit. "I mean... I appreciate what you're trying to do, but I need some time to myself. I'm a mess."

"No, you're not, Em," he laughs, tousling my wet hair. "And I'll give you some alone time. I just want to help."

"I know."

"Listen." He pauses, obviously nervous to bring something up. "Can I talk to you about something?"

"Of course."

"It's about Nate."

"I figured."

"Well, since you weren't able to go to the funeral..." he begins. My heart skips a beat again. Every time someone brings it up, it's like my body just realizes the shock of his death in that very moment. It happens multiple times a day. My brain knows... still doesn't want to believe, but knows... but my poor heart still takes the news as if it's the first time it's been mentioned. I wonder when that will stop.

"Yeah," I say, swallowing hard, letting him know it's okay to continue with the topic. If I cry, they typically won't continue. They've tried to have many conversations with me over the last week, and since I break down consistently, I don't really know what anyone wants to talk to me about anymore.

"Well, we think it would be good to have a memorial service for him, just family and close friends."

"I don't think so, Chris." I immediately hate the idea.

"Why don't you think so?"

"I don't know if I can handle it."

"Well, Emi, it's important for..." He sighs. "Important for closure."

I start crying. The finality of it. Closure. I don't want closure. Closure means I begin to put him behind me. I can never do that.

"I know it will be hard, Emi. We'll all be there for you."

I weep quietly as he rubs my arm. "No," I whisper.

"It's part of the grieving process, Em. The rest of us have already taken this first step. But if you don't get that chance, like we had, I don't know that you'll ever begin to... heal... and we're worried."

"It's too soon," I plead. "It's only been a week and a half."

"I know, and we're not trying to rush you. I know this is going to take time. A lot of time."

"Okay, then when?"

"Next weekend..." he tells me. "Do you think you could do that?"

"No, I don't think I can. I'm not ready."

"Not ready for what, Emi?"

"I'm not ready to let him go."

"Well," he says gently, "you're going to have to start this process sooner or later..."

"I know," I say angrily. "But don't tell me when. You can't put a time limit on this."

"You're right, I can't tell you when to heal," he concedes. "But we're going to have the memorial next Saturday, and we'd like you to be there."

"I won't go," I cry.

"You don't have to decide now," he says.

"I have decided," I continue. "And I won't go."

"Okay," he squeezes me tighter. "Shhh... it's okay."

"I miss him so much, Chris," I barely manage to whisper.

"I miss him, too, Emi." He starts to cry again, too. "Emi, it hurts me so much to see you like this. I had never seen you so happy since you started dating him. Not since we were younger, before Dad left Mom. I mean, anytime you were with him, over the years, as friends, you were a happier person, more content with life... in brief spurts, when he'd come home with you on holidays, or on the trips we'd all take together. He brought out a wonderful side of you, Em. He was so good for you."

35

"He loved me," I explain, "like no one ever could. Ever *will*. And he loved me all along. And I didn't realize it. I could have had years with him. Years! And I only got weeks... because I was stupid or stubborn... or selfish, I don't know."

"Emi, you just have to cherish the time you *did* have together. And those other years, you had him as a friend, your very best friend. And those years made you who you are now," he says. "Those years as friends made your love so much stronger, so much better."

"That's just what Nate would say," I cry harder. "He never lived with any regrets."

"And you shouldn't either," he explains to me. "Nate wouldn't want that. He wouldn't want you to be so sad. He would want you to remember how happy you two were together."

"That's *all* I think about. How happy we *were* together," I say spitefully. "I'll *never* have that again."

"You don't know that, Emi."

"He called us soul mates. I don't think I get more than one of those." Chris has no comeback for that one.

"Are you tired?" he asks.

"Yes," I tell him. I feel completely drained. My head hurts, as it does at the end of every day– and every morning– from crying. "I need some aspirin."

"Let me get some for you." He gets up and leaves the room. Anxious to smell Nate, I reach under the mattress and grab the bag. I open it quickly, inhale deeply. The scent of him takes me back to that non-existent morning. I can still feel his hand, tentative on my breast as he looked over my body for any marks or scars from the accident. There were none. There were none in that dream... and yet here I am, scraped, bruised, bandaged in casts...

"Love ya, Nate," I whisper. I seal the bag up tightly and tuck it back in its hiding place before Chris comes back in. He has changed into sweatpants and a t-shirt. I swallow the two aspirin he brings me with a small glass of water.

"Here," he says, helping me up. "Let's get you tucked in." He pulls the comforter and sheets back and I lie down. He tucks the blankets around me and kisses me on the cheek. "Good night, Em."

"Chris?" I ask before he walks out.

"Yeah?"

"I know I said I wanted to be by myself... but I don't think I want to be alone tonight." Another tear falls from my eye.

"Sure, sis," he says. He picks up a quilt and lies down on top of the comforter, pulling the blanket over him. I lie with my back to him, and he rubs my arm gently, soothingly. He falls asleep before I do.

The next morning I am awakened with a kiss. I know that kiss, those lips. Excitedly, I wake up, sit up in bed– *Nate's* bed– the sun still shining brightly through his floor-to-ceiling windows.

"Nate!" I cry, happy tears falling at the sight of him, dressed in light tan khakis and a white t-shirt. I knew he was just gone. I knew it was all a bad, bad dream.

"Hey, Emi! What's wrong?" he asks, smiling.

"I haven't seen you... I thought you... are you really here?" He pushes a strand of hair behind my ear before kissing my forehead.

"Of course I am, silly. I came to visit you."

"I'm confused," I admit, smiling. "Where have you been?"

"I was with the baby," he tells me. For the first time, I realize he's holding a small child, a little girl. *Was he holding her all along?* She has Nate's gorgeous brown eyes and my reddish-blonde hair, but I don't recognize this baby. She's wearing a little green dress, my favorite color of green. She's bigger than a newborn, though. *How old is she?*

"Whose baby is that?"

"Emi, she's ours!" he laughs. Nothing is making sense to me. I look around the blinding room again. It's definitely Nate's. The last time we were here, his ribs were bandaged from the accident and I was unscathed. Judging by the way he holds the child with his left arm, I assume he is okay.

I shake my head, not understanding. "How are you?"

"I'm fine, Emi. Just fine."

I notice my casts, experiencing a little bit of shock at their presence before vaguely remembering that I had been wearing them before... was it recent?

"How am I?" I ask, gesturing to my bandaged leg with my bandaged arm.

"You're doing great, Emi," he says sweetly. "You're going to be fine." I start to cry out of sheer frustration. *Where had he been all this time?* "Em, what is it?"

"How long have I been asleep?"

"Awhile," he says.

"I don't understand, Nate. I don't know her," I begin to sob, struggling to find some memory of this precious child... a child that I apparently had... some time ago. *What happened to my memory?* With the age of this child, I must have been out for... for more than a year? Or do I have *amnesia* or something?

"Emi, it's okay," he says soothingly. "She knows you." He leans into me as he sits on the bed, and instinctively my good arm reaches out for her. Nate places her small body into my cradling grasp as he rubs my leg, the one that's not bandaged in a cast.

"What happened to me?" I ask.

"There was a car wreck," he explains. "But you're going to be okay. You were in a coma for quite some time. It's good to see you awake again."

"But we were both okay," I tell him. "Was there *another* wreck?"

"No, love," he says, laughing quietly. "Just the one was enough."

I nod, smiling, breathing in the scent of baby powder, examining in detail the little girl's features. She's beautiful. Tanned skin like Nate's, his smile, adorable long eyelashes. She begins to babble, making the sweetest little baby sounds my ears have ever heard. My heart melts as I immediately fall in love with our child.

"And you're alright?" I ask him again, taking my attention from the baby and getting lost in his gaze as he nods, assuaging my fears. He was hurt and I was fine before. Now it's the other way around. I focus my thoughts on what's happening in front of me. We're here in his loft. He's right here. I can touch him. How I've missed him. I reach out to feel his messy hair. It's soft, just as I had remembered it.

"I was so worried," I tell him, now just accepting the situation for what it is.

Strange, unmemorable, but obviously my reality. I don't care that I don't remember the past year. All I care about is that Nate is here, that our little girl is healthy... that we're all together. "What's her name?" I ask Nate.

"Emi," he says, his voice sounding different.

I look at him curiously. "Why did we name her that?"

"I have to go," Nate says, taking the little girl from my arms.

"Go where?" I ask. "Don't leave. Stay."

"We can't," he says. "We have to go."

"Emi," another voice says, and I realize it's not Nate's.

"Love ya, Em," he tells me, walking backwards out of the room, never losing eye contact with me. The child seems to smile in his grasp.

"I love you, too, Nate. Please don't leave," I cry. He turns the corner and walks out of my sight.

"Emi, wake up," the other voice says. It's Chris's voice. He is telling me to wake up? *God, no! Please, God, please don't let this be the dream. I want this to be real. Give me my life back, God, give it back! Give him back!* I just want to scream! I don't ever want to open my eyes, to see that this wasn't real. I need him.

Someone touches me on the shoulder and I open my eyes. I am no longer in Nate's loft. I survey my surroundings, turn to look at my brother lying next to me. I begin to sob.

"Chris," I cry. "He was here."

"What?" he asks, his voice thick with sleep. "Emi, you were talking in your sleep."

"No... no, no, no, no, NO!" I yell, sitting up abruptly, squeezing my eyes shut as I try to bring back the image of Nate and our little girl. "Where is he?"

"It was a dream," Chris informs me. "You're at my apartment, remember?" I know I am, but I don't want to admit it. I open my eyes, trying to acclimate myself to my sad reality again. I can barely see through my own tears. After a few minutes of breathing deeply, I begin to calm down. Chris tugs my shirt, and I fall onto his chest, needing to feel safe in *someone's* arms, but instead feeling completely lost and broken.

"I was with him," I mumble softly as the crying begins to subside.

"Emi, just go back to sleep," he encourages, pulling me closer to him and smoothing my hair down. "It wasn't real."

"Don't tell me it wasn't real! You don't know! I could feel him," I argue, rolling on my side, away from my brother, pulling the covers tighter around me.

"Emi, shhh..." He continues to try to soothe me with his sounds, but he falls asleep before I do, failing miserably. Eventually, my exhaustion wins out and I'm back in a dreamless sleep. I wanted to see him again... feel him again... Instead, my head just swims in darkness... in nothing.

In the morning, I wake up with yet another headache. These days, they're constant, nagging, come hand-in-hand with the tears. I go to the medicine cabinet in the bathroom, but it's empty. *Suicide watch.*

"Chris!" I call down the hallway. "I need some aspirin, like, now. Please." I'm just too impatient, want this pain to subside for good.

"Good morning, Em," he smiles, carrying a glass of water and two pills. "Don't panic." I swallow the pills quickly. "Did you sleep okay the rest of the night?"

"I guess," I tell him. I then remember the dream that awoke me in the middle of the night. "Oh," I say, grasping my stomach.

"Are you okay?"

"Just... feeling empty... again," I explain. "I just remembered the dream."

He hugs me closely. "Do you want to talk about it?"

"No," I tell him, still wanting to believe that it was real. "Not right now."

"Okay. Anna's coming over in a few minutes to help you bathe," he says.

"Chris, I'm pretty sure I can manage myself. Just... please... let me have a little dignity. Plus, who cares if I bathe or not. I've got nowhere to go, you know," I say.

"I guess that's true," he concedes. "But I invited Jack over tonight to watch the Rangers... do you think that will be okay?"

"Who?"

"Jack. You remember him from the party, don't you?"

"I'm not sure. And I'd rather not try to remember that night, if that's okay."

"I'm sorry."

I shake my head, frustrated that our conversation ended up where it did. "Back to the Rangers. It's fine," I tell him. "It's your house... please continue with your life. You could even go to work, if you wanted... I'd actually like that." *Just leave me alone.*

"I'm not in any hurry to do that," he laughs. "You're welcome to watch the game with us."

"No thanks," I decline his offer. "I'm busy," I say sarcastically.

"Come on, Emi, you like hockey games," he tries to convince me.

"No, I like *going* to hockey games," I tell him. "There's a difference."

"You've been spoiled by your rich-" He stops suddenly.

"What?" I ask, taken by surprise. Chris had always teased me about the things Nate and I did together. If Nate wanted box seats to a Rangers game, he'd buy them. When he wanted to travel to a five-star resort, he'd go, often taking me with him if he was without a girlfriend at the time. Chris would tell me that I'd be so used to the "privileged" lifestyle that a normal guy would never be good enough for me. In truth, nothing we did ever felt "privileged." He was always so down-to-earth... seemed normal enough to me.

"I'm sorry, Em." He shakes his head.

"It's fine," I tell him, turning away from him to hide the tears. "He *did* spoil me."

"But I didn't mean to say that," he says.

"It's okay," I repeat. "Really."

He turns me around and nods quietly as we exchange sympathetic glances. He kisses me on the cheek. "Are you sure you can shower by yourself?" he asks, and I'm glad he's changed the subject before I can dwell on what my life used to be like... what it would never be like again.

"I'm sure," I tell him, annoyed.

"I'll call Anna and tell her she doesn't need to come right now, then."

"And I'll go give it a shot," I tell him, returning to the bathroom.

Chris sits in his dining room, working quietly from home, later in the afternoon as I watch more TV. A reality show marathon has kept me distracted all day, but I can feel my brain turning to mush as a result. Eventually I turn off the television and sit in silence.

"You okay, Em?" he asks, coming to check on me.

"Yeah," I answer, numb.

"Can I get you anything?"

"Do you have any wine?" I ask.

"No," he laughs. "This is a beer-only apartment– until Anna moves in."

I sigh. The idea of getting a little buzz was tempting... but not tempting enough for Chris's cheap beer. "How about some water then?"

"Coming up," he says.

"What time is your friend coming over?" I ask when he brings me my drink.

"Seven-thirty," he tells me. "Are you going to join us?"

"No. I'm not really in the mood to change out of my pajamas."

"Emi, hon, I don't care what you wear. Jack's certainly not going to care."

"Good, then I won't change," I state, satisfied to simply remain comfortable.

"Does that mean you're going to watch with us?" he asks, walking to the kitchen.

"We'll play it by ear," I say with little enthusiasm, leaning toward a 'no' but wanting to make it seem like I was trying. "But why don't you guys go out to watch the game. Isn't there a sports bar around here?"

"Honestly, Emi, I think it will be good for you to get your mind on something else."

"And a hockey game with your friend is what you've come up with?"

"He asked to watch the game with me. I didn't figure you'd have an opinion. Did you want to do something else? I'll tell him no and rent a movie or something, if you want. Or we can play poker..."

"No, it's fine, Chris. Hockey night with Jack is fine." I have no intention of hanging around for that. I'm getting tired anyway.

"Good," he says.

"Is Anna coming over, too?"

"Yeah, for a little while."

"Cool." Restless, I stand up and feebly follow my brother into the kitchen. "Is there any mac and cheese left?"

"Sure," he smiles. "Want me to get it for you?"

"No, I'll manage," I mumble, hobbling to the fridge. "Did you want some?"

"Yeah... why don't we heat up some dinner."

"Okay." We both look through the various plastic containers that were left by friends and family members, picking out things here and there that we like. Inevitably, all I want are casseroles and mac and cheese. At least, for once, food is sounding appetizing again.

After dinner, I load the dishwasher with my one good arm while Chris cleans the rest of the kitchen. It feels good to do something productive. Even though it's a small task, it just feels nice to contribute a little. I've grown so tired of being helpless.

I sit back down in the living room as Chris turns on the pre-game show. Anna comes in a few minutes later, and Chris returns to the kitchen to heat up something for his fiancée to eat. She sits next to me on the couch and tells me a little about her day.

"Did you sleep okay last night?" she asks. I remember back to the restless night, the dream... and for right now, I really just do want to keep the dream to myself. I smile, remembering the feeling that Nate was there with me.

"I guess. Chris stayed with me, so that helped."

"He's such a good guy," Anna says.

"I guess he's an okay brother," I tease as Chris makes his way back into the room.

"What did I miss?"

"Emi just told me you stayed with her last night. I thought it was sweet," Anna tells him.

Chris nods and smiles, bringing Anna her dinner. When she finishes eating, they both go back to the kitchen to clean up and discuss their day. The doorbell rings, and I stand up to get the door since I'm the closest one to it.

"Emi, I got it," Chris yells to me.

"It's fine!" I open the door, and Chris's friend smiles warmly, wearing slacks and a white button-down shirt, the top button undone, making me feel monumentally underdressed in my pajamas. He's holding a six-pack of beer in one hand and a bottle of Bellei Lambrusco in the other. Wine. God bless him. Maybe I'll hang out for at least one glass.

"Emi," he says as I reach for the bottle of wine that he extends to me, his eyes quickly scanning my outfit. "How are you?"

"Better now," I laugh, looking down at the Lambrusco. "Did Chris call you?"

"No," he smiles. "Why?"

"Oh. I had asked him for some earlier... and this is my favorite kind of wine."

"Well," Jack begins, "you actually let me try it at the engagement party." His voice trails off, his eyes shifting uncomfortably. I had forgotten about that conversation that we had at Chris's party.

Fuzzy fragments of memories jump around in my head. I doubt I would have remembered that if he hadn't mentioned it, and still, it's not very clear. "Oh, yeah," I tell him, remembering the drink we had together while Nate's band played. I remember the glance that Nate and I exchanged, remembered mouthing the words "I want you" to my boyfriend. I swallow, hoping to rid my throat of the lump. I struggle to smile, keep the tears away. People will always bring up things that remind me of him. I have to get used to this, somehow. I need to prepare myself for it, so it doesn't come as a surprise, forcing the emotions to sneak up on me like this.

I inhale deeply and breathe out slowly, my eyes intently focused on my house shoe.

"I'm sorry," he says with regret. "And, I don't know, you probably shouldn't drink it if you're on pain medication," he adds cautiously. "Are you in any pain?"

"Am I in any *pain*?" I repeat the senseless question, although I'm sure he didn't mean it that way.

"That's not what I–" He shakes his head and takes a deep breath. "Again, I'm sorry. That was poorly... worded..." I can tell he feels awful, and I'm sure my caustic tone with him is only making it worse.

I try to soften my response to put him at ease. "No, really, it's okay... and thank you." A tear escapes, but it's just a lone one, as I gain a little control, composure. I wipe the tear away quickly and start to hobble toward the kitchen.

"Let me carry that, Emi," he says, taking the wine back.

"Thanks," I blush as he tucks the bottle under his arm. He also takes my bandaged arm and lets me lean on him, making my stroll to the kitchen that much easier.

"Jack comes bearing gifts," I announce after clearing my throat, shifting my balance away from my brother's friend.

"Fantastic," Chris says, shaking hands with his friend. Anna hops off the kitchen counter and gives him a hug. I'm digging through their drawers, trying to find a wine bottle opener. Chris interrupts my search, holding out the tool I was desperately looking for. He glares at me, but smiles. "My sister, the wino," he jokes.

"She's not on any medication?" Jack quietly directs his question to Chris. He's trying to be discreet, but I hear him anyway and glare out of the corner of my eye. Chris looks at me for an answer.

"I just took the aspirin when I got up this morning. It's fine."

"You probably shouldn't take anything tonight, then," Jack says with concern, intercepting the corkscrew from Chris, "if you intend to have something now."

I nod. "Yes, doctor," I mock him. He smiles faintly, looking down at me attentively, setting the bottle on the counter and maneuvering the utensil into the cork. "It's been ages," I tell him, suddenly self-conscious, justifying my thirst. *When was the last time I had a drink? Before Christmas... maybe Christmas Eve? It seems so long ago.* "Does anyone else want any?" I ask.

"Me!" Anna says happily as the guys shake their heads. I find two glasses and set them on the counter. Jack pours the wine carefully and hands each of us a glass. Chris opens up two of the beers and hands one to Jack.

"To a Rangers win," he toasts, and we all drink.

Feeling the need to be social since I'm drinking the gift Jack brought for me, the four of us settle into the living room to watch the game.

I try to zone out, shrink back into my own head, but Jack actively engages us all in conversation. "Now, I don't know if you knew this," Jack begins as the puck drops, "but Chris and I used to play some drinking games when we'd watch hockey in college."

Chris moans. "I didn't know that," Anna says.

"Yeah. We'd start the night by flipping a coin to see who would get the Rangers. Heads was Rangers, I think," he says.

"That's right," Chris says.

"So we would have our shot glasses ready and a bottle of tequila on hand... it was one shot for penalties, two shots if the team on the penalty kill got scored on... we each had to drink if there was a fight, right?"

"Yeah," Chris laughs.

"A goal for your team meant the other person had to drink another shot..." Jack laughs. "There was one game that was just penalty after penalty, goal after goal, fights... it had everything."

"Oh, god," Chris says.

"It ended in a shoot-out... now, we didn't have any rules for shoot-outs, and we were both pretty gone by that point in the game."

"And the tequila was gone," Chris adds.

"Yeah, tequila was gone, I forgot about that," Jack laughs. "So we decide that whosever team lost the shoot-out, that person had to run naked to the neighboring sorority house, knock on the door, and ask whatever girl opened the door out on a date– on the spot."

"Oh, god," Chris repeats, laughing. Anna and I are giggling at the thought.

"I guess Chris's team lost..." I conclude, swallowing back my laughter. I immediately feel guilty.

"No," Jack says. "Mine lost." He smiles, and Anna and I exchange confused glances.

"Yeah, so he strips naked," Chris says, "and walks confidently next door...

knocks on the door. He's so wasted that it didn't phase him at all. And this girl opens the door."

"Kaylee," Jack says. "Kaylee Milner..."

"That's right!" Chris says.

"I got lucky..." My jaw drops. "Oh, no, not like that!" Jack adds, embarrassed at his choice of words, laughing. "I got lucky in that Kaylee already had a crush on me. So she actually said yes."

"And since we hadn't thought that far ahead," Chris adds, "Jack brings her back over to the frat house. They sit down on the couch next to me and just start making out."

"I'm not proud," Jack says, shaking his head, laughing harder, "and it was probably a good thing when Chris threw up on her."

"Oh, my god, you didn't," I blurt out, looking at Chris incredulously. Anna and I erupt in laughter.

"I did," he blushes. "The tequila..."

"Yeah, it was bad," Jack adds, his eyes starting to water from laughing so hard. "And after he did, I ran to the bathroom and threw up myself. Oh, we were both so sick."

"Kaylee never gave him the time of day again," Chris says.

"And I think that was the last night we did the drinking game, too," Jack adds.

"Yeah. I don't think I've had tequila since then, either."

"Yeah, now it's only in moderation," Jack confesses. "I'm too old to do that anymore."

"Too old," Anna scoffs. "How old are you?" Anna asks.

"Thirty-three," he sighs.

"Yes, *so* old," Anna mocks him.

"Okay, maybe I'll go with too wise, not too old."

"I'll give you that," Anna says.

Still smiling, I pick up my empty wine glass and start to get up for a refill. All three stand to assist me. "I've got it," I assure them, making my way to the kitchen, stumbling only slightly over the pajama pants that are a little too long, hanging loosely from my thinner body. "Anyone want anything? Not that I can really carry more than one, but..."

"Nothing for me," Anna says.

"Me, neither," Chris adds.

"I'll get my own," Jack responds, following me to the kitchen. He sees me struggling to get the cork out. "Give me that," he laughs, taking the bottle from my hand.

"I can do it," I tell him.

"I don't mind," he says, pouring another glass for me.

"I hate being helpless," I complain with a pout.

"Well, the casts do render you a *little* helpless," he says. "But I'm not really doing it to help you. I'm just trying to avoid an accident... Girl has a glass of wine. Girl hobbles on one leg. Oops, stumbles a little... Girl tries to open wine bottle with one hand. Girl loses balance. Girl drops bottle... or glass... or both... Boy standing next to her has to clean it all up." He shakes his head. "I'd be less reluctant to help then, I think."

"Really?" I ask.

"Yes, I might be too busy laughing."

"So I should take advantage of this, then?"

"Yes," he says, carefully placing the glass of wine into my good hand.

"Well, then, thank you."

"You're welcome, Emi," he smiles quickly, grabbing another beer out of the refrigerator.

"Any more stories about my brother?" I ask.

"Plenty," he assures me as he guides me back into the living room.

By the time the game is over and Jack and Anna have left, I'm feeling a little bad... and a *lot* guilty. I laughed tonight... actually allowed myself to have a little fun. I'm sure the alcohol had a lot to do with that, but a part of me feels like I betrayed Nate... is it too soon to laugh like this? Too soon to spend an hour or two not thinking about him? I feel like it is. *I'm sorry, Nate*, I tell him, feeling certain he can hear me... feeling certain he witnessed the evening. I sit on the bed, staring through the window into the darkness outside. I see something move in the reflection of the glass. Chris is standing in the doorway, watching me.

"You did really well tonight, Emi," he tells me.

I shake my head. "I think it's too soon," I tell him. "I feel bad for... laughing..."

He walks in and sits on the bed next to me. "Don't," he says. "I think it's good for you."

I shrug. "Do you think he's watching me?"

"I think he might... I'm sure he checks in with you, makes sure you're okay. I bet he was happy to see you smiling tonight."

"I don't know."

"I do," Chris says with confidence. "He would always rather see you smile... see you happy than sad... don't you think?"

"It sounds logical, it does... but I don't want him to think I don't miss him."

"Em, he knows that. No matter what," he thinks for a second. "He knew how very much you loved him in life, Emi. He takes that with him... he has that love you gave him for eternity."

"But what does that mean for me, Chris?" I ask, feeling panic. "If he has all my love... am I just destined to be alone for the rest of my life?"

"I don't think he has *all* your love, Emi. He has all the love you could give him in his life... but you have so much more to give. You weren't allotted a certain amount, and then that's it..." he laughs quietly at the thought.

"I just *want* him to have it all," I tell him.

"You can still love him, Emi," he assures me, putting his arm around my shoulder. "That's okay. Normal. No one is going to take that away from you. Someday, though, even *he* would want you to share that love with someone else. If that's what made you happy."

"Thank you, Chris." I smile, believing he's right but still feeling a tinge of guilt.

"Do you want me to stay in here tonight?" he asks.

"Yeah, if you don't mind... I'd really appreciate it." I don't want to need him, need his support, but I do. I want to be alone, but realize I'm in no state to be.

"Sure thing, Em. I'll be back in a few."

"Thanks." As soon as he leaves, I find the tie and hold it closely to my nose, smelling the familiar, comfortable scent of Nate. My heart skips a beat, as if he is in the room with me.

"Love ya, Nate," I whisper, tucking the keepsake away. I close my eyes tightly, the vision of him coming back to me immediately. I'm back in his bed, and he leans over to kiss me, his body silhouetted by the blinding sunlight that filters through his windows. *I love you too, Em.*

CHAPTER 3

Every day I'm at Chris's, I feel a tiny bit better, cry a tiny bit less. Chris has been beyond gracious, helpful... and I can't thank Anna enough for letting me steal his time away from her. It's been amazing, spending this time with my brother, getting to know each other again. I hadn't realized how much of his life I had missed in the past few years as the distance grew between us. I feel closer to him now than I ever did, even when we moved away when our parents separated, when we could only find comfort and familiarity in each other.

Today, I fear I will take a step or two backwards. Chris is driving me to Nate's apartment. Donna called yesterday and asked if we could meet there. Talking to her on the phone was incredibly emotional. She cried just hearing my voice. I cried hearing the sadness in hers.

"I'm going to go to the coffee shop," Chris says as he pulls up to Nate's building. "Just call me when you're ready."

"Okay," I say. As I emerge from his car, still bandaged, I am quickly greeted by Marcus, the doorman. First he hugs me, apologizing, obviously affected by Nate's passing as well. He takes my arm and helps me into the building.

"You look too skinny," he tells me, smiling. "But beautiful as ever."

"Thanks. Is Donna here yet?"

"Yes, she's been here awhile. Do you need help getting up there?"

"No, I can manage, but thank you." He takes me to the elevator, pushes the button for the twelfth floor and waves goodbye.

I take a few deep breaths before knocking. I try to imagine that he's still in Vegas, remembering when I would come over here while he was out of town... just try to pretend that to get myself in the door, knowing that he's not inside. Sometimes I have to play these mental games with myself. Maybe it's not really healthy, but they help.

I knock tentatively, lightly, a part of me hoping no one will answer and I'll just be able to go back to Chris's apartment and postpone this inevitable meeting for another day... if I could ever be more prepared for it.

Donna opens the door, but again, I hardly recognize her. Her eyes are swollen, her hair brushed straight, and again she has no makeup on. She was always perfect before welcoming guests into her home or before going out on the town. She looks so much older, so sad, her eyes showing every ounce of sorrow that she's feeling.

"Oh, Emily," she breaks down, embracing me tightly. I can't help but cry. "How are you doing, honey?"

"I'm okay," I lie. There were times in the past couple of days that I did feel okay... but that feeling was gone as soon as this door opened, as soon as I inhaled the familiar scent, saw the many small reminders of him inside the loft.

"Come in," she says as she returns to the floor next to the Christmas tree. Dry, brown needles cover the hardwood planks. She is carefully wrapping up all the ornaments and placing them in a box. Two empty stockings hang over his fireplace, one with his name and one with mine. These weren't here the last time I was. The lump in my throat grows at the thought of his sweet gesture. I look away quickly when I notice a third, smaller stocking laying on the mantle. The empty feeling assaults me again.

His unmade bed seems to call out to me. But is this really his room? *This* is the place he called home? Gone is the brightness of the sun, replaced by looming clouds and long shadows. A dull grey now stains what used to be his crisp, white sheets. And were his walls always this taupe color? This room was... gleaming white... alive... perfection. Happiness. Full of hope and promise. I barely recognize it now.

Are any of my memories real? Does any part of the Nate I knew remain? I wonder if the bed still smells like him... I try to resist the urge to saunter over, climb in, bury myself in the covers, in the memories, but lose the battle in the end. I amble to the bed and sit next to it, picking up the pillow where Nate typically slept. The other side of the bed is just strangely unmade, my absence obvious. I hold the pillow to my face and inhale deeply. I stand up only to collapse onto the pillow on the bed, moving toward the window and rolling into his awaiting arms as the clouds move out of the way for the afternoon sun.

Why did you leave me, Nate?

I love you, Emi. I feel enveloped by his grasp, my body becoming warm at his touch.

If you loved me so much, why did you leave?

You know it wasn't my choice. I squeeze him tightly.

Then come back.

"Did you say something, honey?" Donna's voice interrupts our conversation. My heart stops beating for a few seconds. I warily open my eyes to see the grey pillow in my arms, and not Nate. His mother sits down next to me, patting me on the leg as the sun shrugs back beneath the clouds. She hands me a tissue to wipe my tearing eyes.

"It still smells like him," I tell her.

"I know." She lets me cry for a few minutes. I struggle to compose myself, but eventually do, focusing on other things that don't have such a personal connection to him. "Let's come sit down," she says, leading me from the bed to the couch.

"How are you getting through this, Emily?"

"Second by second," I tell her. "Day by day is still too daunting for me. To think that he'll still be gone tomorrow is too much for me to think about. I just try not to think about the future... or the past, really. It's just too sad for me. Still too new, too raw."

"I know," she soothes. "It will get better," she assures me. "Soon, it will start getting easier." I nod. "I really want you to come to the memorial this weekend, Emi," she surprises me with this line of conversation. I just shake my head *no*.

"I've already told Chris that I can't. I'm sorry, Donna," I tell her, making my decision sound as final as it needs to sound. I'm not prepared for this.

"You can," she says. "You need to come, sweetie."

"I can't..." I choke back the lump in my throat. "I can't let him go yet."

She takes my hands into hers and squeezes. "You have to, Emily. It's time." She looks at me with caring eyes, eyes that understand every shred of despair and loss that I feel. She lost the love of her life many years ago, and then lost the only thing she had left of him when Nate... left... I sigh heavily.... when Nate left this world. I lost Nate, and the child we would have shared, created out of the most passionate love I've known. I know she is the only person in my life who can really relate to me, and I appreciate that she respects what he and I shared. Even though we weren't married or engaged, she respects the total devotion that Nate and I had felt for one another.

"Nate would want you to have the chance to move on. I know it's hard. But I think the more time goes by before you get that chance to say goodbye, the harder it will be... the more you live with the idea that he might come back. I've been there, honey. I know."

As tear after tear falls to the ground, my head hanging low, I consider what she's saying.

"We're doing this for you, Emi," she says. "We want to celebrate him, all the great things he brought to this world... honor him in a respectful way, just family and his close friends. We want you to feel the love we had for him, and that we all have, in turn, for you. Just as we were for him in his life, we are here to support you. You were his life, Emi. Not just the past few months. For years, you were his life. A mother knows.

"All the other women, Emily... what he felt for them couldn't begin to compete with his love for you."

I remain silent.

"I found one of his songbooks. If you read the lyrics, you just know. Know the songs are about you. Poems... there are even some prose entries where he mentions you by name. Someday you may want to read it.

"He loved you with all his heart, and just wanted to respect your wishes. He just wanted you to be happy."

"He made me happy," I tell her. "Every second I was with him. I just wish I had been willing to admit my own feelings sooner. I would have had so much more time with him."

"I know," she says, "but it wouldn't have made this any easier. The loss would be just as great.... you made him very happy, too."

I smile through the tears. "I had a dream about him," I tell Donna. I want to assure her that her son was alright, so I tell her of my visit from Nate, from the little girl. I give her every detail I can remember, recount every feeling I felt. I tell her that he says he's okay, that he's with her, our daughter. Tears fall from her face, but she remains composed, as if the visit was expected, as if she already knew.

"A little girl?" she asks, smiling.

"Yes. She had his eyes, his skin... his smile."

"He came to introduce you two," she says, then sighs. "And to tell you goodbye." She pauses, squeezes my hands again. She takes a deep breath and continues. "When Nate's dad died, I had a similar dream. I had a very hard time, forgiving him. And I blamed myself, couldn't help but wonder if it was something that I did that made him go that night.

"It was about a year later, though, a year after he died, when he visited me. After therapy didn't convince me. He assured me of his love for me and for Nate. He apologized for his selfish actions. He asked for my forgiveness."

"So I'm not crazy?" I ask her.

"Absolutely not, honey. And the only person I ever told was Nate. He knew how important that was to me. He saw immediate changes in me after that night.

Maybe that's why he came to see you... didn't waste any time to try to put your mind at ease..."

Even though it was a dream, and even though I hadn't fully convinced myself that I could believe in such things, it began to feel more real... more possible. I knew most people wouldn't understand or believe... but this wasn't about them. He did this for me. I could believe or deny. In this moment, and from here on out, I choose to believe.

I hug Nate's mother tightly. "Thank you," I tell her. "Thank you for sharing that."

"No, sweetie, thank *you*." she says. "Since he was able to tell you goodbye, will you do the same for him? Will you come to the memorial?"

I nod slowly, sad to admit that I will begin to let him go. I find solace in the fact that this is just the beginning. It may take years for me to really say goodbye. This is just one small step. I will take it for him.

"And Emily," she says, taking my hand and leading me to the Christmas tree. "I want you to open this small present."

"Now?"

"Yes, if you don't mind. He told me what it is. I want to talk to you about it."

"If it's a ring or something, Donna, I will not be able to survive. I just won't. He said it wasn't jewelry, but..."

"No, honey, it's not jewelry. Go on. Open it."

I take the small box and untie the pretty bow, then lift the lid off of the container. I pull out the lump of tissue paper and begin to unwrap its contents.

It's a key. I start to shake my head.

"Nate was planning to ask you to move in with him," she explains. "He told me on Christmas. Even before he found out you were pregnant."

I stare at the small brass key and allow myself, ever so briefly, to imagine what it would have been like living here, with him. "I would have loved to move in with your son," I tell Donna. More faded memories of the time before the accident become clearer. "The week before... the accident... after I found out I was pregnant... I told him I needed space. God, Donna, why did I push him away?"

She pulls me into her arms and holds me tightly. "It's okay, Emily."

"Every single day that went by, I missed him more and more. I missed spending time with him... just having him near me. Another week, wasted..." My voice trails off.

"He always knew you loved him."

"Here," I tell her, relinquishing the key to her open palm.

"No, Emi. Nate would have wanted you to have this apartment... if you want it."

"I wouldn't feel right taking it," I tell her. "I don't even know if I could... live here... without him..."

"I insist," she tells me, handing me the key. "I don't need it, that's for sure. I mean, I know this would be hard, but please consider it. In a few weeks, maybe we can meet here again and go over a few things. When you're ready."

I take the key back, reluctantly. I'm not sure I can ever come back here, ever live a normal life here, without him. A sacred place. A constant reminder of him. "I'll think about it, Donna. I don't know that I'd be able to move forward living here. It may just be too painful... too many memories... I just don't know."

"I understand, Emily," she assures me, standing up. "It's yours if you want it. And like I said, take your time. If you just can't do it, decide you can't live here, then let me know. This place meant so much to him... was his haven. Maybe we can make a little gallery out of it or something," she laughs. "It's up to you."

I smile, but still don't know that I will ever be able to stay here. She leans down to hug me. I pick up another small present addressed to me and unwrap it. It's a gift card to my favorite home store.

"He wanted to redecorate with you, too."

"Sweet," I mumble, taking a deep breath and holding the card out to Donna, internally cringing at the thought of getting rid of things. "Can you give this to one of your charities or something? I think it would go to better use there."

"If that's what you'd like," she answers. I nod. "Is Chris downstairs?" she asks me, gathering the things she's packed up.

"He's at the coffee shop down the street."

"Do you want me to take you there?"

"No," I tell her. "I think I'll just hang out here for a few more minutes."

"You'll be okay?"

"Yes, Donna, thank you." She hugs me once more.

"I love you, Emi," she says. "I'll see you this weekend. You call me if you need anything."

"You, too." She walks out the door, closing it softly behind her. I take a deep breath and look around the apartment. I walk back over to the bed, picking up the pillow again. I decide to make up the bed, as best as I can with one good arm, wondering how long his scent will stay on the linens. I limp to the window, surveying the beautiful view of Central Park, remembering the afternoon of Nate's birthday, when we first professed our love for each other.

"Why, Nate?" I ask. "Why did you leave me?" I move toward the dresser, in hopes of finding a few of his shirts to take with me. Everything is how he left it. I hold the shirts close to my chest, happy to have another little token of him with me. The blue Tiffany & Co. box sits on top of the dresser. I had brought it over to wear one night when we went out, always keeping it safe in its case when I wasn't wearing it. I pick it up and I tuck it into the shirts. I can't open it. I'm not sure I'll ever be able to wear it again, but I will cherish it forever.

I fight off tears as I open the door to the guest bedroom, finding it odd that the door is closed. He never closed that door. On the bed are our suitcases from that night. I unzip his bag, sad to see that it's empty. Mine contains the red dress I wore to the party, my shoes, lingerie I had packed to wear that night, various toiletries, make up... everything I had taken with me. A plastic bag sits next to my suitcase. Curious, I open it and pull out its contents.

Two chocolate bars.

The Pregnancy Book.

A little yellow stuffed giraffe with the tags still on it. Even with the evidence in front of me, I don't remember picking up the items. I pull the cord on the giraffe, curious.

"Hi little one." My heart stops, cold, surprised at the sound of his voice.

"Thirteen years. One night. Nine months. One small baby will deliver true love. I can't wait to see you."

I feel faint, finding a place on the bed as the missing memories of New Year's Eve come racing back. I fight off the image that's most prominent. I don't want to see it. I struggle to piece together the night, avoiding the image. The only thing I could remember up until now was making love to him... But after that, we had a conversation as we lay in bed, naked.

I remember how he talked to the baby after we made love. I remember suggesting we go back to the party because I was craving chocolate cake. I remember him telling me that we weren't presentable, and suggesting we go elsewhere for chocolate.

I remember sneaking through the lobby. I had apologized when we got into the car. He left me in the store– he left me to get this giraffe that I now hold in my hands. I found the book, couldn't stop reading it, mesmerized with the information, curious, wanting suddenly to know everything I could expect, wanting answers to questions that had already been filling my eager mind.

I remember that the young clerk said that she was pregnant, too. I remember being surprised to see her wearing a wedding band– she just seemed too young, but it made me feel okay about our situation. We would be married. And I decided in that moment, that the next time Nate proposed to me, I wouldn't let a second go by before telling him yes, yes, yes, over and over again. If we were going to be Father and Mother, we could definitely handle Husband and Wife.

Nate had joked about the sex of the baby, that he was sure it was a girl because he would have been an unfit role model to a boy. I smiled briefly at the thought. I think I told him he was a good man. He was.

I remember him encouraging me to open the bag, to pull out the toy, to pull its string. I cried when I heard it then.

I pull the string again, ignoring the words, merely focusing on the tiny nuances of his beautiful voice, the voice I hadn't heard in weeks... the one I would never hear again, except for this token of his love that he had recorded for the baby. If I linger on this, keep playing this, I won't have to see that image.

But it's too late.

We looked into each others eyes. We kissed. We both must have seen the light change to green. I saw it. He hit the gas pedal. But then I saw something he didn't.

I saw the eyes of a younger man, almost a boy, the fear in them matching my own. The eyes, the boy, the SUV he drove, sped for us, raced toward the car, toward the driver's side of the car, toward Nate. Helpless, I yelled his name, feeling the impact and seeing nothing but white, feeling nothing but fire and pain for a few seconds before I felt nothing, numbness, spreading over my body.

I smelled smoke, tasted blood. Even after I opened my eyes, it took me forever to figure out where I was and what had happened. I could barely move the left side of my body, the side closest to Nate. My left arm wouldn't respond. I couldn't understand why. I tested my right arm... and it moved... I unbuckled the taut seatbelt and moved to Nate, to touch his face. I felt his breath, I remember that. I remember thinking he was alive... but thinking to myself... that Nate... looked... broken...

And I wondered how I could fix him. Confusion was taking over, but I knew Chris would know what to do. I called him, I remember dialing his number, when Nate moaned a little, seemed to be trying to say something. Another sign of hope, a sign of life. He was fine, would be fine. I focused all my attention to him. I cried out to him. I cried out of frustration, confusion, more than pain or sadness. The events weren't real to me at that point. I was going to help him. We would be okay.

I leaned over him, as best as I could with my own broken body that wouldn't respond as it should. That fact eluded me, it was more of a frustration to me than an acknowledgment that I was hurt, too. I don't think my own pain or condition ever crossed my mind after the initial impact. It was only Nate. He was all that mattered to me. Not myself. Even the baby never seemed to cross my mind in those moments where our lives hung in the balance.

I remember a tear of mine mixing with blood on his face. And the last sound he made, the most beautiful sounds. He had said, "Love ya, Em." *Love ya, Em.* He had looked at me, was somehow able to focus on me, met my gaze and held my eyes with his. "Hold me," he had managed to say.

And then, before I could even return the affirmation of love, his stare pierced through me, through my heart like a dagger. I had felt a rush of wind sweep over my body in that moment. I knew he had died. I felt it, but was unable to accept it. I kept nudging him, touching him, wishing my lips could reach his, to breathe the life back into him. I was determined to help, but unable.

I couldn't help him. I watched him die. He lay next to me in his crumpled car, lifeless. No amount of pleading– no matter how many tears I cried for him in those moments– nothing was enough to bring him back to me.

Again, I remember his distant stare... the most horrifying image I'd ever seen, not just of Nate, of the man I loved, but of any human being. *Get it out of my head! Please, God, get it out of my head!!!*

I crumple to the floor in a fetal position, crying, yelling, hugging the giraffe and his shirts, wanting to push the memory back to where it had been hiding for the past few weeks. I wanted to rip the image of Nate dying, dead, out of my mind forever. Of all the times I had begged to remember the events of this night, I never knew I was begging for this. *I take it all back! I don't want to remember!* This is not how I want to remember him.

Alive, happy, in bed, in love. That's the picture of Nate I want to hold on to forever. Not this one. *Not this one.* He is dead. Dead. The word is so horrific, so cold, so final, so ugly, so inhuman... *oh, make it go away make it go away make it go away, please, God, make it go away!*

"Emi!" Chris calls to me, hearing my screams, my prayer. "Emi, it's okay," he says, sitting on the floor next to me, lifting my head into his lap. He strokes my hair, repeating that it's okay, over and over and over again. He cries with me.

"He's dead, Chris," I tell him. "I saw everything. I can't stand it. I didn't want to see him like that. I don't want to *remember* him like that."

"Oh, Emi," he says. "I am so sorry."

I have no idea how much time passes, likely hours, but eventually, there are no more tears, my eyes are completely dry, my head pounds, feels numb. I sit up on my own. It's dark outside.

"Are you okay?" Chris asks quietly, clearly worried.

I shake my head. "I don't think so."

"Donna called me when she left. I tried to call you... I came up when you wouldn't answer."

"I don't even remember my phone ringing," I tell him. "I'm sorry."

"No, Em, I'm sorry. Sorry you were in here alone to go through that."

"Can we go home?" I ask him. "I can't stay here."

"Of course, Emi." He helps me up, takes the t-shirts and blue box from my arms and begins to lead me out of the room. I look at the giraffe, left behind on the floor, and start crying again. I yearn to hear his voice again, to pull that harmless little cord so I can hear him confirm his excitement about the baby, and about the changes in our life she would bring. *True love...* I want to hear him...

Chris's arms around my shoulders, he pulls me with him out the door, leaving the painful reminder behind.

On the table sits the key that Donna left. I pick it up, and– through tears– take one last look at this place, wondering if it could ever be my home without him, and walk through the door, locking it securely behind me. Chris holds his hand out for the key, and I willingly give it to him. I'm not sure I will ever want it back.

As we wait for the elevator, I glance back down the hallway. My eyes widen as I see an image of Nate standing in the doorway of his sun-drenched apartment. The tears welling in my eyes finally force me to blink, and he disappears. I tuck my head into Chris's shoulder as he pulls me into the lift.

~ * ~

I wore that sweater the day I flew to LA. This shirt, I had chosen for his birthday. He was with me when I bought the grey jacket. Each article of clothing hanging in my closet has some meaning attached to it. I should have agreed to go with my sister yesterday when she had offered to take me shopping.

I finally just close my eyes, inhale deeply, and take the first thing I touch off the hanger. Nate doesn't care what I wear today. In my mind, he's always with me anyway, watching over me. At least I hope he is. Today will be no different than any of the others that have passed since he died. I'm still expected to go on with my life. I'm getting better, I think. When I'm alone, I normally sleep to dream, and see him often. Nothing earth-shattering. I don't believe he's come to "visit" me again. Most dreams remind of the times we had spent together over the years as friends. Every time I wake up from one of these dreams, I feel a sense of longing for him– but I also feel like I've made it through another hour or two, or another night without him... and I realize I'm one step closer to seeing him again in the afterlife. That's what I believe, and it gets me through the long hours without him.

When other people are around, it's different. No one lets me get lost in my thoughts. A concerted effort is made to distract me, to entertain me, to feed me, to prepare me for whatever plans they've made. Nate may come up in passing, but it's not a topic I'm allowed to spend too much time on. But today, it's different.

Today, I can spend as much time on Nate as I want. I'd dreaded the approaching day, but now that it's finally here, I know it's going to be good to remember him as a group of close acquaintances. To exchange stories of the man we all loved; the only man I'd *ever* loved.

"Emi, that color is beautiful on you, but that blouse doesn't fit you anymore," my sister says from across the room of my apartment. Teresa had left us alone so I could get ready. I realize I still haven't moved away from the closet entryway. I finally look down to see what shirt I had chosen to wear. I smile wistfully, a tear coming to my eye.

"It never did." I button up the shirt. It fits even worse than it did the first time I wore it. I didn't realize I had lost so much weight.

"Then why would you ever buy it?" she asks, moving toward me.

"I didn't." I find a flowing black skirt and pull it on, zipping it up. It barely hangs on to my hips. *Wow. I had no idea.*

"It was a gift?"

"Not quite. I kind of stole it."

"From?"

"Nate. It was his." My sister is silent as she looks at me, moving closer. She touches the ruffle down the middle. *Yes, it's definitely a ruffle.*

"His as in... a girl left it at his place?" Jen asks cautiously.

"No. He bought it for himself."

I take a few steps toward the mirror, standing in front of it as Jen moves behind me. I straighten out the shirt and flop the cuffs, just as I had the first time I recognized how long the ill-fitting sleeves were. I start to smile at the memory, the first time I've smiled all day. My sister smiles back, but can't contain her laughter any longer.

"This was Nate's?" she says, giggling and rolling up my sleeves.

I start to laugh with her. "I know," I say. "I thought the same exact thing. I figured I was doing him a favor by removing it from the loft... god, it seems like yesterday, but it was over a year ago..."

I gulp, realizing the occasion for which he had intended to wear it. The merriment of the moment stops immediately. Oh, God. I never would have thought, on that day, that he'd die a year later... to the day. Everything was so different then. I've changed so much.

I look long and hard in the mirror at my gaunt body, realizing it's not only my physical characteristics that have changed. He changed me. I learned what it really meant to love someone.

"It's time to go, Em," Jen tells me, seeing me on the verge of falling apart. She puts her arm across my shoulders and leads me toward the door.

In the car, my sister sings along to the radio as I stare blankly out the passenger window, returning to my earlier train of thought. He had changed me for the better. He showed me love, like I never knew it... only to have it stolen from me way too soon. We didn't have enough time.

I wasted so many years chasing a feeling that probably never even existed–in sobriety, anyway. I never claimed to be sensible... but I loved him, with all my heart, for so long. I loved him as a best friend would, but kept my heart at a safe distance. When I finally decided to set aside this mystical notion of romance, I was able to see my real feelings for him. I was so nervous before I went to LA. I had no idea what he would say to the idea of dating one another. It was the biggest relief to learn that he still felt the same way.

I'll never forget the way he looked at me that first night in LA, the first night we were together. I thought I had seen Nate in every capacity. I thought I knew all of his expressions, but this one was brand new to me. As I stood naked in front of him, as I never had before, my heart pounded in my chest. The women he chose to date were model-caliber, and I was afraid I couldn't offer him enough. One look into his eyes, though, confirmed it all, and I knew I had no reason to be afraid. As his hands drifted over my body, his eyes finally met mine. In them, I saw commitment. Devotion. Assurance. Pure love. I had his undivided attention, all I had ever wanted from him. The impromptu poem he recited to me touched me deeply. My eyes well up as I realize I can't remember the words any more. *Why didn't I write it down?*

Shaking away the regret, I remember the moments just before we made love. When he joined me under the crisp sheets of the hotel bed, his attentiveness deepened. He was focused, confident, wanting and needing, curious and excited. I could tell it was a moment he had longed for, and one he was happy to see to fruition. His love became lust, an emotion he was ashamed of, but I was happy he felt it for me. It felt good to be wanted like that. I don't think any man had ever wanted me like that.

I start to cry again, realizing no man may *ever* look at me like that again. Jen pulls into a parking spot and hands me a tissue before getting out of the car at the restaurant. She comes around to my side of the car and opens the door, reaching in to hug me.

"It's okay, Em," she whispers in my ear, kissing my temple. "We're all here for you."

"I know," I choke out, grateful to have support from my family and friends. "I'm okay." Her arm across my shoulder, she guides me to the entranceway of Frontbar. Nate's last client, Albert, was more than willing to close his bar for the afternoon for the memorial service.

"You look very pretty, Emi," Anna tells me. I know I don't, but appreciate the effort she's putting forth.

"Thanks," I tell her, wondering why I bothered letting my sister fix my hair and put makeup on me this morning. There is no way that I won't be a sobbing mess in a matter of minutes.

"Are you ready?" Chris asks, his arm around Anna's waist.

"I guess," I say, taking a deep breath. Chris opens the door, and Anna helps me into the building. A large, framed picture of Nate is the first thing I see. It was taken in his apartment, on his birthday. It's a candid that Teresa took from across his loft. He's amid a group of his guests, smiling, actually waving. It was likely taken right before he thanked everyone for coming. It's beautiful, really represents him well, the Nate we all knew and loved. It's like he's waving goodbye. I touch the glass softly, imagining I'm touching his lips. "I miss you," I whisper to him, hoping he can hear me, wherever he is.

Nate's mother is the first to welcome me, hugging me tightly, a long embrace. Other guests follow suit. My parents and their spouses, my sister's husband, Clara, Albert, Kate, Nate's bandmates Eric and Jason, and Teresa. A small grouping of chairs surround a podium, and after everyone greets me, they all begin to find seats. Albert stands behind the podium.

"I just want to thank everyone for coming," he says softly. "I thought we'd just open this up to let you come up and say something about Nate... a memory, a story, a feeling... anything. I'll start." He continues. "When I hired Nate, he was just another contractor to me. I saw talent in him immediately, but I just wanted his art. What I didn't expect was to become friends with him. We were nothing alike, but he was just such a passionate person with his art, and he was really driven. That was what I could relate to. His drive to succeed. He really made an impression on me, and I'm happy I had a chance to know him."

He takes a seat, and Kate stands in front of us next, speaking to his incredible talent, as well. She was followed by Eric and Jason, who speak together about his wild creativity and his ability to bear his soul in his lyrics and songs. They admired his courage, and his dedication to putting on a good show. Teresa talks about his sense of humor. Jennifer speaks for Clara, retelling stories of fun times that she and her Nate-Nate had together. Everyone takes a turn, my parents, my brother, Anna, even Donna. They all say such beautiful things about him. Once everyone has a turn, I begin to panic, realizing I should probably go up to the podium and say something. I am not prepared for this.

I stand up and hobble my way to the podium. I face my audience, and once

I realize they're all staring at me expectantly, I just look down. I stand quiet, looking for words, stories, something to share with these people who also loved the man I loved. It's all too personal, though. I'm not ready to share our moments with anyone else. Maybe I'm being selfish, I don't care.

"I love him," I mumble. "I miss him. There will never be anyone like him. Um... I love him." I start to cry, my knees begin to buckle under the weight of my heavy heart. Chris comes to the podium, leads me back to a seat, puts his arm around me and hands me a tissue. I hear other sniffles around me.

Albert stands and lets us know that he has some food and drinks on the bar. Everyone gets up and gives each other hugs or makes their way to the food. I stay in my seat, feeling unable to move. I see Teresa talking to Donna, handing her a large book. Nate's mom opens it and touches a page gently. I hear her thank Teresa, and then she embraces her warmly.

Teresa looks over at me as Donna walks away from her. Our eyes meet, and she smiles. She walks toward me and sits down in the chair to my left.

"Emi," she begins. "I put together an album of the pictures I took on Nate's birthday... the ones in Central Park."

"That's what you gave Donna?" I ask.

"Yes," she tells me. "I have one for you, too. When you're ready."

"I'd like to see it."

"You sure?" she asks, reluctant.

"I'm sure." She stands and walks toward the bar, where another large book sits. I notice she exchanges a glance with my mother.

"Here you go," she says proudly. I open it up to the first photo, and it's a picture of Nate holding me, my legs wrapped around him. We're smiling, looking into each other's eyes, our noses touching, leaves scattered on the ground below.

"It's beautiful," I tell her, happy but so sad at the same time. This was one of the best moments of my life, when I told him I loved him for the first time. He had been so excited, he picked me up and swung me around. "We look so happy." The next pages are some of the posed shots we took, sitting on the park bench, on the ground, in a constant embrace. In each picture, I see something in

Nate that I had forgotten about... an expression, a gesture, a smile. They all hold something unique.

As I turn another page, there are two pictures that simply cause me to gasp. One is of him hugging me into his chest. He is resting his head on mine, smiling, and I look sad. I'm crying. I remember the regret I had felt in that moment, the regret of not allowing myself to love him sooner. The photo on the opposite page is of us sitting on the bench, our knees angled toward one another. He's looking down into my eyes, I'm looking up in to his, hopeful. His hand is wiping a tear from my cheek. I close the book quickly.

"Are you alright?" Teresa asks me, and I nod. I just imagine him watching over me now, wanting to embrace me, to wipe the tears from my eyes. I know that, wherever he is, he would be wanting to comfort me. He was always so quick to make the tears stop... all my life he had comforted me. I wish he was here now to pick up the pieces, to clean up the mess that was made when he left...

After an hour or so, people come and sit next to me, offer me soothing words, try to get me to eat something. I struggle to be polite, social, just hugging the album tightly. Eventually, people start leaving. Chris walks over to me.

"Emi, Anna's going to get a ride back with Jennifer," he tells me. I nod. "Will you come with me?"

"Yes." He leads me to the car, and as I put on the seatbelt he turns to me, again his eyes filled with sorrow.

"I'd like to take you to the cemetery, Em. Just the two of us. In fact, I can stay in the car. You can go talk to him..."

I burst into tears, knowing that this was coming but still no more prepared. "Okay," I tell him, swallowing hard. I do have things to say to him.

Chris walks me to the gravesite, identified by a temporary marker. The flowers that adorn the grave look fresh, new. I figure they were brought here by his mother, my family. I know that they have been doing everything in their power to prepare me for this. I carry the album with me in one hand, his silk tie in the other, and sit down on a marble bench that is located next to the site.

"Can I have a few minutes?" I ask Chris once I'm settled.

"Of course, Emi. Take your time." He squeezes my shoulders and I hear his footsteps walking away behind me. After a few moments of silence, I flip the album back open to the first page.

"Look how cute we are," I laugh, a tear falling. "I had never been happier, Nate. It just felt... natural... to be with you. Obvious. I felt like I was the only thing that mattered to you." I turn a few pages, finding the photos that had upset me at the memorial.

"I'm still crying today, Nate, but these tears are nothing like the ones I cried that day. I remember being so overcome with emotions, with love, that I couldn't stop the tears from falling. I couldn't contain the way I felt for you any longer. I felt like I had been hiding the words for too long and couldn't wait to tell you, so sure of my feelings.

"These tears today, though, Nate. I don't know if they'll ever stop. I know I'll never stop loving you. I can't imagine not missing you, every minute, every hour, every day. I don't know if it will get any easier. I hope it does... but I hope you know that if I cry fewer tears, that doesn't mean I love you any less. You were my soul mate. No one else can ever be that to me. We were that to each other. We get to keep that part of each other. So, I guess, in a sense, part of your soul will be with me all the time."

I smile, feeling chills at that thought. The thought that I do get to carry a piece of him with me always.

"Nate, I don't know why God decided it was your time... or why He couldn't take me with you. Some days I don't think I'm strong enough to handle it... so if you can, watch out for me... and give me some strength when I need it. You always did when you were here... you made me stronger, better, made me love more than I ever thought possible.

"And if our child is up there with you, if that little girl in the dream was real, please take care of her and let her know that I love her, and that I'm so sad I'll never get to meet her in this life. Someday, though... I hope to know her."

I turn through a few more pages in the album, laughing at some of the funnier moments, sometimes unable to distinguish between the happy and sad tears. The last page are two candids of us walking, holding hands, one from the front, the other from the back. On the latter, our bodies are in silhouette against the setting sun. Walking toward the light... there's no use in asking God again why I had to stay while he left.

"Goodbye, Nate," I tell him, now beginning to sob. Goodbye Emi and Nate. Goodbye to the time we shared, the love we exchanged. He is gone, and I am forever changed, different... never the same Emi. In a sense, I am gone, too.

"Love ya, Nate." In my mind, I only hear silence. I kneel by the marker and fold the tie, tucking it underneath the metal plate. I loved the tie, but I loved it on him. He never looked more handsome than when he was wearing that tie. Without him, it's really just a nice piece of fabric. *He should have been wearing it when...* I can't even finish the thought.

I close the album and begin to stand up, turning around to find my brother. He sees me across the cemetery and walks quickly toward me to offer his support. He hugs me when he reaches me, and says nothing. We are both silent as we drive back to his apartment, forty minutes away.

~ * ~

A few weeks later, after having my leg cast removed, I decide to take the train into the city that I've missed so desperately. I love Manhattan. I miss the sounds and the smells and the people... and I really can't wait to get back there.

I realize I'll probably be forced to take a cab at some point, but I want to walk as much as possible to work the muscles in my leg a little. It still hurts when I put weight on it, but is infinitely more comfortable without the heavy cast.

Bummed that Teresa isn't at the apartment, I just leave her a cheeky note and tell her I'll come back later in the day. I go back downstairs and wander around the periphery of Nate's apartment building, considering going in. Marcus sees me and waves me in.

"Hey, sweetie, how are you doing?" he asks, sympathetic.

"I'm hanging in there," I tell him. "You?"

"I miss him. I miss his stories, his energy. He was a good guy."

"Yeah, he was."

"Did you want to go up?"

"No, I didn't bring the key."

"I can get you one..." I consider the offer, but decide against it. "Not yet, I don't think. But I'll be back."

"I hope so, Emi. You're welcome anytime." I wonder if he knows that Donna gave me the apartment. I'm guessing he knows. I think she had paperwork drawn... I was a little out of it that day, though, just signed on the line mindlessly.

I continue to walk south on Fifth Avenue, going into a few shops along the way. My clothes aren't fitting well, so I purchase some new jeans and t-shirts. When I look through the bags as I amble down the street, I realize everything I purchased is either black or grey. Guess that fits my mood.

"Emi?" a man's voice says to me as I feel a hand on my arm.

"Oh, hey, Colin." I'm repulsed at the mere sight of him.

"I'm glad I ran into you," he says.

I remember the last night he and I were together.

Colin had an insatiable appetite for sex, something I was well aware of, and something I naively thought I was satisfying for the nearly four months that we dated. We spent at least five nights a week together, all that time, and every night, I obliged to his increasingly strange sexual requests of me. He was into things I had never tried, and I had decided to just go along with it, most of the time, for the experience. I didn't always enjoy it, but he did. I was making him happy. That knowledge was about the only thing I got out of the relationship. It was very lopsided. To this day, I don't know what drove me to date him for as long as I did. I didn't love him. In fact, I was astonished that I could be so intimate with him, and not really feel any real emotional connection. At the time, I thought it was very adult of me... I felt as if I was coming into my own. The more time that passed, though, I just became more and more disappointed in myself, vowing to never have another boyfriend like that one. And I won't. For more reasons than one.

I still shudder at the thought of that last night we were together. We had been drinking– like always– and we went back to my apartment. Teresa had made plans to go out of town for the weekend, so Colin and I decided to stay at my place instead of his apartment that he shared with two other guys. The advantage to their place, though, was that they all had their own separate rooms... with doors... novel concept.

Colin was always a little rough with me when it came to sex. How could he not be, though? He was two-hundred-ten pounds of muscle. When he would pick me up, it was if I was completely weightless. But that night, as we turned on some rock music– his mood music– and settled into my bed to start making out, things started to go downhill, quickly. He had pulled my hands over my head and was constricting them at my wrists, hard. So hard that I knew I would have bruises to hide in the morning. I had been wearing a thin t-shirt, which he literally ripped open to reveal my breasts. More bruises on my neck. I asked him to slow down, to be a little more gentle with me as he kissed me, hard, pressed himself against me repeatedly, harder and harder. More bruises.

I stretched my fingers and flexed my wrists when he let go. He kneeled over me and quickly took off all of his clothes. Before I knew what was happening, he had flipped me over on my stomach. He finished taking off my shirt and threw it on the floor. I tried to turn back over to look at him, talk to him, but he pressed my shoulders into the bed. When I started to kick my legs, he pulled his feet in and rested them on my calves, stilling my motion. Leaning up, moving one hand to the middle of my back, pressing hard, he took off my panties.

"Colin, stop," I had said, scared.

"Baby, what's the matter?" he said. "I thought you liked it this way."

"Colin," I swallowed, feeling completely helpless with my situation. I couldn't fight him. "Are you at least going to wear some protection?"

"Haven't we been seeing each other long enough that we don't need to do that anymore?" he asked.

"No. Colin, please stop, you're scaring me." I told him, still unable to make eye contact with him, which I always thought was necessary when he got rough. Without eye contact, I wasn't sure he even respected me as another human being. His eyes would get wild, often angry.

"I know you want this," he said as he leaned over me, his breath hot in my ear. "You've been flaunting yourself all night in that little skirt you were wearing."

"No, I don't want this."

"What the fuck is going on?" Colin moved off of me quickly, covering himself with my sheets, leaving me lying there, exposed, in front of my roommate, who I couldn't have been happier to see.

"I thought you said she was gone for the weekend," he seethed.

"I missed the train," Teresa said. "And I'm not going anywhere. So I suggest you go."

"Come on, babe," he said, dropping my sheets while he stood up, naked, and pulling me up with him. "We'll go to my place."

"Get your hands off me," I said, pulling away with all the strength of my body. I propelled myself to the other side of the bed and grabbed the comforter off of it, wrapping it around me.

"Don't act like you weren't enjoying that just 'cause she's here," he smiled. "You don't have to be embarrassed."

"Hey, fucker!" Teresa yelled loud enough for our neighbors to hear. "Get the hell out of here!"

"What are you gonna do, bitch?" Colin smirked, picking up his clothes.

"Well, I've got friends at the police station, and I've got 9-1-1 on the phone right now. So what are *you* gonna do, *bitch*?" she retorted, holding her cell phone out to show him she was serious. Colin quickly dressed. Quickly left. I had hoped I'd never see him again.

"Why are you glad you ran into me?" I ask, taking careful steps away from him on the crowded sidewalk.

"I've missed you," he says. "What happened to your arm?" he asks, gripping the part exposed above the cast.

"Car accident."

"Man, that sucks." Yeah, it does. *It sucks far worse than you could imagine.*

I nod in agreement. "Did you need something?" I ask, agitated.

"Can I see you again?"

"Are you kidding?" I let out a surprised laugh and start to walk away from him. He holds on to my arm tighter. I try to shake him off, but can't. "Let go of me."

"Come on," he says, his hot breath on my neck, my stomach churning. "You know you liked it."

"Frankly," I tell him, "I've had better."

"Bitch," he says, pulling me closer to him, roughly. "*Tease.*"

"Colin, let go of me right now." He starts to pull me with him as he continues his stroll down the street. I struggle with difficulty, feeling exhausted from all the activity. "Let me go, I mean it," I tell him through gritted teeth.

"Emi, it *is* you!" a voice startles us both from behind. We both stop walking, turn around to see Chris's friend, Jack, but Colin just stares, doesn't let me go. I barely recognize him, dressed in sweatpants and a loose-fitting sleeveless grey t-shirt. "I don't think we've met yet," he says to Colin, extending a hand confidently. "I'm Jack, an old friend of Emi's."

"Mind your own fucking business, Jack," Colin seethes.

"I'm pretty sure she asked you to let her go. Did I hear you right, Emi?" he asks, gaining my approval. Nervous for him, knowing Colin's strength, I don't know how to answer him. I don't want him to get in the middle of this. My eyes just plead with his.

"You must have misunderstood," Colin says, turning us away and pulling me farther down the street. Jack jogs in front of us, stopping us again.

"Let her go, man," Jack says sternly. Colin has at least three inches on him... and I hadn't noticed Jack's arm muscles before, but even seeing them now, there was no comparison between his and my ex-boyfriend's. When Colin doesn't relent, Jack adds, "You're on one of the busiest streets in the city. Do you think you can just walk away with her like that, unnoticed?"

"I don't see anyone stopping me," Colin boasts.

Jack straightens up, crosses his arms in front of him. "That's what I'm doing."

"Jack, just..." I plead. Jack doesn't break eye contact with Colin.

"Yeah, and what are you going to do?"

"I guess I'm going to do whatever it takes to get her away from you," he says, now getting visibly angry.

"Let's go, man!" Colin says, still holding onto me but assuming an offensive posture.

"Really? Here?" Jack stalls. "You've drawn quite a crowd, and I'm pretty sure they're going to side with the lady... and not the *ass clown*."

In a split second, Colin pushes me into some of the guys who were standing around watching the scene unfold and lunges for Jack.

"Jack!" I scream, covering my mouth in fear, unsure of what I should do. Out of nowhere come two men from behind me, grabbing Colin by his shoulders and tackling him to the ground before he can get to Jack.

And all the while, Chris's best friend is just standing there, confident, unwavering, ready to be beat to a pulp.

"Are you okay, miss?" one of the men that I fell into asks.

Stunned, I just nod my head. A few other men join the two tacklers and help Colin off the ground. Alone, none of them would have had a chance against him, but Colin knew he was outnumbered.

"Get the hell outta here," the tallest of the four men says, pushing Colin down the street away from me. The small crowd that had formed claps at the spectacle they just witnessed.

"Do you know these guys?" a woman asks me, cautious.

"I know that one," I say, pointing to Jack. "He's safe."

"Are you sure?"

"Positive," I smile, feeling my heart start to beat again.

"Jack to the rescue," the tall one says.

"Another damsel in distress," a shorter one laughs. He has dark hair and eyes the same color as Jack's.

"Thanks, guys," Jack says, shaking the others' hands. "I know this one, though. This is Chris's little sister."

"Ahhh..." another says, disinterested.

"Wait, Chris's sister? Isn't she the one..." his voice fades intentionally.

"That'll really get the adrenaline going," Jack laughs, talking over the other man.

"That was so stupid," I tell him.

"What was stupid?" he asks me. "I was in control of the situation the whole time. Those are my brothers," he says, motioning to the two that tackled my ex, "Matthew and Steven... and that's Thomas, my sister's husband, and Lucas, Matty's partner."

"He could have hurt you."

"He could have hurt *you*," he says back to me. "Looked like he was going to. I wasn't going to let that happen."

I just stare, still in awe. His family starts discussing the altercation loudly as the crowd disperses.

"Thank you?" he asks.

I nod, realizing my legs are suddenly incredibly weak. "Thanks." I stumble back into the wall of a shop behind me and drop the bags I was carrying.

"Whoa," Jack says, coming toward me quickly. "You okay?"

"That was a little scary," I breathe. "What just happened here?"

"Emi, you're shaking," he says. "Emi, look at me." He shakes my shoulders gently.

"I feel like I'm going to faint," I tell him, my breathing speeding up, my heart racing even faster. He puts his arm around me and helps me sit down on the sidewalk.

"Guys, go on without me. I'm going to make sure she makes it home and then I'll catch up with you."

"Alright, man," I hear one of them say. My gaze is fixed on... nothing... somewhere in the distance.

He angles my face to his. "Emi, look at me." Finally, my eyes focus again on his. "Are you okay?" He squats next to me, holding my shoulders to keep me steady.

Suddenly aware of my surroundings, I feel my face flush with heat. I inhale deeply.

"That's good, you have some color again," he says.

"Thank you," I tell him.

"Who was that?"

"Just a guy I dated last year."

"Wow," he says, a little taken aback. "Can I ask you something?"

"Sure."

"Why didn't you fight back?" It's a simple question, but one I have no immediate answer for. I repeat the question a few times in my head. *Why didn't I fight back?*

"I'm still just... weak... and numb..." I tell him. "And honestly, it never occurred to me that I had a choice. That I could beat him. I've felt pretty helpless, for quite some time. Is that weird?"

"I wouldn't call it weird," he says. "Worrisome, though. You've got to have a little bit of self-preservation in there." He touches the back of my hand. "After all, Emi... you're a survivor."

"Sometimes I feel so alone," I confide in him weakly. "Sometimes I feel like no one's paying any attention to what I do. I don't think anyone really listens to my cries for help anyway."

"Now I know that's not true," he says, finally sitting down next to me. "Your brother would live and die for you. I'm sure the rest of your family feels the same, but I can only speak for Chris."

"I know he would," I concede. "I owe him so much."

"He does it because he loves you. He does it because he wants to protect you. He does what any good older brother would do."

"Is that what you did today?" I ask him, smiling. "What any good older brother would do?"

"That's exactly what I did. I'm just glad I was around."

"Where were you headed?"

"Central Park. We were going to play some flag football."

"Well, please, Jack," I urge him. "Please go catch up with them. I'm fine." I lose my balance trying to get up and fall into him. "Sorry," I say, trying to read his expression... *Anticipation? Confusion?* A smile slowly spreads across his face.

"Wow," he sighs, seemingly out of breath.

"Wow what?" I laugh.

"You fell into me..." He shakes his head. "Wow, nothing. Let me help you up." He stands and pulls me up, not letting go until he's sure I'm steady on my own legs. He picks up my bags, the smile still lingering.

"What's with the smile?"

"Really? You don't know?" his smile falls slightly.

"No, I have no clue." He looks at me, questioning me.

"It's really nothing. Sorry." He shrugs as his grin shifts to detached disappointment. "So, um, you've moved back to the city?"

"No, I'm just here for the day. I wanted to get out and see my home, my roommate... do a little shopping."

"Well, where are you off to now?"

"Back to my apartment, I guess... see if Teresa's around."

"Where is that?"

"York and 74th."

"Let me walk with you," he offers.

"I'm okay, Jack, really. He's gone."

"I insist. It's what any good older brother would do."

"Okay then," I acquiesce.

CHAPTER 4

It's the middle of March and the casts are finally off! I feel free, in more ways than one. After staying with my brother for two months, I moved back into my old apartment yesterday. I owe Chris so much for everything he did for me. I don't know how to repay him for the sacrifices he made. He used up all of his vacation time to stay with me, to make sure I was okay. He comforted me daily, listened to me cry myself to sleep nightly. He provided needed distractions, made sure I ate, prayed with me when I needed even more than he could give. I am lucky to have him for a brother.

I started taking on some freelance projects last week, and it feels good to actually be working again, bringing in some money, doing something creative with my time. I'm beginning to feel a part of myself returning, and it feels pretty amazing.

Teresa is happy to have me back. We stayed up all night, unpacking and reorganizing things, talking, getting reacquainted. I missed my roommate, especially the steamy stories of her love life. I could always live vicariously through her. I haven't laughed so hard in ages.

She has planned a small gathering for this evening. A few of our friends are coming, as well as some people I haven't met before, friends of Teresa's. Teresa told me she invited Chris and Anna, but wasn't sure that they would be able to make it. While she naps, I decide to survive on caffeine. I'm feeling mildly optimistic right now, and I'd like to keep the feeling going. Sleep brings too much time to myself, too much time to think about Nate. I've been sleeping much less, and yet somehow surviving, not feeling tired at all. I really feel there has been some divine intervention happening.

I have finally gotten to the point that I can recall events, words, memories without falling completely apart. People are gradually becoming comfortable bringing him up around me, which is a relief. It was awkward having conversations with people, conversations that you know should have been about him, but weren't because of the fear of precipitous tears. There are even moments in the day that I can think about other things, focus on them fully. I had worried that a part of me would always be distracted by the tragic events of that night, but I am somehow able to compartmentalize it most of the time, lock it away safely for my own private time.

I'm working on the freelance project, a few illustrations to accompany a short story in a national women's magazine. It's a pretty big deal. Teresa was actually the one who got me the job. She writes for the magazine from time to time, knows all the right people. She took my portfolio to her last meeting with the editor, and they had a job for me within a few days. I am grateful for the work and for the income. She is, too. After all, I skipped out on the rent for a few months. I know she was struggling, but she would never tell me that. I should make enough on this project to pay my rent and all the utilities for a month, so I hope that gives her a decent break.

When Teresa wakes up in the late afternoon, she encourages me to shower and start getting ready for the party. One thing I have noticed is that I often manage to distract myself so much that I need to be reminded to do pretty basic things every once in awhile, say fix my hair, put on socially acceptable clothes, brush my teeth. After my shower, I find some jeans and a loose black turtleneck. I dry and curl my hair, put my makeup on, some tennis shoes. I sit down on my bed and continue working on the illustrations when Teresa comes out of the bathroom. She gives me one look and rolls her eyes.

"No, way," she says. "Number one, no black," she directs. "Number two, uh, no turtlenecks, and number three, what the fuck is up with those shoes?"

"What's wrong with the shoes?"

"Sneakers, Em? Really. We aren't going hiking."

"I thought this was just a casual gathering..."

"Sweetie, it is. But come on, people want to see Emi, not her frumpy cousin... do you mind?" She pulls me by my arm as I set the laptop back down on the bed. She scours through the closet to find something better for me to wear. After shooting down a few of her initial ideas, tight-fitting low cut sweaters, we settle on a cream-colored v-neck knit shirt with capped sleeves. She goes to her side of the closet for shoes, pulling out a pair of sandals. When I take off my shoes and socks to put them on, she throws the sandals back in the closet.

"Your toes are not sandal-ready," she informs me. I look down and notice my nails, red polish barely clinging on to the tips of them. "I'm adding pedicure to our list of things to do this week." Another good reminder from a good friend. "Here, take these," she says, handing me a pair of sage green mary-jane pumps. "Cute," she says, looking me over. "It's just missing an accessory or two."

We look at each other in silence for a few seconds, obviously both thinking of the same necklace, neither wanting to suggest it. It has stayed in its little turquoise box since the last time I wore it, a week before the accident. I smile faintly and nod my head. "Okay, I'll wear it."

"You sure?"

"Yes, I love it, and it would look perfect."

"Okay," she says, walking to the dresser and picking up the box. She opens the lid, and I have to take a deep breath before lifting the pearls out. I had forgotten just how beautiful the necklace was.

"Oh," I whisper as I feel like I might begin to hyperventilate. I grasp onto the dresser to steady myself. I examine the flower closely, its blossom colorful and alive. I hope to be that again someday. I count to ten, forcing myself to breathe in, breathe out, as Teresa takes it from my hands and clasps it around my neck.

"Perfect."

"Thanks," I sigh one last time, composing myself.

"Alright, help me get some of these snacks ready," she says, again pulling me with her to our small kitchen. She pours us both a glass of wine and takes some boxes out of the freezer. "What temperature do I need to set the oven to?"

"Three-hundred-fifty degrees," I read off the back. I take out a cookie sheet and arrange some mini-quiches on it as Teresa gets out some bowls and fills them with chips and dip. I find a veggie tray in the refrigerator and get it out, arranging the vegetables on a plate. She turns on some upbeat music, and we have a little fun dancing around the apartment with our wine before the guests show up.

The first three to arrive are our closest friends, Patrick, Melisa and Megan. Teresa knew Megan from a previous job and had become fast friends. Melisa was her younger sister, less than a year separating them in age, so they were very close. Patrick was a guy we had all met in a club one night. He was always willing to go out with us at the drop of a hat. What man wouldn't want to hang out with four attractive drunk women? Teresa and I suspected that he and Melisa had hooked up after one rowdy night, but they never confirmed it and we never asked.

I knew that they had gone to Nate's funeral, and Teresa told me that they had visited me in the hospital a few times when I was first admitted. I don't remember a whole lot from that time. I don't know if my brain was just protecting me from something that would be too painful for me, or if there were drugs involved, but I slept a lot that first week. While I was at Chris's, they had wanted to drive out one night, but I wasn't in the mood for company, so I had asked them not to come. This is the first time I've seen them in a few months.

"Emi!" they exclaim, rushing to hug me. "You look gorgeous!" Megan says.

"Stunning even," Patrick adds.

"Too skinny," Melisa scrunches her nose in mock scrutiny.

"Thanks, thanks," I say. "I've missed you!"

"We've missed you! I'm so happy you're home!"

"Me, too."

"Where's the wine?" Melisa asks. I gesture toward the kitchen where Teresa has put out all the alcohol that we have on hand. I guess it's going to be one of those nights.

We only have one couch, and our apartment is so small that our beds serve as living room furniture, too, so most parties turn into a gathering of lounging, drinking guests. We have extra pillows and blankets for the occasions.

After about twenty minutes, there is a loud knock at the door.

"It's the boys," Teresa says, giggling. Boys? Great.

"Who are these *boys*, exactly?" I ask.

"Bradley, of course," she explains. "He's bringing some of his firefighter friends with him."

"Great," I tell her, giving her a scowl.

"Oh, it's not like that, Em," she says. "They probably won't stay long anyway, they were just going to stop by before going to a bar later on."

"Alright," I concede. She opens the door and three young, built, handsome men enter the apartment. Megan and Melisa say hi, and it seems they've all met before.

"Emi," I say, waving my hand to them from across the room. They introduce themselves to me and grab something to drink. One walks over to my bed and sits down next to me.

"Emi, was it?"

"Yes," I smile cordially.

"So, Emi, what do you do?"

"Like, my work, what do I do?"

"Yes," he laughs. "Like, your work."

"I'm a graphic designer and illustrator," I tell him.

"So you draw?"

"I draw a little. On the computer, really. Not so much by hand."

"I draw," he says. "Give me some paper." I open my sketch pad– which is rarely used– and hand him a pencil. He draws a picture of Garfield... I'm pretty sure it's supposed to be Garfield anyway. It's a fat striped cat leaning over a plate of square food– presumably lasagna.

"Not bad," I say politely, but I'm clearly annoyed. *Who is this man? And why is he here, with me? Is he interested in me? Because it's just too fucking soon for anything like this. I mean, if things were normal again... if my life was normal... would this be fun to me? Was it ever? Would he be interesting?* I struggle to remain calm and... normal.

"You draw something," he instructs, handing me the pad of paper.

"Uh, no," I reiterate. "I don't really draw by hand. Mainly on the computer."

"Oh," he responds. "Well, just something."

"Alright." I reluctantly take the pencil and draw a flower, shading it slightly for a three-dimensional effect.

"That's pretty good," he says. "Very pretty."

"Thanks," I blush. This boy clearly doesn't know good art when he sees it. The flower is average, at best. *You're wasting your time, man.*

"So what do you do for fun, Emi?"

I shrug my shoulders. "I don't know, hang out with friends, go out, that sort of thing." I'm short with him for a reason... for a million different reasons.

"Well, we're going out later tonight, if y'all want to join us."

"Thanks, but I'm not sure," I answer. I *am* sure, actually, I just don't want to be rude. "We'll see."

"Good enough," he says. He walks across the room to his two friends, who are talking to Teresa and Megan about something that happened in the firehouse earlier today. They're all laughing. I sigh heavily, feeling a little overwhelmed and a little antisocial. I'm not ready to be happy Emi, not ready to meet new people. I glance at Melisa and Patrick, who are deep in conversation with one another. I pick up my computer and continue illustrating. In no less than five minutes, the artistic firefighter whose name I've already forgotten comes to peer over my shoulder.

"Wow, that's cool!" he exclaims. I'm wondering if he's just trying to be nice, to strike up a conversation.

I laugh nervously and thank him. I close the window I was working in and open up an Internet browser, navigating to a weather site to see what the forecast is. I can't work when people are watching me. I need to feel uninhibited to do my best work. Eventually, he gets bored and walks away.

Needing a boost of confidence from my brother, I pull out my phone and send Chris a text message. *"Are you coming over?"* A few minutes pass before I receive a response.

"Too late," he texts me. I sigh as I hear a knock on the door. Teresa answers it, and it's my brother, Anna, and Jack.

He sees me across the room and says, "We're already here!" I light up and go to the door, giving him a hug.

"Thank God," I tell him. "This all just feels weird," I whisper.

"Em," he says. "It's okay. I'm sure you're doing fine." Anna hugs me before going to the kitchen to get drinks, and Chris follows to help her.

"Emi," Jack says, smiling, nodding his head.

"Hi, Jack. What brings you out tonight?"

"We were actually looking at tuxes, of all things," he says. "Chris seems to be under the impression that I have a better sense of style than he does, so he wanted my opinion on what he had narrowed them down to."

"So, what did you decide on?"

"We're thinking top hats and canes," he says, scratching his chin, his voice contemplative. "And purple and gold, those look pretty sharp."

"Nice," I tell him, smiling. "I can see it now. You'll look just like the boys at my eighth grade dance, circa 1993."

"Eighth grade, huh?" He cringes. "In 1993, that would have been my senior prom."

"Well, hey, old man, a cane may be appropriate for you, then," I tease.

"You hush, little girl," he jokes with me.

"Well, did you pick something out for real?"

"We did," he says. "Just some classic looking tux... oh, hell, who am I kidding? It's a tux, they really all look the same, don't they?"

"No. Is it black?"

"Black."

"Tails?"

"No."

"Bow tie?"

"Um, no."

"Three button?"

"Was I supposed to count them?" he asks.

"I guess it's a good thing Anna was there, or you would look like a gay Mr. Peanut– without the monocle, of course."

"Of course," he laughs. "No monocle." Anna and Chris bring Jack and I drinks.

"So, did he tell you about the tux?" Anna asks.

"As well as any man could," I tell her, giving Jack a sideways glance.

"They're nice," she says. "I took pictures of them on my phone. I'll show you later."

"Cool," I tell her.

"You know, you and I need to go shopping one of these days," she begins. "When you're ready, I mean." She looks at me uncomfortably.

"Sure, Anna," I assure her. "Just say when, and I'll be there. You've only got six months, you know."

"I know," she agrees. "I don't know what we were thinking, setting the date so soon."

"I know. You just can't wait to start your lives together," I say. "I completely understand." I feel a lump growing in my throat, but swallow quickly, keeping it from causing tears to well up in my eyes. The last thing I want to do is take any of the joy out of their wedding planning. They deserve an amazing wedding, and as the maid of honor, it's my duty to help make sure it's everything Anna wants it to be and more. Sure, it's difficult. And yeah, maybe she's having second thoughts on me being a part of her wedding party under the circumstances, but I don't want her to have any regrets. I will do everything a good maid of honor can do to support her bride.

"How are you settling back in, Emi?" Chris asks.

"Just fine. It's like I was never gone. Do you guys want to come sit down?" I lead them to my bed and we all have a seat.

"So, you do graphic design?" Jack asks.

"Yeah, I do freelance work for agencies mostly," I tell him. "Right now I'm illustrating for a story for a women's magazine."

"What's the story about?"

"It's about child care, actually," I tell him. "Sort of the pros and cons of day care versus staying at home versus a nanny... typical women's fare."

"So what are your illustrations?"

"Oh, well, I'm just drawing the children in each situation... children being children... you know."

"Do you have any to show?"

"I don't know," I tell him, embarrassed. "The drawings aren't finished yet..."

"I'm no art critic," he laughs. "I can barely hold a pencil, much less draw. I won't judge."

"I guess... okay." I open up the laptop and navigate to a few of the illustrations.

"Those are amazing, Emi," he laughs with genuine interest. "I love the masks they're wearing."

"Thanks," I tell him. "Just trying to characterize them as the little monsters they can be..."

"Sort of reminiscent of 'Where the Wild Things Are,'" he says.

"Wow," I say, surprised. "That was actually my inspiration. I wasn't sure the reference was relevant enough."

"I love that book! The pictures are really great. I think this is really... great," he tells me.

"Well... thanks," I tell him, blushing. "How do you remember the book, old man? You were a child of the sixties, weren't you?" I joke with him.

"Somewhere around there," he responds. "No, actually, I've got two nieces and two nephews... and somewhere along the way, I became their designated story teller."

"How old are they?"

"Twelve, eight, five and two."

"Wow, a twelve-year-old?"

"Yes, my twin sister, Kelly, started pretty young," he says. "She married her high school sweetheart. She was twenty-one when she had her first son."

"Are they still together?"

"Happily married," he nods.

"So you have a sister, Kelly, and then just the two brothers?" I ask to keep the conversation going.

"How did you know?"

"Remember, they swept in like superheroes to save your life," I tease him, remembering the altercation on Fifth Avenue.

"*Your* life," he says.

"He was going after you at that point."

"Yeah, good point. Yes, just the two brothers. Matthew's thirty-one and Steven is twenty-seven."

"No kids there?"

"Steven's girlfriend has a daughter, but they don't have any of their own. They do both want to have kids someday, though. I guess it's a byproduct of a happy childhood."

I nod, thinking silently to myself, staring across the room until I lose focus. All this talk of children... just makes me... sad. I clutch my stomach and a tear escapes from my eye.

"I'm sorry," Jack says. "Did I say something..."

"She's fine," Chris interrupts before I can respond. I nod and confirm that I'm okay. I'm guessing he doesn't know about the child I lost in the accident.

"Hey, Emi," Teresa calls from the couch. "We're all going to go dancing. Do you guys want to come?"

I look at Chris and Anna, and they shake their heads. I don't really want to go either. The sleepless night seems to be catching up with me. "No, I'm pretty tired. I think we'll just stay here."

"You sure?"

"I'm sure, Teresa. Go out, have fun." I feel a little bad about my anti-social behavior. I just feel like I've been out of our social circle for so long that I'm having a hard time fitting back in. I'm comfortable with my brother and my soon-to-be sister-in-law. I'm sure I'll soon feel like going out again, but I'm not ready for that yet. I just want the safety and security that I get from our little apartment.

Teresa and her friends pick up their things and exit the apartment, leaving me, Chris, Anna and Jack lounging on the two beds. We talk some more, as Chris takes the remote and turns the television on, giving us some background noise. Chris and Anna are lying on Teresa's bed, and eventually resort to talking quietly to one another. Jack and I sit on my bed, looking at the TV. I'm feeling vaguely uncomfortable sitting on my bed with him... but I don't really know how to diffuse the situation. *Do I get up and go sit across the room on the couch? Isn't that rude? I can't do that.* I just decide to pull my legs into my chest, closing myself off.

"I think I'm going to call it a night," Jack announces, possibly reading my body language, relief washing over me.

"You want us to take you home?" Chris asks.

"No, I'll get a cab," he tells us.

"Alright, well thanks for coming out with us tonight," my brother says.

"It was my pleasure," he says, turning his attention to me. "It was good to see you again, Emi."

"Thanks, you too."

"Take care of yourself."

"Thanks, I will," I tell him. I walk him to the door, closing it behind him.

"You guys don't have to stay," I tell my brother and Anna. "I'll be fine."

"I don't know, Emi," Anna says. "We don't have to leave yet."

"Honestly, I'm really tired. I didn't sleep at all last night, and I'm sure I'll be out once my head hits the pillow. There's nothing to worry about."

"You know you can call us at any time, right?" Chris asks.

"I know."

"And here, let me give you Jack's number. He's just a few blocks away. I'd feel better knowing you had someone close-by in case you ever needed anything. He said he wouldn't mind helping out."

"I don't think I'll need that."

"Just take it, Emi. It'll make me feel better about leaving you here alone."

"Alright."

"We love you, Em."

"Love you guys, too. Be careful going home."

"We will."

"Well," I tell them, hugging them both, "good night."

"Sleep well, Emi."

"Bye."

I walk to the dresser and look at myself in the mirror. I have a difficult time recognizing myself at times. It's not just the fact that I've lost weight since the accident. Something in my eyes just seems sad, dull. Will I ever be vibrant, happy? Or has this experience changed me so much that I will never be the woman I once knew, the woman that Nate knew and loved. Would he recognize me today?

I take the necklace off and place it carefully back in the box. I wash my face and put on a t-shirt, one of Nate's that I found earlier in the day. It's clean, doesn't smell like him, but there are two small spatters of paint on one of the sleeves that remind me of him. I crawl into bed, hugging myself tightly as I start to cry. This is the first time I've been truly alone since that night. I suddenly wish I still had the tie with me, so I could breathe him in, and feel him with me again. I want to remember everything about him! I focus on the time we spent in the hotel, making love. When my mind starts to wander to the car, to the crash, I do whatever I have to do to keep the image of him dying out of my head. I know it's there, always in the background, but that isn't how I want to remember him.

I sob heavily, loudly, like I haven't been able to do in weeks. Being alone gives me the freedom to let it all out. I cry until there are no more tears, until my head hurts so badly that even the moonlight is too much for my weary eyes to handle. This is the time of night that I find my over-active imagination to be most useful. I pretend that Nate's arm is around my body, cuddling closely to me. I feel safe, protected, loved. I will fall asleep shortly.

The sunlight is full and bright when I open my eyes the next day. I look at the alarm clock, which states 1:15. I've been sleeping for over twelve hours... I don't remember the last time that happened. Teresa's bed is just how she left it last night, so it's clear she didn't come home last night after dancing. I see a light flashing on my phone and pick it up off the nightstand. Three texts, two missed calls, one message.

The first text is my brother letting me know they made it home okay. The second is from Anna, sent minutes later, asking if I was okay. Teresa sent the third, letting me know she would be staying at Bradley's. The voice message is from Anna, from this morning, again asking how I was doing. *I'm fine, I'm fine, stop worrying about me, people.* I know I should be appreciative... I'll text them in a few.

I decide to get up and shower before leaving the apartment for a latte. I don't bother putting make-up on or fixing my hair. I stuff my laptop in my bag and head out the door. The day is beautiful, not too cool. I pick up the coffee and take it outside, deciding to go for a walk. I end up at Nate's building. Marcus greets me and invites me in, giving me a sympathetic hug.

"Are you moving in yet?" he asks.

"No, not yet," I tell him. "I don't know if I'll ever be able to."

"Well, I hope you change your mind."

I nod. "I guess I'll go up and make sure everything is okay, though."

"Alright, Emi. Let us know if you need anything. My shift is almost over, but our new doorman, Frank, will be here for the rest of the day."

"Thanks." I take a deep breath and head toward the elevator. It seems so quiet, so empty inside, more so than normal. At the moment I feel I may suffocate in the enclosed space, the door opens on the twelfth floor and I quickly escape. I stand outside of Nate's door– my door– fumbling for the key and trying to find some courage. Finally, I'm able to go in.

The quiet and emptiness of the elevator doesn't even begin to compare to the feeling of Nate's apartment. There is no life at all inside. Every step on the hardwood floor sounds amplified, echos. I go to the stereo that sits gathering dust and turn it on. The Zero 7 CD is still in the player. I go through the stack of CDs next to his stereo, finding the one we listened to in LA. I sigh, remembering the night in Los Angeles when everything was finally falling into place.

I put my computer on the work desk and power it on, trying to envision living here. I walk to the kitchen to throw my coffee cup away, see if there is anything in the refrigerator. The only thing left is bottled water, something Nate always had ample supplies of. I take one out and carry it to the desk with me.

Of course there is no Internet access here anymore, all the wireless networks password protected, so if I intend to do work over here, I'll need to look into that. I decide to do some touch-up work on the illustrations. After only thirty minutes, I just feel overwhelmingly tired. I'm not sure why, after twelve hours of sleep, but it's difficult to even keep my eyes open. I look at the bed, and know immediately I cannot lie down on it. There are just far too many memories there. I want to leave those memories as they are, don't want to taint them with new ones. I walk over to the couch and cuddle with a throw pillow. The music lulls me to sleep.

A knock on the door wakes me. When I open my eyes, I'm disoriented and confused. It takes me a few minutes to realize where I am and why I'm here. Another knock. I have no idea who would be coming to visit– no one knows I'm here. Looking through the peephole doesn't help. It's a young woman, but I don't know her. I assume she has the wrong apartment, so I open the door to tell her.

"Can I help you?" I ask her, suddenly realizing that it's Samantha. She looks older, her hair cropped to her shoulders.

"Oh," she says, obviously surprised to see me at the door. She looks behind me at the apartment, scanning the room. "Is Nate here?"

"I'm sorry?" I say.

"Um, Emi, right?" I nod. "Is Nate around?"

"I'm sorry," I repeat nervously, my body starting to shake. "Samantha, why are you here?"

"I just need to talk to him for a second. If he's not here, I can come back."

I shake my head slowly, disbelieving, looking into her eyes to see if she's joking. I gather that she's serious by her eager look. "Samantha... he doesn't live here..."

"What do you mean?" she asks curiously. "I know that's his stuff," she says referring to his apartment furnishings.

"Yes, it's his stuff," I tell her, forcing a smile. "And no, he's not here, Sam." My voice seems to get quieter involuntarily. *How could she not know? How did she get past the doorman? Did she really not know?*

"I tried calling, but his phone was disconnected," she explains.

"Yes," I say, my eyes beginning to water. "Did you need something, Samantha?"

"No," she laughs. "I just missed him. I was hoping to talk to him about things... show him how I've changed." She seems so young, naive.

"Oh, my god," I choke out the words.

"What is it?"

"Come in, Sam," I open the door wider, inviting her into the apartment. "Sit down."

She sits on the couch, tense, her posture straight, looking at me with wondering eyes.

"Samantha," I say, taking her hand in mine. "Nate passed away." I've never had to tell anyone that before, and the words feel horrible coming out of my mouth. It's as if they have their own terrible aftertaste. I swallow the familiar lump in my throat.

"What?" she says, shocked, her face crumpling. She begins to cry, and I can tell that she truly cared for him, for my love.

"It was a car accident on New Year's Eve," I say, trying to be strong for her as others were for me when the news was still fresh and foreign.

She sobs uncontrollably, and I reach over to hug her. She embraces me tightly, clinging to me.

"It's okay," I whisper, telling myself as much as I am telling her.

"I still love him," Samantha confesses.

"So do I," I tell her. "I know it hurts." I remember that Nate had been her first, and recognized that she would always feel a special connection to him. I don't feel jealous. I know that what Nate and I shared was different than anything that he shared with other women, with her. But what he and I had was too sacred to relate to anyone, especially her. She didn't need to know the details.

"It's not fair," she sobs.

"No, it's not," I agree. It feels different to be on this side of the news, the one delivering it. The fact that I'm able to say it out loud makes me realize that I've made significant progress in healing. It's as if this visit from his ex is a test for me. And I feel like I'm passing.

Samantha releases her hold on me and stands up, wandering around the apartment, looking at things that brought back her own familiar memories. As she eyes the bed, I feel panic. That bed is sacred to me. I don't care what connection she feels to it. It holds my memories, and I don't want to think of anyone else having such memories. I don't want anyone's hands touching it. She begins to reach for a pillow, and I can't contain the feeling any longer.

"Please don't touch that," I tell her, order her. She stops in her tracks. "I'm sorry, but please don't touch the bed."

"I just wanted to–"

"I know," I cut her off. "But, please don't. Just, please leave it alone."

She looks at me confused.

"I'm going to have to ask you to leave," I tell her. "This, um... it's my apartment now... and I would appreciate if you didn't come back here."

"But–"

"I don't mean to be rude," I tell her, unable to catch my breath. "I know you're a sweet girl. I know he was important to you. But he was mine. He was my everything, meant everything to me." The strength I felt a few minutes ago drains quickly from my body. The tears begin to flow. "Please go."

Samantha nods, looks at me like I'm crazy and exits the apartment quickly. I fall to my knees, crumple to the floor.

"Damn it, Nate!" I yell. "Why?!"

Over the next few hours, the phone rings a few times, text messages come in. Since the phone is on the desk, and I remain in a ball on the floor, I don't answer anyone's attempts to contact me. There's no point. I feel like I've taken a huge step backwards. I don't want anyone to see me like this. I struggle to find my sanity again, to accept him, his life, his death. I hate that she came over here, reminded me that he had a different life with different women. I hate that I feel a little less special, was reminded that I wasn't the only one who loved him completely. I hate that other women may have known him like I did. I hate that I had to be the one to tell her that he died. *Died.*

Another knock on the door brings me back to reality, but I realize I don't have to answer it. I didn't have to earlier, shouldn't have, in fact. If I had ignored it, I would be functioning in some capacity right now. I'd be designing, or reading, or watching television or something productive. Instead, I remain crippled, motionless on this hardwood floor.

Suddenly the door opens, and I realize I didn't lock the door after Samantha left.

"Emi," Jack says, rushing to me on the floor, his shadow disappearing in the darkness as the door closes behind him.

"What are you doing here?" I ask, unable to see anything in the apartment due to the moonless night.

"Chris has been trying to get in touch with you. We've all been looking for you for hours. I went by your apartment, and this was the only place Teresa could think of that you might be. Are you alright?"

"No," I tell him.

"Did you fall?"

"No."

"Are you hurt?"

"Yes."

"Where?" he asks, his hands lightly touching my shoulders.

"My heart," I exhale in a sob.

Realizing I'm not physically hurt, he picks me up off the floor. My eyes adjust to the darkness in time to see him carrying me to the bed.

"Don't put me on the bed!"

"Okay, Emi," he says, "calm down. Breathe... Is the couch okay?"

"Yes," I tell him. He sets me down and turns on a nearby lamp. He calls Chris, telling him where he found me, how he found me.

"Why did you come here, Emi?" he asks.

"Just to check on things," I tell him. "I went for a walk and ended up here." I tell him the whole story, the happenings of the day, how it made me feel that Samantha showed up, said she loved him. I tell him how it made me feel less important, less special. I tell him more than I intend to tell him, to tell anyone. I am such an emotional wreck I can't stop the flow of words.

"Emi," he says reassuringly. "If you think that you were just another woman to Nate, you are sadly mistaken."

"You didn't know him," I argue.

"No, I didn't. But I know what I saw in his eyes, on more than one occasion. The night I met you, I could see how much he completely adored you. I saw his aside glance to me, warning me to stay away from you. And at the party on New Year's?" he pauses, waiting for me to look at him. "I saw how he looked at you when he came off the stage, the passion in his eyes pierced through me, through everything else in that room. He loved you deeply and completely... and that's rare, Emi.

"He was lucky to have found you. It was obvious that you were his world. And if I could see that, could feel that... me, just some stranger that didn't even know him... well, Emi, you should have no doubt in your mind."

"That's nice of you to say."

"Well, it's true," he laments, then sighs. After a few minutes, my breathing is back to normal and I sit up on the couch, staring at my feet.

"Can I walk you back to your apartment?"

"You don't have to," I tell him as a sudden deja vu invades my otherwise distracted mind. I feel as if we have had this exact conversation before.

"I know I don't have to, but I'd like to... give Chris some peace of mind." A slight grin breaks out across his face.

"Why are you smiling like that?" I ask, curious.

"Just... nothing," he laughs quietly.

"Okay," I smile, still wondering but feeling strangely comforted and... okay. "Let me get my things." I put my laptop in my bag, and Jack takes it from me, slinging it easily over his shoulder. I turn off the lights and lock the door behind us.

"So I was thinking," Jack says as we walk down the street, "that the next time you feel like going over there, maybe you should bring someone with you. I'm sure Teresa would go... Anna or Chris would be happy to come down, I know."

"I don't know when I'll go back."

"Well, when you do..." his voice trails off. "Have you eaten anything today?"

"I don't think so."

"Do you want to get something?" he asks.

"No, thanks. I'll eat something at home."

"Okay." The rest of the walk home is silent, except for occasional street noise. He walks me upstairs to my unit, and familiar sounds greet us before I even get out my keys. Teresa has Bradley over... *fabulous*. I feel my face get hot, blush.

"Uhhh..." Jack says before letting out a small laugh.

"Yeah," I retort, bitterness oozing from my throat.

"Are you sure you don't want to go grab a bite to eat?"

"I'm sure," I tell him, taking a deep breath and grabbing my bag off of his shoulder. "This is my life." I open the door briskly and walk in. As I turn around to close the door, he looks at me, confused, and I tell him good night.

"Bye, Em."

I keep my head down as I walk to the dresser to get some pajamas. Teresa and her boyfriend don't even act like I'm in the room, although I know I made enough noise to make them aware. Quickly, I go into the bathroom, turn on the radio and start running water for a shower. Hopefully that will give them enough time to finish what they're doing.

As I stand under the hot tap water, I consider my options. It seems pretty clear what I need to do. I need to acquaint myself with Nate's apartment again... need to accept it as my home... need to get out of this situation before it drives me crazy.

~ * ~

Two weeks pass, and the occasional night of sex continues in the apartment. I don't know how I ever stood it before. Their feeble attempts to be quiet, discreet, they just aren't good enough. I don't know if I'm angry because I'm not having sex, or if I've just reached my breaking point with her lifestyle, but I don't think I can stay here much longer. I feel like I've been changed too much to go back to this life. I'm not the person I used to be.

As I'm working one afternoon, the phone rings.

"Hello?" I answer.

"Emi, it's Jen," my sister says.

"Hey, Jennifer, what's up?"

"Nothing," she speaks, her voice wavering, noticeably upset.

"What's wrong?"

"Michael..."

"Michael what?" I ask.

"We've decided to separate," she cries. "It's just not working out."

"Oh, Jen, I'm so sorry. What happened?"

"He just doesn't think he loves me anymore," she tells me. "He's bored with me."

"That asshole," I mumble. I never liked him.

"Where are you?"

"I'm at home," she says. "I have to go pick Clara up from Pre-K in an hour."

"Where is he?"

"I don't know."

"Listen, why don't you pick up Clara and come over. I'll make some dinner and we can talk about it."

"You don't mind?"

"Not at all," I assure her.

"Thanks, Emi."

As I wait for my sister and niece to arrive, I straighten up the apartment. As I'm making the bed, I have an idea. I iron out the details in my mind and think that Jennifer will definitely go for it. They show up a short while later.

"Clara-bee!" I say, squatting to pick up my niece and twirling her around. I set her down on the couch in front of the television, currently tuned to an educational channel. She is immediately enthralled. I hug my sister and offer her a glass of wine and a box of tissues. In the kitchen, as I make dinner, she tells me about their recent fights, hurtful things that were said... things that just can't be taken back, and will likely end their relationship for good.

"I think you're better off without him," I tell my sister. I know that she doesn't want another marriage to fail, but they were never good for one another. They eloped so quickly that no one was able to talk any sense into her before they exchanged vows.

"Deep down," she admits, "I know you're right. It's just hard... to be alone..."

I shake my head, give her a knowing smile. "So I have an idea."

"I'm listening," she says.

"Well... I'm thinking about moving into Nate's apartment."

"Do you think you're ready for that?"

"No," I tell her. "Not alone, I'm not, but..."

"Us?"

"Yeah. Maybe you and Clara could move in with me... we could start to make the place mine, create some new memories there... and you could see if the separation is what's best for you... I know the drive to Clara's school would be far, but it'll be summer soon, so you won't have to worry about it for long..."

"Are you sure, Emi?"

I smile, feeling strangely hopeful. "I'm positive. Please, Jen. Let's do this... for both of us."

She shrugs, smiles back at me, and I can see hope in her eyes, too. "Okay!"

CHAPTER 5

Last week, in preparation for the big move, I invited Donna to the apartment to go through some of Nate's things, take items that should stay in her family, things that have sentimental value to her. She encouraged me to keep the furniture, and told me it would be okay if I took the art down. I can't bear the thought of that, though. I wouldn't want it anywhere else. Seeing his art makes me happy... the paintings were a part of him, so they're really something he's left behind for us to enjoy; to bring us fond memories. We've boxed up his clothes, keeping an item or two to ourselves. The rest of the things, we have decided, are going to a local shelter. When Donna leaves, she tells me that I can do whatever I want with anything that's left. We agree to meet for coffee in the next couple of weeks.

I'm now returning home with new linens for the bed. I desperately hope that this will make it okay to sleep in it. I had offered that bed to Jen and Clara, but Jen insisted on taking the smaller guest bedroom. I unpack the sheets and throw them in the washer.

Teresa was upset at first when I told her I was moving out. She was stressing about how she would be able to afford the rent and utilities on her own. A few days later, she announced that Bradley was moving in with her, which would be a much better arrangement for her in the end– as long as they stayed together. He and his firefighter friends helped to move my stuff this morning.

Michael helped Jennifer pack her things, happy that he would get to stay in the house. It was his house to begin with, so I don't think he ever had any intention of moving out in the first place. Jen had hopes that this would just be a trial separation, but in my heart, I think it's over. And I think it's best, especially with Clara in the picture. I can remember the fights our parents had when we were younger. It was difficult to live at home at times. For Clara's sake, I'd love to see her grow up in a happy household.

My sister and niece will be moving in tomorrow. We decided it would be best for me to get my stuff in and start unloading a day in advance, to alleviate a little bit of chaos. What that means for me is that I have to spend my first night here alone. Chris would be calling me later, I was sure... likely multiple times. He had been worried, had even offered to come stay with me tonight, but I really do want to try to do this on my own.

I sort through the boxes, unpacking things here and there, and before I know it, the apartment begins to look and feel different. Maybe I will be able to make this loft my home. I turn on some music and just focus on what I have to do, and the day, evening, they both pass quickly. By eleven, I'm tired– but still not certain that I'll be able to fall asleep without difficulty... no matter what the place looks like, there are memories of him everywhere. I go to turn on the bath water, and as I'm walking to grab my pajamas, someone knocks at the door. All of a sudden, I realize Chris hasn't called at all tonight... and then it dawns on me that I probably never turned the ringer on today. I have been way too busy to even think about that.

Through the peephole, I see Jack and laugh to myself. I open the door quickly.

"What?" I ask, smiling, knowing exactly why he is here and exactly who sent him.

"We've all been calling..."

"I know," I confess. "I guess my ringer was turned off. I'm sorry."

"Are you doing okay?" he asks, lingering in the doorway.

"Fine," I tell him.

"You look good."

"No, I look like hell," I correct him, running my hands through my messy hair. "Come in... let me go turn off the faucet." His hands in his pockets, he ambles through the doorway. "Do you need to call Chris?" I yell from the other room.

"Just texted him," he hollers back.

"I was just going to take a bath," I tell him. "I feel like I have dust all over me."

"Well, don't let me stop you," he says. "I just wanted to make sure you were getting settled okay. I'll go."

"No," I say quickly, secretly thankful that he came, that someone came over tonight. I know I will benefit from a little distraction. "You came all this way. What's your drink of choice?"

"Do you have any beer?" he asks.

"Yep. Just stocked up at the store for the awesome firefighter movers."

"Excellent."

I grab a beer from the refrigerator and take it to him. "Feel free to have a seat."

"Thanks. Do you need help with anything? Hanging pictures, moving heavy objects?"

"No, I think I've got that taken care of already... so where do you live?"

"Upper West Side," he says.

"You didn't walk all the way over here, did you?"

"No," he laughs sheepishly. "I was actually on a date when Chris called me."

"You're kidding me..."

"No," he says. "Is that so unbelievable?"

"Oh, no, that's not what I meant," I explain. "Where is she?"

"I dropped her off at her apartment."

"Well, please, I'm sorry... please, get back to your date," I encourage him. "If I had realized–"

"No, don't make me!" he says. "It was awful. I was so thankful Chris called. It couldn't have ended soon enough."

We both laugh. "Oh, okay. What happened?"

"Oh, god," he sighs. "It was a blind date. Russell, my college roommate, set us up." He groans.

"That bad?"

"I don't know what he was thinking," he says. "The only thing she had going for her was her looks, and that's just not enough for me."

"Yeah, you seem like a guy who likes a little substance," I tell him.

"A lot of substance," he corrects me. "I've been told I'm too picky... that my standards are too high."

"I've been told that, as well," I smile. I was just lucky that Nate met all those standards. Well, he *was* the standard. I swallow thoughtfully. "I think it's okay to have high standards."

"Okay, maybe, but it sure limits your love life," he laughs.

"Yeah, but when you find her, it'll be great."

"Hope so," he says, finishing his beer, looking around the apartment. He reaches for the photo album that's sitting on the coffee table... then retreats, realizing what it is.

"Um, do you want another drink?" I ask him, my attempt to distract him as I move the book to the shelf across the room. *I need to find a special place for that.*

"I don't want to keep you from your bath," he says.

"I can get you a beer and take a bath, you know. As long as you don't think I'm being a bad hostess."

"Well, then, sure, I'll take another."

"Okay, make yourself at home," I tell him. "I don't have a whole lot to eat, but you can probably find something... and here's the remote."

I pour myself a glass of wine and head back to the bathroom, turning on the hot water again to fill the jacuzzi. As I climb in, I can't help but reflect on the memories of Nate, particularly our night together in this very tub. That night was raw and instinctive and passionate. Everything was still new to us. We conceived a child that night. The lump in my throat threatens to surface, but I force a smile, remembering how happy I had been with Nate, not just when we were dating, but for years. I remember his smile, the way he looked at me when he kissed me. *Focus on the happy times. That's what I have to do to move forward.* He would want me to remember him this way, and I intend to honor that.

I slowly drink my wine and relax in the hot water, soothing my sore muscles after a long day of moving and unpacking. After about a half hour, I remember that Jack is still here and decide to get out and be social with my guest. I dry off and put on some flannel pants and a t-shirt, and then I put my robe on over that.

"What are we watching?" I ask as I walk past him in front of the refrigerator, making my way to the couch.

"News," he tells me. "I'm feeling out of touch. Is it okay if I have one more?" I nod my head and adjust a throw pillow on the couch, cuddling with it, waiting for him to return from the kitchen. I notice his phone vibrate and light up on the couch next to me. I don't mean to look, but the message is from my brother, and short enough for me to read in one sideways glance.

"Sure you don't mind staying with her for awhile?"

A part of me wants to admit that I read it, wants me to encourage him to go. I don't want him to feel obligated to stay and essentially babysit me... but another part of me wants him to hang around a little longer. It feels good having someone here. The more I think about it, the more I'm not sure I'm ready to be alone tonight.

He picks up his phone and glances down at it as I pull my feet up on the couch, tucking them closely into my body to not invade his personal space. I avoid his eye contact when I feel him looking over at me, afraid that he'll choose to go. I'd really like him to stay. After a few minutes, he clears his throat and makes comments on the news stories here and there, but over time, I find it difficult to keep my eyes open.

"Emi?" someone says softly, the apartment dark. It takes me a second to realize where I am, who is talking to me, whose lap my feet are in–

"Oh, crap!" I say, sitting up immediately and pulling my legs to the floor. "I'm so sorry, Jack, did I fall asleep?"

"Yes," he laughs. "You've been out for hours. I dozed off, too."

"What time is it?" I ask.

"It's four in the morning."

"Oh, my god! You didn't have to stay," I explain.

"I didn't mean to, Emi. I dozed off, too," he repeats. "I just wanted to let you know I was going so you could lock up behind me."

"Oh, yeah," I say. "I hope you didn't have any plans this morning..."

"Actually, I do," he laughs. "But I'll be alright. Don't worry about me." He picks up his bottles and puts them on the island on his way to the door.

"Oh, I am so sorry," I reiterate.

"Stop apologizing, Emi! It's fine!" he laughs.

"Okay, if you're sure."

"I'm sure. Are you going to be okay?"

"Yes," I tell him, and I know that I will go right back to sleep.

"Alright, sleep well," he says, smiling.

"Be careful," I tell him. "And thank you."

"My pleasure." I close the door and lock it after he leaves. I walk to the bed, pull off the comforter and take it over to the couch to go back to sleep.

Someone poking me on the shoulder wakes me up. My whole body aches as I try to move my limbs. Groggily, I open my eyes and leap into an upright position when I see a face only inches from mine.

"Anni-Emi?" my niece says, realizing she scared me.

"Clara! What are you doing here?" I sweep her into my lap and kiss her on the cheek.

"We used the key," Jennifer says apologetically. "I knocked but you didn't answer."

"Sleeping," I explain. "Really well, apparently. I don't think I've moved at all since I laid down... sorry about that."

"Well, are you ready for us? The truck is downstairs."

"Of course, I'll pull on some clothes to help. I cleared out the guest room for you and arranged it like we talked about."

"Thank you," she says.

We spend the day directing movers and unpacking boxes. The move goes smoothly, and the apartment looks less and less like Nate's as the day wears on. I make sandwiches for the three of us and we all take a break from the hectic day.

"So," my sister begins. "You slept on the couch?"

"Well, I didn't mean to," I tell her. "Funny story."

"Love to hear it..."

"I guess everyone was calling yesterday, and my ringer was off, so Chris sent Jack here. He stayed for awhile and had a beer while we watched some TV... and apparently I fell asleep on the couch... he woke me up at four."

"He stayed over?" she asked.

"He didn't mean to. He fell asleep, too... but he woke me up and after he left, I just decided to go back to the couch where I was already comfortable."

"Mm-hmm," Jennifer says skeptically. "Pretty sure Chris put him up to that..."

"Maybe," I respond vaguely, not wanting to admit that I saw the text that my brother had sent.

"And you're sleeping where tonight?" my sister asks.

"His bed... I think... I'm going to try."

"Good. It's *your* bed, Em. It'll be okay."

"I know. It doesn't really even look like his bed anymore. I just know... but I'm sure I'll be fine."

"Atta girl," she says.

"Emi?" Clara asks.

"Yes, sweetie?"

"Can I sleep with you?"

"Clara," Jennifer says, "we have our own bed in there, remember?" She gestures toward the guest room.

"I know, but I want to sleep with Emi and Nate-Nate like last time." Jennifer looks at me, worried. It is true that the last time Clara stayed here a few weeks before he died, she slept in between Nate and I when she came down with a cold. I smile warmly at my niece.

"Well, Clara," I say softly. "Remember, Nate-Nate's not here." Every so often, we have to remind her that Nate is gone. Still, she doesn't comprehend what happened to him, but she is finally accepting of his absence. She just has to be reminded every once in awhile.

"Oh, yeah," she smiles. "Nate-Nate's in heaven."

"That's right," Jennifer says. I smile, feeling the familiar lump in my throat and my eyes beginning to water. I stand up to get drinks so she won't see me cry. She is such a sweet little girl, she normally cries with me when I begin. And I don't want her to cry.

"Clara," I tell her, carrying three bottles of water. "You can sleep with me any time your mommy says it's okay."

"Yea!" she exclaims. "Mama, can I tonight? Please?"

Jennifer looks at me, and I nod my head. "Okay," she says. "But just tonight." I know my sister is doing what she thinks is best for me. I mouth the words "thank you" to her.

"So, hey, Chris and I were talking about your birthday," Jennifer says to me.

I groan and roll my eyes. "What about it?" I dread my birthday, coming in a little over a month. I will be thirty years old.

"What do you want to do to celebrate it?" she asks.

"Nothing," I laugh. "Absolutely nothing. I'd like to stay in my twenties, thank you."

"Not possible," she says. "We can do a party here–"

"No," I interrupt. "Not here. No party." We had Nate's 29th birthday here just five months ago. So much has happened since then. My whole life has changed, whole world turned upside down.

"Okay, we can go out..."

"I don't know," I consider the options. "What about just a family thing?

Something low key."

"We could do that."

"Maybe at Chris's apartment?" I ask.

"I'll suggest it to him. I'm sure he and Anna would be happy to host it."

After dinner, we continue to unload boxes, and again, I'm exhausted by the day's end. After my bath, I go over to the bed, where Clara is already tucked in and fast asleep. I tell my sister good night and crawl under the covers of the king sized bed. I kiss Clara on the forehead, careful not to wake her. As I try to sleep, I do my best to think of anything other than Nate, but the image of his smiling face keeps making an appearance in my thoughts. I allow myself to think about kissing him goodnight. Instead of feeling sad, the usual longing, I feel okay. Hopeful that the healing is continuing, I focus on sleep.

~ * ~

"Son of a bitch!"

"What's going on?" I ask my sister after she slams the door shut.

"You know how I couldn't find that one box of Clara's toys?"

"Yes..."

"Well, I realized I must have left it in the closet at the house, so I decided to stop by after I dropped Clara off at school. I tried to call Michael first, but he didn't answer." In the past two weeks since she moved in, we had unpacked every box, gone through every drawer, trying to find the toys that were missing. They had been boxed up for awhile, toys that Clara had outgrown, ones that my sister wasn't ready to part with yet.

I have a feeling I know where this conversation is headed. "What happened?"

"There was a *fucking* woman walking around the *fucking* house in his *fucking* robe!" It was just as I had expected.

She sits down on the couch and starts to cry. It's not fair that this has to happen to her, again. Her first husband cheated on her. And even though she was currently separated from Michael, it was far too soon for either of them to move on... at least it was too soon in her mind, and in my mind, as well. They had decided on a "trial" separation, but it was clear to me what his intent was from the start. My sister was hopeful she wouldn't have to survive two failed marriages.

"Jen," I tell her, putting aside my work, "I'm so sorry."

"It's just not fair," she sobs.

"No, it's not," I agree, rubbing her back. "What did he do?"

"Nothing!" she yells. "He acted like everything was normal, like I should expect another woman to be in *our* home! He tried to introduce her to me, but as soon as I saw her, I just stumbled to the closet, found the box, and made my way out the door, as fast as I could." She gets up off the couch hurriedly and walks into the kitchen, finding the nearest bottle of wine and pouring herself a glass.

"Jen, it's not even ten—"

"Emi," she warns. "Do *not* go there."

"Sorry, you're right," I apologize. I'm pretty sure I'd need something to calm my nerves, too, if I was in her position.

"I might as well just file for divorce now," she says. "I don't know what we're waiting on. If he can just move on and start fucking strangers so soon after we split... I don't think he wants me anymore." She weeps quietly, restraining herself from letting it out again. "What is wrong with me, Emi?"

"Nothing," I assure her. "This has nothing to do with you. This has to do with an immature man who rushed into marriage when he wasn't sure it was what he wanted. Period. You guys barely knew each other, remember?"

"But we were in love," she explains. "He accepted me and Clara, both. I thought he loved us."

"I'm sure he thought he did, too. In fact, I'm sure he did. I'm sure he acted on that passion... probably never considered any practicalities... consequences... sacrifices he'd have to make."

"You know," she says, "why couldn't he have been the one to die?" My breathing stops, my heart stutters at her statement.

"Jen, don't say things like that," I try to reason with my sister.

"Seriously?" she says, her voice elevating and words quickening, becoming more and more irrational. "I don't understand why Nate, who was so devoted to you, loved you completely, was well on his way to creating the perfect life for you both... why did he have to go? Why would God take him, one of the few genuinely good men of the world? And why would He leave this piece of shit excuse for a human behind?" She gets up to pour another glass of wine.

"Jen, please," I beg. "You can't look for reason in Nate's death at all. There is no *reason* behind why he is gone. I have just had to learn to trust that Nate was needed elsewhere and that He had other plans for me. It's all blind faith... but it's all I have to explain what happened."

"And you just accept it?" she asks.

"I have to. What other options are there? Live in denial? Pretend he's still here? Be angry at God? Kill myself?"

My sister sits in silence as she drinks.

"In the end, I just think about what Nate would want for me. I believe he's watching me... that he looks out for me... that he really just wants me to be happy. That's all he ever wanted for me in life. I feel certain that he still feels that way." I become a little choked up and begin to cry. I quickly swallow the tears, not wanting to take attention away from my sister.

"I still don't see why God just left me with trash," Jen says.

"Because He knows you can handle this," I tell her. "He knows you're strong enough to take this experience, learn from it, and move on."

"But why me?" she cries.

"Probably because He knows you can do better. There is someone better suited for you, and for Clara."

"But I don't want to be alone," she says through her tears.

"You're not alone," I tell her. "You've got Clara, first and foremost."

"That's not what I mean."

"Okay, so you'll be without a man for awhile. You know, maybe that's the point. Maybe that's 'why you,'" I say. "Because you've never really been alone. You've always just gone from relationship to relationship... you've never been 'alone' in your entire adult life!"

"I'm not like you, Emi," she says.

"What does that mean?"

"I don't know myself well enough. I'm not comfortable with myself like you are. I'm not strong like you are."

"Well, then this is your chance to get that way," I laugh. "I am the way I am because of my past experience. I'm strong and independent because of the many years I spent 'alone.' It's really not so bad."

"But Clara needs a father figure," she argues.

"You know what, we have a great male role model in our family already. Her uncle Chris will be there anytime you need him or want him around. So that can't be the excuse you use. Don't just go out and find another man for Clara's sake. She'll be much happier being surrounded by people who love her and want her around... people she's already built trust in."

"I know you're right," she concedes. "What are we going to do?"

I smile, having thought that question to myself many times over the past few months. *What am I going to do? How can I move forward with my life?*

They were constant questions that plagued me, but every day, I came up with one or two more answers. I was building a powerful arsenal of weapons to fight a sad and lonely existence, living in the past. Some days the answers are earth-shattering; other days, they're barely a blip on my radar. Together, though, they give me hope of some sort of future. At this point, I'll take it. I'll take what I can get.

"We're going to live here together, and we're going to help each other, one day at a time. That's what we're going to do," I tell her. "We're going to help each other make smart choices. We're going to be honest with each other and, more importantly, learn to be honest with ourselves. And we're going to heal, we'll move on from all this pain and find our happy ending... somewhere. Maybe a man will be involved, maybe not. But we're going to be happy with the outcome, whatever it is."

"Where'd you get all the answers?" Jen asks me. "You're my little sister. You're not supposed to be smarter than me."

"I've done a lot of growing in the last few months," I remind her. "Plus, I've had years of self-introspect. That's what being single does to you."

"Scary," she jokes.

"Not scary," I correct her. "Healthy."

After a few more glasses of wine, Jennifer falls asleep on the couch. At two-thirty, I decide to take her car to go pick up Clara. I leave her a note on the coffee table so she won't worry. Maybe a little sleep will do her good... and she'll have some time to pull herself together for her daughter this evening. I decide to spend the afternoon with my niece, and grab a few pieces of bread on my way out.

Clara is happy to see me when she hops into her booster seat. I turn around to buckle her in.

"Where's mommy?" she asks when I start driving.

"She's at home sleeping. She wasn't feeling well."

"She's sick?"

"Just a little," I tell her. "I'm sure she'll be all better tonight."

"Okay," she says, content with the response, as any five-year-old would be.

"How would you like to go to the park?"

"Yes! Yes! Yes!" she exclaims. "Can we feed the ducks?"

I pick up the bread that I stuffed in a baggie before I left the apartment. "I brought the food!"

"Yea!" she cheers.

After a few hours of playing in the park, feeding the ducks and geese, Clara and I make our way back toward the apartment. I stop at the nearby deli and pick up some pasta for dinner. Clara insists on having a pink cupcake, so I get one for each of us as a special treat. When we reach the door, I hand her one of the cupcakes and encourage her to take it to her mother.

"Mommy?" Clara says, navigating to the guest bedroom.

"Hey, baby," my sister says. I peek in and see my sister lying on the bed, reading.

"I brought you a present," Clara announces.

"Is that a cupcake? For me?"

"Yes. But I have one, too."

"Well, that's so sweet! We need to eat dinner first, though," Jen reasons with her daughter.

"I brought that, too," I tell her holding up the bag. "Hungry?"

"I could eat," she smiles, walking toward the kitchen to get some plates. I grab the silverware and some water, and we all meet at the table.

"How are you feeling, mommy?" my niece asks.

"Much better, honey. I don't know how I'll ever thank Auntie Emi for her help today." She smiles and mouths the words "thank you" across the table.

"After everything you've done for me, this is the least I could do."

When dinner is finished, I clean the dishes while Jennifer turns on a children's DVD for Clara to watch.

"I've been thinking," my sister says to me. "I've been trying to figure out what drew me to him in the first place."

"Okay."

"And I remember thinking back then that all the good guys were taken, and literally, as soon as he did something nice for me, I just pushed and pushed to get married... assuming he was one of the good guys, and thinking that I better not let him slip away.

"After I got that in my head, really nothing could convince me otherwise. There were big warning signs all along the way, but once I put him in that "good guy" category, I wasn't moving him anywhere else, no matter what sort of bullshit he put me through. Did you know that he asked me early on in the relationship if Clara could go live with her father?"

"No," I said. "Wow. If only Michael knew *him*."

"Yeah," she continues. "He just wanted me all to himself, and I made promises to him that I'd leave Clara with her grandparents and you and Chris on weekends so we could have that time to ourselves. I never intended to do that. I just said it to smooth things over, so that this fairy tale would continue moving forward. We fought about it all the time."

"He didn't eventually come to accept her as a permanent fixture in your life?"

"Never," she says. "He resented me for 'tricking' him into marrying him, he said."

114

"Well, he's an asshole," I tell my sister. "If he couldn't love Clara like we all do, then Jen, he is not worth crying over."

"I know," she says. "In my mind, I know. In my heart, though, it just hurts."

"Believe me, I know," I assure her.

"So, do you think there are any good guys left?" she asks me.

"I don't know," I tell her. "For years I didn't think so, and then found one staring me in the face all my life. I was looking in the wrong places, or looking for the wrong person. So, yeah, I think there are some good guys left, somewhere. When we're both ready, I'm sure we'll find one for each of us. Right now, though, we just need to focus on us. We don't need men in our lives right now."

"But I want one," my sister whines.

"You've got to be happy with yourself," I tell her. "Let's just focus on that for now."

She nods, but I'm not convinced she believes me.

~ * ~

Who would think that I would actually feel younger on my thirtieth birthday?

Chris and Anna were hosting a casual barbecue at their apartment. It was an unseasonably warm May day, so it was the perfect opportunity to wear the green striped sundress I bought on clearance last fall. It fits me even better now, since I had still not put back on the weight I had lost earlier in the year. Jennifer, Anna, Teresa and I had spent the morning getting manicures and pedicures, just a fun day with the girls. We had a light lunch after that, followed by some window shopping in White Plains. It was probably the most carefree day I'd had all year. The conversation was good, for the most part, except when my sister would begin her "all the good men are taken" rant. Anna and I had become quite adept at changing the subject, wanting the mood to be a positive one today. Teresa supplied her own form of entertainment, catching me up on the tales of her love life. Even Jen found reasons to smile and laugh at her story-telling.

By the time we get to the apartment, Chris, Dad and my stepfather are all gathered around the grill in the backyard drinking beer. My mother and stepmom are in the kitchen with Clara, preparing some side dishes. I love that my parents and stepparents are so accepting of each other. Even though the divorce was tough, my parents' second marriages are much happier, and this crisis seems to have brought the whole family together.

"Honey, you look beautiful!" my mother says excitedly, having not seen me in a few months.

"Happy birthday, sweetie!" Elaine adds. They both come over to hug me, then Jennifer and Anna.

"Thanks, thank you for coming," I tell them.

"We wouldn't miss it," Mom says.

"Emi, you want some wine?" Anna asks.

"Of course," I smile, heading out to the patio.

"Men?" I announce my presence.

"Em!" Chris says, hugging me and kissing my forehead. The dads do the same.

"Happy birthday, baby," my dad says.

"How is the grilling going?" I ask.

"Just fine," Don, my step-father, says. "We've got a little of everything."

"Perfect. Are you guys having fun?"

"It's a nice, relaxing day. The weather's perfect."

"I know," I say. "Well, I'll leave you to your man time," I joke with them. My father grunts, playing along.

The women sit around the dining room, sipping wine and having good conversation. We snack on vegetables as we wait for the main course to finish grilling. I really couldn't have asked for a better day. The weather, the company, the conversation... I just feel at home and at peace. Every day gets a little better. I can see changes in myself daily. I still miss Nate, would have loved for him to be here with me, but I've come to realize that life goes on without him. It has to. At first, I wasn't willing to accept it, but over time, I have learned to. My prospects no longer look bleak, the future no longer shaded by a dark cloud of sadness. There are still moments here and there that I might shed a tear, but having Clara and Jennifer in my apartment, I reserve those moments for my own private time. I have more memories of the happy times, I smile more, I can talk about Nate in everyday conversation and not feel overwhelmingly sad. I am thankful for the years we had together as friends and the weeks we shared as lovers. It was how it was supposed to be. A little regret lingers, but I'm able to push it to the back of my mind most of the time.

The doorbell interrupts our conversation. Anna hops up to answer the door as the rest of us stay seated, chatting quietly.

"Jack!" she exclaims. "What a nice surprise, come in!"

"Just for a second," he says, walking in with a beautiful, exotic-looking woman on his heels. Chris enters through the patio door.

"Jack," he says, shaking his hand.

"Chris, Anna," he says, "this is Marie." The woman waves shyly from behind Jack.

"Nice to meet you," my brother says. "What brings you out here tonight?"

"We were in the area, and I just thought I'd stop by to drop off a bottle of wine for the birthday girl," he smiles, nodding in my direction. Surprised, I stand up and walk over to him. Marie hands me the bottle of wine.

"You didn't have to do that," I tell him, looking at the label of my favorite wine. "Thank you so much."

"Marie," he says to his date, "this is Chris's sister, Emi."

She smiles and says hello, and I do the same.

"Chris said you were having a little family thing, so I hope we're not intruding," he says to me, waving politely at Jen and Teresa.

"Not at all," I assure him. "Can you stay for dinner?"

"No, we're on our way to catch a movie," he explains.

"Well, thank you for the wine. You know I'll enjoy it."

"I know," he smiles. "How have you been?" he asks.

"Pretty good," I tell him. "Jennifer, Clara and I have settled in nicely... we have a routine, which is good. I've got a ton of work keeping me busy."

"I'm happy to hear it."

"How have you been?" I ask politely.

"Great," he says. "Business is good. Listen," he says quietly, careful to not be heard by my brother or his fiancée. "I was thinking maybe you and I could host a dinner or something for the happy couple a little closer to the wedding... maybe sometime in August? Close friends?"

"Oh, yeah," I say. "That sounds good."

"Well, start thinking of some ideas or places. We'll talk about it later."

"Okay," I smile.

"Well, I hope you have a happy birthday, Emi."

"It'll be even better now," I say, holding up the bottle. "Thank you, and it was a pleasure to meet you, Marie," I say to his date.

"Likewise," she says.

"See you later!" Jack announces to the room so that Chris and Anna hear. They wave goodbye and I close the door behind them.

"That was nice," Anna says, giving Teresa and my sister a strange side glance.

"What?" I ask her.

"Nothing," she says, grinning.

"Alright," I say. "Who's going to open this wine for me?"

"I've got it," Teresa says, stealing the bottle from my hands.

"See?" my sister says to me quietly. "Now, he seems like a nice enough guy, but again, like all the good ones, he's taken."

"I'm sure there are others, Jen," I assure her. "There are millions of guys in Manhattan. I'm sure we can find two decent ones."

"I don't know how you're so certain."

"Blind faith," I remind her. "It's all I've got, remember?"

"Right."

CHAPTER 6

By mid-July, my sister and I are both comfortable with our living arrangement and have a good understanding of each other's limits and boundaries. It was hard at first, getting used to one another all over again. When we were younger, we fought constantly. My sister had been the only child for four years, and then my brother came along, with me less than a year later. My brother and I were fast friends, playing together, sharing toys, and as we grew older, we would always team up against our big sister. He and I just had so much time together, but Jennifer was in school by the time we were toddlers, so there was always a little distance between our older sibling and us.

Having her live with me was like another opportunity for me to really get to know her. We had a lot more in common than I ever thought possible. Our beliefs were the same, we just chose to lead our lives in different ways. Neither was right or wrong. I had once judged her and the way she lived her life, but it was just because I didn't understand her choices. Now that I could understand where she was coming from, knew some of her experiences, I could see why she made the decisions she did.

In the summer, for six hours a day, Clara goes to daycare a few blocks from our apartment. Jennifer has gotten a part-time job as a receptionist in midtown. She typically drops off Clara, then heads to work, puts in four hours, then picks her daughter up and comes home. This gives me some much-appreciated alone time to work, or to just clear my head, if needed. In the late afternoons, I'll typically take a break at Central Park with my niece, and give Jennifer an hour or two to herself before dinner. It's a pretty good routine, and I know it's been really good for me, having them here.

Jennifer hasn't been on a single date since moving in. She has filed for divorce, and seems to be well on her way to putting that era of her life behind her. I can see changes in her, good changes. She is finding interests in her own things, making a life for herself on her own. I'm very proud of her, and I can see happiness coming back into her life. In a way, it's been good for me to help her out, focus on her. I had plenty of idle time this year, and really didn't need any more of it. There were times when I felt I was just sinking... but being there for my sister has somehow kept my spirits afloat.

Frustrated with my current freelance project, I dig out my colored pencils and an empty sketchbook from my desk to attempt to "draw" my idea... it's supposed to look like a childlike drawing... surely I can manage that. Or not... page after page, the scribbles don't look like the right scribbles. Too messy. Too sophisticated. Too red. Too black. *Too freaking frustrating!* I begin to rip out the pages, taking my aggression out on the inanimate object that's making me feel like I have no talent whatsoever at the moment.

Holy... *oh my god.* I lose my breath at the image in front of me. It's his sketch. Nate's... his clean lines and detailed illustrations are unmistakeable. I thought this was a new sketchbook. *My* sketchbook. *How... what?*

It's a sketch of a room, a little boy's room. The position of the window and architecture of the beams let me know immediately it's the guest room where Jen and Clara sleep. A crib is positioned to one side, and a large, red dog– whom I immediately recognize as Clifford from one of my favorite books when I was little– watches over the tiny baby's bed. The wall is tinted sky blue, dotted with clouds and birds. Two trees flank both sides of the brown wooden crib, which I now notice sits directly in front of a dog house painted the same brown color. Small, printed letters sit at the bottom of the drawing: "IF IT'S A BOY - 12/27 - Nathaniel J. Wilson"

My throat gets tight and my eyes water, the emptiness I felt in the pit of my stomach so many months ago returning immediately. Were it not for the accident, I would be eight months pregnant.

I turn the page quickly, hoping to find refuge in the solace of another blank page, but I'm instead assaulted by an equally picturesque scene. Pink, purple and red stripes and green and yellow polka dots are the background for this image of another one of my favorite storybook characters. Corduroy, the little bear in his green overalls, is reaching over for what he thinks is his missing button, just like the cover of the book. I look closer and realize the polka dots are all buttons. The crib in this picture is white with tiny bow accents on the four posts. "IF IT'S A GIRL - 12/27 - Nathaniel J. Wilson"

God damn it, Nate! I throw the sketchbook across the room as a loud scream escapes my taut throat before the sobs. Alone in the apartment, I grasp my stomach tightly, cradling the baby that isn't there, rocking my body back and forth... rocking the tiny child that will never be. The mental anguish quickly becomes physical pain.

I thought that I had accepted this loss long ago, when I had made peace that Nate was gone, and that he was with our child. *Our child. Our sweet child.* I was supposed to be a mother. Soon.

People should be throwing me a baby shower right now, celebrating the upcoming arrival of my little girl... I'm convinced it was to be a girl, from the dream I had. We would have a couples shower. Our families would be there, and friends. We would be unwrapping gifts, pink onesies galore and cute little dresses that the grandmas just couldn't resist. It's just not fair.

I crawl to the bed, curl up with a pillow and cry until there are no more tears. *God, please let me see him. Please let him come to me. I want to see him. I want to see our little girl. I want to be with them. Please, God, please. Why did you take them from me? Can't I go, too?* I briefly allow myself to fantasize that another freak accident will deliver me to them. Is it wrong to wish such things? Do I?

I don't wish it. I don't think that I wish it, anyway. I force myself to remember my family and friends, people I would miss, who would miss me dearly.

Staring at the white textured ceiling, the only thing in the apartment that doesn't remind me of Nate at the moment, I try to think of excuses to get me out of this evening's plans. Jen had twisted my arm earlier in the week, and I somehow committed to going out with friends tonight. I want to back out, but I've done that the last two times they've invited me to do something, and I just feel like I have to do this at this point if I want to remain their friend. My brain tells me that the distraction will be good for me. My heart just wants to stay here... try to sleep, in hopes of a dream where Nate will visit me. Even if it's just for a minute... *God, one more minute with him, with them... that's all I'm asking. It's not too much. Is he watching me? Is she okay?*

I close my eyes and sit up too quickly, my equilibrium a little off at the sudden movement. I dip my head into my hands and wonder how I'll be able to keep my mind off of the thoughtful murals that Nate had created... or the small child that would inhabit the space surrounded by his paintings... which just brings me full circle to the man I love. It's like the wounds are all reopened, and I'm bleeding out. Slowly, I make my way to the bathroom and begin running hot water for the shower.

Feeling resentful against my friends– although they have my best interests at heart, I know– I force more tears out of my bleary eyes. I don't want to go to some trendy dance club, but I don't want to let everyone down, either... and I certainly don't want everyone to know that I'm reverting back to the dark place they all thought I was emerging from. I was doing okay. *Why did I have to find those drawings?*

Fuck! I don't want to go I don't want to go I don't want to go. I remember how excited Jen was when I told her I would go, though. And Teresa had promised we would have a good time...

"Emi, you okay in there?" I hear my sister yell through the bathroom door. "You've been in there an awful long time."

I glance at the clock on the wall, wiping condensation off the glass shower door. I'm surprised to see I've been in here for twenty minutes. "Fine," I lie, looking down at my pruned fingers. I take a deep breath and accept that I am not backing out. *Focus on something else, Em.* I let my inner cheerleader try to pump me up. Maybe I will have fun. Maybe something will help me to forget about my everyday existence for a few hours.

Until this morning, I had come to terms with the facts of my life, and I was beginning to feel somewhat happy with my reality– I was learning to be happy again without Nate.

Eight months pregnant. I clinch my stomach again as the cheerleader struggles to push her way back in. *I hate her sometimes.*

Is it fair to hope that the night will have some pleasant distractions? Is it right at all? Or should I still be mourning? And I have to wonder, how will I be in a month, when the baby would have been born? Will I feel different? My head begins to hurt... from the crying, from the questions, who the hell knows why nowadays? I finally climb out of the shower as the hot water runs out and pull a towel around myself.

"Anni-Emi, I have to go potty!" my niece whines from outside the door. I immediately feel bad for hogging our one bathroom.

"Okay, Clara-bee, I'm sorry," I tell her as I open the door, a rush of cool air a vast contrast to the steam room I've been hiding in. She pushes past me and closes the door quickly.

"Sorry," I mumble to Jen, forcing a smile.

"No worries," Jen says. "Chris and Anna should be here in a few minutes to pick her up. Did you decide on what you're wearing?"

I shrug, uncaring, and stare at the contents of my closet in a daze.

Jen went out yesterday and bought a new dress. She had invited me to go, but I was sure I had something suitable. I find some black slacks and a silver chemise in my closet that I hadn't worn in ages. A pair of black heels completes the look.

"Are you alright?" Jen asks me, undoubtedly noticing the puffiness under my eyes.

"I'll be fine. Just a rough day," I tell her. I think she's just so excited to get out that she chooses not to press me further, not wanting anything to spoil the night. Any other day, I might think she was being selfish, but not today. I don't know if it's normal or okay for me to feel like this. I'm not sure what to do about it.

"Mommy, you look pretty," Clara tells her mother, standing on her tip-toes and peering into the mirror that Jen is leaning toward. I feel another pang in my stomach. *Mommy.* Such an innocent word that is doing so much damage to my soul. It's like the air is knocked out of me, as if my lungs have collapsed. I let out a sigh as I walk out of the room to grab a tissue.

"Well thank you, sweetie," I hear Jen say as she finishes touching up her makeup.

"Mommy, can I go?"

"No, you get to go to Chris and Anna's, remember?"

"I don't wanna go," she begins to whine. "I wanna dress up and go with you!" She folds her arms and sits on the floor, beginning to wail loudly. It's rare that she throws tantrums, but when she does throw one, she makes it count. I'm glad that something has happened to require my full attention, even if it is my niece squealing. It jolts me out of my coma-like state. I walk into the guest bedroom and open the chest on the floor by Clara's twin-sized bed. She has dresses in it of multiple Disney princesses, so I pull out a few and take them to her.

"Hey, Clara-bee," I interrupt as she takes a breath.

"What?" she pouts.

"Do you wanna be Cinderella or Snow White?"

"Neither." She furrows her tiny brow.

"I'll curl your hair for you," I offer.

"Can I put on makeup?" she asks. I look at Jen and she nods, picking up some tinted lip gloss and powder and handing it to me.

124

"Yes, if you stop crying and let the tears dry, we can put some makeup on, too."

"Okay," she says, standing up and walking to me. I take Clara into the guest room as we hear a knock on the door.

"I'll get it," Jen announces.

Clara and I put on the Cinderella dress as I heat up the curling iron. I hear Jen in the living room explaining what's going on, and then she adds something indistinguishable under her breath. Anna comes into the guest room with us.

"Clara?" Anna asks.

"Uh-huh?" my niece answers.

"Do you want to go out for ice cream when you're finished getting ready?"

"Uh-huh," she repeats.

"How are you doing?" she asks me.

"Fine," I tell her.

"You don't look fine, Emi," Anna says.

"Thanks," I say, rolling my eyes and biting my quivering lip.

"Em... why have you been crying?"

"Not in front of Clara," I whisper. "Not now."

Anna stands silently, staring at me, her brows angling in curiosity. I just shake my head at her.

"So, thanks for taking care of Clara tonight," Jen interrupts from the doorway.

"Anytime," Anna says. "Hey, Emi, I was wondering if we could go do a fitting next week for the dresses. Are you up for that?"

"Of course," I say, a little annoyed at the insinuation that I might not be okay to do my maid-of-honor duties for her upcoming wedding. "Just name the time and place."

"And maybe go to the florist? I have some final decisions to make and I'm having trouble."

"Sure thing, Anna. We'll make a day of it."

"Cool," she says as I put the finishing touches on Clara's makeup.

"Clara, come sit down so I can curl your hair." She plops down on her bed, smiling anxiously. "Now be still, okay?"

She nods her head wildly. "Not like that, silly. Be still."

"Okay," she whispers, careful not to move at all as I take her fine hair and wrap it around the curling iron. Anna hands me some hair spray when I'm finished.

"You're perfect!" I tell my niece, handing her a mirror. After she inspects herself, I pick her up and hold her tightly, her tiny arms returning my hug.

"Thank you, Anni-Emi!"

"You're welcome, Clara-bee." An errant tear drops from my eye, and I quickly wipe it away before anyone notices. "Are you ready to go have your ice cream?"

Again, she nods quickly.

"Alright, pumpkin," her mom says. "You be good for your aunt and uncle, got it?"

"Got it," she says emphatically. Jen hands Anna an overnight bag and we all hug goodbye. Clara is in high spirits as she walks out the door.

"I'm so excited!" Jen says when the door closes. "I haven't been out in so long!"

"Should be fun," I say, the muscles in my face struggling to form a smile. I'm not as excited as my sister, and have a hard time faking it. It seems a little strange. In addition to feeling sad, I feel guilty. But in the end, I know I shouldn't sit around the apartment and mope. It's just a night out with the girls. Period.

"Let's see if we can find the others," Teresa yells over the crowd. Jen and I met her at her apartment, and Melisa, Patrick, Megan and the other guys were supposed to meet us here. We fight our way through swarms of people until Teresa finds Bradley and his friends. I recognize a few of them from the party we had a few months ago, particularly the young one who seemed so eager to see me draw. We're reintroduced, and I learn his name is Shawn. He singles me out immediately and hugs me as if we are long lost friends.

"How are you doing, Emi?" he asks.

"Great, you?"

"Fine," he smiles. "It's good to finally see you again."

"Oh," I say, a little taken aback, "you too."

"Can I get you a drink?"

"Sure, a glass of merlot, please," I request. I glance to see if my sister wants anything, but she's already being dragged onto the dance floor by another of Bradley's friends. Teresa and her date follow them. I survey the club for the rest of our friends, in near-panic mode that I might have to be alone with Shawn, that I might be expected to have an actual conversation with him. *Calm down. Calm down. You're being silly.*

"Your wine," he says, handing me my drink and setting his glass down on the table next to us. I fight with my emotions to force the sides of my lips to curl upwards. This really shouldn't be so difficult. "You seem sad... or tense," he says, picking up on my mood immediately. He walks behind me and starts rubbing my shoulders. His touch is strange, rough, but it feels nice and I don't have to talk to him while he's massaging the knots out of my muscles. *Calm down.* I take a large, long sip of my drink.

"Thank you," I tell him when he eases up.

"My pleasure," he says. "Do you want to dance, or would you rather hang out here?"

"Sit, for now," I say. He pulls the chair out for me. I don't know if chivalry can be faked, but his actions just seem... selfish? Is that the right word? Like he's only doing these things for personal gain. Poor guy. Maybe I should let him know right now he will get nowhere with me tonight... or probably ever.

"Have you done any cool projects lately?" he asks, and again I question his motives on such a simple inquiry. Have I become so cynical that I don't believe that a man can be genuinely interested in what I do? I try to clear my head of my preconceived notions. *I shouldn't be here. I shouldn't be among other people tonight. I should be home, alone. I'm just not feeling this.*

"Nothing really interesting," I tell him with little enthusiasm. "I'm being considered to be the lead illustrator for a CD, though. That's pretty cool."

"Really? Whose?"

"Oh, it's just some small independent album. Nothing major."

"That's cool," he nods. "So you got your own place, Teresa said?"

"Yeah," I respond. "I have a loft a few blocks from the old apartment. My sister and niece and I share it for now."

"Cool," he says. "Where is it?"

"It's off 5th," I say nonchalantly, but realize any loft off 5th Avenue will raise the eyebrows of people in my circle of friends.

"Wow? You must be doing really well," he laughs.

I shake my head and smile. "No, it's not like that," I say, not wanting to get into the details. "It was a friend's place. I'm just staying there for awhile." Fortunately, he doesn't ask any more questions about it.

"Maybe I can see it sometime," he says... and it just seems... forward.

"Maybe," I say politely as I feel a tap on my shoulder. I look up to see Megan, Melisa and Patrick. "Hey, guys!" I stand up and hug them all, grateful that they're here now, hoping they'll join Shawn and me at the table.

"Em, how are you?" Melisa asks, her eyes filled with that familiar look of concern and sympathy.

I just nod, and that seems to be a good enough answer for her.

"I'm happy to hear it," she says. "Is Teresa here?"

"Yeah, they're already out dancing."

"Well, I think we'll hit the floor, too."

"Are you sure?" I ask with a little too much eagerness. "You don't want to join us for a drink first?"

"I will," Patrick says, "but the girls have been dying to go dancing for weeks."

"Cool. Patrick, this is Shawn, I don't know if you remember him from the party?"

"Sure, Shawn," he says, shaking his hand. "I'm going to get a drink. Merlot, Emi?"

"Please," I say, eyeing my half-empty glass.

"Shawn, you good?" he asks as he starts to walk away, not even waiting for his response.

"I'm fine," Shawn yells, even though his glass is empty. I sit back down.

"So," I start, attempting to find something interesting to talk about. "Have you wanted to be a fireman all your life?" I realize my question almost sounds like I'm mocking him.

"No," he smiles. "I was in college, sort of struggling for direction. And then the attacks happened... and I just felt moved to become a New York firefighter. I actually moved here from Texas, and I've never looked back." *Maybe he's not so selfish after all.*

"That's great," I say warmly. I can't help but feel a little more respect for him... and I feel worse personally for judging him too soon. "Texas, huh? You don't have much of an accent," I notice.

"Well," he says with obvious twang, "I try to tone it down for y'all." He winks at me. "We don't all sound like hicks."

"Obviously," I say. Patrick sets down the glass of wine in front of me before taking a seat next to me, scooting in closely.

"Thanks." I finish my first glass quickly and start on the second.

"So, Patrick," Shawn says loudly across the table. "What do you do?"

"Account executive for an ad agency," he says, barely making eye contact. Shawn nods. Patrick puts his arm across my shoulder and whispers in my ear, "You having fun?"

I shrug and nod.

"Is he bugging you?" he asks. "We can move to another table."

I shake my head. "I'm fine."

"If you'll excuse me a second," Shawn says, standing. "I'll be back in a few minutes."

"Okay," I say, a little concerned that he knew we were talking about him. Shawn walks toward the restrooms.

"Let's go dance," Patrick says, standing up.

"Um, I'll meet you out there, okay? I'm going to go the ladies room first."

"Alright," he concedes. "I think everyone's around that corner," he says pointing across the club, then heading that direction. I finish the second glass of wine and make my way over toward the bar. The alcohol seems to be clearing my mind of the sadness... I know it's not healthy, but it seems like all I can do to survive at the moment. I find a tiny opening and squeeze through, my shoulders pressed against a woman to my left and a man on my right. I just meekly watch the bartenders, in hopes that one will notice me and take my order. It's been awhile since I've done this. I've lost my courage to even order a drink. I stand there at least five minutes, being passed over repeatedly.

The bartender points at the man next to me and asks what he's drinking.

"Stella, and the lady will have a glass of Bellei Lambrusco, if you have it," he says, gesturing in my direction. I look over to see Jack smiling at me. His friendly and familiar face is a welcome sight to my tired eyes.

"Hey!" I say to him, surprised. "Um, thank you. I didn't see you there!"

"How are you doing, Emi?" His eyes are warm, concerned.

"Good," I say instinctively. "You?"

"Fine," he says. "Are you here with friends?"

"Yeah, Jen and Teresa and the whole crew," I tell him. "Who are you here with?"

"Marie and an old sorority sister of hers," he says, and I can sense a little frustration in his voice.

"You don't sound like you're having a lot of fun," I notice.

"I'm not big on this place."

"You don't dance?" I ask.

"I prefer a different kind of dancing," he points out and I nod. The bartender puts our drinks down and I hand him my credit card. He looks at Jack, who takes my card from the bartender and tells him to put it on his tab. "I've got this one."

"Next round's on me," I say. Jack stands up and offers me his seat. "I'm fine," I tell him, but he insists that I take the chair.

"I hope it's not weird for me to tell you this, but you look incredibly beautiful," he says to me, leaning closely toward me, his arm resting on the back of the chair. His fingers brush my arm for a brief second. I'm pretty sure I feel my heart skip a beat... and I haven't felt anything like that in months. I'm immediately confused. I shouldn't feel things like that.

"Thanks," I say softly, looking into my wine glass.

His hand touches my chin and lifts my head upwards. *Whoa.* "Are you sure you're okay?"

"Yeah," I say, trying to look happy, his eyes locking on mine. Again, I feel it. It's the strangest thing. This guy has been in and out of my life for months and he's never had an effect on me. Maybe it's the wine. I'm really not sure what's happening. He clears his throat and looks away.

"So, we've got reservations at Buddakan next Saturday," he says. I look at him, obviously confused. "Chris and Anna's dinner? Remember?"

"Right," I laugh, embarrassed. "Buddakan, Saturday. And did we decide who all is going to be there?"

"Chris and Anna. You and Jen, and guests, if you want. Marie and I. Our college fraternity brother, Russell, and his girlfriend. And one of Anna's friends and her husband. No parents," he reminds me. "Just friends. And I'll give the restaurant the final number on Monday."

"Right," I repeat. "I can say with certainty that Jen and I won't be bringing guests." We had made all of these decisions a few weeks ago over a few email messages, but after a relatively sleepless night, I was pretty– well, absent– from the whole conversation. When he picked up on how tired I was that day when my responses seemed to make very little sense, he said he would handle everything... and obviously he has. "Thanks for putting this all together... it's still a surprise, right?"

"Yes, they don't know. I invited them over to watch a baseball game, so that's where they think they're going... only I'm going to have a driver pick them up..."

"Wow, Anna agreed to go watch a game on TV?"

"Well, I told her Marie wanted to get to know her a little better. You know how gracious Anna is."

"Yes, I do," I tell him. "How are things with Marie?" I remember the gorgeous, dark-complected woman that he had brought to Chris and Anna's apartment on my birthday. I'm just plain and mousey compared to her. *Wait, why am I comparing myself to her?*

Jack hesitates and glances down quickly at his beer. "Uhhh..." he starts.

"Okay, I guess."

I watch his expression and remain quiet, hoping that he'll expand on his answer.

"Maybe it's just too early to say, but I don't feel a real connection with her," he says. "I shouldn't be talking about her like this," he immediately amends his response. "It's rude."

"I'm sorry," I say, feeling bad that I asked the question.

"Oh, no, it's fine. I just need to figure some things out, that's all," he smiles and takes a drink. I sit silent for a few minutes, just listening to the loud music and the hum of the crowd. My eyes catch sight of a couple at the end of the bar. Their faces are close, they're smiling gently, talking. They exchange a sweet, short kiss. I sigh heavily, but can't take my eyes off of them. I remember the picture of Nate and I, the one that he had with him in LA. This couple reminds me of that picture. Reminds me of my love... reminds me of my baby.

"What are you thinking about?" Jack asks. I watch him avert his attention to the couple at the end of the bar. He looks back at me.

"I just miss that," I tell him, sadness taking over. "I wonder if I'll have that again." The tears start to form, and I'm immediately angry with myself for getting emotional.

"Let's go get some air," Jack suggests, taking the empty glass from me and setting it on the bar, picking up my hand, and leading me to the club's private patio. His hand is soft and warm, his grip tight on mine. With how crowded the club is, we're both surprised to find that we're the only two people taking advantage of the quiet outdoor space. He pulls out a chair for me to sit in, and he takes a seat across from me. As he drops my hand, a ring I was wearing falls off. He picks it up and sets in on the table in between us, occasionally fumbling with it between his fingers.

"It doesn't fit me anymore," I explain with a shrug.

"Obviously," he laughs. "So, back to our conversation... you seem a little down tonight, Emi," he says with concern.

"Yeah, I am," I swallow hard. "I'm not really up to talking about it, I'm sorry."

"No, I'm sorry for prying," he says. "But if I may... you will have *that* again someday."

"You think?" I half-laugh.

"Undoubtedly," he says. "Any man would be lucky to have you." Our eyes meet again, linger. This is wrong, crazy. I must be projecting feelings on to him. He's my brother's friend. He's beyond gorgeous, exudes confidence... yet somehow isn't arrogant at all. I mean, he's a nice guy, yes, but I've never thought of him in this way. Maybe it's just because I feel so horribly lonely and vulnerable tonight. It doesn't feel right, though. Yet, it does in a strange way– like there is someone who is actually perceptive enough to know something's wrong, and bold enough to inquire about it... like there is someone that might actually... care? I mean, it feels wrong, but then again, it doesn't.

"Thanks... and you're not prying," I tell him. "I appreciate your concern, really."

He smiles. "If you ever want to talk..."

"Thank you." I glance around, taking in our surroundings, checking out the street below. When I peek back at him, our eyes meet again, and the blush rises in my cheeks. Quickly, I look away.

"Wonder if it's going to rain," Jack comments, filling the silence with a neutral topic.

"It sort of smells like it," I say, eager to join the conversation. "I haven't heard a forecast in days."

"The paper said it wouldn't come until tomorrow."

"Hmmm..." I add. After a few more minutes of silence, we hear the music change to something downtempo.

"Now, this is the kind of music I like to dance to," he says with a small smile. "Should we go join our friends?" he asks. I don't want to leave him, I feel safe with him, comfortable... a way I haven't felt in a very long time. I know it's all wrong. He is here with a date, for God's sake– a date that he wants to slow dance with, no less. And I shouldn't be thinking about him in this way! I can only attribute it to the wine. I don't want to leave him, but at the same time, I know I have to.

"I think so," I say, knowing it's for the best. He opens the door to the club for me and follows me in. "Thanks for talking to me."

"Anytime, Emi." He extends his arms to hug me, and I gladly embrace him. I hold on tightly.

"I needed that," I whisper in his ear, part of me hoping he can't hear, the other part hoping he won't let go of me. He pulls back slightly, a look of surprise evident on his face, but instead of speaking, we begin moving together to the slow song. He pulls me in closer. The way he moves, it's as if we've done this before. *Did we dance at the engagement party?* I consider asking, but remain quiet, wanting to forget that one night that I'll never be able to. Neither of us utters a word. I put my head on his chest, and he gently runs his fingers through my hair, a gesture so simple... and yet, I'm overwhelmed with emotions.

"There you are!" Shawn exclaims, interrupting the intensity of the moment. Jack and I immediately leave our embrace and take a step away from each other. I quickly wipe away a tear. "Where have you been?" he asks.

"Oh, I ran into my friend, Jack, at the bar. We just went to the patio for some fresh air. It's just so loud in here!" I explain as Jack's expression changes from contentment to worry when he sees that I was crying.

"We were looking for you! Let's go dance!" he says, pulling me away from Jack.

Jack finds my other hand before I'm out of reach. He stops Shawn's forward motion, and I feel like I'm trapped between the two of them. "Emi, take care of yourself," he says.

"I will," I tell him.

"So, I'll see you next Saturday at Buddakan?" he adds.

"I'll be there," I smile. "Oh, and I probably owe you a drink." I squeeze his hand before letting it go. "Have a good night."

"You too," he says, a sad smile on his face as he backs away into the crowd, undoubtedly to find his date.

When Shawn and I find our group, we join the circle of dancers. Everyone is having so much fun, and I struggle to match their energy, my own sorrow just weighing me down. Sad about Nate. Sad about the baby. And sad that I had to leave that safe and familiar place that was with... *wait, with Jack?* How did this happen? *When* did this happen? *I'm buzzed. I'm lonely. I don't really feel that way about him.*

Patrick and Shawn take turns buying the next few rounds of drinks, and after another hour, I'm exhausted and more than a little drunk.

"Let's go back to my apartment," Teresa suggests. "The drinks are cheaper." I look across the circle at my sister, whose attention is all but consumed by one of Bradley's friends. They agree to go to Teresa's, as do the other firefighters and Megan, Melisa and Patrick.

"I think I'm going to head home," I tell everyone.

"Do you need me to go with you?" Jennifer asks.

"No, I'll be fine. I'm just tired."

"Okay," Jen says, obviously relieved that she doesn't have to come home with me. "Don't wait up," she leans in and tells me. I roll my eyes, but know she's going to do what she wants anyway. Nothing I've ever said has changed her mind.

"I'll see you home," Shawn volunteers.

"Oh, no, Shawn, really, it's okay. I got it." I trip over my feet as I try to walk away.

"I insist," he says with a laugh. "It's late, you don't need to be out by yourself."

I really don't want the company, but I agree to let him walk me home. On the way, it begins to sprinkle. Shawn takes off his jacket and holds it over my head to shelter me from the rain. This time, I don't question his motives, I just accept that he's a nice guy.

Shawn gawks when we get to my building. "This is where you live?"

"Yes," I say nonchalantly, noting how wet he has gotten as the shower picked up. "Listen, do you want to come in and dry off a little?"

"That would be nice," he says. I'm relieved that Marcus isn't working tonight... I think I would be a little embarrassed, ashamed, if he were to see me bringing a guy home.

When we get upstairs, I go to my closet to find a dry shirt for Shawn to put on. I pass over two of Nate's shirts and find an old concert t-shirt of mine. It would be too small for Shawn, but it was the best I could offer him. He happily takes it and puts it on. I take him a few towels so he can pat his hair dry.

"Thanks for walking me home," I say to him, stumbling as I take off my heels.

"Thanks for letting me," he says wandering to the window that overlooks Central Park. "Great view."

"I know," I say, feeling unclear. "Hey, would you like some coffee or something?"

"Sure, black," he says walking back toward the living room. He puts a towel down on the couch and sits down as I make the coffee.

"You can turn the TV on if you like," I tell him. While the coffee's percolating, I go to the restroom and change into a dry pair of jeans and a polo shirt. I pull on some warm socks before stopping by the kitchen and pouring two cups of coffee and taking them to the living room. I set them on the coffee table and then sit down at the other end of the sofa.

"Thank you," he tells me, taking a sip.

"You're welcome," I smile, still feeling a little strange.

"These paintings are pretty cool, did you do them?" Shawn asks, motioning to the artwork on the walls.

"Uh, nope," I say. "My, uh, former boyfriend was a painter."

"He is really good," he says.

"Yes, he *was*," I correct him.

"Oh," Shawn says. "I forgot that. I'm sorry. He's, uh... he passed away, right?" *Yes, Shawn, he died. I really didn't need a reminder.* I feel a pang in the pit of my stomach.

"Yes," I respond, lingering on the thought, staring at the painting.

"I remember Teresa telling us that awhile back. I'm sorry," he apologizes again.

"It's okay," I sigh, returning to the present... to this strange man sitting next to me on the couch.

"Don't be upset," he says, sensing my mental distance and leaning into me.

Before I know it, his mouth is attacking mine. It takes me a moment to realize what's going on. I push him away, shaking my head and laughing.

"Wow," I say, completely taken by surprise. I look down at my hands to avoid eye-contact. Shawn obviously has something else in mind. He lifts my chin and kisses me again, this time gently. It's been so long since someone has kissed me, and I'm briefly caught up in the moment. I close my eyes and envision myself kissing Nate. When I start to believe it's really him, I gasp and push Shawn away again. "I can't do this," I tell him.

I've betrayed him. I've betrayed Nate, in his own apartment. What is going on? How did this happen? Is it really happening? Am I just drunk? Confused? Generally out of my mind?

"I'm sorry," Shawn says. "I was just trying to take your mind off things."

"No, it's okay. I'm just not ready for this." We sit in awkward silence, drinking coffee. Finally, I apologize for my rudeness and ask him to leave. Glancing out the window and seeing the rain shower outside, I let him borrow an umbrella and tell him good night.

A strange end to a strange night. I close the door behind him and change into some pajamas. The rain turns into a thunderstorm. Lightning flashes in the loft intermittently as I lie in bed, trying to go to sleep. Again, I'm alone, but tonight, I feel that's the way it should be. It's the way I want to be. The way I feel I'm supposed to be. Now... and maybe forever.

Nate, I think, hoping he can hear my thoughts. *I'm not sure what's going on. Please, believe me, I love you. I will always love you. I don't know what's going on with me tonight. I'm sorry. I just feel the need to apologize... please forgive me, I'm begging you... and Nate?*

I tuck my knees into my chest and begin to sob.

How is our little girl, Nate? I miss her so much. I miss you both so much I can hardly stand it. The emptiness is back, Nate! I thought I was past this... but it still hurts so bad. I realized something the other day... in my memories of that night, Nate, the bad ones, the ones I want to forget... I don't remember being concerned at all for our baby. I don't know why. And I feel guilty. Why did the thought not ever occur to me in the car that night, as we both lay there, hurting, dying?

I would have been a good mother. I say this more to convince myself. *Nate... do you ever miss me? Do you feel sadness where you are? Come comfort me, please. I need you... so badly. I can't do this without you. I want you back. I want a family. I would do anything, Nate... Please forgive me for tonight, Nate. Not just kissing Shawn... but for feeling something... for Jack. It had to be the alcohol. My heart belongs to you, will always be yours. I love you... forever, Nate.*

I don't remember going to sleep, but when I awaken the next morning, my eyes are so dry and uncomfortable and the headache has returned. Regardless, I am surprised that I managed to sleep all night by myself in this loft. I would be proud of myself if I hadn't succumbed to the feelings of sadness and loss last night, to feelings I thought I could handle better by now.

I walk to the bathroom to get some aspirin, and am briefly alarmed when I realize my sister didn't come home. I find my phone in my purse and see that I have two messages. I listen to them as I take the pills.

The first is from Jennifer. "Em, I hope you made it home okay. Wish you would answer your phone. I'll be home in the morning... don't worry about me. If you need anything– anything at all– just call me."

The second is from Jack. "Hey... we should talk. Call me sometime." My stomach turns, feelings of regret settling in immediately. *I love Nate.* I quickly delete the message, as if that will erase all the confused memories I have of last night. I grab a diet soda from the refrigerator and head back over to the bed, lying down gently. They're mornings like these that make me wish I had curtains or something to keep the blinding sun out of this place, to maintain the darkness. My head hurts too much for this. I pull a pillow over my head and try to go back to sleep. *I wonder why Jack thinks we should talk?*

I wake up again when my sister comes home. She comes over to the bed and sits down, waiting for me to pull the pillow off my head. When I don't, she does it for me, greeting me with a silly smile.

"What's up?" I mumble.

"Did you have fun last night?" she asks.

"Sure..." I moan, still not ready to get up, lying in silence.

"Well, I did, too, Em, thanks for asking."

"Sorry, Jen," I tell her. "I had a little too much to drink last night... and it hurts."

"So what happened with Shawn?"

"Nothing. He kissed me, it was weird, I asked him to leave."

"Em!" she scolds.

"What? What was supposed to happen?"

"It was raining, and you kicked him out?"

"I gave him an umbrella," I explain, justifying his exile to the wet streets of New York.

She laughs. "Emi, you're a mess."

"I'm just me... so what happened with... what's his name, anyway?"

"Garrett," she says, "and it was wonderful."

"I'm guessing you..." I really didn't need to ask. The smile gave it away at first glance.

"Yes," she grins. "It was amazing, Emi. We–"

"TMI," I tell her. "I'll take your word for it."

She huffs and walks into the kitchen to get some water. "I saw Jack at the club after you left," she says.

"Really?"

"Yeah, he was at the bar... didn't look to be having much fun. He was twirling around a ring or something, just staring at it." I grab my right hand. *My ring!* That must be why he wanted to talk to me.

"Hmmm..." I say, not wanting to talk about him at the moment... I have to sort out some things, feelings. "What time is Clara coming home?"

"I have to go pick her up this afternoon," she says. "I think I'll take Chris and Anna out to dinner to thank them. Do you want to come?"

"I don't think so," I tell her. "I've got a headache to do and some work to get rid of... or the other way around... whatever."

She laughs, then asks if she can take a shower.

"By all means, go ahead. I'm still not getting up." I pull the comforter over my head and attempt to sleep a little more while Jen showers, but I can't help but be curious about Jack. *We should talk,* he said. If he had just wanted to give my ring back, wouldn't he have said as much? I don't know what to think about him. So it's best not to.

"What don't you know?" my sister asks. I hadn't realized I was saying the words aloud. She pulls the comforter back and sits down.

"Nothing," I say, trying to blow her off.

"No, what?" she presses.

"Really, Jen, I don't want to talk about it."

"It's Shawn, right? Do you like him?"

"Jen, no, it's not Shawn, no I don't like him, no, it's nothing... please, just drop it."

Later in the day, after Jen leaves to pick up Clara, I decide it's time to get out of bed and shower. My headache finally gone for the time being, I feel like I'm able to face the day, or what's left of it, anyway. I opt for a bath, relaxing in the hot water until my skin begins to prune. I get dressed and fix my hair, apply some makeup and decide to go to Grand Central Terminal for a bowl of soup and my favorite pie. Comfort food sounds ideal. A comforting hug would be even better, coming from someone I feel completely comfortable with. If only Nate were here to make me feel whole again.

I sit down in one of the big, plush chairs and settle in for some people watching, again hoping for a distraction. I am able to lose myself in the afternoon chaos, wondering where people are going, imagining the great adventures they may be on. It certainly keeps my mind off things I don't want to think about.

I take a bite of pie as I realize my phone is vibrating in my pocket. I struggle to put my hands on it, and answer it before I even see who's calling.

"Hello?" I say, my mouth full of food.

"Emi?" It's Jack. Shit, I'm not ready to talk. He told me to call him. He's not supposed to call me. Shit. "What are you doing?"

"Uh..." I swallow. "Eating pie at Grand Central?"

"The little place with the green awning?" he asks.

"Yes," I admit.

"That place is good. Hey, I have your ring," he says. So maybe I *was* just over-thinking things. Maybe he did just want to give me my jewelry back.

"Oh, yes," I say. "I forgot about that."

"Well, I'm right down the street," he says. "Can I bring it to you?"

"Umm... well-"

"I'm already on my way," he says. "I'll be there in five." He hangs up abruptly.

I was going to tell him no, that I would get it at Buddakan next Saturday, not wanting to see him, not wanting to see if I would feel things I shouldn't– no, didn't want to– at the mere sight of him. I'd rather just believe that those feelings were caused by the wine, and nothing more. I am not ready for this test.

I wrap up the remainder of the pie and put it back in the bag. All of a sudden, my stomach is in knots and I have lost my appetite. I begin to look for Jack around the entrance to the food court level. When he finally comes down the stairs, the feelings I had been dreading return. I stand up to meet him half-way across the walkway. He's dressed in a suit, looking handsome, put together, every strand of hair perfect, his skin smooth from a recent shave.

"Hi," I smile, wondering if I should hug him or shake his hand or greet him in some other fashion. I do nothing.

"Hey," he says. "Can we sit down for a second?"

"Sure," I tell him.

"First, here's your ring," he says, holding it out and dropping it in my open palm.

"Thanks."

"So, did you have a good time last night?"

I smile a little and nod, remembering the way I felt with him.

"I mean, after our talk, with your friend?"

"I, um–" I'm not really sure what he's asking.

"God, I'm sorry, that's really none of my business. God," he laughs. "I mean, are you okay? I wasn't sure, the way we left things."

"What's none of your business?" *Did he see Shawn and I leave together? Surely he doesn't think...* "He just walked me home," I blurt out subconsciously, my eyes wide at my strange admission.

"No, I–" he hesitates, a subtle smile on his face. "I didn't–" He shakes his head, his cheeks turning a soft shade of pink. "I just want to know if you're okay, that's all."

"Of course, yeah," I nod, embarrassed. "Yeah. It's just... I don't know. Some days I'm just... sad. I can't really help it. It was one of those days yesterday," I explain.

"I'm really sorry. I wish there was something more I could do..." Again his tender eyes envelop mine.

"And I wish I knew how people could help me," I tell him. "I just think this is something I have to do alone."

"You're never alone, you know that, right?"

"Sure," I smile.

"One other thing... I just want to apologize for last night. I don't know what got into me," he says, no longer looking me in the eyes.

"What do you mean?"

"It was just... I don't know... awkward, wasn't it?" he laughs.

"Oh," I manage to say, shaking my head. "I don't know..."

"We're okay, though, right? We're good?"

"Oh, of course," I say confused, not knowing why we wouldn't be. Could he sense that I had feelings for him? And maybe he feels he was leading me on? Fuck, this is so embarrassing. Shit. My face gets hot, my palms sweaty.

"Good," he says, abruptly standing. "I'm on my way to Marie's, so I need to get going. I'll see you Saturday!" He watches me intently.

"Okay," I say, even more confused now than I was last night. It's one thing to think I have feelings for someone who might be interested in me... but he's not? Really? Great.

When he's out of sight, I quickly open the bag and scarf the rest of the pie. Before I leave, I go and buy another one to take home. A little emotional eating might do me some good. Maybe my ring would fit again soon.

By the time I get home, after wandering the streets of New York, my sister is already home with Clara. My niece greets me with a big hug and kiss. I grab two forks and sit down at the table with my pie. Clara pulls up a chair and picks up the extra fork.

"How was your stay with Uncle Chris?" I ask.

"Good," she says, matching my sombre mood and picking out the apple slices in the pie and eating them one by one.

"Hey, Emi," Jennifer says. "Anna wanted me to remind you that you're going to do the fitting tomorrow."

"Crap," I say, eying the pie I shouldn't be eating. Ever since the accident, I just seem so absent minded. I forgot that we had plans to do that. "Right, what time?"

"Noon," she says. "She's going to pick you up."

"Alright," I say, sighing.

"What's with the pie?" my sister asks. "And the frown?"

"Nothing," I tell her. "Just feeling a little down." About Nate? About the baby? Could it be about Jack? All the feelings are getting mixed up at this point.

~ * ~

"What time will you be back?" Jen asks the next day as Anna and I are walking out the door.

"By five," Anna says. "I've got an early morning tomorrow."

"Um, Em," Jen whispers to me. "Do you think you can watch Clara tonight?"

"Garrett?" I ask. She nods her head. "Sure. We'll see you later."

"Thanks," she says. "Bye!"

At the dress store, Anna stands on a raised platform, modeling her elaborate wedding gown. It's strapless, a pale champagne color with gorgeous beading and intricate embroidery with a mocha-colored sash. "That dress is perfect. It looks so amazing on you, Anna. Chris's jaw will hit the floor when he sees you walking toward him in that."

"You think?" she says.

"I know. Do you want me to take a picture to send to your mom?"

"Please, she's dying to see it on me." I snap a few pictures with my phone and show them to Anna for her approval. She nods. I'm expending so much energy on keeping the mood happy that I'm worried she'll see right through me... see how fake I'm being. If she notices, though, she doesn't bring it up. Perhaps she just wants to be happy today... she deserves that.

"Okay, your turn," she says, stepping off of the platform.

I groan, feigning annoyance with the fashion show.

"Hey, Maid of Honor, you're going to like this, damn it!"

"Just kidding, Anna," I smile. "I really am excited to put it on. It's just the modeling part I hate." My dress is like a simpler version of hers, with the colors reversed. It's beautiful, likely the prettiest dress I've ever worn. The salesperson helps to dress me, and when she zips it up, I can feel that our last alterations are perfect. I stand on the raised platform in front of Anna.

"Ohhh," she squeals. "I'm so excited! That looks perfect! Turn around!" I walk in a slow circle for her and her smile just grows larger. "Do you feel like a princess?"

"Maybe a little," I admit.

"Yeah, all the single guys are going to go nuts! Um... I'm thinking we might need to dress you in something frumpier," she jokes. "I don't want you getting all the attention."

"Oh, shut up," I tell her. "Come up here, let's get a picture of both of us." She steps on the platform and the saleslady snaps a few shots of us. "What color are the guy's ties?"

"Chris's will be this champagne color, and Jack's will have the mocha color."

"Wow, I can't wait!" I'm now getting very excited. Happy to see my brother marry this wonderful girl, and a little anxious to see Jack in his tux and mocha tie. I shake the thought out of my head.

We change out of our dresses and back into our street clothes and head over to the florist. Anna's biggest dilemma is whether or not to add any color to her white and off white arrangements. Since the wedding is formal, I convince her that simpler is best, so she goes with her gut instinct and keeps the colors the way she had initially chosen.

We stop at a restaurant for a glass of sparkling wine to celebrate. I propose a toast to Chris and Anna. She proposes one back, simply to love.

At four, she drops me off at my building and I go upstairs, anxious to show Jen the pictures of the dresses. She becomes just as excited when she sees the photo of Anna and me on the platform.

"I'm so happy for Chris," Jen says. "I just love Anna. She's perfect for him."

"Yeah," I agree.

"Hey, listen, Emi," Jen says. "You know the dinner thing next weekend? Didn't you say I could bring a guest?"

I sigh. I hadn't considered the thought of her bringing a date... because if she did, I'd be the only single person there. "Yep," I say curtly.

"Well, would you mind if I invited Garrett?"

"Really? You just met him, don't you think that will be weird?"

"Not really," my sister says.

"It's fine with me," I tell her, unable to hide the dissatisfaction in my voice.

"Is it?"

"Sure, Jen," I say, frustrated. "It's fine. I'll be the only one without a date, but it's fine."

"Why don't you ask Shawn?" she says quietly.

"Because I think that *would* be weird... and I don't really want to see him again."

"Oh," she says. "Well, I don't have to invite him."

"No, Jen," I tell her. "I'm sorry... that's just selfish of me to even say anything. Please, invite him. I really don't mind going alone."

"Are you sure?"

"I'm positive. Now I'd feel bad if you didn't invite him."

"Okay," she smiles and hugs me. "Thank you."

In truth, though, I do mind going alone. I shouldn't have to go alone. More than anything, I'd like to have a date... and I don't like that feeling at all. I've never felt like I needed a man in my life. Why do I now?

Later that night, after I put Clara to bed, I send a text message to Jack. *"Add one more to the guest list. Reservations for 11."* I wait for a response, but after an hour, I decide to go to bed.

In the morning, there's a message from him that simply says, *"Great. Eleven. Thanks."*

CHAPTER   7

"Seriously, Emi, come with us!"

"Jen, I'll be fine. I need to get there a little early anyway to make sure the flowers made it." Honestly, I just want a little sliver of time alone... I'm not asking for much, I have been feeling suffocated this week. My sister, sensing my sadness, has been around far more often than normal, calling in sick two days this past week when she was feeling perfectly fine.

I have been afraid to say anything to her about why I am upset, though. I don't know that anyone would understand this loss that I'm feeling... I wonder to myself if it's weird to mourn the loss of my child now... I'd spent so much time mourning Nate, but even though the baby crossed my mind, I'd never really mourned. I had only known about her for a week... does this mean that the loss isn't as great? As mid-August creeps closer, when the baby would actually have been due, it gets harder and harder to think about. I am actually beginning to feel physical pain... don't know if it's psychosomatic or real... and I don't know who to talk to about it. I'm just afraid my family won't understand... will think that I'm reverting back to where I was when this horrible year started. I don't want to worry them... and I don't want to seem weak to them.

"You're being silly to not ride with us," my sister tells me. "Garrett really wouldn't mind."

"No, I'm taking the subway," I tell her. "I'll meet you down there in an hour."

"I don't know why you're so stubborn." I shrug my shoulders, grab my bag and leave the apartment.

"Wow," Marcus says as I walk past him. "Got a date, Emi?"

"No," I tell him somberly. "Not me," I force a smile.

"Well, you look really nice. You *should* have a date."

"Thanks, Marcus. Have a good night."

"You, too," he tells me. I take my time going to the restaurant. Instead of hopping on the subway at the nearest stop, I decide to walk a few blocks to clear my head. The last thing I want to be is sad tonight. This is a happy occasion. I just need to keep reminding myself of that.

At Buddakan, the hostess takes me to the long table on the lower floor, and I'm happy to see that the flowers I picked out have arrived and are placed perfectly on the table. I wonder what Chris and Anna must be thinking by now. They had planned to go to Jack's to watch a baseball game, but Jack was to call them this afternoon, let them know that plans had changed... he was requesting that they dress up, and he told them that a car would be picking them up. He also suggested they pack for an overnight stay. Jack and I had decided to get them a hotel room in the city so they wouldn't have to deal with a forty-five minute car ride back home after dinner. They deserved a little bit of an escape from their day-to-day lives.

"They're on their way," Jack says, sneaking up behind me.

"Oh, hey. I didn't know you were here," I laugh. There's a slight flutter in my stomach again. I had *so* not wanted to feel that tonight, but he looks so handsome, the color of his blue eyes made bluer by his shirt. "Were they okay with the change of plans?"

"Of course," he says. "Would you like something to drink?"

"I owe you," I tell him, remembering that I offered to buy the second round the other night. "What are you and Marie drinking?" I scan the restaurant for his girlfriend.

"Heineken for me," he says. "And I'm alone tonight. Speaking of which, where is number eleven?"

I look at him, confused. "Number eleven?"

"The eleventh guest. Your date?"

"Oh, not mine," I laugh. "Jen's."

"Of course," he smiles and sighs, running his hand through his thick, dark hair.

"Yeah," I mutter, watching his hair fall back into place, only slightly mussed, but begging to be caressed by my fingers. I fight the urge. "So, Marie," I say, tearing my eyes away. "Is she okay?"

"I'm sure she's fine," he tells me. "We've sort-of parted ways."

"What happened?" I fight a feeling of hope that sweeps over me.

"We both just agreed it wasn't working out."

"Well, I'm sorry," I say. He nods, and my eyes get lost in his. "Drinks," I say, walking toward the bar. "A Heineken and a glass of merlot, please," I tell the bartender. As I look in my bag to find my credit card to open a tab, Jack slips in beside me and hands the bartender his card.

"You're not buying the drinks, Emi," he laughs.

"Yes, I am! I said I would the other day."

"Absolutely not," he says emphatically. "Please, let me."

"But–"

"I won't take no for an answer."

I shrug my shoulders. "Well, then, thanks again. Someday, I'll make it up to you."

He smiles a slightly sly grin. "I'll take you up on that." Now my stomach does actual flips. The look on my face must convey the absolute confusion that's coursing through my veins. I laugh it off.

"How are you feeling tonight?" he asks.

"This is a happy occasion," I say, more to myself than to him.

"Excuse me, are you Emi?" a woman interrupts our conversation. I turn around and see a couple I've never met before.

"Yes," I say, "you must be Mae and Andy?" I ask.

"Yes, it's a pleasure to meet you," Mae says. Mae went to high school and college with Anna. They lost touch over the years after graduation, but had recently reconnected online. They haven't seen each other in years, so I'm sure Anna will be surprised and delighted to see her friend again. "And you're Jack, I presume?"

"Yes, nice to meet you both," he shakes their hands. "Would you like some drinks?"

"Please, yes, uh... Chardonnay for both of us," Andy says.

"Coming right up," Jack says, heading toward the bar as the rest of us take our seats at the table.

"So, Mae, did you manage to keep it a secret? You didn't tell her, did you?" Mae and her husband had traveled from Philadelphia and were spending the weekend in New York.

"She has no idea," she says. "I am so excited to see her, and to meet Chris... now he's your brother, right?"

"Yes," I say.

"And how long have you and Jack been together?" she asks as Jack hands them their drinks and sits down next to me.

"Oh, no, um, Jack and my brother are old college friends," I explain.

"So you're not dating?" Andy asks.

"No," I say, a little uncomfortable, hoping Jack will say something. When he doesn't, I look at him, a strange expression spreading across his face. He smiles and very slightly raises an eyebrow, as if to signal that it's not such a bad idea... or maybe I'm just reading too much into it.

I already feel like I'm on the verge of a breakdown. I don't need these other feelings complicating matters. Why am I thinking things like this? Surely this just isn't right. Surely it's too soon to be thinking about this... thinking, yes. But feeling... I can't help how I'm feeling. Do I want to feel this? I'm not positive.

"Oh, well, I just assumed since you were both hosting the dinner tonight," Mae explains.

"Just a joint effort," Jack says, smiling. He looks across the room and stands up abruptly as another couple enters the room.

"Jack!" the man yells from the bottom of the stairs. Jack walks assuredly to greet the man and his guest. I assume this is Russell, Jack's college roommate who was also in Chris and Jack's fraternity. They hug, and Russell introduces Jack to the woman who is accompanying him. He shakes her hand and then leads them both to the table.

"Russell, Nicole, this is Anna's friend Mae, her husband, Andy," he says, before gesturing to me, "and this is Chris's younger sister, Emi."

"I remember meeting you at the engagement party," Russell says. "Red dress, right?" Russell smiles. Nicole glares at him out of the corner of her eyes.

"Yes," I force a smile. "Good to see you again." As we're all making introductions and getting to know each other, my sister and Garrett come downstairs and join in the conversation. Jack asks me to help him with some drinks at the bar.

"Can I get ten glasses of champagne?" Jack asks the bartender. "They should be here any minute," he says to me as we wait. I tap my fingers anxiously on the bar as I watch the bartender popping the cork and carefully pouring the drinks into flutes. I can see Jack watching me in my peripheral vision. I glance quickly to meet his gaze, but he looks away hurriedly. The bartender hands us the drinks and Jack asks him to put them on his card. I need to figure out what he does for a living to be able to afford all of this. He had offered to cover everyone's dinner tonight, but hadn't mentioned the bar tab, but it appears he'll be paying for that, too. And he insisted on putting the hotel room on his card, as well, even though it was my idea and we agreed that I could give him half. I seriously doubt that he'll let me do that at this point.

Jack takes six glasses and I take the other four. He hands all of his out to the couples that have arrived, letting them know that we will toast Chris and Anna when they come downstairs. He walks over to me and takes two of the glasses. "They're here," he says, walking toward the staircase. I watch him cross the room and become entranced with his posture, his thick, dark hair, his confident stride, the way his clothes fit his athletic body... *I should not be thinking these things!* I quickly drink one of the glasses of champagne that I'm holding. I watch Jack hand my brother and his fiancée their drinks and we gather around for the toast. Jack speaks confidently, his voice smooth as his blue eyes sparkle, his enunciation perfect, but his words... my god, his words. His toast couldn't have been more eloquent, more perfect for my brother and Anna. I watch him, slightly in awe, as he lifts his hand toward the sky. I lift my flute, with the rest of the guests, and drink. He walks over to me and eyes the nearly-empty glass of champagne I'm drinking and the empty glass I'm holding in my right hand.

"Um, did you save any for me?" he laughs. I look down, realizing what I've done, and immediately blush, mortified.

"I am sooo sorry," I say. "Here, you can have the rest of this," I tell him, then think to myself that he may actually want his own glass. "Wait, no, let me go get one for you. I am so embarrassed." As I start to walk away, he catches my elbow and stops me.

"Are you alright?" he asks.

"I'm fine, just completely absent-minded for some reason, that's all." We walk together to the bar.

"You seem a little... off."

"No, um," I start. "Well, yes, *off* maybe... I'm not sure what I am," I laugh before finishing off the rest of the champagne and ordering another glass for Jack and a glass of wine for myself. I feel like my emotions are just taking me from one extreme to another today. Sad to... what? Turned on? I'm beginning to think I'm going slightly mad. Surely they have medication for this. Alcohol will have to do in the meantime.

"And two sparkling waters, please," Jack adds to the order. "It's okay," he says, standing behind me and rubbing my shoulders. Jack takes both of the alcoholic beverages to the table and leaves me to carry the water. Is this his way of cutting me off? I guess I have had a lot to drink in the thirty minutes we've been here.

"Is this for me?" I ask him, embarrassed.

"If you're thirsty," he says. "You can even have mine."

I. Am. An. Idiot.

"If you'll excuse me," I say, setting the glasses of water down. I half-run to the ladies room, hoping that a bolt of lightning will strike me along the way. I am so embarrassed. I walk over to the mirror and look at myself, eye-to-eye with my reflection, a million thoughts racing through my head.

I shouldn't have come tonight. I was not up for this in the first place. I'm burying my real feelings by distracting myself with this attractive man. I wish I had stayed home. I want to talk to Nate some more. I want to dream about him. I want to see our child again.

No, I definitely should not have forced myself to come here, to be social, to be happy. And furthermore, I should not be feeling *anything* for Jack. He thinks I'm a drunk. I'm completely mortified...

And I shouldn't care one way or the other because it's *just too fucking soon to move on!*

I sit down on the couch in the lounge area and put my head in my hands as I feel tears forming in my eyes. Now I don't know if I'm crying because I'm just an emotional wreck or if it's because of the alcohol I sucked down in a matter of mere minutes.

"Emi?" Anna asks, concerned. I quickly wipe the corners of my eyes, hoping she doesn't see me crying. "Is everything okay?"

"Fine," I smile.

"The mascara trails say differently," she says, sitting next to me. "What's wrong?"

"I don't want to talk about it," I tell her. "I'm sorry I'm in here crying. I'll be right back out, I just need a minute."

"No," Anna says. "I'm not leaving you in here. Jack was worried enough about you to send me here, so something's going on. What happened?"

"Really, Anna," I plead. "I can't talk about it." She puts her arm around my shoulders.

"Please don't be sad, Em," she says, standing up to get a tissue for me. "Is it Nate?" she reluctantly asks.

"I don't know," I tell her. "I'm just confused about... things... life."

"Well, we're all that, Em. That's nothing to cry about."

"I know," I say. "Really, I'm fine." I take a deep breath and swallow the lump. "I'm good."

"Hold up," she says, getting out her phone and sending a text. "Let's put you back together." A minute later my sister appears with my bag.

"What's going on, Emi?" Jen asks.

"Really, nothing, I think I've had too much to drink already this evening and I'm crying for apparently no reason."

"Em," she says to me, hugging me, knowing there's something deeper going on. She gets out my makeup and hands it to me. "Anna, I've got this. You're the guest of honor, go on."

"I don't mind," Anna argues.

"We'll be out in a second, really. I'm fine," I tell her. She hugs me and returns to the table.

"Jen," I start, then hesitate. It's not the time or place for this, but I feel I might explode.

"What Em?"

"Never mind."

"What's going on with Jack?" she asks.

"Nothing, it's not him. Jen, I miss Nate... and I miss our baby." I break down again, setting the makeup aside.

"Is that what's been going on with you?" I nod and she embraces me again. "I had a feeling."

"I want to go home," I tell her, clutching my stomach.

"We can take you if you really want," she says. "But I'm sure Chris would be sad to see us leave."

"I would be," my brother says, his head peeking in through the door to the lounge. "Is it safe to come in?"

"You probably shouldn't," Jen advises, "but there are no other women in here."

"Did Jack do something?" he says, walking in and squatting down in front of me.

"Jack's getting a bad rap tonight," I concede. "Why does everyone think that?"

"He's the only one you've been talking to since I got here," he says. "And he just came to ask Anna and me if you were okay. She said you two were in here."

"Emi's just a little sad about things," Jen says on my behalf.

"Do you really want to leave?" Chris asks.

"I don't know if I can go back out there. I'm a mess and I'm having a difficult time putting on my happy face for everyone... and I'm trying to mask that with alcohol and I'm probably moderately drunk right now, which isn't helping matters..."

"We can get you some water–"

"Jack already got me some... no subtle hint there."

"He's probably just looking out for you," Chris says, smiling. "He's a nice guy that way. He was always the responsible one."

"Well I'm mortified," I tell my siblings. "I made a fool of myself in front of him."

"What do you care what he thinks?" my brother laughs. *I care a lot. I wish I didn't, but I do.*

I simply shrug as my sister hands me a tissue. "Chris, I've got this from here," Jen tells him.

"Are you going to leave?" he asks me.

"I'll convince her to stay, somehow. Don't worry. Just get out there to your guests."

"I love you, Emi. And you, too, Jen."

"Love you, too," we say in unison as he leaves the ladies room.

"I tell you what," my sister says. "Let's put your make up back on... let's try not to think about what's upsetting you... let's try to have a nice time tonight, for Chris... and after, you and I can go back to the apartment and eat cookies and drink wine and you can cry all night if you want. Can we try that?"

I sigh heavily before agreeing. I blot my eyes again with the tissue and my sister picks up the makeup bag and gets to work.

When we get back to our table, Jen takes her seat and Jack stands up to pull out a chair for me.

"Thanks," I say, afraid to look him in the eyes, fearing he'll see the evidence of tears in my own. I look down at my empty plate and take a long drink of water. Conversation is loud and cheerful as everyone eats appetizers, and I force myself to join in, even though I'm still embarrassed and a little confused. *It's a happy occasion. I can cry later.*

After dinner and dessert, the guests begin to leave. My sister and Garrett are among the first to leave, and Jen stops by to talk to me before they say their goodbyes.

"Do you want to ride with me? I just need to drop him off," she tells me.

"I can take her," Jack says quickly. "If you'd like," he says to me. "I think Chris and Anna wanted to talk about some wedding stuff with us before they leave..."

"Oh," I say. "Um, yeah, I'll catch a ride with him, then," I tell my sister. "I doubt we'll be long."

"Okay," she says. "I'll stop by the store and get some supplies," she winks at me.

"Thanks, see you in a few."

The rest of the guests file out, couple by couple, and at the end of the night, it's just me, Jack, Anna and Chris. We all order coffee and sit around one end of the table.

"Thank you both so much," Anna says. "This was really fun."

"Well, we couldn't be happier for you both," I tell her. "I'm glad you enjoyed it."

"So much better than baseball," she says, winking at Jack. "So why did we have to pack suitcases?" Anna asks.

"Well," Jack says, getting a card out of his wallet, "here is a key to your hotel room. The driver will take you there."

"You really didn't have to do this," Chris says.

"We wanted to," Jack tells him. "Enjoy yourselves."

"Well, thanks, man," my brother says, standing up. Jack stands, too, and they shake hands across the table.

"Didn't you want to talk to us about something?" I direct my question to both Anna and Chris.

"Um, no, I don't think so," Anna says, looking confused at my brother. He shakes his head.

"Oh, okay," I say, glancing at Jack, who's looking down at his wallet, as if not paying attention to the conversation.

My brother and his fiancée both hug me before exiting.

"I'm sorry," Jack says, sitting back down, signaling to the waiter to bring the check. "Listen, I sort of made that up. I just wanted a chance to talk to you, alone." My heart rate speeds up as I wait for him to say more. "I'm sorry if I upset you earlier, before dinner."

"Oh, no," I stammer. "I don't know what has gotten into me lately," I tell him, attempting to brush off the incident. "It's nothing you did... and I probably had a little too much to drink."

"Is there anything I can do to help?" he asks, his voice full of concern. *He seems like such a nice guy.* In my current state, I consider telling him everything– but fear that I may scare him off in under twenty words.

I think to myself and sigh. "No, I don't think so. But thank you." I squeeze his hand, just a casual gesture to show I appreciate his concern. He looks down at our touching hands and flips his over so we're holding hands. I pull mine away quickly when I realize what's going on. I look at him and smile, unsure.

"I–" he begins.

"Here you go, sir," the waiter interrupts him with the bill just as he begins to speak. Jack simply hands him his black credit card and clears his throat. He takes a drink of water and laughs quietly to himself.

"So, this was nice," he says to me, and I nod in agreement. I know this is not what he had intended to say before he was interrupted. The waiter quickly returns with the card. Jack signs and stands up, as if impatient and ready to leave. "Let's go," he says. I lead the way up the stairs and out of the restaurant. Jack gives the valet his ticket and we stand, not talking, awkward, as we wait for his car, a practical four-door Volvo. He opens the door for me and shuts it gently before walking around to the driver's side. He turns up the volume on the radio, drowning out the silence of our ride to my apartment. Once there, he parallel parks and lets the car idle, lowering the music's volume.

"Emi, I don't know if it's too soon, but I really like you and I wonder if it would be alright if I asked you out sometime?" he says in one hurried breath, as if he was gathering the courage all the way from the restaurant.

His question catches me completely off guard. My stomach leaps into my chest.

Even *he* thinks it's too soon. But of all the people I know, I've met, he is the only one who knows the loss I've experienced. He doesn't know everything, of course, but he has been in my life through it all, from the night it happened to the hospital stay, to the suicide watch at Chris's apartment, to tonight. Tonight, where I have proven to myself and the world that I need more time to heal. *Sure it's too soon.*

Logically, I know this. But he knows I have baggage... and still, he wants to go out with me. I don't know if I'm ready. I don't think that I am. But something in me takes control and blurts out an answer that surprises even myself. "I'd really like that." *What did I just say? Was that really my voice?*

"Good," he smiles with a sigh of relief. "I'll call you."

"Okay," I stammer and blush, shaking my head in disbelief. He gets out of the car and walks around to my side, opening the door for me. He offers his hand to help me out.

"Have a great night," he says, pushing a strand of hair out of my face and tucking it behind my ear.

"You, too. Thank you." He walks me to the entrance of the building, his hand on the small of my back, barely touching me but eliciting something in me that I haven't felt in a long time. I get chills as Marcus opens the door for me.

"Bye," he says, turning to walk away. I wave, surprised at the ending to the night, at my response to his question... surprised at the warmth that washes over my body.

"Your face is flushed," Jen says as I enter the apartment. "Are you okay?"

"Fine, I think. I'm going to change into something more comfortable." I grab some pajamas and head to the bathroom to wash my face and change clothes. I can't believe I said yes to him. Surely everyone will tell me it's too soon. I don't have to go, though, when he asks. I'll come to my senses before then. I'm certainly not going to say anything to Jen about it.

My sister has set out a bowl of chips and a plate of cookies next to the bottle of wine she has just opened. She pats the seat next to her, inviting me to join her at the table.

"Do you want to talk about it?" she asks.

"I don't know that it will help..."

"Well, what happened? What brought this on?"

I tell her about my discovery of the mural sketches, and about the subsequent physical pain that I've been feeling ever since that day.

"Do you think it's normal to feel like that?"

"Probably," she says. "Do I think it's real or imagined pain? I'm not a doctor, I don't know. It's possible that your body knows that something's... missing. I know you miss it. I think you have every right to feel this loss and this pain."

"Shouldn't I be over it by now?"

"I don't think so," she says. "I expected you to have another wave of depression around this time. We all expected it, the whole family. I mean, I'm sad for you, Emi. There have been times when I've even cried about it. Being a mom... I can't even imagine that kind of loss. It's okay to be sad."

"But when will it stop?" I cry.

"I don't know, Emi. I know you've been so strong and so self-willed to get through all of this on your own... but maybe it's time to get some help... to go to therapy or something."

"I don't need therapy," I tell her.

"It just might make you feel better. It's one thing for me to say, 'hey, it's okay, you're normal.' It's another thing for an impartial third party– a doctor, even– to tell you that... or to tell you you're *not* normal," she laughs.

"Maybe that's what I'm afraid of," I admit to her.

"Emi, there is no timeline for grief, no one-size-fits-all plan for healing. Everyone has different needs," she says. "I'm here for you, no matter what. But I can help you find someone else to talk to, if you want."

"I think I'll just try to work through this on my own," I tell her. "I'm sure after mid-August it will get easier. Maybe I need to just take this time to mourn."

"I'll give you a little space," she says. "But I'm worried about you. Whatever you need."

"Thank you," I tell her. "I think I'm just going to go to bed."

"What? No cookies? No wine?"

"I'm just tired," I explain. "I'll get my share tomorrow."

"Alright," she says. "I think I'll stay up and read awhile. Try to get some sleep."

"I'll try. I love you, Jen, and thank you."

"Anything for you, Emi," she smiles.

~ * ~

A week and a half passes before I hear from Jack.

I was beginning to think he had changed his mind, but it gave me time to deal with my conflicted emotions.

After crying for days in a row, and beginning to think my stomach was going to dissolve itself from the amount of aspirin I'd been taking for the headaches, I have been doing my best to find distractions. Part of me feels that it's not healthy to do that, but another part of me thinks it's *unhealthy* to just wallow in the sorrow. There's a sane part in me somewhere that knows that therapy would be a good option, maybe the only one, but I am still determined to get through this alone. I was doing very well dealing with Nate's death. I just didn't go through the same sort of mourning for our child. It was just a mistake I made early on. I was accepting it now and handling it as best as I could. And right now, the best I can do is *not* think about it.

160

In my quest for distractions I decided that going on a date with Jack was a good choice. I would be nervous enough to focus most of my attention on that, but in reality, I knew it would be no different than hanging out with friends... because at this point, that's all he is. Sure, he's a friend who makes my heart beat a little faster, but he's still just a friend. If I have no expectations of our meeting, it just makes it easier for me to accept. One day at a time. If we go beyond "friend" territory, I'll deal with that when it happens.

When he finally calls, I let the phone ring three times before answering, even though it is sitting in front of me and alerts me immediately when his call comes in. I don't want it to seem like I was waiting around for this.

"Hello?"

"Emi?"

"Hi," I say through a smile, careful not to reveal who I'm talking to. I have decided not to tell anyone that Jack and I had planned to go out. I don't want any of my friends or family to think that I'm 'dating' again. I'm not sure that's what this is... and it's just easier this way, to not have to explain or justify anything to anyone. I feel a little guilty, but I've decided that this distraction is necessary for my own well-being. I think I've earned a few hours of happiness, and I'm hopeful that it will be fun, comfortable. I don't want anyone to change my mind, and I have a feeling one glance of uncertainty, judgement from someone, one reminder of the relationship I shared with Nate could do just that.

"How are you?" he asks me.

"I'm good, you?" Small talk. *Breathe, Emi.*

"I'm fine. Listen, I'm sorry I didn't call sooner, but I had to go to London on business last week. I just got in yesterday."

"Oh," I say nonchalantly. "It's okay. I've been putting in a lot of hours, too."

"So, do you have any plans on Friday?" he asks.

"Um, no," I tell him.

"I was wondering if you'd like to come to my place for dinner... maybe we could watch a movie."

"That sounds nice, sure," I answer.

"So, I'll pick you up around seven?"

"I can take the subway," I offer.

"Emi, what is your fascination with public transportation?" he laughs.

"It's what I do," I tell him. "I don't have a car."

"Well, I do, and I like to use it every once in awhile, so humor me."

"Alright, I'll see you Friday at seven, then."

"Thank you," he says. "I'm looking forward to it."

"Me, too. Bye."

"Bye," he says. I put the phone down and try to get back to work, as if the phone call didn't just stir up a swarm of butterflies in my stomach.

"Who was that?" my sister asks me.

"No one," I tell her.

"Whatever!" she says. "Friday at seven?"

"It's nothing," I tell her. "Just please don't make a big deal out of it. I'm afraid I'll back out."

"Is it a date?" she asks. I glare at her, not wanting to answer her question. "It is," she smiles. "Please, tell me who!"

"No," I whine. "It's no one you know, and it's not really a date. He's just a friend, and we're just meeting for dinner. Period."

"Alright, I won't push you now, but I may want details by Saturday."

"Jennifer, please, just forget you ever heard any of that. I'm having a hard time dealing with this decision."

"Emi," she says. "Stop beating yourself up. I think this is good for you."

"I'm trying," I tell her. "But this is my own personal battle... so I'd rather fight it alone, okay? I'll give you all the details when I'm ready."

"Okay," she says. "But I *will* stop you from backing out. Seven. Friday. I'll make sure you're ready."

"Okay," I concede. I will likely need her help by then.

~ * ~

On Friday, I'm dressed and ready to go by six-thirty. I have had no thoughts of backing out, but my sister has been following me around all afternoon, just in case.

"So what are you doing?" she asks.

"Just going to his place for dinner and a movie," I tell her. "Just a casual night."

"You know him well enough to go to his house on the first date?"

"I do," I tell her.

"And I don't know him?" she asks, skeptical.

"He's an old friend," I lie.

"Well, dinner at his house... you're very dressed up for that," she says, commenting on the knee-length black and white striped dress I'm wearing.

"Is it too dressy, really?" I ask, panicked.

"No, you look good," she says. "Don't change."

"Are you sure?"

"Positive."

I pace the loft as my sister continues to give me encouragement. At six-fifty, I decide to go downstairs, wanting to avoid the meeting between my sister and my date.

"Emi, have a good time. Just remember to have fun," she says.

"I will," I smile, looking forward to this more than I thought I would be.

"And just call me if you're not coming home–"

"I'll be home," I snap at her. "God, Jen, I'm not ready for *that*."

"Well, have an open mind." I glare at her again.

"I will see you later tonight, unless you're asleep."

"Wake me up," she says.

"We'll see," I respond.

After the ride down the elevator, I pace around the lobby until Jack comes in. He's dressed in grey slacks and a long-sleeved white button-down shirt, the top two buttons left open. He's got a white t-shirt on underneath.

"Hi," I say, smiling and walking toward him.

"Good evening, Emi," he says, hugging me. "You look amazing."

"Thank you. So do you," I tell him, blushing.

"Are you ready?" he asks.

"I am." *I am. I am. I am.*

"Let's go, then." He links my elbow into his and leads me to his car, opening the door for me like a perfect gentleman. Two simple white daisies lay in the passenger seat. He picks them up and hands them to me.

"Wow..." I tell him. "Thank you so much."

"You're welcome."

When he gets in the car, I decide to ask a few questions that I've prepared, wanting to avoid awkward silence.

"So, you graduated from college in, what... 1998?"

"Uh..." he hesitates. "No. I graduated from NYU in 2000. I took a few years off to focus on a company I started in college." He shrugs shyly. "Then I went to grad school and got my MBA in 2004."

"Impressive... what do you do now?" I ask him.

"I am a technology consultant," he says.

"And that means..."

"Well, let's see... the company I formed in college was an Internet start-up that I sold a few years later. So, um, the sale of that company afforded me a pretty decent living. And after I got my Masters, I was able to take on consulting jobs from time to time for other new technology ventures."

"That's pretty nice," I comment. "It sounds like you have a lot of freedom."

"I do," he says, "but I don't really like down time. I like to stay busy, so when I'm not working, I'm helping my sister out with her kids, or I like to volunteer around the city."

"Really?" I'm impressed, but he's sounding too good to be true... if my brother hadn't known him for over ten years, I'd be worried... but I know the friends my brother keeps are good people, so he must be true.

"Yes, really," he smiles. "What are you working on these days?"

"I'm illustrating a book," I tell him. "A children's book... well, obviously."

"Do you enjoy doing that?"

"I really do," I smile. "I like the work and I like the freedom. I tend to be more creative at night, so I like that I can work my own hours."

"Do you always do children's books and articles?"

"No," I tell him. "It's a variety of things. But I like doing children's books the best. My niece really likes to give me suggestions."

"Do you spend a lot of time with Clara?"

"After she gets out of school, most afternoons," I tell him. "She loves to go to Central Park."

"Well, you're right next door," he comments. "That's convenient."

"Yes, but I hope she doesn't get too spoiled. I don't expect she'll be living there forever."

"Is your sister planning to move out anytime soon?"

"No, we haven't talked about that. I don't think I'm ready for her to go yet."

"So, is she serious about this Garrett guy?"

"Who knows," I mumble. "This is Jen. She just can't stand to be alone."

"I take it you're not the same way."

"Polar opposite," I tell him.

"You can't stand to be with someone?" he laughs.

"Oh, I wouldn't go that far," I say. "I just don't have that need to be with anyone. I don't mind being alone."

"Have you always been that way, or is that... recent?"

"Always," I say. "But I have to admit, I never really knew what I was missing until I started dating... um... Nate." I hope I don't make him uncomfortable, bringing him up. "And the last couple of months, I think I can honestly say that I've felt a little lonely. I never used to feel that way at all... I was always pretty self-sufficient." I swallow hard, surprised at my own honesty and openness, my trust in Jack, so soon.

"Now, you and Nate hadn't been dating for very long, had you?"

"No, just a few months," I tell him.

"But you had known him since high school?" His voice is soft, cautious.

"Yes, we were best friends for years."

"And why didn't you date, all that time?"

"Um... timing? Stubbornness? I don't know. And we made a silly pact in high school that we wouldn't... because love ruined people." I laughed. "That's what we thought when we met, anyway."

"Wow. That was probably a pretty good foundation for a relationship," he smiles gently. "If it upsets you to talk about this–"

"No, surprisingly, not at all," I say. "It actually feels good to talk about him... with you..."

"Why with me?"

"I don't know. I mean, I've been avoiding the subject for months. My family's too scared to bring it up... and most people who didn't know him just don't seem genuinely interested. But you..."

I struggle to figure it out. *Yes, why with him?*

"You seem interested, I guess. And I just feel more comfortable around you than most people. And I've been having a hard time coming to terms with this whole date-thing."

"This 'whole date-thing,'" he mocks.

"Yeah. You know, a part of me thinks it's too soon, and then another part of me just wants to experience life again."

We arrive at his town home in the Upper West Side, a gorgeous, newly-renovated three-story building with red brick and taupe shutters. He has a small garden in the front, and it's immediately obvious where the flowers came from.

"This is so cute," I tell him. "And all the daisies, they're beautiful!"

"My sister loves to garden," he remarks. "When she brings the kids over on the weekends, she'll typically spend a few hours planting or pruning or doing something. There's a small yard in the back, too."

"Daisies are my favorite flowers."

"I know," he admits. "I asked your brother. I hope you don't mind, but I did talk to Chris about going out with you."

"Seriously?" I ask, panicked, wondering why Chris didn't mention it when I talked to him earlier today. Maybe I shouldn't have trusted him after all... I really didn't want my family to know anything.

"I'm sorry," he says. "I did ask him to keep it between us, though."

"Does Anna know?"

"Probably. I'm sure neither of them will say anything to you. I just felt it was important to let him know that I had asked you out."

"What did he say?"

"Honestly?"

"Yes, of course, honestly."

"Well, he first threatened my life... said that he didn't want to see you hurt again... and then wished me luck."

"That sounds like Chris."

"He has been so worried about you. He just wants you to be happy."

"I want that, too," I tell him.

"So are you mad that I told him?"

"Not mad, no. I really can't keep much from him anyway. Now if *he* goes and tells everyone..."

"I don't think he will," he assures me. "Can I get you a glass of wine?"

"You sure you want to do that?" I joke.

"It might help with this 'whole date-thing,'" he returns.

"Then yes, please." We go inside his split level town home. It's tastefully decorated, very simple, with very little clutter.

"Have a seat, if you like," he says from the kitchen. I decide to take a look around. He has a bookshelf that seems to be dedicated to his nieces and nephews. There are framed photos, all black and white, of each of them individually, and then various poses of them all together, some with their parents, others just with Jack, and some with what I assume is his whole family. The bottom shelf is organized with children's books.

"That's the family," he says from behind me.

"You really do love those kids, don't you?" I comment.

"Yes," he says. "I hope to have my own someday." I nod and try to smile, but can't, feeling my forehead crumple with defeat. I feel overwhelmed with sadness, immediately recognizing that yes, it's too soon since I just want to burst into tears. I take a deep breath before taking a long sip of wine.

"This place is amazing," I tell him, focusing on something else, *anything* else.

"Let me give you a tour, come on." He guides me downstairs first to the basement, which is a decked-out media center. The lack of windows makes it perfect for a decent-sized personal theatre. The room has plenty of comfortable seating, from cushioned leather chairs to large bean bags on the floor. He has a wall full of DVDs, with just about anything anyone could ever want to watch.

"Amazing," I say. I've never seen anything like this in someone's home.

"Yeah, Kelly's kids spend a lot of time down here," he says. In another room, there is a pool table and dart board, as well as children's toys. There are two more rooms downstairs, both small bedrooms, one decorated in pink and brown polka dots, the other with a baseball theme. There are two daybeds in each room. I didn't think I'd be confronted with so many images of children in this bachelor's home... had I known, I would have suggested going out.

"Spoil them much?" I ask, trying to act as normal as I possibly can under the circumstances.

"Hey now," he laughs. "I had this whole extra floor, I had to use it for something."

"Of course," I say. He takes me back up the stairs to the main floor and shows me the kitchen, dining room and his office. I breathe a sigh of relief, happy to leave the kid's area behind. The dining room and kitchen overlook the backyard, which is perfectly landscaped with flowers and small bushes. A few benches sit in the far corner. The office is on the side of the building, facing a busy street with a grocery store on the opposite corner.

"That window's great for people watching," he says.

"This is such an awesome home," I tell him.

"Let me show you the upstairs."

"Okay."

"It's the bedroom," he says cautiously. "Is that alright?"

"Should I be worried?" I laugh.

"No," he smiles. "I just didn't want you to be uncomfortable."

With four rooms on each of the previous floors, I expect much of the same on the third floor. Instead, it is a huge open space for his bedroom; attached to it, a large balcony with a table and two chairs that have a view of the backyard and the street. I wander around the room as he watches me. A few skylights are installed on the ceiling. The bathroom has a huge walk-in shower and a large tub, as well, with two sinks in the marble countertops. This leads into a separate closet, obviously too large for Jack to fill on his own. Half is filled with suits, pants, shirts, shoes. The other side is bare.

This town home is fit for a family, plain and simple. Most living spaces in Manhattan are small, made-for-one (but which typically housed more-than-one for budgetary reasons). This is quite the exception. Jack knows what he wants in life, and is ready for it. That is obvious.

"I'm a little jealous," I admit. "And I love the loft I live in... but it doesn't compare to this."

"It's nice," he says, "but a little too big sometimes."

"How long have you lived here?" I ask.

"About two and a half years," he tells me.

"And what made you decide to get such a big place?"

"Hmmm," he laughs. "That's another story for another time." He smiles. I let it go.

He leads me back downstairs into the kitchen. He pulls out a barstool for me to sit in and goes to wash his hands. "So, I'm going to make you my signature dish," he says.

"You have one of those?"

"Yes," he states. "It started as a family recipe, but I perfected it over the years. It's chicken, is that okay?"

"Sure... can I help?"

"Absolutely not," he says. "I will be doing the work tonight. I just want you to relax and enjoy yourself." He tops off my wine and sets the bottle next to me. "Can I get you anything right now?"

"Water?" I request, vowing to myself to drink water between every glass of wine. I don't want him to think I'm a lush.

He sets down a glass of ice water and says, "I hope you don't think it's weird that I invited you over. I just wanted somewhere quiet, where we could actually carry on a conversation. It seems like every time we spend time together, we're yelling over crowds."

"Not weird at all," I tell him. *Just wish you had warned me about the playroom downstairs... and your love for children...*

"So, Emi, do you cook?"

"Not well," I tell him, forcing myself to try to enjoy the evening. "I can follow instructions most of the time, but I'm not very imaginative in the kitchen."

"So no cooking..."

"Well, wait, I make breakfast really well."

"Cereal and toast?"

"Not just cereal and toast," I laugh. "I can make an assortment of eggs... and breakfast casseroles... do you like eggs?"

"Sure," he smiles, glancing up briefly from stirring something in a bowl. "Now I'm curious about this breakfast casserole..."

I nod my head and smile back. "It's pretty good, I have to admit... I'll have to make it for you sometime." He raises his eyebrows at me before I even realize what I said, what I seem to have implied. I laugh nervously and blush. "So, uh, yeah... um, so I wrote down a list of questions to ask you to avoid awkward silence," I blurt out to him.

He laughs. "Now would be a good time for one, then... shoot," he says, winking at me.

"So, um..." Still nervous... "What was one of the questions? Oh, yeah. So, Jack, what do you believe in?"

"Is that how you wrote it on the paper?" He smiles, his eyes kind, clearly playing with me. His smile makes me smile.

"Shut up!" I laugh back at him, picking up a wooden spoon from a container on the island. "So, Jack," I repeat, talking into the spoon like a microphone. "What do you believe in?"

"What do I believe in?" he repeats back to me, taking the spoon and talking into it. "Interesting question."

"Yes. Ghosts? Love at first sight? Aliens? I just need to understand what I'm dealing with."

He laughs, using the spoon to stir the dinner he's preparing. "I've never been asked that before... here goes. I don't believe in ghosts. I think it's entirely possible that aliens exist, although I doubt they've visited our planet. I do believe in love at first sight– Chris and Anna are proof, remember? I believe in soul mates. I don't believe in a JFK conspiracy. I believe in God, in Heaven and Hell... and I believe in karma..."

"Karma?" I interrupt.

"Yeah, sort of a what goes around, comes around belief."

"I know what karma is," I smile. "I just find it interesting that you make a point to mention that."

"Well," he says, "I make it a point to live that way. It's kind of important to me."

I've thought a lot about karma recently, having been a believer in it before the accident. Nate was a good man, though, and didn't deserve to die. His mother had survived tragedy before, and never hurt a soul. In fact, she was well known for her philanthropic endeavors. Why did she have to see the two men she loved the most pass away such sudden deaths? And then there's me... I think I've lived a pretty decent, honest life– even a good life. Why was Nate taken from me? What did I do to deserve that?

"So what are your thoughts about karma and bad things happening to good people?" I ask.

"I don't know the answer to that," he smiles gently, seeing exactly where this line of conversation is coming from. "I believe all things happen for a reason, though... and sometimes it takes a while to figure out that reason."

"A lifetime, maybe..." I'm temporarily lost in my own thoughts. I ask *Why?* daily, hourly... but answers never come.

"Maybe," he agrees after a few seconds of silence. "Hey, would you mind handing me the salt?" he asks, bringing me out of my daze.

"Sure," I answer, handing him the spice. "Please, what else can I do to help? I hate that you're doing all the work. I need a task," I laugh.

"Can you make a salad?" he asks with a smile.

"I can manage that."

As we sit down to eat, Jack glances up at me, his hands in his lap. "Do you, uh, pray before meals?"

"Uh..." I blush, dropping my fork. "I haven't since I lived at home. But you can–"

"No, I don't, much to my parents chagrin. I just wanted to ask." He picks up his wine glass. "A toast then?"

I smile and nod, picking up my drink. "It's all you, I know you excel at these things."

He clears his throat. "I haven't really prepared for this one. Here goes. Umm... to the most entrancing green eyes I have ever had the pleasure of gazing into... may they never be blue again."

My eyes immediately begin to water at his sweet toast, a smile growing on my lips.

"That was the exact opposite reaction I had been hoping for," he sighs, setting the glass down and rubbing his forehead. "I'm sorry–"

"No, it was... it was perfect, thank you. I'm just really emotional sometimes." He looks up at me apologetically. "Really. I'll drink to that." My heart racing, I lean over the table, extending my glass to meet the rim of his. "Come on. Cheers," I encourage him.

"Cheers," he says as he picks up his glass and clinks it to mine. His smile is remorseful, but it's still a smile. Our eyes lock as we take a drink. He hopes my eyes are never blue again, and at the same moment, I get lost in the deep, almost turquoise color of his.

"Speaking of blue eyes," I break the silence– and our gaze. "Sinatra fan?" I ask as I tune into the background music he's selected. *Three Coins in the Fountain.* My favorite song of his.

"It's a prerequisite for any man from Hoboken."

"Ahhh," I smile. "I thought I heard a little Jersey in there."

"Yeah, right," he rolls his eyes, taking a bite of the salad.

"So, you're just playing his music as an homage to your hometown hero, then?" I quirk an eyebrow at him playfully.

"And what exactly are you getting at, Poppet?" I look at him curiously, searching my memories for the moment I first heard this term.

"Wait, you called me that in college, didn't you?"

"I did," he tells me. "Remember?"

"Vaguely," I admit. "Do you remember that night?"

"I remember it like it was yesterday," he says.

A warm blush settles on my cheek. *I barely remember him from that night at all. Thanks, jello shots and quarters.* Jack takes another bite of the salad and compliments me on my contribution to the meal.

"Lettuce, tomatoes... cheese... kinda hard to screw that up."

"Oh, it can be done," he laughs. "When we were younger, Kelly loved to experiment in the kitchen. And my parents were always very supportive of her. They'd let her be in charge of one dish, every night... and most the time they were fine.

"One night, though, she let me help. She was trying to be encouraging of me, so she let me pick the ingredients... and just trusted that I knew what I was doing." He takes another bite of salad.

"I knew lettuce was the base. I got that. I figured that much out. But when I was a kid, I hated most vegetables, and I decided I was going to make a salad that I liked, with my favorite ingredients... I was too young to understand that flavors should actually go together..."

"Mmmm... this sounds like it's gonna be tasty."

"Let's see... I felt it was very important to represent the same colors in the salad. Like that would fool my parents. So instead of tomatoes, we had gummy bears. Only red ones. I couldn't stand celery, so I chose lime chunks because I loved lemon-lime soda. Carrots were out, but we had some apricot jelly, so I put a few dollops of that in. One of the few vegetables I did like was onions. So I made sure to add huge chunks. I liked them that much. And I added cheese, nice, big, square blocks of cheese. Loved cheese, too. Instead of croutons, we had Cap'n Crunch. Oh, and there were marshmallows, too."

"Dressing?" I ask, cautious.

"Oh, Ranch, of course." I cringe. "Exactly."

"Did they eat it?"

"My parents wanted to be so supportive... but no. Can I tell you how painful lime juice can be when the roof of your mouth is torn up by Cap'n Crunch?"

I nearly spit my wine out at the thought.

"I wanted it to be good. I ate my entire serving, hoping to find that one magical bite, but it was horrendous."

"You know," I tell him, "you're really not giving me a whole lot of confidence in your signature dish."

"There may have been some limes involved. And onions. But I promise you, the flavors go together. I don't know you well enough to experiment on you quite yet."

I laugh and raise my eyebrows at him.

"Yeah..." he laughs back at me. "Your turn. Embarrassing childhood memory."

"Oh, I don't have any," I say brightly.

"I don't believe that for one second." Oh how true he is... so many to choose from.

"Okay, I have one. This is filed under the category of 'when art projects go bad.'"

"Wait, did you taste it yet?" he interrupts, signaling to my plate. I cut a piece of chicken and pop it into my mouth. Thank God it tastes nothing like marshmallows and ranch dressing.

"It's really good! And I'm not just trying to encourage you, I promise." I take another bite of his savory dinner. It truly is good.

"Thank you," he says. "Continue."

"Okay, this story stars me and a sweet, little, naïve neighbor-boy."

"Name?"

"Jeffrey Fisher."

"How old?"

"Mmmmmm..." I ponder back. "First grade. Seven?"

"Okay."

"So, we had this project, where we had to lie down on big sheets of craft paper. We had to partner up, and in all honesty... I kinda had a thing for Jeffrey."

"You started young."

"Shut it," I tell him, pointing my fork at him before trying his asparagus. "Mmm, this is good too!"

"Thank you. Keep going," he encourages.

"So, I lay down, and Jeffrey had to trace an outline of my body on the paper."

"Kind of early for crime-scene training, wasn't it?"

I laugh heartily, nodding my head. "I did the same for him. When we had our body shapes drawn, we got to decorate them... you know, clothes, eyes, hair...

"So we took them to his house to finish them, and I went to get some supplies from my home to jazz it up a little. I was always a little too creative for my own good."

"What sort of supplies?"

"Finger paint. Glitter. Glue. Stickers. Pipe cleaners for my pigtails. Deodorant."

"Deodorant?"

"Yes. I said deodorant."

"You were very concerned about hygiene back then, huh?"

"I had no idea what it was. To me, it was this awesome container mom had in her bathroom that I used as a microphone sometimes when I played Madonna. I wanted to find a way to attach it to my hand because I wanted to be a singer."

"Yes, because pipe cleaners and glue can attach an object like that to kraft paper," he chides me.

"I was never a science buff. Physics is still a foreign concept to me," I rationalize my first-grade thinking.

"So what happened?" he asks.

"Well, at some point, we realized there were distinct... ahem... differences between boys and girls."

"What did you do?" he laughs.

"It was all innocent. When we finished with our decorating– and after I gave up on attaching the makeshift microphone to my hand– at Jeffrey's

175

prodding, I opened up the deodorant and rolled it on to, um, highlight a couple certain girl assets... and one certain boy asset."

Jack busts out laughing. "That's great."

"Oh, it gets better. Jeffrey changed his tune immediately. His face crumpled and the loudest wail I've ever heard came out of his mouth. *'Mommmmmyyyyyy!'* he was yelling. And I had never climbed under a bed so fast in my life.

"I scooted to the farthest corner, away from any hands, and I hid there, scared to death of what his mother would do to me."

"Did she get you?" he asks, his eyes bright and interested.

"Eventually, after picking up his mattress, she found me. She was crying, appalled that I ruined her son's work of art. She wouldn't listen when I said it was his idea."

"Was it?"

"I doubt it, but he still encouraged me," I laugh slyly, knowing how boy crazy and curious I was at such a young age. "She marched me over to my house, handed my mom the deodorant bottle– which she was just mortified that I had– and she made me make new shorts for his paper doll."

"Shame on you, Emi Hennigan." He winks at me.

"I know. Our relationship never went anywhere after that."

"I guess that's good news for me." The look on his face tells me he didn't mean to say it aloud, but I just smile back. *Maybe it is.*

"So, Sinatra, huh?" I ask, changing the subject as we both finish eating. "I think there's more to this music than you just wanting to support your fellow Hobokenite."

"Are you asking me to dance, Poppet?"

"Is that why you're playing Old Blue Eyes?"

"Come on, Em. How can anyone turn down *Night and Day?*"

"I don't know, Jack," I smile, putting my napkin on the table as I stand up and straighten out my dress. "I'm not sure anyone can."

After laughing and dancing through a few songs on the kitchen floor, I help

Jack with the dishes. When we're finished, he takes my hand and leads me downstairs to the small theatre.

"You can pick the movie," he says, closing the doors to all the kid's rooms. It's as if he could sense my apprehension of being down there, but I am immediately comfortable again.

"There are too many," I comment. "I don't know where to begin." I browse the selection, worthy of its own video store, and find a movie I haven't seen, but have heard that it was funny and a little romantic. Not too heavy, not too girly... "Have you seen this one?"

"Actually, no, but I've heard good things." He takes it from me and puts it in the DVD player. I find a place on the love seat while he goes to a small refrigerator in the corner and takes out two bottles of water. After he turns off the main lights, he grabs a blanket and hands it to me. "It can get a little chilly down here."

"Thank you." I take off my shoes and spread the blanket out over my bare legs. Jack sits on the other side of the sofa, farther away from me than I had secretly hoped he would sit. He is such a gentleman, though, it shouldn't surprise me. What does surprise me is how much more comfortable I am with him than I've been with other men after multiple dates. Other men except Nate. With Nate, once we decided to date, we already knew everything there was to know about one another. There was no period of discovery. It was easy to just... love him.

About thirty minutes into the movie, I ask Jack if he's cold, hoping to share the blanket with him. He plays along, although I doubt he is actually cold. I move closer to him, wanting to be comforted by him. He makes me feel at ease, and he makes me forget things. With my feet tucked onto the couch, my arm touching his, I arrange the blanket over both of our laps. A few minutes later, he puts his arm across my shoulder. I lean my head into his chest, my hand draped in his lap and touching his knee, and continue to watch the movie.

This is exactly what I want. I want to feel close to someone again. I want to feel safe. I felt safe before, with Nate... comfortable... but it was too comfortable. I could never have anticipated what would eventually happen. I now have to contend with those what-ifs for the rest of my life. I'll always be a little guarded, learning the lesson that all things end the most difficult way possible. I notice my thumb involuntarily rubbing his knee at some point. His thumb, in turn, is rubbing my shoulder. Aside from these small gestures, neither of us makes a move through the rest of the movie.

When it ends, though, Jack turns on some music. Small bulbs along the wall, similar to those on the aisles at movie theaters, are the only source of light in the room. I take a deep breath and look at him, impulsively deciding that I want to kiss him. He leans into me as I position myself on the couch and put my hands on his shoulders, pulling him toward me.

"Emi," he says, hesitating, as I remove my hands from his neck and place them into his lap.

"Yes?" I look up.

"I need to tell you something."

"Sure, go ahead," I encourage him, swallowing hard and standing up, now embarrassed to look him in the eyes. "Do you mind if I get another bottle of water?"

"Not at all," he says, then hesitates again.

"Ouch!" I exclaim, feeling the corner of the coffee table dig into my shin. In the dark, I misjudged the distance between myself and his furniture.

"Are you alright?" he asks, getting up and turning on the lights.

"I'm sure I'm fine," I tell him, limping toward the refrigerator.

"No, you're not. You're bleeding," he laughs.

"Crap," I mutter as I stop walking, seeing the blood begin to trickle down my leg, not wanting it to get on the carpet. "Band-Aids?"

"Upstairs," he says, then swiftly sweeps me up into his arms before I can protest. He removes my shoe as the blood inches toward it and hands it to me. "I didn't think I'd need to child-proof the basement tonight," he jokes.

"Yeah, I can be pretty dangerous," I tell him, his face only inches from mine. He pauses as I push some strands of hair off of his forehead, smiling gently as he looks into my eyes. Excitement pulsates through my body. "Um, you were going to tell me something?"

"Let's get you taken care of first," he says as he ascends the stairs to the second floor, and then the third.

"Is this how you lure women into your bedroom?" I joke with him.

His laughter is slow to begin, then he pauses in thought. "I guess it would make more sense to have some bandages downstairs, but I don't." He sets me down on the edge of his bed and makes his way into the bathroom. I examine the cut. The wound seems pretty shallow but is bleeding more than I would expect.

"Does it hurt?" he asks as he kneels down in front of me with a few bandages, some alcohol and some cotton balls.

"It just stings a little," I tell him, embarrassed.

"This is going to make that a little worse," he says as he dabs the alcohol-soaked cotton ball on the cut. I cringe as the pain sets in, but it goes away quickly. Jack applies two large bandages to cover up the wound, then wets another cotton ball. Slowly, he traces the line of blood from my ankle up to my shin, which tickles and makes me shiver. "You okay?" he asks as he gets up to take the supplies back to the bathroom.

"Definitely," I tell him as I feel my cheeks get hot. I can't deny how good it feels to have a man touch me again, even if it is to clean up after my clumsy injury. He walks back into the room and kneels down again in front of me to inspect his work. I begin to put my shoe back on, but he takes it from me and sets it on the floor. He puts his hands on my leg, as if to see my shin in better light, then runs them down my leg to my ankle. He sighs heavily, his head angled as he curiously stares at a scar on my knee. I put my hand over it, self-conscious.

"Is that from the..." He clears his throat. "Is that from the accident?" He looks up at me and places his hand on mine, moving it out of the way.

Looking into his eyes, I nod my head slightly. He looks away, back down to the scar and traces his thumb over the four-inch mark.

It is impossible for me to hide from his hands the physical effects that his touch has on me as goosebumps arise all over my body. He glances back up to me, and the look on his face shows conflict, indecision. I run my fingers through his thick, dark hair, wanting him to kiss me, wanting to nudge him in that direction. I begin to lightly rub his thigh with my toes. He laughs lightly, shakes his head, puts my shoe back on and sits down next to me on the bed.

"God, Emi," he pauses. "Remember I said there was something I wanted to talk to you about?"

"Yes," I say, encouraging him to continue.

"It's something that's been bothering me for awhile." His look is serious and almost sad, full of regret, maybe.

"What is it, Jack?"

"Emi, that night..." He purposefully puts his hand on my knee, his finger outlining the scar again.

"Which night?" I immediately know.

"*That* night... um, New Year's Eve." He pauses, gauging my expression before he continues.

"Yes..."

"Right after Nate took you off the dance floor..."

Why is he bringing this up? And now?

"God, Emi, I'm so sorry. I don't know how to say this, I just feel so bad..."

"What do you feel bad for?" I can't imagine now what he's going to say. I search his blue eyes for a clue.

"After he took you off the dance floor, I wished to myself... that he... that Nate... wasn't in the picture."

My brows furrow as I stare at him, questioning him, disbelieving him. I don't understand. I don't know what to say to this.

"What?" I barely manage to choke out, the familiar lump swelling in my throat, my eyes watering. I let go of his hand as I remember his apology from that dark night in the hospital.

"No, Emi, please don't cry. I didn't mean it, of course I didn't mean it, but it's been eating me up for months and I had to tell you before this goes any further." The lights outside the window spread out as the tears blur my vision. I feel my head become cloudy, too, as a rush of memories comes flooding back, beginning with that night, then into the hospital, to the gravesite, to Nate's apartment, my apartment, and finally to this place, Jack's house, and this night. This night that had been perfect up until this very moment.

"Say something, please," he adds.

It's not that I don't know what to say, as much as I don't know how to feel. I say nothing and feel... everything. Sad, angry, betrayed, fooled.

"If I could take the thought back I'd do it in a second... even if it meant he would still be here," he explains, pleads.

"Why would you think such a thing?" I ask quietly, wanting to understand.

"I just felt something between us that night... it was the same feeling I had on the night I first met you," he begins, "and I desperately wanted another dance or two or twenty... another chance. I didn't want to let you go... like I let you go in college... and his determined posture, that look in his eyes, and the way you looked back at him... I knew I couldn't compete."

I remembered with perfect clarity that moment exchanged between Nate and me. It was the only thing I could see clearly at the moment. "I have to go," I tell him, feeling sick to my stomach. I stand up hurriedly. As I begin to leave the room, he gently grabs my wrist.

"Let me go," I whisper to him through clenched teeth, my angry eyes pleading with his, and he drops my arm.

"Please, don't," he says.

"Just leave me alone," I warn as I turn my back to him, heading downstairs to the couch in the living room to grab my bag. I begin to hyperventilate. *Why the fuck did I come here? Who the hell is this man?*

"At least let me take you home," he says as I hear him following me down the stairway.

"No, that's alright," I say stubbornly. "You've done enough."

"Emi, it's late, I don't want you out there alone at this time of night." He puts his shoes on hurriedly.

"What do you care? You don't care about me!"

"I do, Emi. I do, I'm sorry," he begins before I stop his horrible excuse for an apology that could never be good enough.

"You know what, Jack?" I laugh quietly through my tears, "I can take care of myself. I've been doing it all my life."

"Emi..." He opens the door for me and I stop to stare into his eyes once more. I'm sad, angry, but I can see every bit of regret in his eyes through my blurry tears. I don't care.

"Goodbye, Jack." He winces at my words and I turn quickly away, unable to witness the look of sorrow spreading across his face. I wipe away the falling tears as I begin my walk home. With decent shoes, I can make this trek easily, but I'm not sure that these heels will take me all the way home. I'll try, but I'll catch a cab if I have to.

I wished he wasn't in the picture, Jack had said to me. And a few hours later, he wasn't. Jack got his wish.

His wish was granted, and all of my hopes were destroyed in that one night. How could he want such a thing? How could he want Nate, the love of my life, to be gone? If he had only known what Nate and I shared... if he could have seen how happy he made me, and how happy I made him, Jack would never have wished such a thing. Our love was forever. Everyone who knew us knew that for certain. Nate and I were meant to be together. A part of me died with him that night.

Jack felt a connection with me that night? Is that what he had said? I scoff at the idea, remembering my feelings of desire and complete infatuation that I carried with me for Nate that one night, the anticipation of being with him causing the blood to pulse rapidly throughout my entire body. I struggle to even remember the time I spent with Jack last New Year's Eve. For three songs, Nate and I were separated, and for those three songs, I spent them with Jack. We talked about the night in college. We talked about Nate. It was always about Nate. And as soon as I saw him approach me, everything else in the entire world disappeared. He *was* my world, and I couldn't wait to see our future unfold in front of us.

Even if there had been something there with Jack, he would have had no chance with me that night. Is it possible that I had felt something? That we did have a connection?

And what was that about college? How he wished he hadn't let me go? I don't even know what he's talking about. We only spent one evening together in college, at the frat party. I had been too drunk to really remember anything. He sat with me without talking while I waited for Nate. The time I spent with Jack that night was little more than a blur. It was Nate that had made such an undeniable impression on me when he kissed me. So how could that night stand out to Jack? I mean, I barely even *recognized* him ten years later.

My feet ache after about ten blocks, and I slow down a little to give them a break.

How could he have thought that? Still, the words echo in my mind. *I wished he wasn't in the picture.* Jack had said it had been bothering him for months. Months! Then why the hell didn't he tell me before? How many chances has he had? How many times has he posed as this man who cared about me? Didn't he see my pain? Didn't he see how much I had lost?

I imagine what my life would be like right now if he hadn't been taken from me. Pregnant. I'd be pregnant. I begin to sob, clutching at my stomach to stop the cramps that come with the memory. The few people that share the sidewalk with me begin to stare, and I try to hold my emotions back, but it just hurts so badly. I stop, retreating to the corner of a shop entrance, attempting to take some deep breaths, my vision now completely obscured by the heavy tears in my eyes. A figure walks slowly across the street, and as it gets closer, I see that it's Jack.

"I'm fine," I tell him, pulling myself together and beginning my walk home again. "You can go back home."

"Let me get a cab for you, at least."

"I can get one myself," I fight back, but no sooner than the words are out of my mouth, he sees a cab approaching, and he hails it for me. Looking down the street for another option and seeing no other taxis, I relent and walk toward the door he holds open for me. He begins to pull out his wallet, as Nate would always do, but I shove it angrily away into his stomach, pushing hard enough to force him back a step or two.

"I've got it from here, Jack. Thanks." He stands back as I slam the door and tell the driver where to take me.

CHAPTER 8

"I just need another few days," I plead. "I can probably have it done by Monday."

"We don't have any more time, Emi," the magazine editor says. "We already gave you an extension."

"I know, but I had to make some changes—"

"I'm sorry," he interrupts. "We're going to go with another artist."

"Please," I beg, "I need this job." I don't need the money, but I need the distraction, for my attention to be anywhere other than Nate and the baby and this crushing pain in the pit of my stomach.

"I'm sorry, it just didn't work out this time. Take care." He hangs up the phone.

Fuck. This is the second job I've lost in the past three weeks. I put the phone down and stare at the illustration in front of me. I close the file, choosing to not save the changes I've made to it. I stand up to look at myself in the mirror.

I've been in the same pajamas for two days now. I consider taking a shower, but decide to climb into bed instead.

September is just a few days away. I was about six weeks along when I had lost the baby... I would have been a mother by now. The cramp in my stomach assaults me again, causing me to pull my knees up into my chest. I haven't been able to do much of anything in the past few weeks. The pain is unbearable. The memories are devastating.

I imagine what Nate would be like as a new father. He would be so excited. The spare bedroom would be decorated and prepped for our child. I remember the colorful mural Nate had designed, imagine it painted on the wall. The graphic images would stimulate our baby's eyes. He would want to foster creativity in our little girl from day one.

I had taught Nate to change diapers when Clara was a baby, but I doubted he would be much help in that department. He was purposefully bad at it back then to get out of doing the unpleasant task, and I wonder if it would have been a source of tension between us. He would, undoubtedly, be helpful in so many other ways, though. He would have baby-proofed the apartment, putting all of his paints and chemicals on a top shelf somewhere, out of harm's way. He would be spending all of his free time with our daughter. If I was tired, in need of a break, I had no doubt that he would relieve me of my motherly duties and give me however much time I needed. He would take her on walks through Central Park, showing her off to all of the passers-by.

Had he still been here, I imagined we would have taken on the task of babysitting my "niece-monster," as he so lovingly called her, more often. He would have wanted our little girl to have lots of friends. And we wouldn't have stopped with one child. I had no doubt he would want more than one, to avoid the loneliness he felt as an only child.

I miss you so much, Nate. I want you back, and I want our little girl. I want our family. It's not fair.

I'm overcome with tears again, and I reach over to the nightstand for my bottled water and aspirin, knowing what is coming.

"Anni-Emi?" my niece says, waking me up with a jolt. She's lying on her stomach on my bed, her elbows propped, her head resting in her hands.

"Clara, what are you doing?"

"Are we ever going to go to the park again?" she asks.

"Not today, honey," I tell her. "Maybe tomorrow."

"You say that every day," she pouts.

"Clara-bee, why don't you let Mommy take you to the park?" Jen asks her daughter.

"No," she says. "I want Anni-Emi to get up and take me."

"Anni-Emi's not feeling well," I tell her.

"Maybe you should go to a doctor," Clara says. "You've been sick for too long." *She's probably right.*

"Clara, remember what Mommy told you in the car?" Jen says. "About someone coming over?"

"Yea!" she exclaims, hopping off the bed. "Uncle Chris and Anni-Anna are coming tonight! Yea!" She continues to jump up and down on the hardwood floors. I pull the covers back to see my sister.

"Chris and Anna are coming?"

"Yeah, I hope that's okay," she says. "I thought I'd make dinner."

"I wish you would have told me," I scowl. "When will they be here?"

"Seven-thirty or so," she says. "You have plenty of time to get dressed." *But I don't want to get dressed.*

I look at the clock, unsure what time it is. The days just seem to drag on, and I've sort of lost the concept of time lately. Five o'clock. I pull the covers back over my head and cuddle with my pillows to go back to sleep.

I don't wake up until I hear Chris's familiar knock on the door.

"Shit, Jen, why didn't you wake me up?"

"I'm not our mother," she says to me as she opens the door for my brother and his fiancée. "And your language?" she suggests, nodding to my niece. I hurry to my feet and cross the room to the closet to find something to wear. I wave to the guests before shutting myself in the bathroom.

"She's been like that for weeks," I hear my sister say before I start running

187

the water.

"I figured something was up," Chris says. "She hasn't returned any of our calls since that night with Jack."

"Do you think that's what's bothering her, or do you think it's... the baby," I hear Anna ask.

"I say both," Jen says. "I know she was upset about that even before their date, but she's completely pulled away from me since she came home crying that night."

I remember back to the night of my date with Jack, and the discussion I had with my sister when I got home. Still sobbing by the time I came up to the apartment, I awoke her from her sleep and she hurried out of her room, hoping that Clara didn't hear.

"Emi, what happened?" she asked, barely awake.

"God, Jen, I can't stand it anymore," I had cried out to her, collapsing on my bed. "I miss them so much."

"Shhh, Emi, calm down. Slow down. Tell me what happened." I had lain on my side, in the fetal position, as my sister stroked my hair to soothe me.

"I just shouldn't have gone," I told her. "I'm not ready."

"Did something happen?"

"He wanted Nate to die!" I choked the words out dramatically.

"Who did?"

"Jack!" I told her, expecting her to know whom I had been with.

"Jack? Emi, you were with Jack?" she asked, surprised.

I nodded quietly.

"So, then what's going on? Start from the beginning."

"Everything started out fine. He made dinner and we talked... we watched a movie, and I just thought, okay, I really like this guy... you know, he seemed like a really decent guy... and I tried to just let myself *be* in that moment. I was doing okay."

"And then what?"

"I was going to kiss him," I admitted with a blush. "And then he stopped me, letting me know he needed to tell me something about the night that Nate died." My sister was silent as she waited for me to continue. "He said that, after we had danced, that he felt something for me, and wished that Nate wasn't in the picture." The sobbing returned.

"Oh, Em, honey," she consoled me. "Well you don't think that had anything to do with what happened, do you?"

"Logically, no... but what if?"

"Emi, that's just silly," she told me. "And poor Jack," she added. "He must feel awful."

"Poor Jack? What about *me*?"

"What *about* you, Em?" she asked quietly. "This shouldn't affect you like this."

"Why not? It's about the worst thing he could have done, short of driving that SUV." I shook my head to make the memories vanish.

"Because think about it. Think about how bad he must feel. You know he meant nothing by it. He would never wish him dead, Em."

"Well, then why would he say such a thing?"

"Because he likes you, I guess," she said plainly. "And he must *really* like you... really *respect* you... to be so upfront about this. He never had to tell you, and you'd be none-the-wiser.

"And instead, he risked everything just to be completely honest with you. If you ask me, it's a pretty honorable thing to do."

"Honorable, my ass..." I wiped my nose with my sleeve.

"Did he bring you home?"

I shook my head. "I walked half-way..."

"He let you walk home this late?"

"He didn't *let* me, I just did... and he didn't let me go alone. I didn't realize it, but he was following behind me. He caught up to me when I stopped for a second... and then he hailed a cab for me."

"Yeah, I'm sticking with honorable," my sister said. "You shouldn't be angry at him for this. It was one errant thought. One that I'm sure he regrets above all other regrets in his life. I can't even imagine..."

"Well, you can believe what you want. It's unforgivable."

"Oh, Emi," she groaned, getting up and moving across the room. "I think you're just scared to like him."

"Okay, now you're just talking nonsense. I'm going to bed."

"My work here is done," Jen said smugly.

And I had gone to bed that night, replaying her words in my head over and over... not his. *I think you're just scared to like him. What was there to like about him?*

He brought me flowers– not just any flowers, but my favorites.

Our conversations flowed naturally.

He was easy to talk to.

He was a great cook.

He made me laugh.

When he touched me, my skin prickled in goosebumps.

He truly was a gentleman.

He made me... happy... if only for a few hours, but still...

And when I had danced with him that night at the party, in the briefest of moments, I *did* feel something for him. I would never have admitted it before. I may not have ever remembered it, either, had we not shared another moment just like it in the final notes of *In the Wee Small Hours of the Morning* in his kitchen. I had stopped breathing. So had he.

What wasn't there to like about him?

Oh, yeah. His death wish for Nate. I gritted my teeth and gripped my pillow tightly, covering my head with my blanket.

In the other room, the conversation about me continues between my brother and sister. After my shower, I emerge from the bathroom clean, dressed, with wet hair and no makeup.

"Where's Clara?" I ask Jen. "I think maybe we'll go for a walk now."

"Oh, Anna just took her," my sister tells me. She and my brother are sitting on the couch talking. "Come sit down."

"I think maybe *I'll* just go for a walk then." My brother stands up quickly and blocks the doorway.

"Sit down, Emi," he says, walking a few steps toward me, then putting his arm around my shoulders. He guides me to the couch and practically pulls me into the sofa next to him, in between him and my sister.

"Tell me you weren't in bed all day, Em," Jen says.

"I got up to take a call from my editor... and when he told me I couldn't have more time for the project, I went back to bed. I had nothing else to do." I shrug my shoulders, acting like it doesn't bother me.

"You lost another job, Em?" my brother asks.

"They wouldn't give me enough time for it," I explain.

"I'm really worried about you," Chris says to me. "Can you talk to us about it?"

"I'm not feeling well," I tell them both. "I have these constant pains in my stomach... and my head hurts...."

"Is it the same pain you told me about a few weeks ago?" Jen asks.

"Yes, but worse..." I start to cry, and Chris quickly takes me into his arms. I've missed my brother. "I'm just so sad."

"Sweetie," he says, "you have every right to be sad. But you can't keep it all inside. Let us help. Or, if not us, let *someone* help."

"I'm just so tired of thinking about it and can't bear the thought of talking about it. I just want to be able to put it behind me. But the pain is constant, and I can't ignore it. Believe me, I want to heal, I do. I just don't feel like I can."

"I really think you should consider therapy," Jen says. "You can go to my shrink, she's great... or we can find someone else. Just consider it, please. I don't know what to do with you anymore, and I don't like how it affects Clara."

I nod and wipe away the tears. "I'll think about it."

"Thank you," my brother says, again pulling me closer to him to hug me.

Jen gets up to start cooking dinner, and a few minutes later, Anna and Clara return to the loft.

"Anni-Emi!" Clara yells, jumping into my lap. "Are you feeling better?"

"I will be," I tell her, kissing her on the cheek. "I'm better with you here, anyway." Somehow I have to come to terms that my niece will be the only child in my life for now. I'm thankful she is in my life and grateful that she is living with me.

Anna comes over to give me a hug. "Jack keeps asking about you. He'd like to see you. Chris and I are organizing a happy hour for his birthday in a few weeks..."

"I don't know..." I waver.

"Are you still mad at him?" Anna asks. *Am I?* I don't think mad is the word. And if I were mad, it certainly wouldn't be at him. Over the past few weeks, as a distraction, I did revisit that night in my head many times. Do I think he meant any harm? No. Was it wrong for him to think that? I've even accepted 'no' as a response to that question, as well. It was a thought. He wasn't driving the car that killed Nate. No matter what he thought, he had nothing to do with Nate's death, and I can accept that rationally.

I'm frustrated with myself, though, for a multitude of things. For going out on the date in the first place. For talking about Nate with Jack. For cuddling with him on the couch. Mostly, though, I'm frustrated that I allowed my unstable emotions to ruin a perfectly good evening. It *was* too soon. That's the plain truth. But that doesn't change what happened. I'm surprised that he would want to see me again, and I don't know that I could suffer through the embarrassment of apologizing for my insane behavior. Not right now, anyway.

"No, I'm not mad," I tell her. "I'm not ready to see him, though."

"Ever?"

"Not in the near future."

"Well, you do know the wedding is in a couple weeks... and you'll have to walk down the aisle together..." Anna says.

"Yeah, are you going to be okay with that?" Chris asks.

"It will be fine." Chris gives Anna a glance from across the room. I can tell she's worried.

"I wish you could talk to him," my brother says. "He's called me a couple of times just to find out if you're okay since you aren't taking his calls."

"What did you tell him?"

"I didn't tell him that you weren't taking *my* calls either... I just told him you'd be fine... that you needed some time."

"Well... thank you."

"You will be fine," my brother assures me.

"Emi, don't forget that our final fitting is next Tuesday," Anna says. "I'll pick you up around four?"

Of course I had forgotten. "That's fine."

"And do you have a dress for the rehearsal dinner?" Anna asks.

"No, I haven't thought that far into the future," I tell her.

"Well, good, I don't have one either, so you and I are going to go find them together. How does the tenth sound? Can you pencil me in?" she asks.

"I'll put it on my calendar," I tell her. I feel so bad... her maid of honor should be happy. Her maid of honor should be keeping track of these dates, keeping everything on schedule. She should be keeping the bride on task, not the other way around. I wonder if she's regretting asking me. She's too polite to ever say so. But I bet she feels that way.

I want to be happy. If not for me, for my brother and for Anna. This is the day she's been dreaming of since she was a little girl; and Anna, she is the woman that my brother has been hoping for all of his life. They're perfect together. The last thing I want to do is ruin their day... or cause them any worry that I might do just that.

"By the way, that's the day of the happy hour, too, so if you decide to go, I could give you a ride..."

"I'm committing to shopping, but that's it."

After Chris and Anna leave, I get the number for Jen's therapist. I have to get better, for them... and for me.

~ * ~

"I really wish you would change your mind, Em," Anna says to me from the dressing room next door. On our last planned shopping trip before the wedding, which is now only ten days away, we are both trying to find dresses for the rehearsal dinner.

"Sorry, Anna, I just can't." Even though I've told Anna and Chris repeatedly that I would not be accompanying them to Jack's happy hour, she keeps bringing it up. I didn't receive an official invitation from Jack, but there was one relayed through my brother and soon-to-be sister-in-law. I still wasn't ready to talk to him.

"And convince me again how this wedding isn't going to be completely awkward," she demands, audibly frustrated.

"Anna, plenty of weddings happen every day where the best man and maid of honor don't even know each other. Maybe it'll be like those."

"Emi, please–"

"Anna, come on. You promised we wouldn't have to talk about this again today."

"Well, I lied," she says. "This is supposed to be the happiest day of my life, and I don't want it to be riddled with tension between our two best friends. Can't you just talk to him? Hear him out?"

"I'll talk to him soon, I promise. And I'm not mad at him, I told you. I just need to figure some things out first."

I've been to two therapy sessions with Jen's psychologist. It's been helpful having someone to talk to. The pain has lessened, both the stomach cramps and the emotional toil.

"I'm pretty sure he thinks you're mad at him. We've told him that you're not, but since you don't answer his calls..."

"I'm just not sure what to tell him yet, that's all. But I promise you, the wedding will be fine and we'll both look happy in the pictures. We might even *be* happy. You have my word."

"I just wish you'd let him off the hook."

"I will. I have a present I want you to give him tonight. Could you do that for me?"

"I'm sure he'd rather get it from you."

"Anna, please," I demand.

"Alright, I'll do it."

We step out of the dressing rooms at the same time. "Anna, that's fabulous!"

"I think I like this one," she smiles, looking down at the off-white strapless dress. "And that looks amazing, too," she tells me, eyeing my outfit. "Those black heels we saw earlier would be perfect."

"Yeah, I think you're right. This is the one," I say, looking back in the dressing room mirror and standing on my toes to check the length of the black and pink dress. "So we just need to find shoes for your outfit and something blue, right?"

"And some lingerie," she adds. "Then I think that's about it."

"I also need to get a card for him..." I mumble.

"Jack?"

"Yes, a birthday card, to go with the gift."

"Let's do that first," Anna says enthusiastically. We go into our respective dressing rooms and put our clothes back on.

After paying for our dresses, we make our way to a stationery shop. I just want a simple, blank card. I know what I want to write in it. There are no store-bought words for what I want to say in this card. We stroll the aisles looking around the store.

"So what did you get him?" Anna asks, picking up a package of "Thank You" cards.

"This watch I found when I was out shopping last week. It's no big deal."

"Hmmm," she ponders. "A watch can say a lot of different things."

"Stop adding meaning to it," I tell her. "It's just a watch." Of course there's meaning behind it.

"Where'd you get it?"

"At that watch place down the street from the therapist's office," I explain.

"That's a nice place," she comments.

"It's not that nice," I counter. "He'll probably never wear it. He probably already has a slew of nice watches. I just thought this one suited him." The truth is, I've put a considerable amount of thought into this gift for Jack. I deliberately got him a watch and sought one that I thought he would wear... one that's simple and classic. I hope he does wear it.

"Do you have it with you? I want to see it."

"Yeah, but it's already wrapped... sorry." I finally find a card and ask the cashier if I can borrow a pen to write a note to Jack. Anna begins to peer over my shoulder. "Do you mind?" I joke with her.

"Alright, alright."

Jack, the message begins, *I don't expect you to wait for me, but I hope that you will.* I sign my name and tuck the card safely in the envelope.

A text message from him comes later that night. *"I will. Thank you."*

CHAPTER 9

"Emi, come on," my sister says, standing next to me in the ladies room.

"I'll meet you in there, I just need a minute, okay?"

"You're coming though, right?"

"Yes, of course I'm coming." She nods her head and picks up my niece and my eyes follow them as they head out the door into the restaurant hosting Chris and Anna's rehearsal dinner. I turn back around to check my makeup one more time. I reapply my lipstick and smile courageously at myself. *I can do this.* The therapist I've been seeing suggested some positive reinforcement when I started doubting myself.

The first three weeks of therapy were spent dealing with the grief of losing Nate and losing our child. I cried a lot, and recognize that I still have more tears to cry... and that it's okay. Things will make me sad, I just have to learn to accept the sadness and put it aside. I can no longer let it consume me.

When the psychologist had questioned what I was doing to for myself, I told her that work was pretty much my only distraction. She encouraged me to find other things to do, and to surround myself with friends. I explained that it was my intent to do just that when I fell apart after my date with Jack. I told her that I was trying to focus on other, happier things, when I accepted the date with him. I told her that I felt betrayed by him and by his words. I knew, logically, that he meant nothing by them. I also knew that his words had nothing to do with the outcome of that night. I still had a hard time opening myself up to the idea of dating, and particularly dating him, because of this.

The therapist and I talked for quite some time about him. When I tried to find bad qualities in him, I couldn't. I could only refer to this one phrase, the thought that he wished Nate wasn't around so he could have a chance with me. He thought it because he felt something between us. He told me about it because he wanted to be honest with me about something he felt immense guilt about. I had to let him off the hook tonight.

Tonight at the botanical gardens was the first time I had seen him since the date. At the rehearsal, Jack and I assumed our positions and were shuffled around by the wedding planner, but neither one of us spoke and barely made eye contact. Anna and I had been running late, delayed by the lack of cabs on this Friday night, so the mood was a little stressed and we were all in a big hurry to just get it over with.

Over the past month, I've needed to be alone to deal with my past and to figure out my feelings for him. It still seemed too soon for a relationship with him, but I decided that I wanted to be his friend, at least. I knew he would be a good influence in my life. If he could just accept a friendship for awhile, maybe it would turn into something more. At this point, I think that's all I can give him.

I take a deep breath and picture his smile, feeling butterflies in my stomach. My brain is telling me to befriend him, but I really think my heart is saying something else. I don't trust it, though. I don't trust that it knows what's best for me.

Stepping out of the restroom, I take a few more deep breaths before entering the main lobby of the restaurant. I adjust the knee-length black and pink dress as the hostess welcomes me.

She takes me to the private room reserved for the party. It's dark and takes a moment for my eyes to get used to the dim setting. Flower centerpieces don every table, and groups of candles cast deep shadows on the walls. In a setting more romantic than I would have anticipated for a casual dinner, I can't help but scan the room for a particular familiar face. It takes me no time to find him.

He smiles warmly as soon as he sees me. He is standing among a group of men across the room, talking and laughing. Although he seems to be in mid-conversation with the other guys, his eyes never leave mine. Eventually, his friends turn to see what is distracting him. I blush and quickly look for my brother or sister or parents or *anyone* to talk to so I'm not just left standing, staring, blushing. I finally see Jen, Clara and my mother gathered around the dessert table. Clara is eating a chocolate-covered strawberry, her little fingers messy with her delectable treat. As I walk toward them, I find a napkin and take it to my sister.

"Thanks," she says, wiping her daughters hands and face as she puts the last morsel in her mouth.

"Was that good?" I ask Clara, who nods vigorously as she reaches out for me to hold her. As I extend my arms to take her from my sister, Jen holds her tighter. She looks over my shoulder and then back at my mother.

"I think we're going to get drinks, Em, do you want anything?"

"I think I'm okay right now, thanks," I answer. As I turn around to see the rest of the room, I realize why my family left.

"Hi, Emi," Jack says, walking cautiously toward me.

"Hey." I lean forward, hugging him awkwardly.

"It's good to see you again."

"You, too."

"Do you mean that?" he asks, his eyes uneasy.

I nod as a smile spreads across my face. "It's *really* good to see you."

"Emi," he begins, taking my hands in his. "You have to know–"

"Not here, Jack. Not tonight," I plead with him. "I've got a million things to say to you, but this isn't the right place."

"Okay," he says, "as long as I know you intend to talk to me, I'll wait it out."

"Thank you. Let's get this wedding out of the way first."

"Can I get you a drink?"

"Um, sure, a diet soda?"

"Coming right up. I'll be right back." I watch him walk toward the bar and see Anna coming toward me out of the corner of my eye.

"Yea!" she says quietly to me. "Thank you thank you thank you thank you thank you."

"I told you it wouldn't be awkward, silly."

"I know. What did he say?"

"Nothing," I tell her. "This is your night. We'll talk when it's time, and I will fill you in on every last detail." Jack is on his way back when she hugs me, excitedly. He laughs to himself.

"Diet soda," he says, handing me the beverage. Anna, full of energy, turns around and hugs him with the same intensity. She says something in his ear that sounds a little like, "Told you so." After their embrace, she returns to my brother's side.

"Thank you. Water?" I ask, eyeing his glass, suddenly nervous to be alone with him, feeling as if I'm being watched.

"Starting off slow," he says. "I've got to be the sensible one at the after-party tonight."

"Right," I say. "What's the plan?"

"Just your average bachelor party fare... Russell kind of took the helm on this one. I've never been much for planning these sorts of things. What are you girls doing?"

"We rented some movies... I'm sure we'll do girlie slumber party things," I tell him, looking forward to my night in a luxury hotel suite with Anna, Jen and Anna's friend, Mae. "Hopefully we'll get a little sleep so we'll be ready for our early spa appointments in the morning."

"A pillow fight, maybe?"

"Yes, because that's what we girls do at slumber parties."

"Hmm, and what room will you be staying in?" he asks.

"Nope, no boys allowed," I state adamantly. "So, um, back to your party... I'm guessing you have a 'no girls allowed' policy?"

"Did you want to stop by?" he seems to invite.

"I was referring to women who get *paid* to stop by..." I clarify.

"Oh, well, my only input was 'no strippers,'" he says. "But it's Russell, so I'm guessing there will be one or two."

"Great," I reply, unable to hide my general displeasure and annoyance at the idea of him with another woman, a naked one, at that. "But you're the sensible one..."

"Always," he grins widely, a glint of mischief in his eyes.

"Well, just make sure Chris keeps his hands off, I guess," I direct him.

"Yes, ma'am," he mocks me, flirting. "No rules for me, though?" he asks, hopeful, wanting me to be jealous. I *am* jealous, but I carefully plot out what to say to him. After all, I just want to be friends for now. Brain says friends. Speedy heart-rate says something else, but I do my best to ignore it.

"Something tells me you have the decency to know what you should and shouldn't do. That's all I'm going to say. I have no claim on you." His expression changes slightly, disappointed, and I immediately want to take the last sentence back. I didn't want to feel so conflicted tonight. I had prepared myself all week for this night. I was going to keep my distance, refrain from telling him that I wanted to be friends for now. And now that I've seen him, I want to abandon *that* plan altogether. I want to make him smile, to relieve him of any doubt he may have about me... but this is my heart talking... not my head... I didn't plan to *feel* anything for him.

"Jack, I-"

A loud clanking noise, followed by a whistle, interrupts our conversation.

"If everyone could take a seat..." my father announces. The guests eventually break from their small huddles and find chairs at the many tables. I look around the room, and see Anna waving for me and Jack to come and join her at their table. He's watching me, waiting for me to finish my thought. If I knew what to say, I would have said it, but instead, I just take his hand in mine and bring him to the table with me. I squeeze his hand tightly and look at him as he pulls my chair out for me. He seems to be a little more at ease... but I wonder if I'm doing the right thing...

We settle into our chairs as my dad begins a toast to Chris and Anna, standing in the center of the room. Jack picks up an open bottle of red wine from the table and pours two glasses, one for him and one for me. I watch my mother, across the table, wiping her eyes as my father recalls endearing moments from when my brother was just a little boy. My step-father puts his arm around her shoulder to comfort her. Her eyes meet mine, and she just gives me this strange, hopeful, almost apologetic smile. I look away quickly, and as people start to clap, I realize the toast is over. I sip my wine and set it down gently as my dad invites others to say a few words. Anna's friend, Mae, congratulates the couple, and a few of Chris's fraternity brothers have prepared a funny song for the occasion.

Jack picks up his glass and makes his way to the middle of the room, then faces Chris and Anna. I watch him as he begins to speak, his words as eloquent as they were at the engagement party...

I bring myself back into present-day, trying to listen to the words but getting caught up in the confident yet gentle timbre of his voice, so strong, yet so comforting. I force myself to focus.

"...and most of you know the story of how they met..." he continues. "but what you may *not* know is that Anna was running late for a blind date when she met Chris on the street that day. When Chris told me this story a few days after their meeting, I had a whole new respect for him. They talked for just a few minutes, and when she declined his invitation for coffee because she had a date, he wouldn't let her go. He did everything short of begging–"

"No, he begged!" Anna said.

"Okay, yes, he begged her to go out with him instead. Chris was so sure about her... that he wasn't about to let her walk away from him. There was no way he would let Anna walk out of his life."

Jack looks at me, serious and intense, and speaks his last line.

"He knew *exactly* what he wanted, and he wasn't about to let another day go by without getting it." His eyes shift briefly to the guests of honor, but then return to mine. "To Chris and Anna..." he raises his glass and drinks. I get chills and break away from his gaze, averting my eyes to the empty plate in front of me. *How can he be so sure about me? Can he really even know me? There are days when I don't feel like I even know myself!*

Dinner is eventually served, and I remain quiet through most of the meal, not speaking unless spoken to. I have way too much going on in my mind to really keep up with any conversations. When the waiters come to clear the tables, and people start to stand to say their farewells, Jack leans to me and asks, "Is everything alright?"

I nod my head, but I'm unsure. "That was, um, impassioned... your toast..." He senses my discomfort. He looks into his wine glass and finishes it off, then pours more into the goblet. I look for him to say something, but he restrains and has another drink, his gaze fixed across the room, away from me.

"Can you excuse me for a minute?" he asks, standing up abruptly. I fold up my napkin and place it on the table, sighing, feeling as if the conversation between Jack and I needs to happen sooner rather than later. Chris and Anna get up to say goodbye to their guests, and to one another. I watch Jack talking to Russell at the bar. Russell speaks to the bartender, who pours something into two shot glasses. He pushes one to Jack as his friend takes the other. They drink quickly, and Russell pats Jack on the back before walking away.

"The limo's here," my sister tells me. "I think we're all about ready to go."

"Okay."

"I'm just going to say goodnight to Mom and Clara... see you out there?"

"Yeah, I just need to wrap something up. I'll be there in a few minutes."

Jack waits for my sister to leave before coming back to the table I'm sitting at. I pick up my bag, getting ready to leave.

"Can I walk you out?" he asks as we watch all the other friends and family members file out the door.

"Of course." We both take slow, deliberate steps, each presumably waiting for the other to say something. "So promise me Chris won't be hung over tomorrow."

"I'll do my best, but I make no guarantees," he half-heartedly laughs. "What

I *can* do is deliver a very eager groom to the alter tomorrow to marry the woman he loves. Will that work?"

"I think so. And I'll make sure his bride is the most radiant woman in the room, waiting anxiously to marry him."

"Second most..." he corrects me.

"Jack..." I begin as we exit the restaurant, the last ones to leave. I feel the heat rise to my cheeks. Jack checks the time, and I realize that he's wearing the watch I had given him for his birthday. I pick up his wrist and pull it toward me to take a closer look. I raise my eyes, full of uncertainty, to meet his.

"I'm waiting, Emi." I nod, and as he drops his arm, he takes my hand. We continue to slowly walk toward the white limo where the rest of the women are waiting. I feel my pulse quicken, my heart beating faster. A part of me wishes we could have a few hours alone to talk about things, but we both have people relying on us tonight. When we reach the limo, instead of helping me into the car, Jack closes the door that had been left open for me.

I turn to face him, my back pressed against the car. He leans in closer, his lips so close to my ear I can feel his breath on my neck.

"I'm waiting," he repeats, soft, ardent. "But I want to remind you of something."

"Yes?" I whisper, breathless. *Is he going to kiss me?*

He pushes my hair back, tucking strands behind both ears, his fingers lingering around my jawline.

"Emi, I know what I want," he says intently, his look reminiscent of the one he gave me as he toasted my brother and Anna. My heart jumps. *He is going to kiss me!* He draws his face closer, cautiously, his eyes measuring my reaction along the way, until the very last second, when he closes his eyes and lightly brushes his mouth against mine. A memory flashes quickly in my mind, so quickly I barely catch it. The way his lips tease mine leaves me wanting more, a certain longing I've felt before, and as we pull each other closer, a distant but familiar wave washes over my entire body.

In that instant, everything in my world changes.

I have kissed this man before. I have been in search of these lips, this kiss, this touch, this feeling, for over ten years. At the frat party in college, we kissed. I didn't remember kissing him– *how could I not?!*– but I've always remembered this feeling. The details of that evening have been a blur since the night it happened. My unclear memory led me to believe that I had kissed Nate, although he and I had never talked much about it, but I now realize that *it wasn't him*. Now that I've experienced this sensation once again, I remember exactly what happened that night... remember exactly who I kissed by the picnic table that night. It was Jack. *Holy shit.*

I'm clutching his jacket tightly for support when he begins to pull away, holding my face in his hands. My eyes open and meet his once more. I draw him into me again, kiss him deeper, feeling his tongue with my own. I feel numb, and I cannot breathe. When he pulls back a second time, I stare at him, my mouth agape, completely dumbfounded.

The horn of the black limo honks wildly as the guys inside of it start to holler at us. No matter how much noise they make, I am entranced with him... with his kiss.

He stares at me inquisitively, but confident in what he has just done. He does not seem shaken at all, one corner of his lips curling into a knowing smile... like he expected this all along.

"What's that look?" he asks.

I smile broadly at him. "Oh, my god." Those are the only words I can use to express my shock.

"What is it?" he laughs.

I quickly stand on the tips of my feet and close my eyes, hoping he will kiss me again. He lightly touches his lips to mine, but doesn't linger. I open my eyes and he smiles, brushing my hair aside once more to kiss my forehead. He pulls my body toward his, embracing me, as he opens the car door for me. I hold on to the door to steady myself, and as he slowly backs away, I am sure he can hear the faint squeals coming from the girls in the limo.

"I'll see you tomorrow, Emi," he smiles. He takes a few more steps backwards before turning around to walk toward the noisy car that awaits him. Still blown away, knees weak, I can't move; but if I could, I would be running toward him to reacquaint myself with that feeling once more. He opens the door and turns to face me one more time, a huge smile on his face, before getting in and closing the door.

The girls pull me into our limo, jolting me out of my daze.

"He kissed you, didn't he, Emi? Did he kiss you?" Anna asks, and I realize that, from their vantage point in the car, my friends couldn't see what was going on. I touch my lips, and eventually answer simply by nodding my head. I'm still in awe and can't contain the feeling.

"What?" Jen says. "Really, Emi?"

I continue to nod.

"I'm guessing it was good," she comments. She watches me for a response.

"Good?" I ask aloud. "It was better than good. It was..." I struggle to find the word, but finally do, mumbling it quietly, "transcendent."

My heart still pounding, head spinning, I begin to think about what just happened... and what happened in college.

Holy shit. It wasn't Nate that I kissed in college that brought about those feelings in me. This new realization clears up a question I'd had ever since that night. I wondered why his kiss was always different from the first one we'd shared. I'd wondered what had changed. And for years, I'd wondered why he wouldn't discuss that night with me.

Transcendent. The word reverberates in my head as I think back to that night in college. I had first kissed Jack outside, by a picnic table. Later on that night, in my drunken stupor, I remember kissing Nate in my apartment. I remember being confused at the emotions it evoked in me– or rather, *didn't* evoke. I remember our kiss feeling platonic in nature. I remember wanting to feel the butterflies in my stomach, to feel my racing pulse as his soft lips brushed against mine. It never happened with Nate, though.

His kiss was not the *transcendent* one. *One transcendent kiss...* These words seem familiar, but out of context to me.

No wonder Nate never wanted to talk about it. He must have seen me kiss Jack. We were talking about two entirely different realities– mine a complete fabrication of my drunken mind. I laugh quietly to myself, realizing how different my life would be right now if I had been remotely coherent that night. For a moment, I am almost overcome with thoughts of a life that might have been. I push the thought out of my mind before it cripples me with tears.

It wasn't that kissing Nate wasn't great. It was. But ever since I first started to have feelings for him last year– feelings that went beyond the confines of our friendship– I had longed to feel the way I felt that night, when I experienced *that kiss* at the frat party. When I finally did kiss Nate, and *didn't* feel that same sensation, I'd wondered if time and other experiences could change something like that so drastically.

I'd theorized that what set that kiss apart from all the others with Nate was the thrill of doing something "wrong." Even though I had found him attractive from the first day I met him, we had vowed to remain friends. We had the perfect friendship and I never wanted to mess with what we had. It was scary to do otherwise; dangerous, exciting.

"Em, talk to us!" The sound of Anna's voice snaps me out of the trance I had fallen into. I look around to see all three of them staring at me in anticipation.

One transcendent kiss... oh, my God. That was how Nate's haiku began. That poem I couldn't remember. *One transcendent kiss...* but how did the rest of it go? And why is this coming back to me now?

"Can I have some of that?" I ask, noticing that they each have a bubbly glass of champagne in hand. Jen hands me hers and I drink it, quickly, wanting to find that happy place I had been mere minutes ago. I want to find that high from the kiss again, but feel guilty using Nate's words to describe Jack's kiss. No other word can describe it, though.

"Come on, Emi!" I shake my head, unwanted tears forming in my eyes. I'm unable to hold them back. How dare this sadness creep in when I want nothing more than to feel happy! "No crying!" Jen says. "No, no way."

"I just need a few minutes. I'll tell you everything at the hotel." I sniffle quietly to myself, wiping away the tears as they begin to fall. Anna and Mae begin a conversation between themselves while Jen sidles next to me, arm around my shoulders, sipping on her newly-poured glass of champagne. She rubs my arms quietly and lets me have this moment to myself.

We stop by the hotel lounge to have a few more drinks before heading up to the room. After I have a glass of wine, I start to feel more calm, more like myself.

"So, out with it, Emi," Anna demands. "What happened? I thought you were just going to be friends... isn't that what we talked about?" Her smile reveals hope. I knew she had been cheering for Jack all along.

"That was my intention," I tell her. "I didn't see this coming... at all..."

"What do you mean?" Mae asks.

"I've only been kissed like that one other time in my life. And I thought it was Nate... a long time ago... but I guess it wasn't." I swallow hard, coming to terms with an entirely different reality that I'd never known.

Their curious looks encourage me to continue. "I didn't realize it, but we've kissed before," I reveal to them.

"What?" Jen asks. Anna looks confused.

"In college," I start. "I kissed Jack."

"You didn't know?" Anna says. I shake my head. "*I* even knew that," she says, surprised. "How drunk were you?"

"Very," I admit. "But it was the most incredible kiss. For years I tried to recreate that moment, with all of my boyfriends. When I finally made the decision to go out with Nate last year, I thought there was a possibility that I might feel that again." My eyes water again and I look into the eyes of my friends. They look sad, almost worried, waiting quietly for me to continue. Jen hands me a tissue.

"It was wonderful with Nate, really, but I wondered why I never had that sensation again."

"And tonight?" Anna asks.

"Exactly like I had remembered it... and the memories of that night came flooding back. No wonder I could never piece together the details. I was trying to recreate something that never even happened."

"So did Jack tell you what happened that night? Did he tell you how he felt?"

"No," I answer. "I couldn't speak after he did it."

Her smile hides something. "Well? What are you going to do?"

"I don't know. Try to stick to the original plan? And see if that works?"

"You should follow your heart," Anna says.

"Yeah," Mae agrees.

"I think he cares about you a lot," Jen adds. "I melted when I saw how he looked at you when he got into the limo."

"Yeah, I did, too," I tell them. "I think it's just too soo–"

"Stop, Emi," Anna interrupts. "You think too much."

We order another round of drinks before going upstairs to the suite. Unfortunately, my brain keeps working overtime, trying to digest what happened, and to figure out what I should do. The bittersweet memory of Nate remains in my mind, but something seems altered. The relationship didn't change, my feelings for him haven't changed, I still love him... but the perception of what we were is somehow different.

The kiss I had experienced in college was surreal. It was what I measured all future intimate moments against. Over the years, after trying and failing to recreate that feeling, I attached to it a special designation. The person I shared it with was whom I was meant to be with. I had believed it for some time. I had believed that person to be Nate. My inability to find it with anyone else was one of the things that eventually convinced me to go to him, to be with him.

When I couldn't recreate it with Nate, either, it didn't affect how I felt about him. Our love for one another was stronger than some fleeting sensation I felt one drunken night in college. That was my rationalization, and it was true. If Nate was still here, I had no doubt we would be together for the rest of our lives.

But Nate wasn't here anymore. And this kiss... this *one transcendent kiss...* it changes everything.

~ * ~

I can't believe it's already nine o'clock in the morning. I've been watching the clock most of the night, unable to sleep. Anna was on an adrenaline high until about three, until we all convinced her to lie down and try to sleep. With the help of some relaxation music, she finally dozed off. Jen and Mae fell asleep soon after, but my mind wouldn't rest.

I don't know what I'm going to do about Jack. My stomach still flutters every time I think about him kissing me last night. I want to allow myself to feel this for him, but I'm still carrying around so many other emotions at this point that it just seems... well, complicated.

After taking a shower, I awaken the other girls and encourage them to get ready for our spa appointments. We'll start with massages, then come back to our room for lunch and a little rest. I have a feeling Anna will be a bundle of nerves and energy today. At two, we'll go to the salon to get our hair and makeup done, with plenty of time to mentally prepare for the ceremony at six.

The massage is just what I need. An hour of time devoted solely to me. I indulge myself in the possibilities of the day, sifting through my options and hoping to gain a little direction on which one is right for me.

I could succumb to my heart's desires and commit to a relationship with Jack.

I could agree to start dating him, knowing in my heart what I want but allowing myself time to get used to the idea.

I could request that he give me some time and space to sort through things.

I could let myself sink further in despair over the loss I've experienced this year. A part of me feels I owe it to Nate, but I don't give this option a second thought. I've devoted so much time to my grief and sadness. I need hope. I need the possibility of happiness again, or I may never find myself again.

I know for a fact that I want to feel that sensation again... and I know that I *will*. It will just be a matter of time. This, how much time, is what I need to decide. By the time the treatment is over, I feel a little clearer of my options.

We all meet back in our room and order room service.

"I can't wait to see Chris," Anna says, excited. "We agreed to not talk today... but I'm dying to know how he's doing."

"Let me worry about that," I tell her. "Just relax and I'll check in with him."

"Thanks, Emi."

I pull out my phone to send Jack a text message. *"Do you have a few minutes to meet me in the lobby?"* As I wait for his response, I try to do something with my messy hair, but give up when I sense there's no hope.

About five minutes later, he responds, *"I'm on my way."* I didn't anticipate him being ready right away... but anxious to see him, I decide to just put some powder and lip gloss on. Au natural. My yoga pants and tank top complete the look. *He's got to accept me for who I am... and this is pretty much it!*

"I'll be back in a few. I'm going to confer with the best man," I tell her. "Any message you'd like me to send along?"

"Put some lipstick on, Em," my sister encourages. I roll my eyes at her.

"Tell him to tell Chris I love him and can't wait."

Too impatient to wait for the elevator, and feeling a burst of nervous energy, I take the stairs to the lobby. He's standing near the elevators and doesn't see me across the room. He looks perfectly put-together, as always. Today, he's wearing a pair of khakis and a short-sleeved plaid button-down shirt, no buttons fastened, with a crisp, white t-shirt underneath. His hands are in his pockets, he's shifting his weight to one side. I walk to a set of couches in the middle of the lobby and sit down, crossing my legs and folding my arms in my lap.

"Pssst..." I get his attention. He smiles and walks toward me, taking a seat on the couch opposite mine, a small coffee table separating the two of us. He leans toward me, clasping his hands in his lap, his posture mirroring my own.

"Good morning," he says.

"Hi," I say, almost giddy with excitement.

"Hey," he returns. "What's going on?"

"I just wanted to check in... make sure Chris is okay, everything's on track... no stripper mishaps..."

"No mishaps," he states. "And Chris is fine. He woke up this morning feeling a little nervous about the ceremony, I think. He keeps thinking he'll mess up his vows... I told him I'd keep a printout with me and whisper them in his ear, if he needs it."

"That's romantic," I chide. "He's not hungover?"

"He won't be," he says. "He went back to bed for a bit. You can censor that for Anna if you think she'll worry."

"Probably will," I laugh. "I'm sure he'll be fine, though. Anna wanted you to tell him that she loves him."

"I'll give him that message. I'm sure he feels the same."

"Okay." I look around the room, anxious.

"How are *you* feeling this morning?" he asks, clearly alluding to our kiss.

"I'm tired," I admit. "I didn't sleep at all."

"Was that my fault?"

"Maybe just a little."

"How can I make it up to you?" he asks.

"Catch me at the alter if I start to collapse of sleep depravation."

"I will definitely do that for you. Shall I bring a pillow?"

"That would be nice, thank you."

"I'll assign that task to the ring bearer."

I smile broadly. "And you?" I ask him. "How did you sleep?"

"Better than I have in a long time," he brags.

"Did you now?" I ask.

"I did."

"Was that *my* doing?"

"It was all your doing, my sweet Emi." My heart skips a beat. "Feel free to do it again, anytime."

"You wouldn't rather *sleepless* nights?" I blush at my brazen suggestion, surprised the words came out of my mouth. My question shocks Jack as well.

"Well, when you put it that way..."

"I can't believe I just said that," I admit, covering my mouth.

"I'm a little shocked myself. But I like it."

"It's the sleep depravation, I swear."

"Excellent. Then I *definitely* hope to hear more."

My jaw drops, a surprised laugh escaping my lips. "Jack!" I bite my lip, completely fascinated with him.

"You started this," he says smugly, his kind eyes capturing mine as he stands up and takes my hand in his, helping me off the couch.

"I did. Bad me."

"Yes, bad you," he agrees, kissing the back of my hand before weaving his fingers between mine. "Hey, maybe you can hang back tonight after the reception... maybe we could talk a bit?" he asks as we walk toward the elevator. "I'll drive you home."

"Definitely. I'd like that."

"Great," he says, pushing the button. "You look cute, by the way." His eyes scan my casual attire.

"I'm a mess," I tell him, turning red, wishing I had put on lipstick.

"Not at all," he argues. "And you're even cuter when you blush like that." I feel my face getting even hotter as the elevator door opens. He brushes two of his fingers against my cheek. "Can I walk you back to your suite?"

"Okay." I feel his hand lightly touch my back as he guides me into the empty elevator. I'm a little apprehensive to be alone in this car with him. *Will he kiss me again?* My overactive imagination runs rampant with various scenarios, all leaving me breathless. I lean on the railing for support, and have a feeling my constant blush is giving my thoughts away.

He leans against the opposite side of the enclosed space as I tap my fingernails on the metal bar. "Are you nervous?" he asks.

"A little," I admit.

"It'll be fine," he assures me. "*Everything...* will be fine."

"Okay." I take a deep breath as the door opens to the fourth floor. He follows me down the hall to the suite.

"Thanks for meeting me," I tell him.

"Thanks for asking me... I'll see you tonight," he says, pulling me toward him and wrapping his strong arms around me. I embrace him tightly, feeling safe in his grasp.

"I'm looking forward to it."

He releases me and begins to walk back down the hall. He turns around one last time as I watch him leave. "I am, too, Emi," he states, smiling, before continuing toward the elevator. He waves as he goes inside and I wave back, opening the door to my suite and walking inside, feeling as if my feet aren't even touching the floor.

"Chris is great, and he loves you," I announce to Anna, closing the door behind me.

"Is he nervous?" she asks.

"Just about remembering his vows. Not about you."

"Six o'clock can't get here fast enough!"

"I know," I concur.

After we eat lunch, my mother, Anna's mother and Clara join us for our salon visit. The afternoon seems to drag on as I get more nervous by the hour, and it takes all my concentration to not mess with my hair and makeup once it's done to Anna's specifications. I try to keep it together for Anna's sake. I don't want my nervous energy rubbing off on her. I stop by the hotel lounge as soon as we get back to have a glass of wine. I notice my brother is seated at the bar, so I decide to join him.

"Chris?"

"Hey, Em!" he exclaims, standing to give me a hug and a kiss on the cheek. "Wow, you look great."

"Thanks. You should see Anna. She is gorgeous."

"I can't wait," he says. "Why aren't you with her? Is she alright?"

"Her mom's here," I tell him. "I've got butterflies for some reason and I don't want to let her see me like this. Hence the wine..."

"Ahhh," he says.

"You okay?" I ask him, wondering why he's drinking alone in the bar.

"Fine," he says. "Just thinking about some things."

"But you're okay?"

"Sure," he assures me, then quickly changes the subject. "So, Jack?"

"What about him?" I ask, coyly.

"Last night?"

"That?"

"Yeah, *that*, Em. How do you feel about it?"

"Umm..." I dwell on my thoughts. "We've apparently kissed before," I tell

214

my brother, "in college."

"Yeah, of course you have... at the frat party."

"Yeah, well I had been under the impression that I had kissed Nate that night, not Jack."

"What?"

"Yeah. You know how drunk I was," I reason with him. "But that moment was amazing, and it stayed with me all these years... and as soon as he kissed me again last night, I remembered everything. But I always thought it was Nate that made me feel that way. So it's a little weird... to know that it was Jack... and it's strange to feel it again, because I had accepted that I never would, since it never came back to me when Nate and I were together."

"Huh," he comments.

"A little hard to wrap my brain around, really."

"Well, you made his night," he says. "He never stopped smiling."

"I guess that's good," I say, unsure.

"Are you having second thoughts?"

"Of course," I tell him, the only one who I feel can really understand. This year has brought us even closer than we ever were. "But not about him so much... I feel pretty certain about him. I just feel like I'm still carrying around a lot of baggage... and I don't want to mess anything up."

"So what are you going to do? You know I love you both... I feel like I have to protect you both."

"We're going to talk tonight, after the wedding. I'm going to tell him what's been going on with me."

"The miscarriage?" he asks.

"Yeah, among other things... I just think he needs to know what he's getting himself into."

"Just so you know, I don't think anything you tell him will change the way he feels about you."

"How can he be so sure?"

"He felt something when he kissed you, too, however many years ago that was. He told me about his feelings for you after you left the frat party. I gave him a black eye for it."

"Really? You hit him?"

"Yeah. All the guys wanted your number, though." He looks at me and rolls his eyes. "You were the highlight of the night for most of them. I didn't know Jack felt any differently than any of my other brothers."

I want to laugh, but feel... *robbed.*

"But Jack? What did you tell him then?"

"I told him to forget about you, Em. I told him that you and Nate were meant to be together."

"What?" I ask.

"I told him if you ever brought him up, I'd tell him. But you never did. I knew you never would."

"Why'd you think that?"

"Because I really believed you and Nate were meant to be together. I wasn't making it up."

"Wow," I say, taking in the new details. "Huh." My thoughts start spinning wildly out of control, question after question gushing to the forefront of my mind. Would Jack and I have worked out as a couple in college? Would we have had the last ten years together? Would he have been the same person he is today? And what about Nate? Would he and I have remained friends after all these years?

I allow my imagination to swim in the what-ifs... I imagine what it would have been like if Jack had asked me out those many years ago. He would have reminded me of the kiss... or he would have kissed me again. Either way, I would have immediately known how drawn to him I was. The feeling was palpable, unmistakeable... enduring ten years, the feeling as fresh as it was the first time we kissed. Sure, we were different people back then, but the chemistry we have now was present back then, too. Where would I be today? Happily married? Maybe a couple of beautiful blue-eyed children?

Maybe Nate wasn't my soul mate after all... I think about the things I would have missed. I would have never known how Nate truly felt about me... and maybe his feelings would never have developed into anything more than friendship, anyway. I never would have recognized my own curiosities about our relationship. I smile inwardly. If Jack and I had started dating long ago, would I be sitting here, today, wondering 'what if' about Nate? It's possible I would never have known the joy of being pregnant... nor would I have known the immense devastation of losing that baby... or losing him.

He wouldn't be gone. My heart jumps at the thought. He would still be alive today. We only left because I wanted chocolate. Fucking *chocolate*. Such a trivial thing in hindsight brought such a tragic end to his short life. He might even be married to someone with children of his own... Smiling, I imagine that our friendship would have lasted all this time, and that our kids would have played together.

One tiny moment, one moment of unclarity...

"How could you not tell me?" I choke out through a few tears, but I know it's not his fault. So many variables kept Jack and I apart all these years. My drunkenness that night. Nate's misunderstanding the following morning, and his decision to never discuss that night with me. Chris deciding not to tell me anything.

My brother stares into his drink for a few minutes before answering. "I'm not proud, Emi, but how could I have known?"

"I don't guess you could have," I finally assure him, patting his arm. It wasn't his fault. It wasn't meant to be... then... We both take another sip of our drinks.

"Last night, Jack got to relive that moment, and he was completely euphoric all over again. I hadn't seen him like that since that party." Chris laughs, but then a serious look replaces his smile. "If you're not sure, Emi, be honest with him. If Nate is still holding that place in your heart, tell him."

"I will, I promise."

"He'd be good for you, though." He takes another long drink. "It's kind of hard for me to say that. It was always supposed to be you and Nate." My brother's eyes begin to water, and mine, in turn, follow suit. "Even after he died, I never could see you with anyone else, even though I hoped for it. I'd never seen two people *so in love*. I don't think I even have that with Anna," he says.

"Chris," I begin, "I know Anna loves you with all her heart. And I know you feel the same. Of course you have that with her."

"It just... *looks* different."

"Nate and I were friends for years and years. We had a certain familiarity with one another that only comes with time. You'll have that with Anna, I have no doubt..."

He sits quietly and takes a few more sips from his pilsner glass. "I do love her." He smiles.

"I know you do. And if it makes you feel any better, I look at you guys and think, '*Man, I want that.*'"

"You'll have it."

"I hope," I tell him.

"You will." Chris pulls out his wallet and leaves a few dollars on the bar. "Thank you, Emi," he says, smiling and assured. "Love you." He lightly kisses the top of my head.

"You, too," I return. "See you at the wedding!" He walks out of the lounge, and after I finish my glass of wine, I blot a lone, remnant tear from my cheek and return to the suite, hoping my makeup still looks okay.

CHAPTER 10

At the arboretum where the wedding will take place, Anna's mother sits next to her as the photographer snaps some photos before the ceremony. All the finishing touches have been put on, and the bride is anxious to make her trip down the aisle.

"Okay, Emi, can you do one last thing for me?" she asks, rummaging through her suitcase and pulling out an envelope.

"Of course."

"Can you take this to Chris? And tell him to read it before the wedding."

"Sure thing." I check myself in the mirror, straightening out a few wrinkles in the bridesmaid gown and tucking a strand of hair back into place. I reapply my lipstick and take the card from Anna, nervous but excited to see the men.

I knock on the door down the long hallway that has been designated as the men's dressing room. Hoping to see Jack, I'm a little disappointed when my father answers.

"Wow, Emi, you look beautiful," he says, my eyes scanning the room. *No Jack.*

"Thanks, Dad, you look pretty handsome yourself." He hugs me and I wander over to my brother who's sitting stiffly on the couch. I pick up the piece of paper that sits in front of him as I sit down.

"Still memorizing your lines?" I ask.

"I'm gonna screw this up, I know it," he says.

"Your brother's a little nervous," Dad comments.

"Don't worry about it, Chris. If you forget the vows, just look in her eyes and tell her how you feel. It will come to you."

"I know, I know," he says standing up and beginning to pace.

"You'll be fine," I tell him as I interrupt his stride, holding out my arms to hug him. His embrace is tight as we hold on to each other. "You look amazing." I take a step back and straighten his tie, then hand him the card from his bride. "Here, maybe this will help. It's from Anna. She says to read it before the ceremony."

"Thanks," he smiles, digging into his pocket and handing me a rectangular box. "Will you take this to her?"

"Oooo, what is it?"

"You'll see, just take it to her, alright?"

"Okay, fine. I love you, Chris."

"You too, Em."

"Love you, Dad, see you in a few!"

I take the box and leave the room, quietly closing the door behind me. As I walk down the silent, otherwise-empty hallway, I see Jack approaching, his head down as if he's concentrating on something, carrying a flask that I assume is for my brother. My heart thuds loudly in my chest. He looks even taller in his tux, the bottom button of the two-button jacket unfastened, his hand in his pocket. He seems completely comfortable in his formal attire. I, on the other hand, can't stop fidgeting with the sash of my dress and have a difficult time walking in the shoes that Anna insisted I wear.

When he looks up, he stops in his tracks as he sees me.

"Wow," he says quietly, a smile quickly forming, his hand reaching to his face, drawing attention to the faint five o'clock shadow. He looks incredible. I continue my stride toward him on the way to Anna's dressing room, gaining confidence with each second he stares in my direction. My eyes are drawn to his, the excitement inside of me obvious by the grin on my face. As I reach him, I allow my gaze to wander, checking him out completely and nodding flirtatiously when my eyes meet his again. I don't stop, just keep walking, his eyes following me until I reach my destination. I linger in the hallway, watching him, before entering the room. I wave briefly as the door closes. *Oh, my god, I can't breathe.*

"Yeah, good call on the tuxes, Anna," I tell her, my face obviously flushed. "The men look amazing." She laughs.

"I know," she smiles. "How's Chris?"

"Great. He sent this for you." I hand her the box. Inside is a delicate diamond bracelet. She gasps when she sees it. "It's beautiful. Let me put it on for you."

Her eyes begin to water. "That was so sweet of him," she says. "I saw this at a jewelry store right after we got engaged! I can't believe he remembered it." It does seem strangely sentimental and romantic for my brother... I grab a handkerchief and begin to blot her eyes before the tears can escape.

The wedding planner enters the room, letting us know that the guys are ready in the outdoor garden where the wedding is taking place.

"Are you ready?" he asks. Anna nods, taking the handkerchief from me, tucking it under her bouquet.

"Let's go!" she says, making her way out the door, her mother and I in tow.

From behind the seated guests, as I wait for my cue, I see Jack, standing slightly behind my brother, his hands clasped in front of him. He watches me intently, his eyes never leaving mine, and whispers something in my brother's ear that makes him laugh. Chris looks much calmer now. I, now aware of Jack's steady gaze, become nervous.

When the music begins, I slowly walk down the aisle, nodding to family members and friends as I pass them. I'm careful not to look at Jack, afraid that if I do my heart may stop beating or my feet may stop moving. I make eye contact with my brother, who smiles warmly at me, and finally reach the alter.

The song changes, and the crowd stands and turns to see Anna and her father. I hear Chris inhale slowly, loudly. I study his face as he watches his bride approach. He starts nervous, then excited, then happy, then completely taken with this woman that he has chosen to be his wife. Just seeing her beautiful form walk down the aisle has given him all the courage in the world.

After Anna's father has given his daughter's hand to Chris, she sneaks in a kiss before the minister begins, her excitement overflowing. I laugh at the cute way she is with him.

Man, I want that.

Both bride and groom remember all their hand-written vows and deliver them with such love and devotion that I hear sniffles from the audience. After the officiant presents them as husband and wife, and after they share the sweetest of kisses– my heart melts– I hand Anna her bouquet and watch them travel back down the aisle. I look up at Jack, for the first time since the ceremony began, his expression hopeful and composed. My heart flutters again and I smile nervously. I take his arm and we follow the bride and groom. About halfway down the aisle, he slides his arm back slightly and takes my hand into his, squeezing it gently.

After posing for what seemed like a hundred different photos in another spot in the garden, we finally make it to the reception. Jack and I go inside and immediately find something to drink. The DJ announces the bride and groom and invites them onto the dance floor for their first dance. A verse into the song, the DJ asks for the parents to join, as well as Jack and I, as the maid of honor and best man. He takes our drinks and sets them down at the head table.

"May I have this dance?" he asks, in mock formal speech, knowing I won't say no.

"Of course." Again he offers me his arm and guides me to the dance floor.

"How do you know how to dance like this?" I ask him as he leads me in a waltz, one hand on the small of my back, his other clutching mine loosely.

"I've been in many, many weddings," he says. "One of my cousins required me to go to ballroom dancing classes with him as one of my groomsman duties."

"You make it seem easy," I tell him.

"You're a natural," he says, and I smile, remembering the dance classes Nate and I took years ago. I'm pretty certain I was everyone's source of entertainment in the class. It took me much longer to learn steps than everyone else. Nate would try to hold back his laughter, but he wasn't always successful... but he would always invite me over to practice during the week so I'd be better by the following class. "You look breathtaking tonight, Emi," Jack says as he brushes my cheek with his fingers, his hand still holding mine.

"So do you," I tell him as another song begins. Chris taps Jack on the shoulder and asks if he can cut in, offering Anna as a partner to him. My brother, not as skilled a dancer as Jack, pulls me closely into him, our form resembling a hug more than a dance position.

"I love you, Chris," I tell my brother. "I am so happy for you. She is amazing and I know you two will have a wonderful life together."

"Thanks, Em," he tells me. "I just want you to know that this year has changed my life, and getting to know you better has been a big part of that. With everything we've been through, it just makes me want to live my life to the fullest and keep close all the people I love." He looks at my face to see my eyes begin to water. "No, Em, please don't be upset. I'll tickle you, don't, I mean it."

"Don't you dare tickle me!" I playfully slap his shoulder and wipe away the tears. "I know what you mean, though. I'll always be there for you, Chris, especially after all you've done for me."

"I wouldn't have had it any other way," he says. "You know you mean the world to me... always have. And I'm so glad you and Anna have become so close. She's never had a sister, and I know she thinks of you as one... and Jen, too. I'm happy you've welcomed her into the family."

"Well, she's a perfect fit. Thanks for picking someone we like." Anna approaches us slowly and I graciously give her groom to her. Jack is dancing with my mother and I decide to return to my wine for a second and take a seat. I discreetly kick off my shoes, the hem of the dress hiding the evidence.

Jen and Clara find their way to the head table and sit down with me. Clara munches on a small plate of appetizers that her mom prepared for her. I pick up a cracker and take a bite.

"He's gorgeous," Jen says, nodding to Jack. "I think you may have to fight Mom for him." I laugh softly, watching, mindlessly eating the wafer. "You're going to talk to him tonight?"

"Yeah," I tell her. "I'm still working out the details in my mind."

"Has he kissed you again?" she asks, a certain giddiness in her voice.

"No. I hope he doesn't."

"Why not?"

"I can't think clearly when he does that," I say, remembering the daze I was in last night after it happened. "I get butterflies just thinking about it."

"All the more reason to do it again!" she exclaims. "Let loose a little, Emi. It can't hurt."

"Actually, it can," I tell her. "Getting that close to someone again, trusting him completely, believing he'll be with me forever... and then... it ends. Somehow, it always ends..."

"That's tragic, Emi," she says, obviously disapproving of my reflective mood. "What would be more tragic is if you let that fear make all your decisions for you. You'll never be happy." She shrugs her shoulders.

"Well, that's harsh," I argue.

"It's just true. I'd hate to see you let him go for that reason..."

"I never said I was. But you know what? This is my business, and I don't appreciate–"

"Why are you fighting?" Clara interrupts. "I thought weddings were happy."

My sister and I glare at one another briefly, and I take a deep breath.

"I just want you to be happy again, Em, that's all. I just want what's best for you."

"I know," I concede. "I've given this a lot of thought... so you have to just trust that I know what's best for me."

"I'm not sure you do," she says with sincerity. "I hope you do..."

"I do."

"Anni-Emi, will you dance with me?" my niece asks.

I stand up and pick her up into my arms, moving to the song and swinging her around. She giggles loudly, then requests that I take her on the dance floor. After I slip my shoes back on, I start to walk with Clara toward the parquet floor. I twirl her around and she takes the opportunity to show off some of her ballet positions she's learned in her dance class. When a fast song comes on, she squeals and jumps up and down, and I take her hands and lead her around the floor.

"Can I cut in?" Jack asks.

"Well, Clara wanted to dance–"

"I meant with Clara, thank you very much," he smiles, directing his attention at my niece. I expect Clara to shy away, as she does with people she's not very familiar with, but she immediately holds out her hands to him. "Here, you can stand on my feet." He helps her settle on his patent leather shoes and dances around the floor. Clara can't stop giggling. I back off the floor to watch them, standing next to my sister.

"He's good with her," Jen says.

"He's got two nieces and two nephews that he adores," I tell her, sighing heavily. I fight the thoughts that try to creep into my head and decide to take a break. "Hey, I'm going to go take some food to Anna. I don't think she's had anything to eat all night."

"Okay."

I go over to the amazing spread of food and pick out a little of everything, enough for both her and Chris. Eventually I convince them to take a seat so that the toasts can begin.

After my father, Anna's father, Jack and I have saluted the bride and groom, Anna and Chris cut the cake and take a few moments to relax with their dessert and drinks. Jack and I join them as the rest of the guests mingle, laughing about the day and listening to them describe what they're going to do in Hawaii on their honeymoon. Jack excuses himself to talk to Russell, and shortly after, the DJ announces the last dance. I look at Anna and Chris, busy nuzzling one another, quietly enjoying each other's company. They glance at me briefly and both give me encouraging nods and I stand up to go to Jack. No one else is on the dance floor. When I'm half-way across it– half-way to him– he sees me walking toward him. He just stops and watches me, a completely content look on his face. He holds his hand out to me and leads me back onto the floor.

This time, his hand draws my body closer into his, his arm seeming to envelop me more completely. We stare at each other, the song slow, romantic, seductive– clearly selected for the bride and groom, whom I briefly glance at. They're both smiling at us. When I look back at Jack, he's also seeing their consent. He looks back down at me and lets go of my hand to touch my face once again. As much as I want him to kiss me, I'm too conscious of all of my family members watching us dancing. I wrap both of my arms around him and put my head against his chest, listening to his heartbeat. The fingers of one of his hands expand and contract slowly on the small of my back. He plays with my hair, brushing his fingers against my ear, with his other hand. I close my eyes, blocking out the vision of everyone else in the room. This moment confirms everything.

When the song ends, I pull back slightly to look at him again. He cradles my face in his hands and stares into my eyes. Slowly, I take his hands from my face and hold them close to my heart. I see Anna get up out of the corner of my eye and realize it's time to get ready to go.

"I'll meet you back here in a bit," I tell Jack. He nods and quickly kisses the back of my hand before letting it go.

Hurriedly, I help Anna change into a different dress before we send them off to the hotel.

"Thank you so much, Emi," she says.

"You're welcome, but I really didn't do much," I tell her. "I thought you might demote me to bridesmaid or just plain-old Chris's sister a few times in the past year. Just... thank you... for putting up with me."

"Oh, Emi," she says. "I love you so much and I never once had second thoughts about you being my maid of honor."

"Well, thank you. And welcome to the family." We hug tightly. "I hope you guys have a great trip."

"Oh, we will, I can't wait to leave in the morning."

"Is there anything you need before you go?" I ask. "Anything I can get you?"

"No, Em. Your role is done," she smiles and hugs me. "I need you to stop hanging out with me and go talk to Jack. And then I need you to remember every detail, because I want to know what happens."

"Don't worry, I'll tell you as soon as you get back."

"Good luck," she says, embracing me once more. "Be strong... but be open..."

"Okay. Have a wonderful time."

I take her to Chris's dressing room and then head to the entrance way where all the guests have gathered, armed with rose petals to shower the happy couple. Jack and a few of his fraternity brothers are making last minute touches to the limo. Chris and Anna walk halfway through the crowd, then stop and kiss before continuing to the car.

The rest of the guests leave soon after. I give Jen all of Anna's things to take back to the loft, and she and Clara take off after I tell her that Jack will take me back home. As the waitstaff begins to clean the reception room, Jack grabs a freshly-opened bottle of wine and two plastic cups he finds in the bar, then signals for me to follow him into the garden. *Gladly.*

He leads the way down a secluded rock path, an approaching small waterfall making its presence known by a soft bubbling sound in the distance, getting louder. The moonlight dances on the water, unobstructed by a single cloud in the sky. The chirping of crickets add to the soundtrack, the sounds of nature making louder the silence between Jack and me.

He speaks from behind me. "So, Emi, a little over twenty-four hours ago, I wasn't sure I had a chance with you." I remain quiet, wanting him to continue. "And tonight, I know there is something here... between us. What changed?"

I take a deep breath, my back still to him. "Kissing you. It sounds cliché and stupid, but I felt something."

"Well, we kissed ten years ago, and I felt it back then. Didn't you? Why did it take you so long to come around?"

"Honestly?" I ask.

"Of course."

"I didn't remember kissing you in college." I purposely don't turn around, not wanting to see the look of hurt he may have on his face. It takes a while for him to recover from this.

"Really... huh..." More silence, but frustration seeps out in his tone. "How could you not–"

"Wait a second, let me finish," I interrupt.

He thinks for a second. "Sorry," he says. "Go ahead."

"What I said is that I didn't remember kissing *you* in college."

"I heard that." I turn around to see him. "I got that."

"No, you didn't hear me. I *said* I didn't remember kissing *you*... but I remember the kiss... in every fiber of my body, I remember that kiss."

"I'm not following you."

"Jack, I thought I had kissed someone else that night. I thought it was Nate."

I turn around to stand on the edge of the pond, peering into the shallow water. I hear Jack set the wine and cups down on the ground. The memory of Nate floods my mind. Saying it out loud– to Jack– just feels like a betrayal. *I'm sorry, Nate.*

I inhale and continue. "It wasn't until last night that I remembered it was you. As soon as you kissed me, the memory of that night came back to me. For years, I just assumed it was Nate. But since we had vowed to not date, I tried to put it out of my mind... or I tried to recreate it with other men. But I couldn't... not even with Nate when we decided to get together. I never thought I would feel that again."

His hands on my shoulders, he turns me around to face him. He has removed his jacket and loosened his tie, looking more relaxed. Without warning, his hand lifts my chin and his lips brush mine, the most alluring of kisses, his mouth teasing me. I hold his head in my hands, pulling him closer to me. We break apart when we are both out of breath.

"You can't keep doing that," I tell him, stunned.

"Are you kidding? Now that I know how it affects you..."

"No, really," I say, smiling slightly, "I can't think straight when you do that. And I need to think straight for this conversation."

"Okay, Emi," he says, understanding my serious tone. "I'm sorry." He walks over to the park bench where the wine is. He pours us each a glass, and pats the seat, requesting me to sit by him. He hands me a cup and I take a long, slow drink.

I straighten my dress before assuming my place next to him, stretching my legs out and kicking off my heels. My painted toenails peek out from under the dress. Nervous, I curl my toes in and cross my feet.

"I will cry tonight. I just want you to be prepared."

"I am, actually," he says, reaching into the pocket of his tuxedo jacket. "Handkerchief." He holds it ready in his hands.

"So, you know, I lost a lot last year... when he died." I sense Jack is going to let me do all the talking. "My best friend, my love... I lost a part of my identity when it happened. I hadn't realized so much of me was tied into him, but it was... and he had become a part of me... um, quite literally, actually.

"That night, I had this insatiable craving for chocolate... so he took me to the store to get some. I don't like chocolate... it was a craving... I..." Sadness overwhelms me as I hear him exhale heavily.

"You were pregnant," he says.

"I *was*... but you knew?" I ask.

"I didn't know, for sure," he says, his eyes distant. "I thought I overheard."

"How could you know?"

"I was at the hospital... Nate's mom came in. She told your mother something about a baby. I think she was trying to be discreet, but it was difficult since she was in near-hysterics. No one really knew if she had any grasp on reality at the time. While your family tried to sort through things, I decided to leave. It had been a bad night... and that was a private matter that I didn't need to be privy to.

"But you never started showing, so I hoped I had mis-heard... and hoped that you hadn't miscarried after the accident. Although I was curious, I never asked Chris. It wasn't any of my business. And I also didn't want it to be true, for your sake." We're both silent for a few minutes. "How far along were you?"

"About six weeks. I lost the baby five days after the accident."

"God, Emi, I am so sorry. Oh, my god." He takes one of my hands into his, and puts the handkerchief in the other one.

"The baby would have been due a few weeks ago," I think to myself, aloud. "And I would have had a part of him with me forever." I cry quietly to myself as he puts his arm around my shoulders and pulls me into his chest.

"I'm so sorry," he repeats. "I just don't know what else to say."

"There's nothing to say. But this is what I've been trying to deal with for the last month or so. I didn't deal with that loss in the beginning. I guess I could only handle one thing at a time. I guess I somehow knew that."

"That's understandable... but Emi, I'm here for you."

"I know you are," I smile through the tears. "And I want to be able to go to you for support, I do. But I don't know if I'm in the right place to do that."

"What do you mean?"

"I have a lot of healing to do still," I explain. "It would be so easy to jump into a relationship with you, Jack. Sooo easy. You're everything I want, need... but I want to be whole for you. I want to be able to give you every part of me... you deserve nothing less... but I don't want to take away from what I still have to do."

"And that is?"

"I need to get past this sadness and loss. I need to get beyond the fear of losing more people that I love. A part of me doesn't want to get that close to anyone again... because I don't think I could make it through anything like that again."

"What can I do?" he asks.

"Be patient," I tell him. "Be a friend to me, for now."

"A friend," he says, the word lingering on his tongue.

"And this whole kiss thing..." I continue. "I'm really holding it all together, but... it's bittersweet. You know, what Nate and I had, it was wonderful. Our friendship laid a foundation for... what could have been an incredible relationship. But I went searching for that feeling, believing it was him... believing I was *meant to be* with him... so it's a little earth-shattering to accept that it was your kiss that did that to me, and not his.

"I mean, I'm happy about it, believe me. I can't believe that I have a chance to have that again, after all these years. But it sort of alters everything I believed in."

"How so?"

"I've never felt anything like that, Jack. I had convinced myself that I was meant to be with Nate– based on that kiss, and the fact that I couldn't feel anything like that with anyone else."

"What happened when you were with him? Did you feel something like it?"

"No," I explain. "Like I said, it was wonderful, and we would have been happy together, I have no doubt. But when you kiss me... I feel it in every cell in my body... like a current running wildly through my veins, nearly stopping my heart..."

"I know," he says. "That's why I'm not sure I can *just* be your friend at this point."

"I just need you to try. That's all I can do, too... try. I just don't want our relationship to be based solely on how you make me feel when you kiss me."

"You know it wouldn't be," he reasons.

"I don't know," I counter. "I know I could escape everything by running to you, and letting you be my everything."

"Then do that..."

"Running to you is running away from my past... and it would catch up with me over time. I'm going to therapy. I'm really working hard at this... and I'd really like your support– your friendship– through this."

"Anything you want, Emi," he says, resigned. "I would do anything for you, you have to know that."

"Thank you."

"But please don't hate me if I slip. You just do something to me."

"Well... ditto..."

"Oh, no, if you slip, I can't be held responsible for what may happen. That's too much temptation."

"Well, it's not going to be easy for me, either. I'm going against my heart at this point... it seems unnatural, but necessary."

"I don't have to agree," he tells me. "Unnatural, yes. Necessary?" He shakes his head.

"For me it is."

"Alright, Emi. Can I ask a favor, though?"

"Sure," I tell him, open to anything if he can do this for me.

"I'll ask you later," he says. "I think it's about closing time here." He takes the bottle and cups to a nearby trash bin, then kneels down and picks up my shoes. "Did you want to put these back on?"

"Not particularly," I answer.

"Alright," he says, leaning down. "Hop on," he says, his back to me.

"No," I tell him, laughing. "No way."

"Come on, Em. Get on!"

"Jack..." He stands up straight and turns to me.

"I could just pick you up and carry you, but I'd be a little concerned about the strapless dress..."

"Alright, alright," I say. He leans down again and I hop onto his back, allowing him to carry me to the car.

"I need to pick up my stuff from the hotel and check out," he tells me. "Do you mind if we go by there?"

"No, that's fine," I answer. "So what's the favor?"

"I'll tell you at the hotel," he says. "I'm going to need your undivided attention."

"Alright," I say, curious.

When we pull into the hotel, I put my uncomfortable shoes back on before getting out of the car. They pinch my toes so tightly that I'm beginning to walk with a limp. I lean on Jack as we go inside, into the elevator. His room is at the far end of the hallway, and I can't wait to get inside to sit down for a break. I wish I had other shoes with me.

When he opens the door, I immediately make my way to the bed and sit down, resting my feet. He pulls up a chair from the desk in the room and sets it in front of me, backwards. He sits down, folds his arms on the back of the chair and rests his chin on his arms. His face is close to mine. "So the favor..." he begins.

"Yes..."

"I'll do the friend thing on a few conditions," he says.

"Okay..."

"First, I'd like to see you... so do you think we can make some time to get together every week?"

"I think that would be fine," I tell him, liking his first condition.

"And secondly, can this friend thing... can it start tomorrow?"

I raise my eyebrows and fold my arms across my chest. As I stare into his blue eyes, my resolve crumbles, and I want to– no, have to– say yes to his request. I slowly inch toward him and kiss him softly. "Is this what you meant?"

"Yes," he says. "Just something to tide me over." He kisses me again, this one a little more passionate, and when he backs away, I stand up, numb, and start gathering his suitcases, attempting to shake off the feeling.

"This is dangerous," I tell him. "We must leave this room."

He laughs under his breath and says, "Yeah, I wasn't asking for *that*."

"Well, good," I say. I wasn't asking either, but the desire inside of me has been dormant for so long that I can barely contain it. It feels so amazing to be touched by a man again. A part of me just wants to drop the whole well-thought-out plan and just let myself follow my heart... let myself *be*– with *him*– in the moment.

When we reach the loft, he insists on walking me in. He carries my shoes as we ascend the elevator to my floor. We share a short kiss on the way, stopping when the door opens suddenly on the seventh floor and another passenger gets in the car. We deliberately separate ourselves until we hit the twelfth floor.

"Did you want to come in?" I ask against my better judgment.

"No, thank you," he says. "Too tempting."

"Okay, well..." *Disappointed... but this is what I want, right?* "Thank you for tonight."

"No, *I* should thank *you* for tonight. You can thank me for the friendship thing... however long that's going to last..."

"Thank you for both," I tell him.

"I really care about you, Emi," he says running his hand through my hair.

"I care about you, too, Jack," I return.

"One last kiss," he says.

"Please," I smile and lean in to his wanting lips, feeling that sensation throughout my body.

"Wow," he says and smiles. I just nod my head, unable to speak. "Goodnight, sweet Emi."

"Goodnight, Jack." I open the door and step inside, watching him as he waits for, and eventually enters, the elevator. We both wave goodbye as the doors close. I sink to the floor once inside the apartment, my knees weak and unable to hold my weight any longer. I hope that the last kiss will hold me over for awhile, but realize quickly that this "friendship thing" is going to be a lot harder than I thought.

CHAPTER 11

Why is he wearing a tie?

After peeking at Jack from around the corner, I look at my reflection in the shop window and pull my stringy, damp hair up in the clip I brought with me.

He said this was a casual lunch... a tie?

When he called me to push back the time by an hour, I was hoping he was calling to postpone our date for another day, but he sounded so excited to see me that I couldn't back out. Not that I didn't try. And it's not that I don't want to see him, I do. I'm just not feeling like myself today.

Breathe, Emi. Just smile, you can do this.

I peek back around at him and hide quickly before he sees me. He looks so handsome, so professional, so perfectly put together. I'm a wreck. I scan my jeans and t-shirt and take a deep breath.

No, I can't do this.

I pull my phone out of my bag and begin to type out a text.

"Why did you wear a tie?"

I look down the street at the approaching cars, looking for a taxi.

"Where are you?" he responds.

"I'm not dressed for this. I'm going home."

Where are all the fucking cabs? It's one o'clock on a Friday!

"Ha ha. I'm sure you look great."

"I'm not kidding." My heart starts racing as a lump forms in my throat. I can't meet him looking like this. As my phone begins to ring, I stuff it back into my purse as a cab finally pulls up to the curb. I open the door and begin to step in, but hesitate when the ringing ceases. I hear the phone chime, notifying me of another text message.

"Just a second," I tell the cab driver.

"C'mon, lady, I ain't got all day."

"Just a second!" I reiterate. "Start the meter!"

"I've been looking forward to seeing you all week." Heat rises to my cheeks as I simultaneously smile and sigh. In truth, I've been looking forward to seeing him, too. I just didn't expect him to look like *that*.

"Sorry, go on," I yell to the driver, shutting the door as I start to think of how I'm going to respond to Jack. I turn around, distracted by my phone, and run right into a man... dressed in a nice, crisp white shirt...

...and that *damned red tie.*

"Where were you going?" Jack asks, gently taking me by the shoulders to reorient me to my surroundings.

"I have never felt so monumentally underdressed," I blush again. "I was going to go home."

"You look great, Emi, don't be silly."

"You said we were going somewhere casual."

"We are. My meeting just ran long and I didn't have time to go home and change. I'm sorry. Is there anything I can do to make you feel better?"

I straighten my t-shirt out and look up at him apologetically, contemplating how I can feel okay about this... um... friend-date-thing.

"For starters," I tell him as I take the knot of his tie under my finger, "we're going to loosen this." He laughs quietly and lets me pull on the knot. I unbutton the top two buttons and back up to look at him. "Better..."

"Are we okay now?"

I stand on my tiptoes and run my hands through his hair, messing it up just a little.

"I think... maybe."

As I'm looking down at his obviously expensive dress shoes, I feel him pull my hair out of the clip.

"I didn't have time to dry it," I begin to make excuses, running my fingers through it. I didn't have time, even though I had an extra hour to get ready today. Yeah. Most of that hour was spent trying to come up with a reason not to go. And yet, here I am, feeling completely inadequate in the presence of a man I really do like.

"It looks beautiful."

"Thank you," I say, resigned. He hands me my clip and crosses his arms in front of his chest. He still looks too nice.

"Are you hungry?"

"I could eat..."

"Okay. Good, let's go." We walk down the street quietly. We both steal glances at one another and smile.

"Wait, it's still not right," I tell him, taking his tie again. I unknot it and pull it off his neck, draping it over my shoulders.

"Now?" he asks again, giving me an incredulous look.

"Now," I grin, a little more comfortable with the situation. He opens the door to a tucked-away sandwich shop and follows me in. The menu hanging on the wall is overwhelming with options. I scan the tables to see what other people are eating.

"Mr. Holland," a man behind the counter greets Jack. "You look different without a tie." I look at him and swallow, playing with the ends of his neckwear, offering it to him. One side of his lip curls up in a smile and he shakes his head minutely at me.

"How are you, Ethan?" Jack asks.

"I'm good, let me go see if JR is available."

"No, I'm just here for lunch today," he explains.

"Jack, I thought I heard you," another man enters from the next room, his hand extended over the counter to shake Jack's hand. "Can I get you the regular?"

"Thanks, JR, sure, that's fine." He looks down at me. "Did you see something you wanted?"

"What did you get?" I ask him quietly.

"The number seven with the works. It's a club, but they have a whole lot of other things-"

"I'll just have the same."

"Are you sure?" I nod in consent.

"Is this a social visit?" JR asks.

"Actually, yes," he smiles. "I promised my friend, Emi, that I would bring her here eleven years ago. It just took me awhile to get her here."

I look at him curiously, then remember the conversation we had that night at the party. I *do* remember him suggesting a place near the campus as an alternative to the bad cafeteria food. I laugh, amused at the fact that he would have remembered that after all these years.

"I'm a man of my word," he says as an aside to me. "JR, this is Emi. Emi, JR and Ethan."

I nod to both of the men who are now wearing gloves and busy preparing our sandwiches.

"Chips or fruit?" Ethan asks Jack.

"Fruit," he answers before checking with me.

"Fruit's good," I agree.

"I'm sorry, I should have asked–"

"No, it's okay," I say awkwardly.

"What would you like to drink?" he asks, blushing.

"Diet soda?"

"Water and a diet soda, please. It's all to go."

"Business is up over last year," JR tells Jack. "By a lot."

"Maybe the renovations had more of an impact than you thought," Jack says, smiling. "I'm happy for you."

"Thank you," JR says to Jack emphatically. Jack just nods. When they hand Jack our food, he just puts some bills in the tip jar they have on the counter. *Large* bills.

"Keep it up," Jack says, nodding, leading me out of the deli.

"Thanks, Jack. Pleasure to meet you, Emi."

"You too, thank you," I tell the men behind the counter.

"Where would you like to eat?" Jack asks, pausing beside a table in front of the sandwich shop.

I shrug. "It doesn't matter to me."

"Doesn't matter..." he repeats. "I was thinking maybe we could take these to Washington Square. Eat by the fountain?"

"That sounds fine."

"Okay." He smiles as he begins to walk toward campus. "How are you today?" he asks, breaking the silence.

How am I? Let's see. I didn't get much sleep, both anxious and nervous about seeing you today. All week, I've been having internal arguments about whether or not it's too soon to move on. Today, I woke up thinking it was too soon. Now that I'm with you, though, I don't think it is. But if I think about Nate... Gah! Stop, Emi! I've been getting constant butterflies in my stomach every time I think about you kissing me. And I can't stop thinking about you kissing me, except I have to because I told you I didn't want that yet. And I don't. Yet. I don't think.

"Fine." I sigh heavily, dropping my shoulders in defeat.

He doesn't press the issue until we're settled by the fountain in the central plaza with our lunch. Jack opens his water, then my soda, and hands it to me. "To a nice afternoon on this beautiful day." He taps my bottle with his and takes a sip. I drink some soda and eat a piece of cantaloupe.

He takes a bite of his sandwich and watches a group of kids playing near the water. "You don't seem fine."

"No, I am," I smile. "I just have a lot on my mind."

"Anything you'd like to talk about?"

Do I tell him about all the second-guessing I've been doing since the last time I saw him? I decide not to and shake my head, more curious about the interaction between Jack and JR. "Why didn't you have to pay for lunch?"

He sighs, accepting my reluctance to talk about myself. "I'm a silent investor in the shop."

"Oh. That makes more sense."

"...than?"

"I was beginning to think JR was going to hand you an envelope full of cash over the counter..." I smile slyly and look into those pretty blue eyes. "I thought I might need to warn you that I have a strong distaste for guns and severed horse heads."

He laughs heartily. "It sounds like you watch too many mafia movies."

"That may be true," I admit. "I went through a phase."

"I must admit, I don't like guns or severed horse heads, either. I'm glad we're on the same page there."

I laugh back at him. "Were you an investor back in college?"

"No, just their best customer. My frequent visits probably kept the lights on many months."

"Well, how'd you become an investor?"

"I always liked the food," he begins. "Initially, that's what kept me coming back. And it used to be run by an older man. Victor. He'd been in business for thirty-something years. He would often come and sit with me at lunch when the deli was slow. He was a good man. Loved his wife and his sons, would do anything for them. Honestly, he would do anything for anyone... he was generous to a fault. Even in those years when business was bad, he would host free Thanksgiving meals for the homeless. I would come and volunteer every year.

"I didn't see much of him while I was away at Harvard. Every time I came back to New York, I'd stop by and we'd have lunch or dinner together. He was having a difficult time making ends meet. I tried to help him out, monetarily, but he was too proud.

"He died peacefully in his sleep one night."

"I'm sorry," I tell him. He smiles and nods.

"His son, JR, took over for him, but there was a lot of debt. I had a little extra money, and I offered to invest in the deli to get it up and running again. I never wanted to see the place close down. Victor loved that business, and I could tell JR wanted to make his father proud. JR and I went over the numbers... I gave him some good business advice and a little cash, and he was able to turn that place around."

"It's a great shop."

"Is the sandwich good?"

"Yeah," I tell him as I set aside a few olives.

"Not a fan of olives?"

"Not so much," I admit. "But it's still really good. And the fruit's really fresh."

"I'm pretty proud of what JR's accomplished. We still meet on occasion to talk about the business, but he really runs it on his own. He doesn't need my advice anymore... he just needs someone to let him know he's doing all the right things."

"That's really nice of you."

"It's what I do."

"I thought you did technology consulting..."

"I do that, too. I like to help people out when I can."

"Good to know." I smile and take another bite of the club. "Wait, can we back up a second? Did you say *Harvard*?"

"I did."

"Wow. There is so much I don't know about you." I grin more at the prospect of getting to know him better.

"What has your brother told you?"

"Hmmm... he told me he punched you. And he told me you were crazy about me. That's about it."

"Both true," he smiles.

"What has he said about me?"

"He just gave me some advice. He told me to be patient."

I roll my eyes, then sigh. My eyes begin to water as I feel a bit defeated. "I guess that's good advice these days."

Jack puts his hand on my knee gently. "Well, I'm nothing if not patient," Jack says.

"Well, good. Because as you can see, you're gonna need to be. I'm an emotional wreck these days."

"I don't see that at all. What I see is a woman who has been through a lot this year... a woman who is handling it all strikingly well, actually. I mean, you made it here today. You didn't back out. That's a step."

"A baby step..."

"You told me this wouldn't be easy. It shouldn't be, and I certainly don't expect it to be." I nod before looking across the lawn at a couple having a picnic in the grass. *They look so happy and normal.* "In time, Poppet. I'll be here. You can come to me."

"Thanks," I tell him.

"Would you like to go for a walk or something?"

I nod to him before answering him. "I really would."

He stands up, picking up our trash and throwing it into a trashcan nearby. I hand him his bottled water, ascending the steps and following his lead.

"Ten questions?" I ask as we begin to walk the perimeter of the park.

"What?"

"We can ask each other ten questions. Get to know each other better."

"Okay, you first."

"Are you a cat person or a dog person?"

"Dog," he says definitively. "But I don't have one. I had a fox terrier when I was younger. God, I loved that dog." He shakes his head and laughs to himself. "Was that the right answer?"

"Is that your first question?" I cleverly ask.

"Is that your second?" he shoots right back.

I squint at him playfully and stick my tongue out at him.

"Nice," he says. "Cat or dog?"

"Let's just say the cat and I didn't get along growing up. I've never had a dog, but I like them."

"Never? Wait, no, that's not my next question."

I shake my head at him and smile. "What band dominates your iPod?"

"Ah, what a wasted question," he says. "I don't have an iPod."

"How could you not have an iPod?"

"Hey, it's my turn to ask a question."

I let out a frustrated groan.

"Professionally, are you doing what makes you happy?"

"Easy one, yes." We stop for a few minutes, watching a young man play the violin. His eyes are closed as he concentrates on his music. Jack places some bills in the violin case next to the performer. At the end of the song, we continue walking. "Let's see..." I begin. "If you could have any other career, what would it be?"

"Hmmm... that one's tough. Maybe a dive instructor? Or a doctor... I don't know."

"Those are pretty opposite."

"Well... they both make lives better. In different ways. Have you ever been diving?"

"No. I'm scared of sharks."

"Oh, come on," he tries to sound convincing. "It's exhilarating. A whole other world lives down there, it's fascinating. There aren't always sharks..."

"Can you guarantee that?"

"I would never put your life in danger. I can guarantee *that*." He glances at me briefly, then faintly smiles.

The way he says it, his voice so earnest and sweet, his eyes so captivating... Without any doubt, I believe him. I sigh and bite my bottom lip, the butterflies returning in full force.

"My turn?" he asks. "Where is one place in the world you'd like to visit that you haven't been before?"

"Just one? Wow. I'll pick a continent, then. Europe."

"You've never been?"

"No. My life is seeming very sheltered all of a sudden..."

"I've been a lot on business. I think I'm actually going again next year."

"Lucky."

"If you play your cards right, Miss Hennigan..." he says shyly, and I can tell as soon as the words come out, he's not sure if he should have said them. I smile, watching his posture relax.

"I wouldn't want to be a bother," I tell him. *But I'd go in a heartbeat!*

"It would be an honor to have you come with me, Emi."

"You don't even really know me yet," I joke with him, nudging him with my shoulder. "We haven't even made it through *five* questions."

"I know how you make me feel," he says seriously, slowing to a stop and taking my hand in his. His motion is cautious, and he looks at me for approval. My heart starts to pound in my chest as I start to melt under his gaze. "Is this okay?" He glances briefly at our hands.

God, I want him to kiss me. *Ignore everything I said to you, Jack, and just kiss me! Ugh!*

I weave my fingers between his, feeling myself blush. "It's nice." I start walking again, pulling him along with me. He catches up quickly.

"It's your turn," he tells me.

"Okay... who are you closest to in your family?"

"That depends. Kelly and I have a natural bond, really. We sense things about one another from time-to-time. And I see her most, she's the only relative that lives here... but Stevie and I have similar temperaments."

"He really looked up to me, growing up. And I always wanted to set a good example for him. If you put all four of us in a room together, Kelly and Matty normally end up in some animated conversation, and Stevie and I just sit back and listen."

"Sounds like you're all pretty close, though."

"We definitely are. Along with your brother, they're the best friends I've got."

"You seem like the type who'd have a ton of best friends."

"I have a fair amount of friends... acquaintances... associates..." He's quiet for a few seconds. "I think I'm a pretty good judge of character. I can pretty much tell if a person is being straight with me, or if they're just being friendly for personal gain. I have to be wary of that. I mean, really, everyone does."

"Yeah," I agree, spotting a few girls a couple yards away looking in our direction. "Speaking of friends, do you know them?"

Jack slows down and slowly changes our course away from them, but nods politely at them. "No, I don't."

"They're probably thinking, 'What's a guy like that doing with a girl like her?'" I joke with him.

"Hush. Stop putting yourself down. You have no reason to."

"You're right, I *am* wearing the tie now." I throw one end over my shoulder dramatically.

"Okay, Emi, what's the most daring thing you've ever done?"

"Hmmm..." I ponder. "I know you're thinking skydiving or bungee jumping, but I haven't done either of those... I don't really know."

"Surely there's something."

"I ride the subway alone, at night, all the time," I deadpan.

"That's something, but..."

I think long and hard, for those moments in my life where the adrenaline just took over and actions came before thoughts. One stands out above all others.

"I confronted my dad and his mistress at a restaurant."

Jack doesn't know how to respond. He looks at me curiously.

"Yeah, my friends and I went out to eat after some theatre performance. My mom and dad were actually *at* the performance, *together*, but the woman with my father at the restaurant was certainly *not* my mom. And he was very... um, cozy, with her.

"I just got up from the table and walked slowly to theirs, just waiting for him to make eye contact with me. I stood at the edge of the table while they kissed. Elaine saw me first," I tell him. "She said, 'Can I help you with something?' And my dad looked over, and the look on his face... it was just shock and remorse and shame and sadness, all covered with her lipstick, and I just cried.

"It took Dad a minute to find the words, and then he just said, 'Emi, honey, we're in love.'"

"Wow," Jack comments. "I'm sorry, Emi, that must have been horrible."

I shrug and nod. "I just said to him, you know, in between *sobs*, 'Are you gonna tell Mom, or am I?'"

"And he did, and they divorced... and Dad married Elaine a few years later, and Mom found a new husband... and they're all living happily ever after now."

"Yeah, your family dynamic is very interesting," he says to me cautiously.

"Yeah, it is. But it's good. *Now*, it's good."

"Good." He squeezes my hand a little harder. "Maybe we should go skydiving sometime so we can get you a more uplifting answer to that question," he says with a smile. "Or shark hunting..."

"I do not believe shark hunting would have a happy ending," I respond to his playful suggestion. "I'm not sure I'd live to answer that question again if you made me go shark hunting. If the shark didn't kill me himself, I'm pretty sure the fear alone would stop my heart."

"I *will* take you diving someday," he vows.

"Over my dead–" I stop myself before finishing the sentence. We both stop walking as I lose the words, and my breath. I look down at the ground before Jack angles my body toward his. Not wanting him to see me sad, I take a deep breath and try to compose myself. I glance up and smile at him as he looks at me with concern.

"I'm fine." I begin to tap my foot nervously, willing the tears to stop forming and the lump in my throat to go away. He tucks my hair behind my ear and rubs my arm gently. When I blink, two tears escape, and he envelops me in a soft embrace and kisses the top of my head. I hold on to him tightly, continuing to breathe deeply and deliberately, concentrating on my surroundings, on Jack, on how safe I feel in his arms, on things that make me happy. As the tears dissipate, a shop across the street comes into focus.

"I want some pie," I mumble into his shirt.

"What?" he asks.

I pull back and look at him seriously. "Pie," I repeat. "I'd like some."

"Okay," he begins, obviously unsure how to handle me. I take his hand in mine once again, and begin walking toward the bakery across the street.

"Do you like pie?" I ask in hopes of moving on in the conversation.

"Is that ten?" he responds.

"Ten what?"

"Questions. Surely that one was eleven." He smiles at me smugly, now leading the way across the street to the shop.

I really think I could follow him anywhere. Again, butterflies. And I *love* them.

After we eat pie– mine, the traditional sour cream apple walnut; his, key lime– he asks me if I'd like to join him for a little shopping.

"Are you forcing me to find some date-appropriate clothes?" I ask with a laugh.

"Absolutely," he answers. "I saw this impossibly short skirt earlier today, and these heels. Wow. They were all at this lingerie store, I think it was this way," he says, pointing and beginning to walk that direction. I laugh and take his hand, pulling him back to me.

"Is that what you like your women to wear?" I tease him.

"My *women*?" he asks. "Emi, honey, I don't have women. And I only want you. And I don't care what you wear. Ever." He picks up our linked hands and kisses the back of mine.

"That must be true, remembering what I wore to that frat party..."

"You were adorable."

"I looked ridiculous."

"No, you didn't see yourself through my eyes. Trust me."

"I–" he puts his finger over my lips.

"Shhh... stop arguing with me," he whispers lightly, smiling. *When he looks at me like that, I'll do anything he asks.* I just nod. "Thank you. So, you're in for shopping?"

"What for, for real?"

"My niece's birthday. Jacqueline's turning six on Sunday."

"How fun! Sure, I'm in. Where to?"

"I was hoping you'd tell me," he says, looking for a cab. "What do six-year-old girls like?"

"Well, Clara just turned five. She loves dolls and stuffed animals. And books."

"Jackie has a whole library of books. We go to the bookstore every few months to get more. Those kids devour books."

"That's great."

"I think so. So let's talk stuffed animals." A cab pulls up to the curb and Jack opens the door for me.

"Fifth and Forty-Sixth," I tell the cab driver. "We're going to make Jackie a bear. What is she interested in?"

"Um..."

"Like, what does she want to be when she grows up?" I ask him.

"A mom," he tells me. "She wants to have twins, like me and her mother. She's fascinated by twins. She was devastated last year when I told her there was just no possible way for her to actually *be* a twin."

"Killing the dreams already," I joke.

"I was there when she was born," he admits. "I saw with my own two eyes. I can't lie to her," he shrugs and smiles.

At the bear shop, we both start looking around at the options.

"What are these, stuffed animal carcasses? How morbid is this?"

"Shut up!" I hit him playfully on the arm. "Look, there are bears, and dogs, and cats... just find one you think is cute."

"Emi, please. I don't know..."

"Oh, my god! They have Hello Kitty!"

"Do you think she'd want that?"

"No, *I* do! She was my favorite when I was little."

He picks up the white cat by the scruff of her neck and holds her pathetically in front of me. I grab her from him, looking over her sad, limp body.

"With a little stuffing... and the right outfit..." I say dreamily.

He takes the animal from me and continues to look. "Come on, focus. What about Jackie? She *does* like bears."

"Personally, I like the curly one. It looks kind of vintage." I pick one up and model it for Jack playfully.

"Yeah, that's it," he says, picking up one of his own.

"I'll do the honors," I say, trying to put his back.

"We're getting twins," he tells me definitively. I smile at him, falling for him just a little bit more with every thoughtful thing he does. I take both of the bears to the stuffing station, and make sure they're both filled equally.

When they're done, I wander to the clothes and try to find a couple of matching outfits. "Are they twin boys? Or girls? Or one of each?" I look up when Jack doesn't answer and see him approaching with a fully stuffed Hello Kitty doll.

"Jack, really, you don't have to do that," I blush.

"Are you kidding? To see you that excited about something so small? If it makes you happy, I want to."

"Really, you never have to buy me things to make me happy. You do a pretty good job just being... *you*."

"You're taking this cat home," he states in a commanding tone. "I stood there and approved the amount of filling, for heaven's sake. Look, it even laughs," he says, squeezing the doll to generate a giggling sound, making *me* laugh.

"Alright," I concede.

"I hope you get along better with this cat than you did with the one you had when you were younger."

"Well, I see you've declawed her, so we're half-way there."

He starts looking around at the clothing and accessories.

"You didn't answer, is Jackie having boys, girls, or both?"

"One of each," he tells me. I find a cute pink plaid dress for one bear and a matching blue plaid top for the other.

"Do we have a price limit here?" I ask.

"They don't have diamond-encrusted watches for these things, do they?" he laughs. I shake my head. "Go crazy," he says, still browsing. I eventually find matching shorts, socks and shoes for the bears. I finish them off with a Happy Birthday cupcake for the girl and a baseball for the boy. I lay everything out on the counter for Jack to approve.

"She'll love them," he comments, picking up the cupcake and baseball. "They're actually quite perfect."

"Well, thank you. I hope she likes them."

"Here," he says, handing me a gift box. "Make sure this one looks okay," he says, urging me to open it.

As he pays, I take a look inside and pull out the Hello Kitty doll. He has taken the liberty of dressing her in one accessory.

She's wearing a red tie.

"She's perfect," I smile.

Once all the animals are in their boxes, Jack leads me out of the store and up Fifth Avenue. I purposefully walk slowly, not wanting our day together to end so soon. The sun is just beginning its descent, and the shadows cast off of St. Patrick's Cathedral make it look even more majestic than normal.

"I love that this church stands here in the middle of all these boring buildings. It really breaks up the monotony and makes me just want to stand in awe of it every time I pass it."

Jack nods silently. Moving both boxes to one hand, he takes my free hand into his and begins to cross the street toward it. "Have you ever gone in?"

"It's been years," I tell him. "I stopped being a good Catholic a long time ago."

"I think they'd still welcome us," he says. "I'd like to go in and light a candle. My grandfather loved this church, and he passed away three years ago... wow, three years ago, yesterday."

I swallow hard, but agree to go in. I know Nate's funeral was here. I wasn't able to go, but I know he was here, shortly after he left me and left this world, he was here. I can't stop the tears this time.

We set our boxes down just inside the door and walk to the table full of candles. I watch Jack as he lights a candle, then bows his head in prayer. I take a deep breath and light one of my own, bowing my own head and swiping at tears.

I still miss you, Nate. I sniffle, the sound incredibly loud in the cavernous chapel. I feel Jack's hands on my arms as he stands behind me, which just makes me cry harder.

I miss you, but I'm trying really hard. And I think I'm doing okay.

Jack hands me a tissue, and I blot my nose, breathing in heavily and finally opening my eyes.

"Glad I didn't wear much makeup," I whisper to him. I can feel him chuckle quietly against my back. I lead the way out of the chapel, and we both pick up our boxes as we head out the door.

"How'd your grandfather die?" I ask Jack after we've descended the stairs and begin walking toward my apartment. He's quiet for a few seconds, looking out in front of him.

"Shark attack," he says seriously before his grin betrays him. I, again, slap him on the arm and laugh. "It was actually a killer whale."

"Stop!" I laugh harder. We both reach for the other's hand at the same time this time, interlacing our fingers together.

"Lung cancer," he finally admits. "He was a smoker till the day he died. He just wouldn't give it up."

"That's sad. I'm sorry."

"It is pretty sad. I would have loved for my kids to meet him. I have so many great memories with him."

We both walk quietly for a bit. At the next cross street, I take a left, pulling him with me.

"Where are you taking me, Poppet?"

"I don't want to go home quite yet. I don't want this day to end on a sad note. Wanna grab a drink?"

One corner of his lip rises slightly. "I don't know if we should take the twins into a bar, you know?"

"Oh, we can stick them in the coat closet," I tell him. "They're too young to remember anything."

"I guess you're right," he says.

I take him to my regular wine bar and offer him a seat at a table near the window. I pull my chair close to his before sitting down.

"Emi," Mandy, one of the bartenders, greets me. "Haven't seen you in awhile, girl! You doing okay?"

I nod and smile. "How are the wedding plans coming?" I ask her.

"Great," she answers, glancing at Jack.

"Mandy, this is my friend, Jack. Jack, Mandy."

"Good Evening, Mandy," Jack says, standing up to shake her hand. As he sits back down, Mandy looks at me with raised eyebrows. I can't help but smile. *Yes, this incredibly polite and gorgeous man is here, with me.*

"Do you want to start with your regular?" she asks.

I begin to say yes, but Jack cuts in. "This is a pretty impressive place," he says, scanning the many bottles they have on display. "It looks like you have a lot of good wines on hand."

"We do."

"Any Chateau Margaux on hand?" Mandy's eyes glance to mine and back to Jack.

"Umm... yes, I think we do. I'd have to check the cellar."

"Would you mind? I'd be interested in a 2000... maybe a 2005."

"I'll be right back," Mandy says as she quickly strides toward the cellar door.

"I'm going to show you what a *really* good wine tastes like."

"I like my normal stuff," I tell him. "I'm kind of set in my ways."

"I can appreciate that. Your normal stuff has its place. But this? I promise you wouldn't be disappointed. And if you hate it, you can follow it up with your sparkling girlie stuff."

A few minutes later, Gary, the manager, comes to our table with a bottle. "Sir, you requested the 2005 Chateau Margaux?"

"Yes," Jack answers. Gary hands Jack the bottle to inspect. "That's the one," he says, smiling.

"Fine choice, Mr. Holland," he says, producing a corkscrew from his pocket and opening the bottle. He sets the cork on the table. Jack looks it over thoroughly and nods. Mandy shows up with two glasses and sets them both on the table.

"You'll love it, Em," she assures me. Gary pours a small amount into a glass and hands it to Jack. He smells the wine, then drinks a sip.

"It's wonderful," Jack says, allowing Gary to pour us both full glasses. "Thank you."

"My pleasure, Mr. Holland." Gary and Mandy both head back to the bar to tend to other guests.

"Did I tell them your last name?"

"I don't think so."

"How does he know you?"

"I slid her my credit card," he whispers, then winks.

"I was going to treat," I tell him with only a slight whine.

"Not tonight, you aren't. Next time."

"You keep doing that..."

He strokes my hand on the table and lifts his glass. "Ready?"

I pick up my drink.

"To twins..." I offer.

"And sharks..." he returns.

"To extreme sports I'll never do..."

"To those that you *will*..."

I laugh at his assumption.

"To Europe?" I shrug my shoulders.

"Definitely to Europe." I blush at the thought, and reflect on the rest of the afternoon we've spent together.

"To good families..."

"And good friends..." he adds.

I breathe in the scent of the wine and smile.

"To the friendship..." He smiles back and we both drink slowly. It is the best wine I've ever tasted.

"To more..." he says hopefully, intensely. We both take another sip, then set our glasses down. His elbow on the table, he touches my cheek with his fingers.

He leans in slowly, his eyes never leaving mine. My breathing quickens and the butterflies go crazy. "Emi, I know you said you just want to be friends," he whispers.

I lean into him, his hand guiding my face to his. I moisten my lips in anticipation and nod my head.

"Just once?" he asks quietly with the kindest eyes, the most eager look on his face. I couldn't say no to that– even if I *wanted* to, and I *don't*.

"Yes," I say softly, closing my eyes and finally feeling his lips brush against mine lightly. He runs his fingers through my hair, then massages the nape of my neck. I hold his face to mine, willing him to continue. He kisses me chastely, nothing obscene or tawdry, nothing that speaks of the obvious sexual tension between us. It's sensitive and attentive, gentle and sweet... and seems to still go on forever. Maybe it's because I don't want him to stop.

"I could do this all night," he whispers against my lips the words that have been dancing around in my own head.

"Okay," I tell him. Three more thoughtfully placed kisses and he finally pulls away first. I blush as he smiles at me.

"Thank you."

I smile back at him and pick up my wine glass. "To more..." We drink again, and eventually finish the entire bottle of wine and a cheese plate before the streetlights begin to glow brightly in the otherwise dark street.

"Should we get you home?" he asks after paying the tab. My eyelids feel heavy, undoubtedly from the wine. I'm a little drunk. I just answer with a nod.

He grasps my hand tightly and leads me out the door, our gift boxes in tow. "I could get a cab, if you'd like," he suggests.

"I'm okay. Maybe a little stumble-y, but I'm fine. I'll lean on you." He lets go of my hand and puts his arm around my shoulder, pulling me into his side, and laughs lightly. I feel him kiss the top of my head again.

"I had a great time today," I tell him when we reach the door to my apartment.

"I'm glad," he says. "I did, too. We're on for next week?"

"Yep," I say pertly.

"Is there anything in particular you'd like to do?"

"Nope." I smile. "Just something with you."

"If you think of something, let me know." I nod. He sets his boxes down and takes both sides of the tie that still hangs around my neck. He pulls me toward him and leans down until his eyes are level with mine. "Can I–"

"Yes," I say to him, pressing my lips to his anxiously. He laughs as he kisses me back. This time, I may have felt a little tongue. I may have been the cause of that, too.

He finally pulls back and rubs the silk of the tie against my nose. "What I was going to say, before I was so pleasantly interrupted," he begins, "is 'Can I have my tie back now?'"

"Oh," I whisper, blushing with a tinge of embarrassment. "Of course."

"I only asked for one kiss, Emi. I wasn't expecting any more. I know you need time, and I don't mean to confuse things."

"I know." *Friendship, Emi. That's what you asked for.*

"But you can interrupt me like that any time you want."

"No, you're right," I say to him. "I don't want to send mixed signals. Let's take it slow."

"Okay," he agrees. "Anything you want."

"Thank you."

"No, thank you. Sweet dreams, Poppet." He takes his tie from my neck and kisses me on the cheek. After picking up the boxes, he begins to walk away.

"You, too, Jack. I just..."

He stops and looks back at me.

"Just..." I don't know what I'm trying to say. "Just, thank you for everything. Really."

"You're welcome, Emi. Good night."

I go into the apartment and remove the stuffed animal from the box, setting it on my bed. After changing into my pajamas, I crawl under the covers and cuddle with my gift from Jack. I reflect back on our day, beginning to feel a bit of guilt about how little I thought about Nate. He's always on my mind, but today, there were huge spans of time when he simply wasn't. I start to feel a little sad, and hold the Hello Kitty tighter in my arms as the toy begins to giggle. I can't help but smile and laugh myself.

I think this is normal. I think I'm going to be okay.

CHAPTER 12

For the last month and a half, there have been two weekly appointments that I have penned onto my calendar and been anxious to keep. The first appointment is my therapy session, every Tuesday at two o'clock. The second appointment takes place every Friday afternoon. Jack and I have continued to spend that time together, as friends, getting to know each other.

Therapy has been wonderful and I feel a little more like myself after every session. This week's appointment was no different, but I've been issued a challenge by my psychologist. Still conflicted with the fear that starting a new relationship now may be too soon, she has encouraged me to revisit the place in Central Park where Nate and I went last year on his birthday. It is the place I feel closest to him, probably because of the pictures I have of us from that day. It's where I first told him I loved him. She hopes that I can somehow accept that he would want me to be happy, no matter what. It sounds logical... I just can't envision him ever encouraging me to be with another man.

The mild summer we had seems to be issuing a much cooler fall than I can remember in recent years. When I exit the building, I consider turning back for a jacket, but figure I'll get hot with the exercise and continue on to the park. The whipping wind pulls the leaves off of their branches, swirling them on the sidewalk in front of me. When Clara and I come here in the afternoons, we typically stay pretty close to my normal entrance into the park in case she gets tired, as she tends to do after a long day. I decide to circle the whole park for the first time in a long time.

There are times, in the midst of this park, that I don't even realize I'm engulfed in this huge city. The street noises just seem to fade away, seemingly less to do with actual sound, and more to do with the distraction of new scenery. I can get lost in this park. There had been days when I wished it would just swallow me whole.

I spot the familiar park bench, empty, inviting me to take a seat. This isn't the first time I've been back to this bench since Nate and I professed our love for each other here last November. Earlier in the year, I had spent a few mornings sitting in this very place, coffee in hand, my face lowered to the ground to hide the tears in my eyes... questions swimming in my mind. Today, my heart isn't as heavy, by now used to the idea that he is gone and accepting that there are no answers to my many questions.

It's not the first time I've been back, but it is the first time I've seen the view from this bench. Even last year, I was only looking at Nate, seeing his assurance of love staring into my hopeful eyes. The view is breathtaking. From the small hill, the park spans out in front of me. Grass brown with only speckles of green here and there, leaves flying in the gusts, ducks swimming in the rippled pond, blue with the reflection of the clear, crisp sky above. The trees stand tall, strong, orderly but without pattern. A few squirrels dart across the lawn gathering nuts and climbing the large trunks, pieces of bark flaking off every so often. One gets a little too close, stares curiously at me when I move my foot, just slightly, before running quickly away, his tail fluffed and alert.

It's the first time in a long time I've seen true beauty in the world around me. I take a deep breath, then fight the lump in my throat, angry that sorrowful emotions are beginning to overwhelm me, threatening to blur my vision with wet tears. I'm not allowed to be sad. I struggle to remember the time before Nate and I dated, when we were only friends. I didn't date often, but when I was seeing someone, he would always find some fatal flaw in him. No man was ever good enough for me... and I typically listened to him, convinced myself that his judgment of character was sound, and I would move on to the next. What would he think about Jack, though?

From what he knew of him, or thought he knew of him, I didn't think he would approve. I remember that Nate thought that Jack was taking advantage of me the night of the frat party. If Nate had known what actually happened, though... I smile to myself, my skin breaking out in goosebumps as I remember the kiss. *He's a good man, Nate. I think you would really like him. I love you so much... nothing will ever change that. But he'll take care of me, like you would have. He wants to... doesn't that say a lot about him? He knows about you. I think he accepts that a part of me will always be with you. Would you accept him, too, knowing that you both have the same ultimate want for me— for me to be happy?* I shake the tears away, swallowing hard, wanting direction... wanting to see this beautiful day... wanting to see what the future might hold for me. Overwhelmed by the sights in front of me, I thank God for this day.

There are still days that I wish that Nate would visit me again in a dream. I wish he would tell me if I'm on the right track. I wish he would give me advice. Most of all, I wish he would tell me it was okay to be with another man... to be interested in Jack. I shouldn't need his approval like this, I know. But he will always be a part of me, a part I can never forget and would never want to. I oftentimes feel damaged without him here on earth with me, but sometimes I feel whole when I realize he is always with me in spirit, and I want to keep him close to me. I'm not sure that it's good or bad to feel that way. Am I just holding on to him, to that safety I felt with him, to fill a void I'm missing in reality? A void that I could attempt to fill... Do I have to give him up to move on? Or can I separate these feelings, define a space for two different men that I care about? Love doesn't die, but people do... my love for Nate is something I will carry with me forever. And the next man who loves me— the next man I decide to love– will have to understand and accept it. Is Jack that man? Does such a man even exist?

I pray for clarity often. I pray for courage. And I pray for a man who will love me and be confident in the love I give him, even if it's not *all* of my love. I will give as much as I can... and hope it will be enough not only for him, but for me. I used to believe that Nate might have been the great love of my life... and I would dwell on what little time we had together, wondering if that was really all the world held for me. If he was my great love, we would have had more time, wouldn't we? So *was* he?

Before long, the sun sets and the lamps that are scattered in the park become the only source of light in the middle of the park. Darkness brings a chill to the air, and I decide it's time to go back to the apartment. I stop by the nearby coffee shop before going home.

I shouldn't be surprised to see her here, but the sight of Samantha nearly knocks the wind out of me. Visions of my crumpled self on the floor of the apartment after she left come rushing back... and for a second, I'm amazed and proud at the progress I've made over the last few months. I take a deep breath and smile sheepishly at her, not knowing if she will remember me or acknowledge me after the way I treated her that night.

"Emi," she says from behind the counter, kindness in her eyes and a comforting expression on her face. "What can I get you?"

"Hi, Samantha. Non-fat chai, please."

"I should have known," she comments. "That was his drink, too."

"Yeah," I remember. After she passes on my order to the barista, I hand her my debit card.

"It's on me," she says. "Do you mind if I join you?"

"Oh, um, no, not at all."

"Rob, I'm going to take a break," she tells a co-worker. When my drink is made, she brings it around the counter and leads me to a couch in the corner.

"Thank you," I tell her. "How are you?"

"I'm good," she says. "How are *you*?"

"I'm doing pretty well.... look, I'm really sorry about what happened... how you found out and how I treated you."

"Oh, my god, don't apologize," she says. "*I'm* sorry."

"You don't need to apologize either." We sit uncomfortably for a few minutes before she breaks the silence.

"He was my first love," she tells me, shrugging. "I guess I'll always feel something for him."

I smile and nod, understanding her feelings. "Of course you will."

"About a week after I found out, I went back to Marcus and talked to him for a long time. I felt so distanced from Nate, from the situation. I was sad that I had missed so much of what was going on. The way we split up was bad. I acted very childish. I was embarrassed and I really wanted to apologize to him. I needed some closure, but really didn't know anyone else who knew him... anyone who could fill in the blanks. I'd never met his mother, I didn't know any of his friends... and I knew I couldn't– or shouldn't– go back to you."

"One thing about Nate, he really did care deeply for all the women he dated," I tell her. "He fell in love easily. He thrived on being in love. You can rest assured knowing that you were very special to him."

"I know. But after talking to Marcus, I realize that you were his soulmate. I didn't understand why you were so upset– why you were in his apartment in the first place... so I had to ask someone. Nate sort of kept you from me. He'd mention you, but there were few details... like he was keeping them all to himself. Marcus said you had been a part of his life for a long time. He said that he could tell Nate loved you from the start... said that he acted different, looked different when you came around. Marcus remembers the day that he came back from some trip, to Las Vegas, I think it was? Nate dropped his bags in the lobby and went over to Marcus and hugged him, he was so happy. 'I love her,' he had told him. 'And I'm pretty sure she loves me. I'm going to marry this girl.' That's what Nate told me. He said he had never seen him so elated, it was like he was walking on clouds. And then he said he was like that every day until..."

My eyes water, a longing in the pit of my stomach beginning to resurface. Marcus had never mentioned that to me. What a beautiful story to hear... from this young girl that I had once thought was so immature and manipulative.

"Thank you so much for telling me that."

"Oh," she says quickly, "I didn't mean to make you cry."

"No, it's okay," I laugh. "I've never heard that story. I'm constantly amazed that new memories still surface... but no matter what, I cherish them all. The tears are a small price to pay for them."

"Anyway. I just wanted you to know there are no hard feelings or anything."

"Oh, same here. Thank you, really."

"You're welcome," she smiles. "I've got to get back to work."

I extend my arms to her and we embrace. "Take care of yourself."

"You too. I'll see you around?" she asks.

"Probably so." We both stand up and part ways. I walk back to the apartment grinning, imagining Nate and Marcus hugging in the foyer and letting out a quiet laugh to myself.

After taking a bath, I lie down in bed and stare out the window, the city lights casting a warm orange glow through the apartment. It's been a very Nate-centric day, and I'm positive I'll dream about him tonight. I just feel it. Maybe I'll get the visit I was hoping for.

When I awake from a very sound sleep, the bright morning sun greeting me at first sight, it's Jack that fills my groggy visions. Again, I've dreamed about *him*. Still in that area between conscious and unconscious, I roll over and smile, trying to remember the details. In hopes of continuing the dream, I try to go back to sleep.

No, I don't want to go back to sleep! It's Friday! I'll *see* Jack today. I am suddenly energized and hop out of bed. My time spent with Jack is the highlight of my week, every week. He picks me up mid-afternoon and always has something different planned each time. We've been to museums, to the movies, to tourist haunts, shopping, to various parks and restaurants around the city. Last week we volunteered with a local organization that helps children of broken homes. They had a fund-raising fair, and Jack and I worked at one of the booths on the fairway. After an exhausting day, after our shifts were done, we played some of the carnival games and noshed on junk food. Jack's high school and college baseball days helped him win an insanely large stuffed dog for me, which now has a permanent place on my bed next to the other stuffed animal he gave me on our first outing.

The dog and cat have spent significantly more time on my bed than Jack has. We have stayed true to our friendship so far, keeping any physical activities to a bare minimum. We'll hold hands from time to time, put our arms around each other... but we haven't shared any more of the kisses that make my body unsteady and my mind bewildered. Sometimes our conversations will drift to those feelings when we talk on the phone. The anticipation is growing... I'm getting more and more used to the idea of dating him every day. And as far as dating goes, I had told him early on that he was free to date other women if he felt like it... but he has made it clear that no other women interest him, and that he is committed to waiting for me. I really do feel lucky... and safe with him.

Today, it's Halloween. In his family, it's become a tradition to have his sister's family over for trick-or-treating. This year will be no different, except for a few additions. Jack has invited Clara, Jen and I to go with them. Jen, anxious to spend some time with a new suitor, declined the invitation, but I told my sister I would happily take Clara with me.

I'm anxious to spend a little time with Jack's twin sister, Kelly. My sister is an acquaintance of hers, having lived in the same area of Westchester, their kids going to the same school, and Jack has told me a lot of good things about her and her children... and I'm anxious to see how he is with them.

Fridays are my most productive day, work-wise, as I just want the hours to fly by while I wait to see him. Today is no different. I finish up revisions on two freelance jobs a week before they're due and submit them to the agency that hired me for the work. I've been much more motivated lately, and I've been getting so many offers that I've had to turn a few down.

Jen comes home around four o'clock, having waited until the very last minute to buy a Halloween costume for her date tonight. Clara is tired from the shopping trip and full school day. I help her take part of her costume off– her pink butterfly wings– and she collapses on my bed, snuggling up to the stuffed animal.

"Are you still up to going trick-or-treating tonight?" I ask my niece. She yawns but nods to me, her eyes closed.

"Just let her nap for a bit," my sister says, examining the sexy nurse costume she had purchased. "He's a doctor," she smiles.

"Clever," I comment sarcastically. I've never gotten into Halloween... I don't know why... it's just a weird holiday. "I'm going to take a shower," I tell my sister.

"You haven't been in bed all day, have you?" she asks, concerned, noticing my pajamas.

"No, just really busy with work... I was in a zone and didn't want to interrupt it," I smile at her.

In the hot shower, I get more and more anxious to see Jack. He makes me laugh, and when I'm with him, I don't have time to dwell on anything sad. I don't know if he plans for constant distractions, or if it's just in his nature to keep going, going, going... I know he said he doesn't like idle time... and that probably helps with our friendship. Idle time can lead to other things... I ponder those other things for a few minutes, feeling a flash of warmth spreading over my body.

"What time is he picking you up?" Jen asks when I come out of the bathroom.

"Five-fifteen," I tell her. "His sister is making dinner for us first, and then we'll go and beg on all of his neighbor's doorsteps."

"Make sure Clara eats something decent, okay? I'm pretty sure they just fed them candy at school today. She was super-hyper when I picked her up, and then really grumpy and tired about an hour later."

"Got it."

"And I'll pick her up after my date, right? What did we decide, nine-thirty?"

"Yeah, are you sure you don't mind?"

"She's my daughter, of course I don't mind. Plus, she has gymnastics in the morning, so I want her to get a good night's sleep."

"Okay. Well I'm sure I won't be *that* late," I tell her.

"We're fine," she says, smiling. "You're an adult, you can stay out as late as you want. Just keep your phone on you."

"I know, I know." I go to the closet and pull out some new distressed designer jeans that I bought with some extra money last week. Because they're a few inches longer than what I usually wear, I have to wear some abnormally high heels with them. I found some comfortable wedge sandals that look pretty cute with the jeans. I choose a black and white silk camisole to wear underneath a white belted jacket that I haven't worn in ages. The jacket isn't very heavy, so I hope it's not too cool out tonight. When I look in the mirror, I smile with self-satisfaction. This is the outfit... if it's cold, too bad, I'm not covering this up with a silly coat.

I wake up Clara and help her get back into her costume. I put makeup on her, which has become her favorite part about Halloween and playing dress-up. She is the ultimate girlie-girl. She puckers her lips and playfully threatens to kiss my cheek.

"Go kiss your mommy," I encourage her. "Jack should be here any minute." She runs into her bedroom and finds my sister getting ready, her costume not exactly kid-friendly, but Clara's still too young to think anything... I hope.

I answer the door quickly when he knocks, welcoming him into the apartment. I meant to straighten it up a little before he came over, but forgot. *It's not too bad.*

"Hey," he says, smiling broadly, arms outstretched for a hug. "You look great."

"You, too," I tell him. I watch him as he walks across the room, noticing how well his jeans fit him. Jen comes out of her room, her short white skirt barely covering her. I'm somewhat embarrassed by her right now. She looks great in it, but it almost seems desperate.

"Jen," he says, barely seeing her, as he walks to the window to look outside.

"Hey, Jack!" she says, clearly wanting attention. I narrow my eyes in her direction, and she retreats to her room and sends Clara out. Jack turns around, likely seeing the butterfly wings reflected in the window.

"What a beautiful butterfly!" he says as he kneels to meet her at eye-level, his tone playful.

"Thank you, Jack," my niece says shyly.

"Are we ready to go?" She nods excitedly and he looks up at me. I copy my niece's response.

"You both might need jackets," Jack says. "It's a little chilly."

"I'll be fine. And Madame Butterfly has a wrap for just such an occasion," I tell him. "Mustn't hide the wings." I wink at him, picking up the shawl.

"Of course," he smiles back.

"Bye, Jen!" I yell on my way out. "Nine-thirty, right?"

"See you then," she says.

"Nine-thirty?" Jack asks, closing the door.

"She's going to pick Clara up... isn't that when you said your sister would be taking off?"

"Oh, yeah," he says, interest piqued. We haven't been truly alone together since the night of the wedding. I simply wonder to myself if I'll be able to maintain the friend distance. I grab his hand as we follow Clara to the elevator.

"Is that a good idea?" he asks, as if able to read my mind.

"I'm not sure," I admit, shrugging my shoulders and smiling coyly. "We'll find out."

When we walk into Jack's house, the familiar smell of Italian food fills the space. He leads Clara and I into the kitchen, where Kelly is taking a large dish of lasagna out of the oven.

"You're just in time," she says.

"It smells wonderful," I comment.

"Emi, it's good to finally meet you," she says.

"You, too."

"And Clara," she adds, "you look very pretty."

"Thank you," my niece says, ducking behind my legs.

"Jacqueline and Andrew are downstairs," Kelly tells her, "with Maddie and Brandon and his friends. Do you want to go play with them while we get dinner ready?" She nods.

"I'll take you down there," Jack says, but she hangs on to my jeans.

"Let's all go," I suggest. "I'll be right back to help you," I tell Kelly.

"Oh, we've got it covered," she returns. Jack leads Clara and I downstairs into the basement. Jack introduces me to all of Kelly's kids, as well as to her oldest son's two friends. The older sister is helping the younger two color on a large piece of craft paper on the floor. The older boys are playing pool in one of the side rooms.

Clara immediately joins Jackie, who had become her friend last year at day care.

"Will you be okay down here?" I ask her. She nods, picking up a crayon and beginning to draw. Jack and I go back upstairs to join his sister. A man is in the kitchen helping her.

"Emi," Jack says, "this is Thomas, my brother-in-law." He seems to be a few years older than Jack and Kelly, probably around forty. I shake his hand, quickly recognizing him as one of the men who helped Jack when he confronted Colin... that seems like so long ago.

Jack and I set the table for four, and then put plates and silverware at four more seats at the bar. Thomas gets out three paper plates, apparently for the older boys who are going to eat downstairs.

After dinner, Thomas volunteers to do the dishes while Kelly, Jack, me and the four younger kids go trick-or-treating. The older boys, not interested in collecting candy, are watching a movie in the home theatre in the basement.

"Jacks is so nice to let the kids come over every year," Kelly says as we wait at the end of the sidewalk, watching the children and checking out all the other costumes walking the street that night. *Did she call him Jacks?* "We're pretty spread out from our neighbors where we live. Trick-or-treating isn't as much fun when you're driving door-to-door."

"I can imagine not," I agree. "Jen used to be in the same situation."

"How is she doing?" Kelly asks. The tone in which she asks the question makes it obvious that she knows about the divorce this year.

"She's great," I tell her. "She and Clara are living with me."

"And how are Chris and Anna?" she asks.

"Fine," I say, smiling. "They had a hard time getting back into the flow after two weeks in Hawaii. And Anna started a new job here in the city... they're thinking about moving to Brooklyn."

"I bet you'd like that," she says.

"Definitely."

Jack doesn't say much as we wander the streets in his neighborhood, letting his sister and I get better acquainted. She's very warm, very open, definitely suited to be a mother with obvious nurturing skills. It's easy to talk to her.

As the night wears on, cooler weather sets in, and I begin to wish that I had brought another jacket to wear. Jack, noticing that I'm cold, stands behind me and rubs my arms.

Each time we take a break from walking to the next house, he wraps his arms around me. I wonder if he can feel my heart beating faster in my chest.

"Why didn't you bring your coat again?" he asks smugly.

"Because it didn't go with this outfit," I explain, knowing it's a silly reason. "But I don't regret it at all." I snuggle further into his embrace.

After an hour and a half, Clara, Jackie and Andrew are beginning to tire and complain that they're cold, so we head back to the house to sort through the candy. After determining that the guys are watching a scary movie downstairs, we keep the other kids upstairs to go through their loot. They each pick out their favorites and do a little creative swapping, eating a few pieces while they're sorting through the pumpkins. Andrew goes to the bookshelf and pulls off a book, taking it over to Jack to read. His youngest niece and nephew take seats on either side of him on the couch, both leaning into him while he reads. Clara comes to sit in my lap in a club chair on the opposite wall while Kelly and Maddie go into the kitchen.

Clara listens to Jack's soothing voice as he reads, but she soon falls asleep, the long day finally catching up to her. I watch Jack, admiring how good he is with the children. And it's clear that they adore him. He looks up from the book and makes eye contact with me, my heart jumping a bit when he winks at me, not skipping a beat with the words since he likely has this book memorized.

The doorbell rings, waking my niece.

"I'll get it," Kelly says, walking across the room to the door. She invites my sister in, and I'm relieved that she's wearing a coat over her revealing costume. Clara hops up to greet her mom and I wave to her.

"Did you have fun?" I ask.

"Sure," she says. "I think I'll see him again." I nod. "Jack, your house is incredible," she comments, looking around the living room into the open kitchen space.

"Would you like a tour?" he asks.

"I'll take her," I volunteer. He agrees and continues reading. I show her the remaining rooms on the main floor, then take her downstairs to the basement. Jen picks Clara up and shields her eyes from the movie on the large television, recognizing the classic horror movie from our childhood years– and remembering the nightmares I used to have after seeing it. She makes a comment about the kids rooms, noticing all the toys and how nice it must be to have an uncle like Jack.

When I come back up the stairs, I ask him if it's okay to show her the top floor, his bedroom.

"Sure, it's fine," he says. We go up to the top level, and I can tell my sister is very impressed with the room.

"Okay, this is gorgeous," she says, taking a seat on his bed and bouncing lightly, "and comfy." She smiles, raising an eyebrow at me.

"I wouldn't know," I tell her as I roll my eyes at her.

"You're telling me, all this time you two–"

"No!" I say, blushing.

"Nothing?"

"No... I'm not... I don't know."

"Emi," my sister looks at me in disbelief, "has he kissed you again?"

"Ewww..." Clara interjects.

I shake my head. "It's not like that. We're just friends."

Her eyes widen as her jaw drops. Eventually, she stands up off the bed and walks away from me to the bathroom. I follow her curiously, until she abruptly

269

turns around to face me.

"Emi, remember our conversation about all the good guys being taken?"

"Yeah..."

"Well one of them is downstairs, waiting for you... and I swear, if you don't do something soon, some other girl is gonna come along–"

"Alright, stop it," I discourage her. "This is my business, and we're not discussing it. Come on, let's go back downstairs," I suggest, suddenly uncomfortable with my sister being in his private space. Jen huffs, obviously annoyed, but follows me downstairs.

By the time we get to the main level, Kelly and Thomas are gathering up all of the kids and their things, saying goodbye to Jack. Kelly gives me a hug goodbye, saying she hopes to see me again soon.

"Well, I just hope there's a reason we're leaving you two alone," Jen whispers to me, too quiet for anyone else to hear. "He won't wait forever."

"Goodnight, Jen," I whisper back. Jen and Clara hug both Jack and I before descending down the steps to her car. Jack follows me back into his home, closing the door softly behind him, slowly locking both deadbolts. I'm suddenly nervous to be alone with him. It feels very different than it did the last time I was here with him, on our first date. So many things have changed since then. It seems as if many walls have been torn down, as if most of our secrets have been exposed, and accepted.

"Wanna watch a scary movie?" he suggests.

"Horror movies really freak me out," I tell him. Anxious to have a reason to curl up tightly in his arms, I answer, "Let's go." He smiles and takes my hand, leading me first to the kitchen to grab some wine, and then taking me downstairs to the home theatre. I take off my jacket, wanting to be more comfortable.

"You're going to be cold," he tells me, noticing my thin camisole, smiling. As I start to put my arm back in my jacket, he stops me and takes it from me. "I'll keep you warm." He grabs a blanket, and instead of sitting on the couch, we take our place on two reclining movie-house chairs, joined together. We recline back, and he puts his arm around me.

When the movie begins, we both predict what's going to happen, the story line obvious, following the plot of all other horror movies before it. We add our own silly dialogue, laughing together, until the first truly scary part happens, at which point I jump and immediately bury my head into his chest. *Exactly where I want to be.*

He laughs at my reaction, pulling me closer to him in an embrace with his other arm. I lightly scratch his chest through his shirt with my fingernails, peeking at the television but ready to duck back into him at a moment's notice. He puts his hand on mine, clasping it loosely, stopping me from scratching him.

"What's up, Emi?" he asks after turning the volume down.

"What do you mean?" Propped up on my elbow, I look at him intently, trying to read him.

"I mean... you arranged for us to be alone... here... what are you thinking?"

"I don't know," I say honestly.

"Because I've been avoiding this exact scenario."

"For the friendship?"

"Yes, for the friendship," he answers with a slight laugh. "Per your wishes. I don't trust myself alone with you."

"I know." He waits for me to continue. "I don't want to lead you on, Jack. That's not what I'm meaning to do. I've been wanting to be closer to you... I guess I'm testing the waters a little. I can't hide the fact that I'm incredibly attracted to you. I feel like I've been denying obvious feelings for you for weeks, and it's exhausting. The restraint and the waiting. And I just want you to kiss me again. I want that so badly."

"I'm fine waiting, Em, you know that," he begins. "But having you here, like this, with you touching me, like this... it's a little tempting."

"I guess maybe... it's meant to be tempting." *I want this. I do.*

"Meaning... what?"

"Meaning... please kiss me."

"Are you su—" I don't let him finish his sentence. I can't wait any longer to feel his lips on mine, so I lean into him, kiss him. It's even better than I remember it. He takes control, gently guiding me back into the chair, his body now leaning into mine. He strokes my cheek, his touch electric on my skin, then kisses it. The next kiss is on my temple, then my ear, which is my weakness. I smile and sigh heavily, causing him to back away, look at me curiously.

"Was that a good or bad sigh?" he asks, tucking my hair behind the other ear.

I blush and laugh. "Very good," I tell him, encouraging him to continue.

His kiss travels from my ear to my neck. My arm around his neck, I run my fingers through his hair as he slowly moves one of the spaghetti straps of my shirt off of my shoulder, his finger continuing down the length of my arm until his hand finds mine. He entwines his fingers into mine, both of our hands resting just below my stomach. He kisses my collarbone softly, then my shoulder. I release my hand from his and begin to unbutton his dress shirt. Once unfastened, I reach under his t-shirt, gently scraping his torso until I arrive at his muscular, smooth chest.

His hand clutches my hip bone tightly as he positions one of his legs between mine. As his thigh makes contact, feelings awaken in me that I hadn't expected to return so easily. I inhale sharply, surprised. I take my hand from his chest and lift his head back up. His eyes, cautious, meet my gaze. He lowers his face to mine, watching, possibly waiting for me to signal to stop. I should. I can't. I want to feel more. I want more.

When his lips finally meet mine, I angle my body toward his, putting my leg on top of his and pulling myself closer into him. I can feel him against my body, leaving me no doubt that he wants more, too. He kisses me more deeply, holding my head to his. I put my hand back under his shirt, this time massaging the firm muscles in his back as my hand tries to grasp him, clutch him, bring him even closer into me. I move my body against his leg and try to get his shirt off of him. I want to feel his warm skin on mine. We separate so that I can take both of his shirts off, exposing his tanned skin and toned abs. While my hand explores his body, he puts his hand up the back of my shirt to unfasten and remove my strapless bra, leaving my camisole in place. Tentatively, his hand travels around my body, first holding on to my ribs, but finally touching my breast, gently. I look into his eyes, my heart racing and body aching, and I see something in them that makes me pause. He removes his hand, putting my shirt back into place and rubbing my back.

Hopeful, I make a suggestion. "Do you want to go upstairs?"

He smiles faintly at me, the look in his eyes concerned. I sense that he is stopping me from going any further. I drop my eyes, not wanting to stop, but knowing immediately that I will not have him tonight. He lifts my chin up, sitting up slightly to press his lips against mine once more.

"Emi, I would like nothing more than to make love to you right now."

"I want you to," I plead.

"Really? Is this what you wanted to happen tonight?" he asks. I think about his question. It's not. I had wanted to kiss him, only kiss, to feel that amazing feeling again. It was just so easy to get lost in that, get carried away. I shake my head and roll off of him onto my back. He leans back over me, his hand traveling down my torso, resting on my thigh... dangerously close... I can tell he isn't completely set in his decision, either. *I hadn't planned on this, but what if?*

Just when I think I may be able to persuade him, he pats my leg playfully and puts his dress shirt back on, leaving it unbuttoned. I touch his chest one last time, dejected, but knowing deep down that we're doing the right thing by waiting. I do want to be sure about myself, about him, about where I want things to go with him... before we take things any further. I've never been one to take sex lightly. I sense that he isn't one, either.

Still, knowing this is the best decision, I feel rejected. I totally put myself out there for him. How can he just... stop? Is he not attracted to me? Is he not sure about me? I honestly believed that everything hinged on my decisions... that he would move forward when I wanted to. A part of me wants to... he senses that... but a part of me has doubts.

He obviously senses that, too.

Damn him and his perceptiveness... and his conscience. What man says no to a woman he really likes who's throwing herself at him?

Jack. That's what man. He's an inherently good man, and although I thought I was in control of this situation, his decision to be level-headed and thoughtful about moving forward reminds me that he is in charge. Deep down, I do know it's for the best.

But I have to wonder: is he just doing this for me? Or is something holding him back, too? Does he have fears like I do? Is he feeling uncertain about us? Because I feel positive that he and I will be good together, that we'll work out. With Jack, my fear is simply losing another lover.

"Are you okay?" he asks me, his voice startling me, bringing me out of my thoughts.

"I'm okay," I answer, nodding, after a few moments of silence. I sit up in my chair and find my bra. "Excuse me," I smile, retreating to one of the bedrooms in the basement and closing the door. I put my undergarment back on and check my hair in the mirror. I touch my swollen lips, missing him already.

He knocks on the door.

"Come in," I laugh, a part of me hoping he's changed his mind. He enters the room, now fully dressed. His hair is disheveled, something it never is, and I want so badly to make it even worse. I hear music coming from the main room in the basement: my favorite singer, her sultry voice encouraging us both back into each others arms.

"I love this song," I tell him. "How did you know?"

"You left your iPod on the table," he says. "I just hit play."

"I must warn you, this music has a tendency to make me do foolish things... keep in mind I was listening to it earlier today, and look what happened."

"It wasn't foolish," he assures me, walking slowly toward me, each step in time with the song's beat.

"Bad timing, then?" I ask.

"I don't think I'd go that far, even," he says. "I want you, Em." We each put one arm around each other and begin dancing. My other hand rests on his chest, feeling his rapid heartbeat. He cups my face into his hand and kisses me again.

"I'm confused," I whisper. "Do you want me, or not?"

"Definitely want you," he answers, "very badly. I want you to know that. I just don't think tonight is the right night for it."

"Well then stop seducing me," I plead, only half-joking. "It's been awhile, you know."

"I assumed that," he says. "I don't want that to be the reason why we sleep

274

together, though."

"It wouldn't be the reason," I say, still dancing with him. "You know how I feel about you."

"Actually, Em, that's just it. I'm not sure how you *do* feel about me. We've never really talked about it. I know when I kiss you, it does something, physically, to you... which is great, don't get me wrong. I feel it, too."

I think about his words and consider the truth behind them. I feel like we've had conversations about this, but he's right. I haven't told him how I feel about him. He's told me how he feels... and hell, he's waiting for me to get my life together. What assurance does he even have from me?

"Wow, Jack," I begin. "First of all, if you want me to talk sensibly to you, you've got to turn this music off." He takes my hand and leads me to the home theatre room and turns the volume down. "Secondly, let's go somewhere with light," I comment. "It's too private, too secluded, too 'I want to take advantage of you' down here."

"Well, where to?" he asks.

"Bedroom?" I joke.

"Kitchen it is." I groan but follow him upstairs. "Do you like cake?" he asks as he reaches into the refrigerator. I take a seat on a barstool on the opposite side of the kitchen island.

"What kind?"

"Spice, I think. Kell brought it over. Would you like some?"

"Cake... you... cake... you..." I ponder the choices. "Alright, cake." He cuts one slice of cake and puts it on a plate, setting it halfway between us on the kitchen island with two forks.

"Milk?"

"Why not?" I smile, picking up a fork and stabbing a corner with a lot of icing. He pours two glasses of milk and brings them over. "This is really good," I say, wishing I had swallowed the bite I had taken before talking. He laughs at me and nods.

"Kelly does this for a living," he says. "Pastry chef."

"She's in the right business." I take another bite. He watches me in silence for a few seconds.

"You were going to talk sensibly..."

"Yes," I agree. "Jack, I think you are amazing... and you're right, something happens to me physically when you kiss me, or even touch me. I told you, I've never felt anything like that with anyone else. You're incredibly smart and driven. And caring and considerate. And you're beyond handsome, too much for your own good, I might say... except that you're completely humble and have no ego whatsoever. You put others before you... you care about those kids... and me... and you're patient and tolerant. I could think of a thousand reasons why we should be together. I know in my heart that we are good together... but..."

"But?" he asks.

"But there's a big reason why we shouldn't... and that's the part that's holding me back, the only part."

"And that is..."

"Nate," I tell him, swallowing hard. He looks confused.

"Nate?" He stares down at the granite countertop. "I still can't compete," he mumbles.

"Are you kidding?" I ask him. "Because it's not a competition. There are no winners or losers..."

"No, I know, Emi, but can you ever... *love* me... like you loved him?"

"*Love* him," I correct him. "I will always love him, Jack. It's impossible for me to stop just because he's not here."

"I feel a little like a consolation prize," he says. "I don't like that feeling."

"I wouldn't like it either," I explain. "But this is my challenge. To prove to myself that I can love like that again, without reservation or hesitation... and to prove to you... that it's you I can be with."

"And how's that going for you?"

"It's a challenge," I shrug my shoulders. "I think I'm going about it backwards."

"What do you mean?"

"Well, I know it's you," I tell him. "Please don't doubt that. I just hope that I can like you... enough for *you*... and the one thing that holds me back isn't

Nate, as a person, it's what happened to him. Losing him... the thought of ever going through that again makes me really cautious. I can feel myself holding back... and that's not fair to you."

He comes around the counter and stands behind me, rubbing my shoulders. His hands stop briefly as I feel him kiss the back of my neck.

"This is about... living..." he speaks softly, carefully. "About being alive, and feeling alive... and sharing your life with someone."

I nod, knowing where he's taking the conversation.

"And I feel so alive with you, Emi." *I know exactly how he feels.* "I wouldn't forego that feeling for anything in the world. There is nothing better than being in love." He kisses my neck again. "There is nothing better than being in love... with you."

My stomach drops, my heart stutters. *He's in love with me.* A part of me is excited beyond belief... and the other part is completely frightened. I knew he cared about me. I guess I even knew he loved me. But he's never said it. And I don't think I can say it yet.

I swivel in the barstool to face him, taking him by the collar and pulling him toward me. We share another incredible kiss, and for a moment, I've actually forgotten that he might be expecting a verbal response from me. I compose myself with a few small breaths. "Jack," I say, my eyes avoiding his, "I'm not ready."

"I didn't think so," he says, kissing my forehead quickly and picking up the empty plate and putting it in the dishwasher. I watch him intently, trying to read his expression, but he keeps his face angled away from mine while he immerses himself in household chores. "Listen," he says, "I've got an early morning tomorrow, and it's getting pretty late. Are you ready to go?"

Okay, so, I'm not ready yet, but I'm not ready to go home, either... He's clearly upset, put out with me and my response. My sister's words echo in my mind. *He won't wait forever.* "Alright," I say, unsure.

"I'll go grab your jacket," he says, leaving me sitting alone in the kitchen. The last thing I wanted was for us to fight tonight. The last thing I wanted to do was hurt him. I feel horrible, but have no idea how to make it better. I put my

277

head in my hands while I wait for him to return. "Ready?" he says, holding my jacket out to help me put it on.

"Jack–"

"Emi, it's okay," he says before I can try to smooth things over. "I'll wait." He still looks disappointed. "Come on." I follow him quietly to his car. *How long will he wait? I can't leave him hanging.*

"So, what are you doing tomorrow?" I ask to break the silence on the way to my apartment.

"I'm actually helping Marie move," he tells me. He stares straight ahead, and I'm sure he can feel my stare boring into him. *Marie? I didn't know they still talked.*

"Oh," I say, unable to hide my surprise. "Okay." More silence, the rest of the way home. He pulls up to my building and lets Marcus open the door for me. He normally gets out to open my door. "Please don't be mad," I plead with him.

"I'm not mad, Emi," he assures me, his tone still short, aggravated. I put my hand on top of his, rubbing his fingers with my thumb. He picks up my hand and kisses the back of it slowly. "Good night." I had wanted him to *really* kiss me, but I guess we were finished with that, for tonight at least.

Marcus helps me out of the car, and I tell Jack good night before closing the door.

Once upstairs, I quietly change into my pajamas and wash my face, not wanting to wake my sister or Clara. I grab a bottle of water before heading to the bed, pulling my computer into my lap to surf the web for a little bit. My mind is still churning, processing, and I know I won't be able to go to sleep for awhile.

Marie? Really? He hadn't mentioned her in all the times we've hung out... it seems strange... like he's hiding something. Surely he's not seeing her again... right? He had told me he wasn't interested in anyone else... but have I been making him wait too long? He reiterated it tonight that he would continue to wait... but what if he's just referring to a relationship? Maybe he's sleeping with her. Maybe that's why it was so easy for him to stop things tonight.

No way. I can't let myself think like this. And so what if he is sleeping with her? I told him he could see other women until I made up my mind. I can't be jealous. I can't be mad. But the thought of him with someone else is driving me insane. No, we're not "together" but I consider myself seeing him exclusively. I don't want to be with anyone else.

I don't want to be with anyone else. That's it, isn't it? That's really all there is to it. I want to be with him, and only him. I have been worrying about feeling whole first, so I can love him enough. But the truth is, he makes me completely happy... and I don't feel like I'm missing any part of myself when I'm with him. I may be missing the part that Nate took with him, but there is a whole other level of satisfaction, pleasure, happiness that comes when I am with Jack.

But the thought of losing that, too, is just too much to bear. I couldn't live through loss like that again. But I think I'm in too deep at this point. My heart stops at the realization. Here I have been putting off being with him while I make the conscious choice of putting myself out there to be hurt again... and in the process, this process of becoming his friend, considering the options, kissing him... I've already made that decision. Losing him to anything, anyone, would be too much to bear. Not just death... that's just one way of losing him. The thought of telling him, 'No, Jack, I don't want to see you anymore because I can't give you enough,' makes me sick to my stomach. Thinking of him with Marie makes me angry. It hurts me no matter what.

These are variables I can control, though. I can tell him that I do love him, enough. I can tell him that I don't want him to see anyone else. I can give him all of myself, and avoid this inherent loss. The only thing I can't control is... death... and although it's inevitable, it's unlikely to happen soon.

Unlikely, but not impossible. God, I'm torn. I don't ever want to lose him.

I stop staring at the computer and shut it down, feeling as if something is resolved in my mind. A quiet knock on the door startles me.

After checking through the peephole, I open the door for Jack, putting my finger over my lips and nodding to the room where Clara and Jen are sleeping. He walks past me, across the room, to the window. He sits down on the love seat, and I follow him.

"You left this," he says, handing me my iPod.

"Thanks."

"Listen, Emi," he says, holding my hands in his.

"No, let me apologize first," I interrupt. "You've been so patient with me, and I think I took advantage of you tonight. Once you kissed me, I just wanted more. I had asked you to wait, and then I sort of moved forward without telling you. I'm sorry."

He sighs heavily. "I don't mind," he says. "Really. I want you to be sure about me. I just want what you're feeling to be about me and not about what you've been missing with him gone."

"Wow, is that what you think is going on?"

"Some days," he says. "I really appreciate that you confide in me your deepest feelings... I'm just not sure if they'll ever be for me, instead of him."

"They will," I say, then shake my head. "No, they *are*. They're just different... It's complicated." I don't know what I'm saying... I'm probably making this all worse. "Jack, about Marie. I understand I said you could see other people, but honestly, I'm not okay with that anymore. Maybe that's not fair of me... but I can't stand the thought of you and her together."

"It's not *fair*, Emi," he says, "if you're not going to decide to commit to a relationship with me."

"I know." I know I'm wrong to even bring it up.

"It's not *fair*, but it's such a *non-issue*... I'm not seeing her. She lost her job and has to move, and she really doesn't have any guy friends to help her. I had planned to tell you about it tonight... but the night didn't exactly turn out how I expected it to. In fact, you caught me completely by surprise, Emi."

"I know."

"You have to know that you are the only woman I want to be with," he says. "I want you, *so badly*, you have no idea how difficult it was to say no to you tonight... and I sense something's still holding you back, but damn it, Emi... I'm ready. And I get that us sleeping together is a turning point for you. I understand that. I respect that. And it's not something I would take lightly, either... but it's a natural progression of things, and I think we're there. I love you, Emi. I *want* you that way."

I nod. I want him, too. "Sometimes, I just feel like I'm being pulled in a million different directions– by my own emotions. In any given hour, I go through grief and sadness and happiness and love and hate and loss and sorrow and desire and regret and indecision... and if I stop long enough to focus on one of them, I'm okay. I can digest that emotion, commit to it, act on it, and then move on. But most of the time, it happens so fast that I can't quite grasp on to one long enough to really feel it. I know that probably doesn't make sense."

"Yeah, Emi, it makes sense, but it sounds like you know what you have to do. Take control. Let yourself... feel.. *something*... for me."

"I'm trying," I explain. "I am."

"You have to start putting the past behind you. I want a *future* with you. Don't you see that?"

"Yes," I whisper, a lump forming in my throat.

"I want you so badly, Emi, in every possible way. You can understand that, can't you?"

"I can."

"Well, do you feel the same?" His frustration is palpable, seems to be filling all the air around me, taking away all of my oxygen.

My heart pounding, my eyes watering, I barely manage to whisper my answer. "Please don't rush me, I'm just not ready..." When I blink, a tear falls down my cheek. His shoulders slump, his head bows to the floor.

"I shouldn't have come over." He begins to walk toward the door.

"Jack, why are you doing this?" I cry to him, following him, holding on to the back of his shirt. He turns around in the middle of the living room and pries my hand away, dropping it quickly.

"Good night, Emi." He doesn't even look at me when he says it.

I watch, frozen, as he continues to the door, unlocks it, and shuts it quietly behind him. "Jack..." I squeak out, my voice stolen by the sobs that have settled in the back of my throat.

What have I done? Why did I let him leave? The one person that has brought me true happiness this year just walked out the door, and I didn't stop him. I couldn't. I can't let him go. I want him just as badly. I want to be ready. I want to be enough for him. I want him back.

I rush to the door and fling it open, ready to run after him... but here he stands, leaning against the door jamb, his eyes sad.

"Don't go," I whisper, relieved to see him.

"You didn't lock your door," he informs me.

"Oh," I respond. "Is that why you stayed?"

"I don't want to go, Emi. I didn't want to leave you. I got half-way to the elevator and turned around."

"Then please, stay. Stay until we can work this out. Please don't leave me, Jack. I can't bear it." Another tear falls.

"God, Em," he exhales, nearly falling into my waiting arms, his head leaning against my shoulder, defeated. "Don't cry. I didn't mean to do that to you. I want to be the one who takes those tears away... I don't want to be the cause of them."

"Jack," I sigh against his neck, more tears falling at his statement. "I'm sorry."

"Don't apologize," he says. "I shouldn't have pushed like that. I just want to be able to... show you... how much I care about you. I know this must be difficult for you... I have no reference point, Em. I want to understand you."

"You do," I tell him, taking his hand and leading him back into the apartment. "You really do get me." I close the door softly, and he locks it up behind us. He follows me back to the love seat.

"I haven't always," he laughs, sitting next to me. "You continue to be a challenge to figure out..." He smooths my hair down and I nuzzle my head into the warm palm of his hand. "It's a good thing I like challenges."

"I'm sorry," I tell him, taking both of his hands into mine, my eyes pleading with his.

"It's been worth every second, Emi. You're complicated, but the more I learn about you, the more I want you." He kisses me slowly. "I want you to want me like I want you. I want you to feel what I'm feeling... I just want to share this with you."

"I do want you," I tell him. "Don't think that I don't. I just want to be sure... that I'm ready..." *Ready for what? I'm ready to have sex again. I want that. I'm ready to move forward with him. I know that. To tell him I love him? Why is that so difficult? Is it Nate that's stopping me? Can I leave him behind? Is that what's keeping me from being ready?* I sigh in frustration. "You are *way* too good for me."

He shakes his head and rolls his eyes, disagreeing. "So where does this leave us?" he asks, standing up and looking out the window. "Do we forget tonight happened and refocus our efforts on the friendship?"

"I certainly can't forget it," I tell him. "Maybe pretend it didn't happen, but forgetting it is out of the question. Nothing that happened tonight is forgettable."

"Is that what you want to do then? Just pretend it never happened?"

"Yeah, I don't think that's possible either. I don't guess there's any going back."

"Maybe there is no going back... but I guess we shouldn't go *forward* quite yet, either... until you're sure."

"I'd probably agree with that. When I'm thinking sensibly, that is." I stand up and walk behind him, putting my arms around him, my hands up his shirt to feel his firm chest, and leaning my head into his back. I lightly scrape my nails over his warm skin. He shivers and holds my arms tightly in place.

"You can't keep touching me like that if you're not ready, though. I honestly can't take it." I can hear the serious undertones in his voice. He turns around in my arms, facing me, his eyes warning me, but his smile, soft and sweet.

"Like this?" I whisper, massaging his back, pulling my body closer to his, leaving no space between us. His arms envelop me and our lips meet at once, eager, thirsty. A small whimper escapes my lungs. I pry my mouth away, our foreheads touching and eyes gazing. "Well, *you* can't do *that*," I set my own rule out loud but know deep down I'd never want him to stop.

"What, kissing me makes you irrational?" He brushes his lips against mine and I attack them, wanting more. He moves his hands to my hair, weaving his fingers through it, his need evident in the way he grasps it. Our breaths are quick when we break away.

"If I say yes, does that mean you won't do it anymore?"

"Do you not want me to?" His voice aches with need.

"No, that's not what I want at all." Quickly, he grabs my waist and presses tighter against me, letting me feel his desire against my stomach, and resumes our kiss after whispering something like "Thank God." *How did this conversation turn in to... this? Fuck it, who cares?*

He picks me up as I wrap my legs around him and lock my feet together. He turns back around so he's facing the window, presses my back up against it, my fingers frantic in his hair.

"So all of this is off limits then. We're agreed?" he whispers in my ear hurriedly before kissing, then sucking, my earlobe.

"Fuck, Jack," I gasp as he props me up, rearranges me a bit so I feel him where I want him most.

"Mmmm... say that again." His tongue traces my collarbone.

"Fuck. Jack." My shallow breaths only allow one syllable at a time. "Mmmm..."

"That is such a turn-on, Em." His eyes penetrate mine, my heart spluttering in my chest.

He shifts his lower body again, slowly, carefully studying my reaction. "Oh, god. Jack," I manage to say although he's completely taken my breath away. I barely have time to see his lips form into a smile before they crash into mine once more. He turns us around, our tongues tangled together, and walks back over to the small sofa, laying me down on it. He kneels on the floor next to me, unbuttoning my flannel pajama top quickly. His eyes pause, taking in the sight of my nakedness for the first time.

"You're beautiful," he says, seemingly entranced, cupping one of my breasts in his hand. I grasp his hair in my hands as his lips and tongue gently survey the other.

As his left hand slowly travels up my leg, I raise one knee and angle my body toward him, wanting him to touch me. He doesn't keep me waiting, his palm rubbing gently, my body moving in rhythm. I take his right hand in mine and weave our fingers together, squeezing tightly as a flash of heat spreads across my body. He increases the pressure, speed.

"Oh, my god, Jack... oh... oh..." His lips cover mine, likely an effort to mask my unsteady outbursts. I hold his head to mine tightly, pulling his hair and moaning into his mouth. "I'm–"

A cough comes from the guest room. Both of our heads jerk to look at the closed door. *Now? Really?*

"It's Clara," I whisper, both of us stilled and silent, holding our breaths, as another cough follows. He turns back around, his amorous eyes begging permission for more. His thumb traces my bottom lip. I lick my lips, my curious tongue wanting another taste of him.

"I don't want to leave you like this, Emi," Jack says quietly, our breathing resuming together before he takes my breath away again with another desperate kiss.

"Jack, we can't," I try to stop him. "Jack," I say again when he keeps going. He finally sighs against my breast, sneaking in a few more lingering kisses before he climbs onto the couch next to me. He reluctantly buttons my pajama top.

"I know," he tells me, his eyes warm and understanding. My gaze gets lost in his. Clara coughs again. "What are we doing?" he asks, running his fingers through his hair.

"I don't know," I laugh.

"What do you want to do?"

"You should probably go," I tell him.

"I know," he laughs. "I will." He smooths my hair, tucks a few strands behind my ears. "I mean about... us... this..."

I shrug and shake my head. "I don't know."

"I think there's only one thing to do... until you're sure that you're ready."

"What is it?" I ask.

"How about we don't put ourselves into situations that could lead to this... no more alone time..."

I ponder his suggestion. "But you'll still kiss me?" I flirt as his hands grasp my waist beneath my shirt and he stares intently into my eyes. "Like this?" We kiss again.

"Don't start that again," he warns. "But yes, just like that," he says, smiling.

"Just not in a setting like *this*." He smiles and stands up, holding out his hands to help me up.

"Okay," I agree. "So when can I see you again?"

He weaves his fingers in between mine and caresses my thumbs with his. "Can't wait until next Friday?" He kisses me sweetly.

"God, no, can you?"

"Not after that. I just want to see more of you now." I catch his double entendre. "Why don't we see if Chris and Anna want to go out next week? I haven't seen them at all since they got back from Hawaii."

"Perfect," I agree. "I'll call them in the morning and let you know when. What time will you be done tomorrow?"

"Hopefully early afternoon," he says. "You know, I could just stop by on my way back to the house."

"I'd like that."

He picks our hands up and kisses both of my thumbs as he walks backwards toward the door. "Will you be alone?" he asks, suspicious.

"I will not," I tell him, jutting my lip out in a pout.

"Do that again," he dares me, and I comply. His lips capture my bottom one, his tongue tracing it lightly.

"Okay, stop," I laugh, pushing him against the door.

"Sorry," he smiles sheepishly. "I couldn't resist. So you won't be alone tomorrow?" His question is plaintive, but teasing. I shake my head, careful not to pout this time because his kisses are driving me insane at this point.

"Then I'll be over as soon as I'm done." He kisses my cheek. "Sleep well, Emi."

"Sweet dreams, Jack."

He smiles an impish grin. "Of you..." he adds. "Thank you for giving me something to dream about." He kisses me once more, my knees growing weak, before he leaves. After locking the door, I can feel myself blush again, a big smile breaking across my face as I think about the way he touched me... about how close we were... how close I was...

In hopes that I may catch another glimpse of him, I look back through the peephole. I can see the neighbor's door across the hall and nothing else... I turn around to walk away when I hear a faint tapping on the door.

I rush back, probably making too much noise as I anxiously unlock the door.

"One more thing," he says as he leans in the doorway.

"Yes?" I grasp the ends of his shirt, holding him close to me.

"Please tell me the second you're sure." He holds my head steady while he looks deep into my eyes. "I want you more than I've wanted anything in my life." The sweetest of kisses follows. "And I know you feel the same way." He pulls away to see my reaction, which is my natural blush and a stubborn smile. "Just let me know when you figure that out." He kisses my forehead and turns around, leaving me staring down the hallway, my eyes following his every movement.

I lean, weak, against the door frame. When the elevator doors open, he finally looks back at me, putting two fingers up to his lips and blowing me a subtle kiss before disappearing from my sight.

CHAPTER 13

I'm running late to the restaurant, having changed clothes about ten times trying to find the perfect outfit. I wanted to find something that would tease Jack just enough... but I didn't want it to be obvious that that was my plan. I finally decide on a lightweight button up silk blouse with a corduroy jacket over it... and I purposefully leave the top three buttons undone. If I lean over just right, the new pink bra I bought earlier in the week peeks out. The airy skirt I selected barely flirts with my knees, and my high-heeled knee-high boots were chosen to deliberately draw attention to my legs. I pull my hair back and tie it loosely, tendrils not quite long enough to fit in the hair ties hanging casually on each side of my face. I put on minimal makeup, knowing that he likes me without it. I finish off the look with a little mascara and light pink gloss.

Our romantic relationship has been just that: *ours*. We have not invited friends or family into the mix yet, not wanting any pressure from over-eager siblings or parents. We want to take our time getting to know one another, at our own pace. Or rather, at *my* own pace. We aren't ready to show physical affection to one another in front of people we know, still keeping a little distance between us. We've chosen to keep the details of our relationship as private as possible since Chris and Anna's wedding. It helps that Jack isn't too big on public displays of affection, either. If this works out, though, he'll just have to get over that. He's been doing pretty well so far.

Since Halloween last week, we've seen each other every day but one. We've been meeting for dinner and spending the evenings together. We've gone for walks, gone to movies... and every night ends with more than one amazing kiss at my front door. We had considered outing ourselves to Anna and Chris tonight– after all, they would naturally be the first to know– but we both decided that it was too soon.

"Sorry I'm late," I announce to Jack, Anna and Chris when I show up.

"Emi, you look great!" Anna exclaims. "I've missed seeing you!"

"Hey, sis," Chris says, hugging me.

Jack eyes me from head to toe and smiles slyly as he stands up to pull out my chair for me across from my brother and sister-in-law.

"Emi," he says politely. We had made a deal tonight. After a phone conversation filled with sexual innuendos this afternoon, we had challenged each other to go the entire night without any physical contact whatsoever. I expected it to be hard. And a little awkward. It already was... and I already wanted to break the rules at one glance. His hair was slightly messy, and he hadn't shaved. He was wearing the jeans I had complimented him on a few weeks earlier. He knows what I like. *He is playing the same game I am playing.*

"Touché," I whisper to him, carefully keeping my distance. He winks and smiles at me.

"I'm going to go grab a drink at the bar, Emi, would you like something?"

"Sure, how about a cherry vodka sour?" He raises his eyebrows, grinning.

"Of course," he sighs. "*Cherry*. Vodka. Sour. Got it."

"Thanks," I say pertly.

"So?" Anna asks, anxious. "How are things going with you two?"

"Okay, I guess," I tell her with a smile and a shrug.

"Jen says you've been seeing a lot of one another lately," Chris adds suspiciously.

"We're just hanging out, that's all," I say casually. My phone vibrates in my purse. I pull it out and notice a text from Jack. "Sorry," I tell my brother and his wife, reading the message.

"You look incredibly sexy tonight."

I smile to myself. "It's Teresa, we're supposed to meet up later," I lie. "Just a sec."

I text back. *"What's with the scruff? You know I can't resist the scruff! Gah! It's like a magnet for my hands, you know that!"*

"Yes," he responds quickly. *"I do know that. Dare ya."*

He sits down next to me before I can respond, setting the drink in front of me. "So, tell us all about the honeymoon," Jack says, inadvertently (but thankfully) cutting short the conversation Anna had started. "How was the resort?"

The conversation at dinner stays focused on Chris and Anna and all the tourist-things they did in Hawaii. Anna passes her camera to us and lets us look at pictures. Jack is holding the camera between us, thumbing through them as we both look at the display, still careful not to touch. He is taunting me, though, trying to angle the camera certain ways so I'll try to grab it from him, accidentally touch him.

I keep my hands to myself, though... and begin to scratch my leg at the hem of my skirt. I continue to carry on the conversation with Anna, not missing a beat. My hand moves closer to my body, slowly, taking the hemline of my skirt with me. I hear Jack inhale between his teeth as he sees my motion out of the corner of his eye, still trying to look at the pictures as he pulls the camera closer into his lap to mask where his eyes are drawn. Finally, my fingers scratching my upper thigh lightly, I feel his hand discreetly pressing down on top of mine. I don't look at him, but can't fight the smug smile from spreading across my face.

After dessert, knowing that I won't be going home with Jack and wanting to– badly– I leave before everyone else, using Teresa as my excuse. Even though Jack already lost the challenge, I just wave goodbye to him after hugging my brother and Anna. I feel like we made it through dinner without raising any suspicions.

I ponder actually calling Teresa to see if she wants to meet up, but decide against it, not wanting to be turned down once again. Ever since Bradley moved in with her, she spends all of her time with him. They might as well be an old married couple... but good for her. It's about time she settled down with someone.

As soon as I get home to the empty apartment– Jen and Clara were staying with our mother tonight– I head to the jacuzzi with a glass of wine for some much-needed alone time.

Feeling strangely smug and happy, and a little buzzed after another glass of wine, I decide to put on my new baby-doll nightie to sleep in. As I turn off the lights and crawl into bed, I hear a light scratching on the door. I flick on the small lamp on my night stand and pull on my short silk robe and my slippers, knowing exactly who is on the other side of the door.

Keeping the chain fastened, I stand behind the door and peek through the opening.

"Not nice," he greets me, smiling.

"I never claimed to be," I tell him, unchaining the door and opening it, revealing my robed body to him in the light from the hallway.

"Now you're *really* not being nice," he says, eyeing my attire.

"One more thing," I tease him.

"What would that be?" he asks, walking toward me. I stop him a few steps in, my hands on his firm chest.

"They're not home," I nod to Jen's bedroom and look at him wistfully. "You can't be here. You know the rules."

He puts his hand to his chin, rubbing the scruff in thought. "Yeah, but I need to sit down for a few minutes. I had a little too much to drink," he says, brushing past me and heading to the couch. I close and lock the door, taking a deep breath, feeling his pull, his desire, and wanting the same... but so unsure, still. I walk to the middle of the living room and stand across from him, fidgeting. He can't keep his eyes off of me.

He stands up and comes to me, his hands running down my arms to still me. He takes the ends of the belt from my robe in his hands. His eyes linger on it before they meet mine, questioning me. "Plus, I've already broken the rules tonight," he says. His glance asks for permission. I hold his stare, watching him, don't stop him. He slowly unties the belt and opens up the robe a few inches, revealing the nightie beneath.

"What is this?" he says, sighing, sounding defeated. He puts his forehead on mine and rests for a second, his lips so close. The pull to his unshaven chin is too much for me to resist, and I touch it lightly, rub my thumb over its rugged texture.

"I wasn't expecting you," I whisper to him. "I was just going to bed... to sleep..." My heart races as I see the lust in his eyes. I recognize that look from Halloween, realizing I'm at an even worse disadvantage tonight. Then, his thoughts were fairly clear– even when my intentions weren't. Tonight, we've *both* had a little too much to drink and we are completely alone. All night.

"I am so attracted to you, Emi," he says, removing the robe and tossing it onto a nearby chair. The baby-doll shirt hangs above the top of my thigh, revealing just a hint of the matching silk panties beneath. "You've got to be kidding me," he says, pulling his head back to scan my entire body. "How am I supposed to not want you, when you stand in front of me, like this?"

"I never said you shouldn't want me. I just don't think you can have me... yet..." He leans in slowly, kisses me softly, his hands on my neck. My body, awakened by his touch, begins to operate on its own, driven by my own longing. I hold on tightly to his shirt, then tentatively untuck it from his jeans, my mind losing the battle with my heart.

"Don't think... yet... it sounds like you're still not sure." He pulls down one strap from my shoulder and kisses it as I move my hands to his hair, running my fingers through it, messing it up the way I like it.

"That's exactly right," I tell him. "I'm not sure." I stare intently at the buttons on his shirt, unbuttoning each one methodically.

"Why aren't you stopping me?" he asks, kissing my other shoulder and then moving his lips to my collarbone.

"I don't know," I whisper, pulling his mouth back to mine.

"Why are you helping me?" He shrugs out of his dress shirt revealing a thin t-shirt underneath, then runs his hands down the length of my body, kneeling in front of me. His hand on the back of my calf, he leans in to me and kisses the scar on my knee, a slow kiss that doesn't miss a single inch of the permanent mark left there by the accident.

He looks up at me, proceeding with caution. I smooth his hair down and swallow audibly, smiling softly. He lifts my top a few inches and kisses my stomach.

"I don't know," I sigh.

His fingers trace the elastic of my panties, and he slowly turns my body, kissing my waistline, until my back is to him. Still kneeling behind me, he puts his hands on my left ankle and drags his fingers up my calf, over my knee, lower thigh, upper thigh. I gasp quietly as his thumb brushes against me. I feel him kiss my lower back as he positions his hands on my right ankle and recreates the sensation on the other side of my body. Again, his thumb grazes me, lingers there. I feel the pulsating grow throughout my entire body.

"Jack," I whisper as I look at him over my shoulder. He gazes headily as he begins to stand up. His hands grip the hem of my top as his lips find mine, gently brush against them. Still watching me, he begins to lift my shirt over my head. I raise my arms, willingly, leaning back into his body, as he slowly feels his way down my arms. He kisses my neck with a soft moan as his right hand takes pause on my breast, massaging it tenderly. His left hand continues down my body, lower. I stop his hand from reaching beneath the silk even though I desperately want him to touch me. He sighs when his fingers feel my reaction to his foreplay through the fabric.

I take both of his hands into mine and turn myself around to face him, exposing my nearly-nude body to him, presenting myself to him. With my hands in his, he steps backwards to the couch, sitting down, pulling me into his lap. He grasps my waist and holds me still while he kisses my neck, then moves his lips to my breast. He skims my nipple with his tongue before taking it into his mouth, sucking lightly, eliciting an involuntary whimper from my lips. He looks up at me and smiles, moves his hands to either side of my face and kisses me passionately. I shift slightly in his lap and feel his response to me through my thin underwear. I move my hips, pressing against him.

"Oh, god," he groans into my mouth. "You are so sexy, like this. Your hair," he says, running his fingers through it. "Your eyes, your lips. Your lips are so perfect. Your kiss..." He mumbles as we kiss again, more, still, the pace quicker, more desperate. "Are you still unsure?" he whispers to me, anguish in his quiet voice.

I pull away slightly, biting my lip, considering his question as thoughtfully as I can with my clouded judgment. Desire in his eyes, his mouth swollen, yearning for mine, I nod my head and press against him, harder.

"Mmmm..." he responds to my motion. "Yes, you're unsure?" he waits for clarification, his thumbs lingering on my ribcage, rubbing circles. I long for his hands on my breasts again, give him permission by moving them there. "Or yes, you're ready?" he smiles, reading my actions as the answer he was hoping for.

I nod again, still in a haze, still moving over his body.

"Emi," he says, stopping my motion. "Please be clear with me. Which one is it? Because if you're not sure, you have *got* to stop doing that." He smiles, pleading, pushing a strand of my hair out of my face. His hands press into my thighs.

I look down in between us, distracted too much by the hopeful expression on his face. The fact that I can't answer him says it all. His fingers under my chin, he lifts my head back up.

"I love you," he tells me, and my heart stops, a strange deja vu playing in the recesses of my mind. "Let me show you." He kisses me again, and I'm almost willing to let myself live in this moment with him. His kiss does that to me.

One transcendent kiss... that later makes lovers...

"No," I whisper to myself. My eyes immediately begin to water, my thoughts drift suddenly back to Nate, replaying in my mind the moment when he first voiced those words to me, as well as the various occasions he had told me he loved me, many times in this same position on this very couch. *This couch!*

My skin begins to crawl, and I shiver at the thought of him seeing this happen in his apartment, on the couch that he bought. I close my eyes, releasing the tears onto Jack's awaiting thumbs.

"Not here," I choke out to him. "Not yet."

"I know," he says, pulling me into his chest and embracing me tightly. "Shhh..." he soothes me. He picks up my robe and drapes it over my shoulders. "But Emi," he says, pushing me away from his body so he can communicate clearly to me, "I *do* love you."

I nod again. I *do* believe him. After we talk for a few hours, Jack feels okay to drive home, but tells me he's not comfortable leaving me alone tonight. Always happier in his company, I let him stay, eventually going to sleep in his arms on the couch.

~ * ~

"Did you do what I asked?" Jack asks when I call him a few days after Thanksgiving.

"It's noon, and I just woke up. So, yes." He had told me last night that he made plans for us. He requested that I sleep as late as I possibly could.

"Good," he says. "Now get up and get ready."

"What am I getting ready for?" I whine, still groggy, but still excited to see him today.

"I told you, it's a surprise. Just dress casually... something comfortable. And *please* bring a jacket..."

"Yes, sir. Do I need to bring anything else?"

"Your license."

"Am I driving somewhere? Because, Jack, I don't like to drive. I barely remember how, it's been so long."

"No, you won't have to drive."

"Will I be getting carded somewhere?"

"I believe it's happened before. Especially if you choose to wear your hair in those two little ponytails... which, by the way, you're more than welcome to do." I roll my eyes at the soft "mmmm" I hear through the phone.

"What is it with guys and pigtails?"

"I don't know what you're talking about. Come on. Get up and get ready! Do your hair however you like," he concedes. "Just be ready by two. Can you do that?"

"Yep. Getting up now. Comfy. Jacket. License. Two. Is that all I need to remember?"

"You forgot pigtails," he says seriously.

"Really?"

"I'm just kidding. But you know they drive me crazy. I guess it's really up to you whether or not you want to drive me crazy today."

"I guess you'll know when you pick me up. I don't know that I'm feeling pigtails today."

"It's fine, Emi. I can tell you're procrastinating now."

"I'm up, I'm up!"

"No, she's not up!" Jen yells from a few feet away. I glare as she giggles.

"Get up, please? I'll be there in two hours."

"Bye," I groan, stretching in the bed. A wide grin spans across my face. *Of course I want to drive him crazy today!*

"So what are you doing today?" my sister asks.

"I still have no idea."

"That would drive me nuts... do you ever get to pick what you two do? It always seems like he's making all the plans."

"He does make most of them. I guess I have veto power... but he's never had a bad idea," I shrug. "Thanks for letting me sleep in, by the way. I didn't hear you and Clara at all this morning."

"I'm surprised, she was a little fussy getting ready. I did bribe her with doughnuts, though. That seemed to do the trick."

"Doughnuts?"

"There's a glazed one in the kitchen for you."

"I'm up," I smile, bounding out of bed for a breakfast treat I rarely let myself indulge in. Not a bad way to start the day.

I take my time getting ready, lingering at the closet for a good ten minutes before picking out a couple of different outfits to try on. I nix the skirt right off the bat after Jen points out an unsightly bruise just above my knee. Jeans it is. I flip-flop between a sweater or layered t-shirts. Sweater is more practical... layered t-shirts are *infinitely* cuter. Easy decision there.

"Are you sure you and Jack are just friends?" my sister asks me.

"Yep," I tell her as I pull on my shirt, my back to her to hide the blush I feel on my cheeks. "Why?"

"You've been with him nearly every day. And you're being a lot more choosey in what you're wearing for him today."

"He's fun to hang out with. And I'm not dressing for *him*. I just feel better about myself when I look decent."

She's smiling when I turn to face her. "I'm happy to see my sister coming back into her own. I've missed you, Em."

I slip on a pair of sneakers, still looking at the heels out of the corner of my eye.

"Heels," Jen suggests.

"He said to dress comfortably. What if we're hiking or something?"

"I would think hiking would be a good recreation for you to exercise your veto power, Miss I-Don't-Like-To-Sweat-and-I-Don't-Like-Bugs."

"True," I ponder. I wouldn't, though. He's been so excited about whatever we're doing... I'd sacrifice a little sweat and a few bug bites for him.

I keep the tennis shoes on, but decide to let him tell me which ones would be better based on our activity.

I curl my hair before pulling it into two low ponytails at the nape of my neck and smile to myself in the mirror. I put on a little lip gloss and press my lips together, anxious to feel his on mine. I kill time while I wait for him by picking up the apartment.

Jen answers the door when he arrives.

"Jennifer," he greets her with a hug. He's wearing his dark jeans that fit him perfectly in all the right places and an untucked light blue shirt. *God, what that color does to his eyes. Beautiful.*

"Hey, Jack. In case she doesn't tell you, she hates hiking."

"Jen!" I scold her. "I don't hate it..." I'm not convincing.

"We aren't going hiking, don't worry." He smiles slyly, and I imagine he's taken note of my hair. I can't help but smile back.

"Can I wear heels?" I ask, picking up the other option.

"There may be a fair amount of walking involved. I would probably keep the tennis shoes." I notice he's wearing some, and he rarely does, so I keep mine on.

"Got it. I'm ready," I say, grabbing my purse.

"What were the four things?" he asks me.

"Comfy. License," I hold up my bag. "Two... oh, right." I return to my closet and pull out a lightweight belted jacket and pull it on. "Now I'm ready."

"Alright. Let's go. Bye, Jen."

"Bye, Jen," I tell my sister, hugging her. "See you tonight."

"Umm..." Jack begins. "Yes, see you later."

He waits until we get into his car before he pulls my head to his by my pigtails and kisses me. *"That's* what I like about them."

"Ahhh..." I say. "Good to know."

We drive through Queens outside the city. "This is an airport exit only," I caution him.

"Is it?" he asks, continuing to drive straight ahead.

"Okay, now what's going on?"

"We are going to the airport," he states.

"I figured that out. Why are we going to the airport?"

"To listen to some music."

"At the airport?"

"Of course not at the airport, silly. We're flying somewhere to listen to some music."

"Jack," I say, concerned. "I didn't pack anything."

"You have everything you need. We won't exactly be staying overnight."

"What do you mean, 'won't exactly?'"

"I mean we're going to a concert tonight, and we have an early morning flight... no hotels, Lord knows I couldn't be trusted in a hotel room with you..."

"Jack," I blush. "Whose concert?"

"I've told you too much already."

"Will you at least tell me what city?"

"Chicago. Have you ever been?"

"Yes, as a matter of fact, I have," I tell him as he parks his car. Teresa and I had gone to a magazine convention there a few years ago. "So we're pulling an all-nighter, essentially," I state.

"We are." He takes his leather jacket out of the backseat and puts it on. "So I hope you're rested."

"Sweet!" I squeal. "How fun!!"

"I'm glad you're excited," he says, pulling me into a hug. A concerned look spreads across his face as he takes the fabric of my jacket in his hands.

"That's the best you could do?" he asks.

"What?"

"This jacket is paper-thin."

"It's fine, I have long sleeves on," I argue. "This jacket *makes* this outfit. Admit it."

He laughs to himself, running his fingers through his hair, considering my clothes. "But there's supposed to be a cold front coming through tonight. You're going to freeze."

I just shrug, uncaring. "Guess you'll have to let me wear yours."

He sighs heavily, then kisses me deeply, toying with my hair again.

"Or you could just do that," I whisper to him. "That works." He leans me against his car and does it again, this time his hands leave my hair and travel down my body, gripping me tightly just below my breasts.

"I can't wait to be alone with you again, Emi." He kisses my neck. "I can't stop thinking about you, about those nights at your loft. You have the most amazing body, did you know that?"

"No," I blush. "So you just want my body, huh?" I ask sarcastically.

"God, no, Emi," he says, serious. "I want all of you. I love everything about you."

"Thank you," I tell him. "You're not too bad yourself." *I want to swallow the words back in no sooner than they left my lips. Just tell him you love him!*

"Let's go," he says, taking my hand and walking a pace in front of me, leading me into the airport.

Once we get to our terminal, he goes to one of the shops to get something to drink. I consider getting out my phone and checking to see who is in concert tonight in Chicago, but I decide to let it be a surprise.

Jack comes back with two sodas and a plastic bag.

"Whatcha got?" I ask.

"Hold these," he says, handing me the drinks. He pulls out a red knitted cap with the I heart NY logo on it and pulls it over my head, tucking my bangs to the side. "And..." He holds up a black zippered hoodie with a matching logo on it to me. "Here."

"I'm not wearing that," I laugh.

"It's the best one they had, I swear."

"I don't care. It's about ten sizes too big."

"Ten? Don't offend me. It fits me."

"Well, then, you can wear it..." I tell him, shrugging.

"You are so impractical and stubborn sometimes!" he says, frustrated. "You'll change your mind."

"I don't think I will... but thanks for the hat. It's cute."

"You're cute in it. Just let me know when you get cold."

"Never," I smile defiantly. He puts his arm around my shoulders as we find a seat in the terminal.

Halfway through the flight to Chicago, I attempt to discreetly get the sweatshirt out of the bag that Jack put under our first-class seats. He had scoffed at me when we first sat down after I asked him if this was the most expensive date he'd ever taken a girl on. I mean *first class?* Flying to another city to see a concert? *Really?*

"Let me help pay you back a little," I had offered.

"I'm sure we can work out a trade of sorts," he said suggestively, making me blush.

He gives me a smug look as I unzip the jacket and lay it across my chest. "Shut up," I murmur. I tuck my knees into my chest and cover them up as well.

"I didn't say anything," he says.

"Thank you," I tell him quietly. He takes his seatbelt off, pushes the arm rest up and scoots closer to me, rubbing my arms vigorously to warm me up. As I look at him to smile, his face inches closer, teasing me. My heart begins to pound in my chest as I anticipate his kiss. He licks his lips and closes his eyes at the very last second. I pull his hand underneath the sweatshirt and place it on my breast. He inhales quickly, and I can feel his lips form a smile.

"Emi," he whispers, taking my breast into his hand and massaging. "Someone might see us."

"I know," I quietly say back to him, lingering on the last word with a sigh. He moans softly into my mouth, his hand applying more pressure. I adjust my hand beneath the jacket deliberately, drawing his attention to it. I move it down my knee, down my thigh, into my lap. His other hand dips under the garment to feel where mine has gone. This time he groans, taking my hand into his.

"Stop, please," he begs. "God, what has gotten into you?"

"I'm not sure," I tell him. "We're taking this trip together... you look amazing tonight... I get to spend the night with you... we're alone."

"We are not alone," he reminds me. "The flight is full."

"But we don't know these people," I say. "Who cares?"

"I care," he tells me. "I care because I know I can't have you tonight, and you're making me want you even more than I already did before we got on this crowded, claustrophobic, cage-of-an-airplane." He moves my hand from my lap and replaces it with his. "God, Emi. Stop me, please?" The lustful look has returned to his eyes, and I realize I'm pushing him too far. I entwine my fingers with his, holding his hand close to my stomach.

"You're right, I'm sorry," I tell him. He closes his eyes again, pulls my head to his with his free hand, and kisses me sensually.

"No, I'm sorry," he says. "I can usually control myself better than this. It's got to be your hair." He shifts back over to his chair and fastens his seatbelt, letting go of my hand. He's quiet as his breathing returns to normal. I rest my head on my knees, looking at him.

"We're going to see the Decemberists," he says, not meeting my bedroom eyes as I try to distract him again.

"Really?" I grab onto his arm, shaking it. "Seriously?"

"Yes," he laughs. "Is that good?"

"I love them! Did you know I love them?"

"You had their entire discography on your iPod, so I had a feeling you did. This theater they're performing at is supposed to have great acoustics... it was sold out, you know."

"But you got tickets..."

"Of course I did. All I could get was a suite, actually... which right now, I'm thinking, is not such a good idea."

"Well," I tell him. "It will be hard to get my attention away from them. I've always wanted to see them... and honestly, most of their music is not... how should I put it... romantic?"

"Okay, that's good. I was afraid this was going to turn into a very long night for both of us."

"Oh, there's still time," I tease him. He rolls his eyes and laughs.

I didn't think he'd be able to pry me away from the band, and he wasn't. He didn't have to. From the moment the lights went down, I just wanted to be near him, to hold him, to kiss him. In the middle of the second song, we retreated to the couch in the private suite and stayed there until the concert was over and all the fans had piled out. We kissed intensely and touched each other innocently– most of the time.

"I think you got me here under false pretenses," I tease him as we're leaving the auditorium. "You said there was going to be a concert tonight. You just wanted to lure me into a private room so we could make out."

"If only I was that cunning," he says. "Hey, Emi," he adds.

"Yeah?"

"I hear they're playing an encore at that hotel down the street."

I giggle as we wait on the sidewalk for a cab. The cold front is moving in, and I shiver at the burst of wind that hits me. He angles me toward him and pulls down on my cap, straightening out my pigtails. He then zips up the huge jacket and pulls the hood over my head. I push it back down, not wanting to hide my hair, my secret weapon, the thing that drives him crazy... and I like it when he's crazy with desire for me.

"So this is supposed to be the best diner in the city," Jack says when we're seated in our booth. We sit across from each other, but lean in closely, holding hands across the table.

"What can I get you two to drink?" the waitress asks.

Jack looks at me for my order. "Just a hot tea for me."

"Make it two. And a couple glasses of water."

"Coming right up."

"So, what time is our flight home?" I ask.

"Five AM. I figure we should head to the airport around three. That gives us about four hours to kill."

"Hmmm," I say flirtatiously, "what shall we do?"

"Eat," he tells me. "Do you like to bowl?"

"I love to. Why?"

"There's an all-night bowling alley down the street."

"Cool!" I say, smiling. "I'll smoke your ass in bowling."

"I'd watch it, Miss Hennigan. I'm pretty good."

"You don't know what you're getting yourself into, Mr. Holland." I stick my tongue out at him as the waitress brings our drinks.

"Did you know what you wanted to eat?"

"I'd just like a bowl of fruit," I order.

"Seriously? We've come to the best greasy spoon in town and you're getting fruit?"

"What?" I shrug. "Okay, and a side of bacon."

He laughs at my request. "I'll have the number three, please."

"Got it," our waitress says, gathering our menus.

"What's the number three?" I ask him, curious.

"Pancakes, eggs and bacon. It comes highly recommended."

"Pancakes?"

"Mmm-hmm... you can have some."

"Maybe just a bite," I answer.

"So, what does your family do for Christmas?" he asks me after a short lull in the conversation.

"Nothing outlandish. We split the holidays... Thanksgiving at one parent's house, Christmas at the other's."

"So you're at your Mom's?"

"Yep," I answer. "What do you normally do?"

"Typically, I'll celebrate with Kelly and her family, but this year, they're going to Thomas's parents house. My parents are pushing for me to visit them, but I'm not sure I want to go to Wyoming. I thought about flying them out, but since they left New Jersey, they really have no desire to come back. They like the country life."

"What about your brothers?"

"We just can't seem to coordinate our schedules. I thought Matty and Lucas might come, but they just decided to go to Hawaii instead. I'd choose Hawaii, too."

"Why don't you go?"

"I don't know," he hedges. "I thought I might like to spend some time with you instead. Do you think you could fit me in sometime?"

How awesome that he wants to spend Christmas with me. My thoughts wander to us, sitting by a tree next to the fireplace at his house, colorful Christmas bulbs providing the only additional light in the room. In my vision, we're both undressed and exhausted, wrapped in a warm blanket. I wonder if I will be ready by then, hope that I will be. I feel like I might be right now. "Of course."

"Good," he says. "I'll work around your schedule. You just let me know." I nod as our food arrives. I immediately wish I had ordered the pancakes. I look up at Jack with pleading eyes. He douses them in syrup and takes a bite, smiling wickedly at me.

Two can play that game. He has something I want, I'll show him something he wants. I pick up a piece of watermelon with my fingers and take a slow bite. I cock an eyebrow at him.

"Want some?" I ask.

"Sure," he tells me. I place the rest of the fruit in his mouth, purposely leaving my finger in there a little too long. He bites me playfully, then closes his full lips around my finger, a small kiss.

"What are you doing, Emi?" he asks me softly.

"I don't know what you're talking about," I reply, fluttering my eyelashes innocently.

"Sure you don't. Did you want a bite of this?" he asks, motioning to the pancakes. I nod slowly as he cuts into the stack and mops up some of the syrup. I lean in to take the bite off of his fork, my mouth open, tongue poised, my eyes never leaving his. My lips close around the fork, and I lick the remaining syrup from them as he pulls the fork away.

"Was that sexy?" I ask as I raise my hand over my mouth, full of pancakes, at which point we both start laughing.

"It was until then," he tells me. "My turn." I pick up a grape and bite it in half, making obvious gestures with my lips, drawing his attention to them. I place the other half on his waiting tongue, and he kisses my finger again.

"Let me try some more pancakes," I say. We continue this, back and forth, until our food is gone. By the end of the meal, I'm completely turned on, and judging from the suggestive glances he's making at me from across the table, it's obvious that he is, too.

"Let's get out of here," he tells me, leaving cash on the table. He takes my hand and I follow him out of the restaurant.

As soon as he starts down the stairs leading to the sidewalk, I pull him back. "I have to kiss you," I plead. He turns around, our faces inches apart as he stands two steps below me. I lean in and pull his head to mine, my lips greedy, his completely willing to give me everything I want.

I squeal, although my lips don't leave his, as he picks me up and carries me the rest of the way down the stairs. When he sets me down on the sidewalk against the brick wall of the building, I take his hands into mine, keeping us close, and pout at him. "I'm not finished yet," I whisper.

"Not here," he tells me. Even though it's the middle of the night, there are still quite a few people on the busy Chicago street.

"Well, where?" I ask, impatient.

"Let's go bowling," he suggests. "You're making me crazy, Emi, with this... like this."

I stand on my tiptoes to meet him again, and he obliges with a deep kiss. "I kinda wish you had gotten a hotel room," I tell him when we part for a breath. He pulls away immediately, possibly considering it.

He looks into my eyes, tugging gently on to my hair to keep me close. "I think it's safe to say this night is ending up very differently than what I had planned it to be," he mutters quietly to me. "This was just supposed to be two friends, going out of town to a concert and hanging out all night... on neutral territory... where they can't get into any trouble."

"And Emi," he adds. "You're getting yourself into serious trouble." He steals my breath again with another kiss, this one more like our first one, the one that drove me crazy with unresolved desire back in college... the same one he eagerly gave me on the night before Chris and Anna's wedding. Sweet, soft, but full of passion.

"Can we?" I ask him, my lips still on his.

"Can we what?"

"Get a hotel room?" I suggest. He finishes the kiss, then sighs.

"Oh, god... really? That's kind of tacky, Emi."

"What's tacky about me wanting to be with you?" I ask, hoping to convince him. "I don't care."

"You care," he says. "I care. I care about you too much for that. We're not going to go get a room for a couple of hours."

"That's not what I meant," I laugh. "Let's just stay in Chicago for a few days."

"I have meetings in New York in the morning, Emi," he tells me, disappointed.

"You have to work tomorrow?"

"I do," he laughs.

"You're going to stay up all night, and be okay to go to business meetings in the morning?"

"I am."

"Why did you plan this, tonight?"

"I didn't pick the date... I picked the concert, which happened to be on this date, this particular Tuesday night... plus, I thought it would be safe for us to avoid exactly what you're suggesting... because we agreed to not put ourselves in these situations until further notice."

"Maybe this is 'further notice,'" I suggest.

"The fact that you just said 'maybe' makes me think it's not."

"You don't want this?" I ask him as his fingers trace patterns on my back.

"It should be painfully obvious how badly I want *you*, Emi. But you shut me down last time we let it go a little too far, remember?"

"I know," I admit.

"What's changed?"

"I don't know," I tell him. *We're not in my apartment, where I still have so many vivid memories of Nate, that's what's changed.*

"Why are you ready now?"

"I don't know," I repeat.

"I want you to *know*," he tells me. I can't hide my disappointment from him. I can't *not* feel rejected.

"Where's the bowling alley?" I ask him, walking down the sloped sidewalk.

"Hey," he says, grabbing my arm and pulling me back to him. "Don't be that way."

"Well," I counter, "be a little impulsive."

"I *am* being impulsive," he states. "I'm making out with you on a crowded street, in front of throngs of people. I don't do that. I'm a planner, Em, and I certainly didn't plan this... so don't say I'm not being impulsive. You bring out a completely different side to me."

"Do you not like being this way?"

"I love it," he tells me. "I love being with you. Everything looks brighter and feels... deeper... when I'm with you.

"But come on, Emi, when I think about our first time together, it's not in some hourly-rate motel... I want you, but I don't want to degrade what we have. It deserves something special. That's all I'm saying."

"Well when you put it like that," I concede. "Okay."

"Okay?"

"Yes, okay," I repeat. "Wanna get your ass kicked now?"

"You're asking for it..."

"Yes, I am," I flirt, taking his hand and pulling him with me toward the large glowing bowling pin in the distance.

Even after our conversation, neither of us can keep our hands off one another at the bowling alley. They have late-night bowling where all the lights are out except for some lines of neon outlining the lanes. We somehow finish the game, even though most of my time is spent in his lap at the scoring table.

On the flight home, Jack takes my hand in his as soon as we take off. I share my earbuds with him and turn on one of my favorite playlists. We both recline our seats back, and within a few minutes, he falls asleep listening to the music.

I want to be with him so badly, and I want it to be special, too. It will be, I know. He deserves the best night of his life... what man waits this long for any woman? And why me? Am I really worth that much to him? I smile, realizing that he thinks so, anyway, and that's really all that matters. I start to imagine different scenarios. At his house... maybe. At my apartment... no, for various reasons. In his car? No, not special. Maybe a trip somewhere, a hotel celebrating a special occasion? Christmas? He likes to plan... he seems to like to be in control of situations, and that's fine.

My stomach gets butterflies and I feel my face blush as I imagine us undressing one another. I feel a little pang of guilt all of a sudden. Would I be able to separate this experience from my encounters with Nate? Would I be sad? I couldn't be sad. Jack deserves the perfect night, period. It would really need to be about him. It would need to be about me thanking him for his patience... for caring... for being sensible... and for loving me even when I couldn't love him back.

Whatever I did, I would have to make sure I was ready to commit to Jack, one-hundred percent, before moving forward. Before taking this next step, I would have to be able to tell him I loved him, too... and mean it with every part of my mind, body and soul.

I wasn't sure I could say that now. I know that I'm falling in love with him. I think it's safe to say that I've already fallen. There just can't be any element of doubt in mind, because once we take that step, we will be moving forward. I will be moving on.

I just hope I can wait until it all comes together, because damn it, he is so incredibly sexy, his kisses so generous and tender, I can only imagine what it will be like to make love to him. *Ugh! I want him now!*

I nudge him softly just before we land.

"Did you sleep?" he asks, half-awake.

"No."

"Why not?"

"I just couldn't stop thinking about... you know... you."

"Mmmmm," he says drowsily. "I couldn't stop dreaming about you. What a relief to see you next to me when I opened my eyes."

"Did you dream I left you?" I ask.

"No... but I was worried you wouldn't be here when I came to."

"I'm here," I tell him, leaning over to kiss him and squeezing the hand I'd been holding for over two hours. I miss it when he finally lets go as the plane rolls to a stop.

As soon as we're in his familiar car, I turn the seat warmers on and close my eyes. Exhaustion is finally setting in.

When I wake up, I look around cautiously, not recognizing my surroundings. It's pretty dark, but I finally realize I'm in Jack's bedroom, in his bed. The curtains are pulled all the way shut over the patio door, obscuring any sunlight if it was trying to come in... and I know it's got to be out there by now. I finally gather enough courage to look beside me, realizing the other side of the bed is still made up. I check under the covers to see I'm still completely dressed in my jeans and t-shirts. On the night stand sits my watch and the rubber bands I had in my hair last night.

How he managed to put me to bed without me waking up is beyond me. I didn't realize I was that tired...

I stretch my muscles and take a deep breath, grabbing my watch to check the time. Two o'clock. *Two o'clock? Shit!* Jen must be worried sick! I tear out of bed in search of my purse. I flip on the lamp and look everywhere in the bedroom, but find nothing. Bathroom... nope. I open the door, wondering if Jack is downstairs. He had meetings this morning, but it's well into the afternoon now. I pass through the living room and his office, both quiet and empty. A pillow and blanket are neatly placed on one side of the couch. Jack's not in the kitchen, either, but my purse is, and my phone is sitting on the counter next to it on top of a note from Jack.

Jen called. She's quite worried. I assured her that you were fine, but she insists you call her as soon as you wake up. I'm at my meetings... I'll call you later. P.S. I enjoyed every second with you last night and this morning. I blush and smile simultaneously before quickly dialing my sister's number.

"Emi?" she picks up before the call finishes the first ring.

"Jen, I'm fine," I tell her.

"I know," she sighs. "Jack took the brunt of my anger and frustration when he called me earlier."

"You didn't–"

"I did... he was very apologetic. It's really hard to be mad at him."

"Yeah," I admit, feeling my heart flutter a little.

"So you're gonna tell me you're still just friends?" she says.

"I am," I lie, wanting selfishly to keep mine and Jack's activities to myself.

"You spent the night with him, though..."

"I did, but nothing happened!"

"Whatever!"

"Seriously!" I confirm. "He slept on his couch."

The line goes silent.

"Jen?"

"I'm ashamed of you," she says, obviously joking.

"Shut up."

"What's holding you back?"

"I don't want to talk about this, Jen."

"I think he really likes you, Em. Don't lead him on," she warns me.

"I'm not," I tell her. "I'm just not ready yet. But he's great."

"He is," she says. "But he can't kidnap you anymore without one of you letting us know what's going on."

"He didn't kidnap me–"

"Emi, Chris and I were worried sick. And neither of you would answer our calls. We thought something had... happened."

"I'm sorry," I tell her sincerely. It was selfish of me, I realize. With my history, it's only natural that my family *would* worry. "For both of us. You're right. We should have let you know. But maybe it's time you don't worry like that anymore."

"We'll always worry, Em. You're our baby sister. You've been through too much."

"Alright," I tell her, feeling bad about what we'd put them through. "I won't do it again."

"Okay," she says, content. "Will I see you tonight?"

"Yes, I'm on my way home now."

I text Jack quickly before leaving. "*Enjoyed your bed... maybe you'll join me there someday. ;)*"

"*Definitely,*" he responds.

Later in the evening, Jack stops by with two pizzas and some wine as a peace offering to my sister. Jen, Clara, Jack and I sit around watching children's Christmas specials on TV, enjoying each other's company. Thankfully, Jack is easily forgiven.

CHAPTER 14

"It can't happen tonight," I tell Jack as soon as he closes the driver side door. He pauses before putting the key in the ignition.

"Ahhh... okay," he nods, taking in my words but avoiding my eyes.

"Does that ruin your plans?" I ask. "I mean, I packed things for an overnight stay, like you asked... but I just don't want it to happen tonight."

"Umm... no, it doesn't ruin my plans. Not *all* of them anyway."

"I'm sorry," I tell him. "I'm, like, ready, I think," I begin, "but today just isn't the right day."

"You don't have to explain–"

"I want to, though."

"Okay, go on," he says as he pulls out of the parking lot. "Wait, before you start... do you mind *sleeping* with me tonight?"

"Sleeping," I clarify. He nods again. "Sleeping is fine. Making out is even okay. I just don't want it to go beyond that. Not tonight. You have to promise me."

"Emi, don't worry. Have I ever pressured you? Ever?"

"No," I say. "But there's a little voice in the back of my head telling me it's time. That you shouldn't have to wait any longer."

"I will, though," he says. "If that's what you want, I will. I promise, Emi, this night is yours. However you want to spend it." He looks over to me briefly and smiles. "Now what happened last Christmas?" he asks.

"How do you know it was last Christmas?"

"Because, when we talked last night, you told me it would all depend on how today went... and I just assumed that the date was somehow important to you from last year."

I frown a little, but take a deep breath. "Last Christmas," I sigh, "is when I found out I was expecting. I've been trying really hard to not get lost in those feelings. It was a horrible night. I was all alone when I took the test... and I was so scared and so angry at him and at myself."

I inhale deeply again. "Like I said, I've been trying to not feel that all over again. But I ran by the drug store this afternoon to pick up a few things, and there was this display of tacky plastic ornaments... but among those ugly cheap things was one pretty silver ball with a pink bow on top. It said, 'Baby's First Christmas.'" I duck my head into my hands and frustratedly fight back the tears. *Fuck, I really didn't want to do this today... I won't do this...*

Jack pulls over to the curb and turns his hazard lights on. He puts his hand on my leg and rubs circles on my knee with his thumb.

"I'm sorry, Emi," he says quietly.

"No, *I'm* sorry," I tell him as I wipe my eyes, the tears not making it to my cheeks. I clear my throat, but feel a little triumphant over my emotions. "I'll be fine once we get to your house. I promise." I smile bravely at him.

"I hadn't planned on taking you there, Em," he says.

"Oh," I say, confused. "Well, wherever... where are we going?"

"I'm afraid if I tell you, you'll think I'm expecting something, but I swear to you... it's fine."

"Crap," I say, realizing I really *had* ruined his plans for our Christmas night.

314

"What did you do?"

"Just in case... you know. I said it should be special, so yes, I was sort of planning for something to happen–"

"Where, Jack?" I press him for more information.

"The Ritz-Carlton Suite at Battery Park," he blurts out quickly, looking at me unsure. "It has incredible views of the harbor and the Statue of Liberty."

"Seriously? The Ritz? That's too expensive, Jack," I plead.

"I know the manager," he tells me, giving me a sideways glance.

"Still... it's too nice. Hell, I feel awful," I tell him.

"Please, don't, Emi. Really."

"Can we do it another time?" I ask.

"Well, the room's already paid for tonight, and my things are already there. I mean, not that it matters, but it would be a nice opportunity for both of us to leave our normal lives behind for a night. Maybe take a break from some of these memories... if you want..."

"But I feel bad," I whine.

"I swear, Emi, you won't when you get there. I checked it out this afternoon, and it's spectacular. You'll be so caught up in the view and service and food, you won't even know I'm there."

"Right," I laugh. "Are you sure you're not disappointed?"

"All I really wanted was to spend Christmas with you. We're doing that. If you want to go to my place, we can. If you want to go back to *your* place, we can. But I guarantee, if we're just going to be sleeping tonight, there is no better place in Manhattan to sleep than this suite. I promise. It's the best room in the city where you don't even realize you're still in the city."

"If you're sure."

He turns off his hazards and checks the mirrors before pulling back out into the street. "I am sure." He smiles, taking my hand and kissing my palm.

The manager of the hotel, a business associate of Jack's, comes to greet us at the check-in counter, and leads us up to the top floor of the hotel to our suite.

"Jack," he says, "don't hesitate to call the front desk if you need anything. And Emi," he says, bowing his head to me, "it is such a pleasure to finally meet you. He's told me so much about you," he adds. My heart palpitates as I laugh softly, looking at Jack as he nods to his friend.

"Thank you," I say. "It's nice to meet you, too." The manager opens the door for us, gesturing for us to go in.

Bewildered, I nearly stumble into the room that's at least twice as big as my apartment. The wall facing us is lined with windows that overlook the harbor, just as Jack had promised. A fully decorated tree is tucked in the corner with presents stacked beneath it. *I hope they're just decorations, because this room must have already cost him a fortune.* The sky is rich with reds and oranges and purples as the sun is setting. It's spectacular. A young man carries my suitcases in and sets them into the bedroom. My eyes follow him into the room, and I notice the lush king-size bed, covered with at least ten pillows, beckoning me.

"I feel so bad," I repeat to Jack once we're alone.

"Emi, don't say that one more time. Please."

"Okay."

"Thank you," he says, pulling me into him. "Merry Christmas, Emi. I hope this is the first of many."

"Wow," I say, my heart nearly full. "Me, too, Jack. Merry Christmas... and thank you for this... for everything you've done."

"You're welcome." He leans in for a kiss. "Hungry?" he asks.

"Starving," I tell him.

"Let's head down to the restaurant for dinner. If we want dessert, they do late-night room service here," he suggests, "and I've already arranged for it."

"Okay," I shrug. "Lead the way."

Our table is overlooking the harbor, too. The night is completely clear, the moon full and bright, casting a long reflection on the water below. Our vantage point also includes some downtown apartments. So many windows are decorated with colorful lights and trees. It's simply beautiful.

A live band is tucked in the corner of the restaurant, playing holiday music. The tables are tastefully decorated in white and silver, small candles flickering in the center of each one. A fire is crackling in the fireplace nearby.

"This is perfect, Jack," I tell him. "I can't imagine a better place to be right now... and I can't imagine any better company."

"You're sweet, Emi. It is nice, being here with you. You did tell Jen you wouldn't be home, right?"

"I did," I laugh.

"Okay," he sighs. "I don't want your family angry with me again."

"They love you," I tell him before taking a bite of my dinner. I nearly choke on the food, realizing I've just professed my family's love for him before I've even admitted my own to him. I do. I don't know why I haven't said it yet.

"You okay?" he asks, handing me my water.

"No, I'm good," I smile. "This place is really nice," I tell him. "Are you sure this wasn't too much?" I ask nervously. "I can pitch in, if you'd like."

He looks at me, almost confused, and then laughs a little. "No, Emi, I'm sure it's not too much. It's part of your gift."

"Part?" I ask. "God, no, this had better be all of it."

"It's not," he answers. "The rest are upstairs."

"The *rest?* I obviously didn't get you enough."

"That's ridiculous, Emi. This isn't a competition."

"I know, but..."

"No 'but,' silly. Plus, you may hate what I got you."

"Okay, this hotel makes up for any bad gifts, for the record. And I'm sure I won't hate it. You seem to be pretty attuned to my likes and dislikes," I add.

"I try to pay attention. But I had to get Kelly's help on your presents. They were a little beyond my expertise."

"I'm sure they will be great," I assure him.

"Why don't we go find out. Are you finished?" he asks, eyeing my nearly-empty plate.

"I'm saving room for dessert," I tell him. "Let's go."

Hand-in-hand, we walk back to our penthouse suite.

"Should we get comfortable first?" he asks before settling in.

"Um... sure. Did you want to go first, or..."

"Why don't we both go?" he smiles, my heart suddenly racing as I think about the incredible jacuzzi tub in our suite... and how much I'd like him to come with me... *but no, not tonight.* I was hoping he wouldn't pressure me... he said he wouldn't...

"I don't think so," I tell him, uneasy.

"Emi," he laughs. "Did you not notice the shower and jacuzzi have their own separate rooms?"

"Oh, no," I sigh, relieved. "I didn't."

"Would you like the jacuzzi?"

"Yes, please," I grin, pleading.

"By all means. Meet you back here in a few."

After my bath, I stall in the bathroom, looking at myself in the mirror. I hadn't exactly planned on hanging out in my nightclothes... I brought the grey and black ruffled sleep shorts and matching camisole to sleep in, so I felt a little like I was teasing him. I chose them because I wanted to have a reason to cuddle in his warm grasp tonight. I was thankful I brought my robe, although it was thin and only came down to the middle of my thigh. I look cute, though. There is no denying that. I had debated pulling my hair back, but I think that might be too much, so I let it fall naturally on my shoulders.

At the last minute, I decide to pull on some striped knee-high tube socks, just to cover up a little more of my body. I don't know why I'm so nervous.

Jack is across the suite in the kitchen, dressed in green plaid flannel pants and a white t-shirt. I can smell the spice of chai tea lattes. *So sweet.* I sneak up behind him and throw my arms around his waist.

"You smell good," I tell him, breathing in his clean scent. He tries to break free of my grasp, but I'm afraid of what he'll think when he sees my clothes, so I hold him tightly. I *so* wish I had brought some yoga pants or something. I debate running back in the room and putting my jeans back on... but I guess it's a little too late for that. I finally loosen my grasp a little, and he turns around to face me, putting his arms around me.

"So do you," he says, kissing me as his hands explore my backside. "What are you wearing?" he mumbles without looking, a heavy sigh following.

"I know, I'm sorry," I tell him, pulling away so he can see.

He scans my body, from the low-cut camisole peeking out from beneath the robe that's too short to my socks. His eyes linger on my feet.

"Are the socks meant to be a distraction?" he laughs.

"Yes?" I say, unsure.

"That works," he smiles. "You are so incredibly impractical, my sweet Emi. But so equally, incredibly, adorably sexy." He picks me up to kiss me again, and sets me down carefully.

"Latte?" he asks, handing me a mug.

"Thank you."

"Why don't you lead the way into the living room?" he suggests, patting me lightly on my rear as he follows me. "So cute," he says as I glare over my shoulder. He's moved the three packages from under the tree to the coffee table, one fairly large one and two increasingly smaller ones. I pull out three much smaller gifts from my bag and set them next to his.

"See? I didn't do enough," I murmur.

"Stop that, Emi," he warns me. "Seriously." He stands up to tune the radio to a station with Christmas music. "How is this?"

"Good," I tell him, patting the seat on the couch next to me. "Open this one first," I suggest, handing him my medium-sized gift. He shakes it ceremoniously.

"Is this the coal?"

"No that's in the big one," I tell him. "Lots of coal for you."

He unwraps the gift, an iPod. "I don't know how you don't have one already. I took the liberty of loading up a bunch of my music on it."

"Thank you, Em, this is great!" he says.

"Open it up and look at it," I encourage him. He takes off the cellophane and opens the box, taking out the music player and staring at it in his hand. "Turn it over," I whisper to him.

"*I like the sound of 'Us, '*" he reads the engraving aloud. His smile grows as his eyes linger on the back of the iPod. His thumb rubs over the sentence. "So do I, Emi," he sighs. "So do I."

"Do you like it?"

"I love it," he says as I lean in to kiss him. "This means a lot."

"Good," I say, bouncing lightly on the couch. He puts the iPod on the table and hugs me, picking me up and placing me in his lap.

"Your turn," he says, handing me the medium-sized box.

"Did you wrap this?" I ask, feeling the crisp edges of the paper.

"Uh, no. I had it wrapped at the department store. It was a fund-raiser for a local school. How could I say no to that?"

"Of course," I smile. "I hate to ruin the paper..."

"Here," he says, ripping through it. "I ruined it for you."

He wraps his arms around me as I open the box and pull out a moss-colored pashmina. "Jack, it's beautiful," I tell him, wrapping it around my neck.

"Let me see," he says, angling my body so he can see my face. "Yes, it certainly brings out your pale green eyes. You are gorgeous."

"Thank you." I feel myself blush as his thumb grazes down my cheek to the corner of my lips. His mouth brushes mine softly before I'm drawn into a deeper kiss. *Not tonight... but... no...*

I break away, sooner than he does, but he doesn't object. I pick up the larger gift that I brought for him. His arms still pulling me into him, he rests his head on my shoulder and asks me to open it for him. When I reveal the top-of-the-line noise-canceling headphones, he lets go of me and takes them from me.

"Wow," he smiles. "I have been wanting these for my trips. Emi, I've priced these, I know they're a lot," he says, concerned.

"If I can't worry about what you spent, you can't worry about what I spent. Period."

"But Emi, it's different."

"No, it's not. So you make a little more than me. Whatever. I can afford this... remember, I don't have to pay rent anymore."

"A little," he mumbles. "Okay..." He hesitates before kissing me on the cheek. "Thank you... now which one do you want to open next?"

"The little one," I tell him as I pick it up. I rip into the neatly wrapped gift, making a production out of it this time. Inside are leather gloves, the same color as the scarf. "I see a theme here," I say, pulling the gloves on. "Very warm. Very nice." I pat his cheeks with the gloves and give him a peck on the lips.

"Okay, last one," I say, handing him the smallest gift. "It's just a gift card so you can buy your own music," I tell him as he opens the present.

"You might have to help me spend this," he says. "I don't really know music... but you seem to have good taste in it."

"Oh, we can find some things together," I encourage him. "I'll help you."

"Very cool," he says, nudging the last box on the table. As I stand to pick it up, he grabs my hips firmly, pulling me back down into his lap once I get the box. His hands skim my thighs lightly as I take the paper off and set it on the floor. I feel his lips move softly across the back of my neck and hear him inhale slowly.

"That feels good," I whisper, distracted.

"Good," he mumbles into my shoulder, kissing it delicately. "Open your present," he adds before wrapping his lips around my earlobe. *My god...* I can feel the blood coursing through my body, speeding up.

I raise the lid and push the tissue paper aside, lifting up a heavy, black, knee-length cashmere coat with three large buttons and flared sleeves. It's the prettiest coat I have ever seen, much less owned.

"Oh, my god, Jack, this is incredible..." I hold it up in front of me, touching the soft fabric lightly. "Kelly helped pick this out?" I ask.

"She did," he says, continuing to kiss my neck. "It's cute *and* practical. Novel concept..." His words are detached and muffled against my skin, his fingers grazing my arms.

"She has excellent taste," I gush, ignoring his playful criticism of my frequent decisions to choose cuteness over comfort.

"Try it on," he urges, snapping out of his daze and prodding me to stand up. "I want to make sure it fits." I walk a few paces away from him as he unbuttons the coat, standing up to help me put it on. I hold out my gloved hand for him to put the first sleeve on, but he pulls the coat in and shakes his head. "We need to make sure it fits without the robe."

"But my robe's thin," I laugh. "Really?"

"Really," he says, the lust in his eyes evident. "For me?" he asks.

"You'll hate what I'm wearing, Jack, I swear."

"I doubt that very seriously," he says. "I've pretty much figured it out by touching you."

"Okay, well, you'll hate me for wearing it, then," I continue.

"Mmmmm..." he hesitates. "I doubt that, too. Please?"

I adjust the pashmina so it drapes over the entire front of my torso before unbelting the robe and taking it off. His eyes scan my body again as he puts the coat on me. I pull it closed, buttoning it up and pulling the pashmina out and throwing the ends over my shoulders.

"Well?" I say, modeling for him.

"I need to fix one thing first," he says, kneeling in front of me and pushing my left sock down my leg. I pick up my foot so he can pull the rest of the sock off, and he does the same on my right side. He kisses each of my knees, paying careful attention to my scar, and I nearly melt right then and there when his tongue makes contact with my skin. He stands up and steps back to see the entire look.

"You're beautiful," he says, his eyes completely sincere.

"So are you," I tell him.

"And for the first time ever," he continues, "I think you're *totally* overdressed."

He approaches me slowly, his blue eyes capturing mine. My heart pounds so hard I'm pretty sure he can hear it. He takes one hand, then the other, pulling on each fingertip of the gloves to take them off. He kisses each finger when he's done, his eyes never leaving mine.

Next, he takes the ends of the pashmina and carefully unwraps it from my neck. He folds it neatly and sets it on the coffee table before kissing the hollow beneath both of my ears.

"My god, Jack," I say in heady anticipation. *Why not tonight?*

"What?" he says, his smile obvious in his voice. I pull his lips to mine, my desire crystal clear, my reluctance to be with him completely... absent.

"I don't want to want you like this," I whisper as he unbuttons the top button of the coat.

"Why not?" he asks, unbuttoning the second one.

"Because I'm afraid I'll let it go too far... and that I'll regret it."

"Emi," he says, his eyes focused on the final button, his fingers slowly unfastening it. I squeeze his hands in mine, my muscles suddenly tense, afraid I'm leading him on too much. "Relax," he tells me, his voice soothing. He kisses my hands again before letting go of them.

He lifts the coat from my shoulders and slides it down my arms, laying it carefully on the back of the couch. He runs his hands from my shoulders to my wrists, picking up my arms and stepping back to see my lingerie.

"So beautiful," he repeats, his eyes again settling on mine. "Emi, you were very up front with me about your boundaries for tonight, and I promise you I will respect them. As I said, this night is what you want it to be. I haven't come this far in this... whatever we are..." he laughs, "without a considerable amount of restraint and willpower. I'm not going to stop that tonight just because you're wearing revealing pajamas."

"It's not just the pajamas," I protest, gripping the bottom of his t-shirt, pulling it over his head. "I don't want to stop kissing you... or touching you... is that too tempting?"

"It's tempting, Emi, but I want you to just relax and enjoy this night with me. When we leave in the morning, I want you to know three things."

"Yes?" I say as I kiss his chest, navigate my tongue to his neck. He picks me up in an embrace to help me reach him.

"That I think you are the most enchanting woman I have ever met... that I respect you, fully, no matter your request... and that I love you, Emi... that I want to be with you."

"That's four," I correct him as he props me up higher. I wrap my legs around his back, locking my ankles, taking his earlobe between my teeth gently.

"I can't count when you're doing that," he explains.

"We're a couple," I whisper in his ear, nibbling again.

"What?" he asks.

"You said, 'whatever we are,'" I repeat his phrase. "We're a couple. I'm committing to you right now. You're the only man I want to be with. So it's official. No more friend-dates."

"Well, our last few haven't been that anyway," he says. "It's been official to me for some time."

"I know... but I'm ready to tell the world you're my boyfriend... and by 'the world,' I– of course– mean my family." He looks at me and smiles before greeting me with another kiss. A knock on the door interrupts us. "Are you expecting someone?" I whisper, breathless.

"Dessert..." he says as he carries me into the bedroom and sets me down before pulling his t-shirt back on and walking to the door.

I glance quickly at myself in the mirror, unable to wipe the smile off my face. I arrange the pillows on the bed and pull the comforter and sheets back, sitting down on the edge of it as I wait for the room service attendant to leave. *I love him. I love how he takes care of me. How he listens to me. How he kisses me. How attentive he is, and thoughtful. I love his sensitive blue eyes, his toned body, how he picks me up to kiss me... I love how he always worries I'll be too cold– how he knows I always will be. I love that he wants children. I love that he's best friends with my brother. I love that he waited... is continuing to wait for me. His patience... how certain he is about his feelings for me, as well as mine for him. I think he's known longer than I have. I love him. I do. Then why is it so scary to say it?*

"I think we have something to celebrate," he says, handing me a glass of champagne. "To us."

"To us." We clink glasses and take a sip. "So what's for dessert?"

"Well..." He takes both of our glasses and sets them on the night stand before crawling on the bed toward me, kissing my left thigh, then my right one. "Mmmm..." he says, his lips creating a vibrating sensation on my leg. "Dessert..." he raises up, kissing my collarbone.

"Dessert," I sputter, my breath gone. He laughs quietly under his breath as he pulls away.

"Dessert. Yes. We have an assortment of fruits, because I know you like fruit..." he begins, "and mango ice cream."

"Sounds..." I murmur, food no longer on my mind.

"Stay there. I'll bring it in."

"Uh-huh," I agree, intoxicated by him, scooting closer to the pillows and sitting cross-legged on the bed, grabbing my ankles nervously. He sets a silver tray in the middle of the bed and sits down across from me. We each take a spoon and share the ice cream and fruit.

"Tell me about your Christmas," he requests, the sexual tension finally settling in the room. *And yet, I want it back.* I nibble quickly, anxious to get back to our previous activity, as I tell him about my Christmas with my family and he tells me about his day spent volunteering at a local shelter. When we're finished, I move the tray to the night stand.

"Thank you," I tell him.

"You're welcome." His eyes are suggestive as I crawl toward his end of the bed. I kiss him before kneeling in front of him and take his shirt in my hands again. I lift it over his head and toss it on the floor. His warm hands clutch my waist before he gathers the ends of my camisole. "Is this okay?" he asks. I nod, raising my arms. He slowly removes my shirt, dragging his fingers along my ribs, breasts, arms, hands.

"You're cold," he whispers.

"A little," I answer, crawling closer into his body and putting my arms around his neck, his lips, tongue finding mine. He moans slightly, feeling my naked breasts press up against his chest. He gets on his knees and puts his hands on my back, picking me up and moving me to the pillows.

"Do you want to get under the covers?" he asks.

"No. I want you to warm me up," I tell him.

When I take my arms from his neck, his fingers intertwine with mine as he pulls one of my hands over my head and grasps it tightly. His other arm is holding his body over mine, his knees on either side of my thighs.

"How?" he asks between kisses as my fingernails trace down his side, to his stomach, his navel, to the waistline of his pants. I waver... *over or under?* He pulls away slightly to look into my eyes. His passion for me is obvious in his gaze. Is this fair? Selfish? *Over...*

My palm gently pressed against him, he exhales slowly, his head tucked into a pillow over my shoulder. My breathing quickens, excited at his arousal, nervous that I won't be strong enough, worried that he won't keep his word.

Why not tonight? I can't think clearly; can't remember why I asked him to wait again. I can no longer trust myself. *I want him. Fuck, Emi, it's okay to want him!* The inner cheerleader back, I begin to let go. His hips move against my hand, which I move lower, closer to my body. His body comes with it.

His lips move to my neck, kissing ravenously. I feel like he's losing control, too. His tongue travels from my neck, across my collarbone to my breasts. As he pulls back, he picks up one of his legs and nudges it in between mine. I moan quietly, unsure if the sound is coming from my own desire to truly be with him, or as a protest to him moving toward the one thing I asked him not to do.

I comply, and allow not one, but both of his legs between mine. His eyes ask for permission before he puts the weight of his body on me. I pull his head to mine, my mouth parted and thirsting for his, granting his every wish. *I will let it go as far as he wants. I only hope he wants it all.*

As soon as his body makes contact with mine, I curse the flannel and cotton that still keep us apart. He slides his body up, slowly, against mine, then down again.

"Oh, god," we say in unison, causing us both to laugh. He moves my hair out of my face, tucking it behind my ear.

"Are you okay?" he asks. I smile and nod.

"Are you?"

"Yes," he says, pushing again. "Are you warming up?" he asks.

"Oh, yes," I tell him as he pulls back again.

"Would you like me to keep going?" Again, a smile and a nod. *Fuck it. Let go, Emi... just let go. He's safe. Let go.*

His lips touch the tip of my nose lightly as he pushes once more. My cheeks are next, as he pulls back. *Push.* Earlobe. *Pull.* Neck. Each motion is unhurried, thoughtful, focused. I can feel my entire body pulsating in anticipation. I am sure he can feel it against him.

His movements slow, eventually stop. His kisses continue, though not as deep as I want them to be. I feel like I can't get close enough to him. I wrap my legs around him, trying to spur him back into action, my hips rocking slightly.

He laughs and kneels up, his hands behind his back to remove my legs. "Jack, it's okay," I tell him, suddenly afraid that he's stopping, afraid he's going to keep his word. He smiles, his hands moving slowly up my thighs, over my panties, up my abdomen and pausing only briefly on my breasts. He moves his hands back to my waist, clutching tightly, and leans over and kisses my stomach. He picks me up gently, my back naturally arching. I exhale, nervously, as his kiss moves to my navel, then to the hem of my panties.

"What's your definition of making out?" he whispers, his eyes focused on the ruffle, his fingers barely skimming the elastic.

"It's okay, Jack," I exhale.

He sighs before continuing, pulling lightly at my panties. "Would you consider this making out?" He kisses just below the hem. "Or would this be crossing a line?" he asks.

"Making out," I answer anxiously. "But Jack, really, it's okay," I encourage him again. "I'm ready." He smiles and nods before gripping the sides of my sleep shorts in his hand and tugging gently. I lift my hips off the bed to help him, tuck my knees in. He pulls the shorts off and sets them next to him on the bed. I study his face as his eyes scan every inch of my naked body.

"You are ravishing, Emi," he says quietly, his hands clutching just above my pelvis.

"Thank you," I blush. He, once again, hovers his body over mine to kiss me. I put my hands in his hair, *wanting him, needing him*. He pulls back and watches my expression as I feel his hand, his warm fingers, touching me.

Oh. My. God. It has been *too* long. I bite my bottom lip before the smile appears.

"Is that good?" he asks, his smile matching my own as he moves his hand slowly.

"Mmm-hmmm," I answer him. He lies down on his side next to me, tucking his other arm beneath my neck, angling my head toward his so our lips can meet. His tongue teases in unison with his fingers. The pressure is deep for a few seconds, then he pulls his lips, fingers, away ever so slightly. Every time he does, I pull his head closer to mine, angle my hips toward him more, *wanting him, needing him.*

I pull his body back on top of mine, and he finds his place once again in between my legs. He moves his lips away from mine, back down my body. Neck. Collarbone. Breasts, where they linger, his soft tongue memorizing the landscape. Ribcage. Stomach. Navel. He skips down to the scar on my knee once more. *God, the anticipation is killing me!* Finally, his lips move back up to my abdomen, just before I decide to direct him where I want him. Fortunately, we both have the same thing in mind.

Fuck, he is amazing. His lips, his tongue, his palm, his long fingers, *fuck*. I am completely and utterly, *wanting him, needing him,* undone.

As I'm coming down, I can't wait any longer to kiss him again, so I lean up and greedily pull him back to me. He eagerly obliges, feeding my hunger, rubbing my temples with his thumbs, wiping away beads of sweat. His hips move slowly, lightly, between my legs, my body grateful for his presence. I push at the hem of his pants, wanting to share this euphoric bliss with him. He finds my hands and pulls them over my head, pinning them down while he continues to gratify the yearning of my lips.

"Are you warmer now?" he asks as I gasp for air, his free hand outlining my body on the sheets.

"Jack," I breathe, "I want to make love to you."

He huffs with a smile and moves to my side. He lets go of my arms and props himself up on one elbow. His eyes are still dark and full of desire, still pining for me. He runs his fingers up and down the center of my body, obviously considering my offer. I entwine my fingers with his and push him onto his back, climbing on top of him.

"Let me make love to you," I repeat, scooting back and taking the waistband of his pants into my hands, tugging. Again, he restrains my wrists, this time shaking his head at me.

"Not tonight, Emi," he says, a small smile on his lips, his eyes playful. "You made me promise."

"But you said tonight was about me. Whatever I want it to be. I want to be with you, Jack. I want you to make love to me." He releases my hands and I lie down, pressing my breasts against his chest, my lips drawn to his. "Please?"

"Emi..." he hedges, laughing quietly, his hands resting on my lower back. "You were... settled... in your... decision... determined," he reasons, his words coming between my desperate kisses, my fingers working overtime to make his hair a perfect mess. He takes my face in his hands and holds it a few inches from his, his eyes searching the depths of mine. "Not tonight, you said," he reminds me mischievously.

"Yes, tonight," I plead.

"No, Em," he repeats complacently, angling his body to push me off of him. He kisses me again, touches my cheek softly. I sneak my hand beneath his pants and feel him. Although his eyes look sated and in control, I learn very quickly that he is not. With more force, he grabs my hand and pulls it to his lips, kissing it.

"No, Emi," he says firmly, biting back a smirk. "I'll be right back." Before I can protest, he leaves me, naked and alone on the bed as he exits the bedroom. "Water?" he calls back to me.

"I don't want water..." I whine softly, frustrated, climbing under the blankets for warmth... and to hide from him the obvious expression of rejection that I can't keep from my face. I pull the sheets over my head, my body still yearning for his touch.

I hear the seal of a bottle of water being broken after something lightweight thuds against my stomach. I peek out at Jack from beneath the covers. He smiles slyly at me, his eyes averting quickly to the thing on my abdomen and back to my face. "You sure you don't want some water?"

I shake my head stubbornly as I sit up a little to see what he has thrown onto the bed... and I have never been so happy to see a box of condoms in all of my life. My smile grows quickly as Jack sets the water on the night stand. I open the box feverishly and take a small package out, tossing the box next to his water.

"Now, Emi," he says, turning off the lamp, undressing to his boxers, slowly, and climbing under the covers into bed with me, his expression one of smug satisfaction. "I don't ever want you to think that I'm not a man of my word."

"Jack, I'm not thinking about your *words* right now." I lie back down, turning on my side to face him, setting the condom down in between us.

"Of course you're not," he laughs, his body settling into the bed, mirroring mine.

"But for the record... you still will be. You said we would do whatever I want... that this was *my* night... remember?"

"So *those* are the words you want me to honor?" He runs his hand through my hair, tugging it lightly to reposition my head. His lips move closer to mine but he stops less than an inch from them.

"Yes," I whisper, my eyes closing in anticipation. "Please," I beg.

"And whatever do you want to do, my sweet Emi?" His breath is sweet and warm against my skin.

"Stop teasing me," I laugh, my eyes now pleading with him. "Take me. Now. Make love to me. Please."

"You're sure?" he asks tentatively, the thumb of his other hand brushing my cheek softly.

"Yes."

He kisses my forehead.

"You're ready?" he adds.

"God, yes, please..."

He kisses the tip of my nose.

"You promise?"

His lips touch mine, able to feel the word "yes" form against them. He moistens my lips as he licks his own. "God, I want you," I tell him, the taste of him pushing me over the edge. His lips brush against mine lightly, teasing me as they always do, but mine press back against his harder, needing more... as mine always do.

A low moan forms in the back of his throat as the kiss becomes deeper, hungrier. Slowly, his body presses against mine, pushing me back onto the bed. His hands planted into the mattress on either side of my shoulders, he pushes away from me and nudges my legs apart with his knees.

"Far be it from me to not give the lady what she wants..." I realize he's still wearing his boxers, and as my hands grasp the strong muscles of his upper arms,

I bring my feet up and hook my toes under the waistband of his underwear, my cold toes meeting the warm skin of his hips, thighs, knees, then calves. He kicks off the garment and smiles, his eyes reflecting the same desire that fills my entire body.

"But it seems like she knows what she wants. God, that was sexy." He lowers his head to kiss me.

"Wait, Jack..." I stop him, my hands now caressing his face and pushing him away so I can see into his blue eyes. "Stop," I whisper. All of his actions cease and he raises his brows in consternation.

"But–" I cut him off, putting my finger over his lips.

"I just wanted to tell you that I love you, Jack. I didn't want there to be any doubt."

He slowly lowers his body onto mine, keeping most of his weight off of me by resting on his elbows. He cradles my face, his thumbs covering the deep dimples brought out by my broad smile. The corners of his lips curl up slowly as he shakes his head.

"I already know, Emi. I never had any doubt. But thank you for telling me." His lips finally reach mine, warm and soft and gentle. "May I continue now?" he mumbles through our kiss, through a smile.

"Please, yes," I giggle.

"I love you, too," he whispers next to my ear, his breath tickling me. "Let me show you."

"Wait, Jack?" I interrupt once more.

"What, Emi?" he says, smiling, but sounding slightly annoyed, his lips continuing their journey across my neck, his hand reaching for the foil packet next to him.

"Merry Christmas."

"Merry Christmas, my sweet Emi." He lifts his head and looks into my eyes, his stare leaving no doubt in my mind about his feelings toward me. He kisses me sweetly, distracting me until I feel the pain– the *good* pain– that I hadn't felt in so long. I gasp at the contact, and he stills and waits for me to open my eyes. Even through his desire, I see his concern.

"Are you okay?" he asks softly.

I nod slowly, biting my lip.

"You're not breathing," he tells me.

Breathe, Emi. ...take soft breaths...

"Oh," I exhale after remembering more of the poem. I concentrate hard on Jack, getting used to the feel of him, closing my eyes again, wanting to think of him– and *only* him– in this moment.

"We'll go slow." His voice envelops me, comforts me.

I nod again, a smile breaking across my face.

"Just relax," he says as I finally feel him rest his body on mine. His lips brush against my cheek, and when I look at him again, he's watching me react to his slow and cautious motions. I put my hands on both sides of his face and pull his mouth to mine. I gasp and wince again at the ache within.

"Does it hurt?" he asks.

"It's fine," I tell him breathily. *Yes, of course it hurts, it's been a year, but god, I don't want you to stop.* "It's good. I'm okay."

"Hold on," he says, pulling away, his sudden absence causing me to inhale sharply. He smiles at me as he strokes my cheek, then lifts my head to his for another kiss as he pulls the pillow out from under it.

"What are you–"

"Lift up," he says, helping me to raise my lower back so he can put the pillow beneath me. He weaves his fingers in between mine, my hands on the bed resting on either side of my head. He watches my reaction to his touch, the connection more comfortable, but deeper, and the new angle bringing a surprising sensation that I had never felt before.

"Oh, Emi," he breathes, closing his eyes for the first time.

"Oh," I sigh with a smile, hungrily pulling him toward me for another kiss as he moves over me. My heart pounds in my chest.

"Better?" he laughs lightly, skimming his lips over mine, touching his nose to mine, teasing me in more ways than one.

"The best," I breathe as he pushes against me again. "I don't... How did... Oh god..."

"I know," he answers quickly. "God, I know..." He continues without hurrying, kissing me with such reverence and care, and at the same time I decide I want this feeling to last all night, I want him more, want him now, want him urgently, want him... *forever*.

I pull my hands from his tight grasp and lightly scrape my nails down his back, feeling a light sheen of sweat on his body. His thumbs rub my temples as his fingers tug my hair gently. I grab his hips, pulling him to me with all of my strength, my nails digging into his skin.

"I love you," he whispers in my ear before tracing the shell of it with his tongue. He knows this drives me crazy.

"Oh, god... faster," I beg him. His pace quickens at my request, and the new sensation begins to build deep within me. "Oh, f..." My heavy breathing steals my words. The feeling is... whole, warm, encompasses every part of me in ways I never knew were possible. "I think I'm coming," I manage to tell him.

"I know you are," he exhales back in my ear. "I can feel you. Oh, god, it's so..." I can hear the smile in his sultry voice as he brings me closer.

"Come with me." He lifts his head and watches me as my eyes plead with his. "Jack," I gasp, beginning to lose myself in him.

"Emi," he answers, this word– my name– shrouded by his desire for me, "I am." And in no time, I know he is. *I* can feel *him*. I can feel him, his shuddering movements only heightening the surge I'm already experiencing, taking in my own pleasure wholly, fully, the feeling inside growing even more intense as I realize I'm giving the same gratification to him.

The sensation is almost *too* intense, *too* potent. It's more than I've ever known. In that moment, everything goes dark as I envision small points of the most beautiful light gently pricking at my skin, trying to escape, the pent-up energy finally getting its release.

The need to yell one or two or a thousand profanities takes over, but all I can do is take his head in my hands and pull his mouth to mine, delivering long, full kisses, stifling every sound but the desperate moans that neither of us can hide from one another.

When I finally open my eyes again– or maybe when my vision is finally restored, I'm not sure– I notice him watching me, the lids of his heavy eyes obscuring part of the beautiful blue I'm used to staring into. I feel my cheeks heat with a blush.

We finally separate, both of us gasping for air, but our gaze continues. We smile together before he leans in for another kiss. "That may have been the most beautiful thing I have ever seen," he says. I blush harder, tucking my head into the crook of his neck. "Don't hide." He guides my head back to the bed to look at me once more.

He slowly pulls back to grab another pillow off the floor and helps to put it under my head.

"Are you okay?" he asks, his hands smoothing my hair, his body settling back onto mine, exactly where I want him.

I nod quickly, still bewildered.

"Can you speak?" he laughs.

I nod again, but don't really register what he's said.

He laughs at my response. "Then tell me, how do you feel?"

I open my mouth to tell him, but words fail me. I just shake my head before smiling and shrugging my shoulders, my face heating up again.

"Nothing?"

"I–" *How can I tell him that I am unfamiliar with any vocabulary words that accurately describe what just happened?* Any words I tell him will come across as less than what I want them to mean. "Everything!" I gush unexpectedly.

"Everything?" he asks confused.

"I don't know what to say," I admit. "I guess, like... imagine every good feeling there is..."

"Okay..."

"Starting with, I don't know, contentedness and going up to, say, pure bliss... and then think of everything in between."

"Got it." He kisses me gently.

"No, so it was, like, *all* of those things happening at *once*– with rainbows and unicorns... and whipped cream... and a cherry on top."

"Rainbows and unicorns, huh?" He laughs at my completely inadequate description. "Definitely better than nothing..."

"Everything," I reiterate. "I don't think you understand. I don't think I can sufficiently communicate what I just experienced, Jack. Obviously..."

"Oh, come on..." he urges.

"Really!"

"Alright, on a scale from one to–"

"Eleven!" I exclaim, pushing on his chest playfully.

"Yikes," he smiles. "That sets the bar pretty high for our future..."

"It was off the charts," I whisper to him seriously. "If it's like this all the time, you will never get rid of me."

"Was there any threat of that?"

"Absolutely not, Jack. I'm here to stay. Always."

"Good," he answers. "Because I'm yours. *Always*." He kisses me before rolling beside me, sharing the pillow with me. He moves one leg and one arm across my body, a possessive posture. *And I'm yours*. He kisses my temple before I turn my head so our lips can meet again.

"You didn't tell me how you feel," I mention to him softly.

"Mmmmm..." he hums contemplatively. "You know how you were worried about the presents you bought me?"

"Yeah..."

"Rest assured, my love, that this was the best gift anyone has ever given me. *Ever*. It wasn't just sexually satisfying," he begins, planting another tender kiss on my nose. "It *was* that, but it was far *beyond* satisfying... and it was precious, and surprising, and passionate, and generous... it was all the things that you are to me.

"And I'm fairly certain the memories that I'll have from this night alone could carry me through the rest of my life. Of course, I hope they won't have to..."

"They won't," I assure him.

"But I will treasure this night forever, Emi, and I will do everything in my power to always preserve and nurture what we have. I don't think this is common. It's not normal. What we have is something exceptional."

I roll over on the bed and press my back into his chest. He pulls me closer, and I take his hand in mine, kissing it softly.

Two tears fall quickly on the pillow, and I swallow hard, not wanting Jack to hear the sadness in my voice.

"It is."

He kisses my shoulder and pulls the comforter over us as my thoughts drift back to Nate. I never thought anything would feel better than what he and I shared last New Year's Eve. I always assumed I would just settle for the next best thing, and I had begun to believe it would be Jack.

But just as his kiss surprised me by surpassing all of my expectations, so has this night. What we have *is* truly exceptional.

As Jack sleeps soundly behind me, I allow a few more tears to fall, again trying to come to terms with what Nate really was to me. I keep trying to assign definitions, words, to what he was– my soul mate? *Really?*

I never anticipated this. I never saw Jack coming. And I never expected to find such happiness again.

I roll over in his arms, rousing him again with a kiss, and without hesitation, he makes love to me again, just as gently, just as passionately... just as I had always dreamed... but never believed would become a reality for me.

CHAPTER 15

"Are you about ready, Emi?" Jack asks as he stands by the door with Jen, watching me select the necklace Nate had bought me out of my jewelry box. I'd been stalling, but I knew we needed to get going.

I clasp the pearls around my neck and nod to him. He puts my duffel bag on his shoulder and grabs my coat, scarf and gloves, helping me to put them all on. It is lightly snowing at the moment, but had been coming down steadily for the past two days. I have my boots on, ready to trudge through a good six- to eight-inches of fresh snow on the ground.

Once in the car, Jack asks for directions to the florist. I had called the one that Nate often used, remembering how pretty and unique the arrangements always were. I requested something clean, modern, not too flashy since it would be sitting next to a tombstone. When the florist asked how I had heard about them, I told them that my former boyfriend, Nate Wilson, used them often. They inquired about how Nate was doing, which caught me off guard. I then explained to them that the flowers were for him... that he had passed away last year. The owner was shocked, audibly sad. "He was one of our best customers," he told me. "We had wondered why he didn't use us anymore."

Jack pulls up to the curb and I get out to pick up the arrangement. The owner comes to greet me personally.

"You're just as beautiful as he said," the florist tells me. "The last bouquet he ordered last year, his instructions were to make it the most beautiful arrangement for the most beautiful woman. I remember the card said, 'Thank you, Emi, my Love. Finally.' He struggled with the words, but settled on that."

I remember the flowers he had sent me two days after his birthday last year... two days after we had declared our love for one another– and then made love in his loft. They were incredible, delivered to my apartment just two hours after I had left his home. They were meant as an apology. They were bought to assuage his guilt. "They were lovely," I tell the florist.

"Let me get the flowers," he says, going to the back room. As I scan the refrigerated case, I pluck the perfect rose from the bin and take it up to the counter. When he comes back, I immediately recognize that this arrangement is something Nate would have appreciated.

"They're incredible," I tell him. "Just perfect."

"I knew what he liked," he says.

I hold up the single flower, and then attempt to give him my credit card. He holds up his hand. "Please, let me get this. I insist."

"Well... thank you. I really appreciate it."

"Miss Emi," he says, "I am so sorry for your loss."

"Thank you," I say, my eyes becoming moist. *I don't want to spend the entire day crying. This has been one of the happiest weeks of my life...* The florist steps from behind the counter and hugs me, then hands me the flowers and opens the storefront door for me. Jack is waiting next to the passenger door and helps me place the arrangement in the back seat next to my sister. He shuts the door and takes my hand, then walks to the back of his car.

"Are you sure you want me to go with you guys?" he asks, his gaze shifting to Jen in the car.

"Of course I want you to go. I couldn't do this without you."

"Are you sure you want to tell them today?"

I just smile, nod, and touch his chin lightly. "I want everyone to know. Here," I tell him, placing the rose into his gloved hand. "This is for you. I love you."

He again glances to make sure Jen isn't watching, then pulls my face to his and kisses me. "I love you, too, Emi." After brushing his lips across my forehead, we part, both getting into the car. My cheeks flush hot when I turn around to smile at my sister.

"Everything okay?" she asks as we begin the drive to the cemetery.

"Yeah," I answer quietly, turning forward and taking a deep breath.

The snow has stopped falling, but it's still very cold and windy by the time we get to the gravesite. I had called Nate's mom, Donna, earlier in the week to see if she wanted to meet us here. She explained that she would be leaving for Thailand early this morning, a gift from her husband, James. I had wondered how she would get through this holiday, the first one without her son, so I was pleasantly surprised to hear that James had made arrangements for them to do something special. Even before Nate died, it was a difficult time for her. At the beginning of every year, Nate and Donna would get together to celebrate her wedding anniversary to her first husband, Nate's dad. They had married on New Year's Day, and his mother felt it important to have one day a year that they would honor his memory. She picked the happiest day they shared instead of the day he died. I think in the future, I might do something similar for Nate.

Donna said she was grateful for the distraction. I asked her to call me when she got back so we could see each other, share some memories. She said she would. I hoped she would. I hadn't seen her in months.

Jack, Jennifer and I wait in his car until my brother and Anna pull up behind us. Chris cuts his lights and engine off, and I sigh heavily, not sure if I can do this.

"Are you ready?" Jack asks, squeezing my hand. Jen massages my shoulder through my coat.

"You can do this, Em," she encourages. "It's okay." I nod and get out of the car, opening the back door to get the arrangement out.

"I'll get it, Emi," Jack says as my brother and Anna descend upon me with hugs.

"Okay," I whisper. Chris and Anna each take one of my arms and lead me toward Nate's final resting place. My sister and Jack follow closely behind.

"Where would you like them?" Jack asks of the flowers. A colorful arrangement sits on one side of his headstone, a ribbon streaming in the wind proclaiming the word *SON*.

"Over here," I point to the other side. Jack brings the bouquet to me, and we set it on the ground together.

I had debated inviting Jack along on this trip. I knew I wanted my brother and sister and Anna there. They were with me from the beginning. I knew Jack had been with me, in some capacity, since that night as well, but he didn't really know Nate.

That's what eventually convinced me to ask him to come. I wanted to introduce them, in my own way. I wanted Nate to see what a good man he was. I knew Nate had his own misconceptions about Jack in life. But Jack was an incredible person, and I felt like Nate should see his selfless ways.

He didn't have to say yes. He would undoubtedly feel out of place, but it was important that he be here with me when I said my final goodbye to Nate. This is significant. This is pivotal. This is the beginning of *our* life together. He needs to know that I'm putting my former lover behind me.

The five of us hold hands and say a few prayers over the grave. I'm grateful to have the four most important people in my life here with me... to mourn the one who used to be my entire life and foundation. It had been awhile since I actually allowed myself to remember the emptiness he left when he died, but I allow it this morning. It still hurts as bad as it did the morning I woke up in the hospital, when Chris delivered to me the news I never expected, never wanted to hear. I sniffle quickly and choke out a few quiet sobs. Jack releases my hand and pulls a handkerchief from his coat, handing it to me. He then puts his arm around my shoulders, pulling my head into his chest. He kisses the top of my head.

Chris squeezes my other hand tightly, his gaze focused intently on the gravesite. I look up at him to see a few tears fall from his eyes, too. Anna leans closer into him for support, but looks at me and Jack curiously.

"Can I have a few minutes alone?" I ask. Everyone agrees, making their way toward a grouping of trees nearby to block the wind. I squat down next to the headstone and adjust the flowers.

I feel like I've told you everything I have to tell you, Nate... and I'm not sure what more I can share with you. I believe that, where you are, you know my every thought anyway. You know how much I've cared for you and how much I've missed you. You've seen me struggle with losing you– with losing our baby– this past year. You know it hasn't been easy. It shouldn't have been easy. We shared something incredible. I've loved you so much.

I'm not sure it's right to ask for things to be easier now... but I hope they are. I've lived three-hundred-sixty-five days without you. Not a single one has gone by that I didn't miss you, wish you were here for comfort or just for someone to talk to. I had grown accustomed to your companionship. I took you for granted. I will never take anyone for granted ever again. I will cherish all the moments I have to share with other people. I will never let another day pass me by. I will live in the present, not mourn for the past or dread the future. I will trust my instincts, and I will act on them, not ignore them out of fear. I didn't do all of these things with you.

I break down and sob.

I didn't do these things with you, but because of you, I will do them for everyone in my future. It's not fair to you. I will always live with that regret. But I hope you know I did the best I could with you. You tried to teach me this in life... I just didn't fully appreciate it until you were gone.

I will never forget you. And I'm sure I'll still talk to you. I can't ignore the person who gave me the best, most heartfelt, most sincere advice for over ten years. I'm sure I'll run things by you sometimes.

But I don't think I can cry for you anymore, Nate. I will always want to, but for me, in life, I have to move on. I hope you can understand. I love you, Nate, and I always will. You took a part of me when you left, and you can have it, forever. But I need to use what is left to live my life.

I stand up and adjust my coat, taking in a few deep breaths.

"Jack?" I call to him. "Can you come here?"

He nods, leaving the rest of our group huddled together under the tree. Chris has his arms around both my sister and sister-in-law. They look like they're freezing.

"If you guys want to go, we'll meet you there," I suggest.

"Okay, Em. You know where to go?"

"I do," Jack answers, waving goodbye as they walk toward Chris's car. As I turn back to the grave, Jack stands behind me, opening his wool trench coat and wrapping it around me as he pulls me into his chest. He kisses my cold cheek, his icy lips providing no warmth. I shiver into him.

"Where's your hat, love?" he asks me.

"In my pocket," I smile at his worry for me, getting the silly cap he bought me at the airport out of my cashmere coat and handing it to him. He pulls it tightly over my ears before throwing his arms around me again.

"Are you okay?" he asks. I nod quietly, staring at the ground below us. I swallow hard before continuing.

"Nate," I start softly, "this is Jack. I wish you could have known him while you were here. I know you would have liked him. And despite what you thought," I laugh, "he was not trying to take advantage of me that night in college. It was quite the other way around," I explain.

Jack rocks us slowly back and forth, an attempt to keep warm.

"You will always be important to me. And he understands that. He's been very patient, very understanding, very supportive... very loving.

"I know he has every good quality you would want me to find in a man. I know you would have wanted me to be happy, Nate. And I just want you to know that I've found someone who makes me truly happy. I hope you can see that.

"I miss you," I barely manage to squeak out. "But he will take good care of me from now on. I hope you rest well knowing that."

"I promise," Jack whispers in my ear.

"And he's a man of his word," I smile. "Trust me, I know." I can feel Jack laugh lightly. We both stand in silence for a few more minutes. I say another prayer in my head.

"I'll never forget you," I tell him, a final tear falling for him. I wipe my eyes with the handkerchief and take Jack's hand into mine, leading him back toward his car.

He opens the door for me and waits for me to buckle my seatbelt before kissing me, softly, sweetly. He shuts the door quietly and goes around to the driver's side, getting in.

"Off to Brooklyn," I sigh.

"To Brooklyn," he repeats. "You'll love their house." Jack had helped my brother and sister-in-law move into their house earlier in the week.

"I'm sure I will. I'm so glad they finally moved closer. It will be nice having them nearby."

"Definitely."

Jack's phone rings in the console. He looks at the caller ID. "It's your brother," he says, answering it. "Yeah, we're right down the street... no, I can go... it's not a problem. Anything else? Okay... See you in a few." He hangs up and puts his phone in his coat pocket. "They forgot to get ice," he says.

"Okay," I smile as he pulls over in front of a house.

"I'll go get it. You go inside. It's that one, right there."

"No, I'll go with you," I protest.

"Emi, I've got it," he insists. "It will take me ten minutes, tops."

"But the roads are bad..."

"Stop it," he says. "The snow is melting. I'll be careful. Just go in, please?" he asks.

"Okay," I pout, undoing the seatbelt and opening the door. He holds my arm, pulls me back to him. He takes off my cap and kisses my temple.

"I'll be right back."

I stand on the curb and watch him slowly drive away. A holiday wreath hangs on Chris and Anna's door, welcoming visitors. The door is unlocked, so I venture inside. Just as I'm about to announce my presence, I hear a conversation that piques my interest.

"No, she packed a bag and everything," Jen says. "She's going to his place tonight."

"I don't get it," Chris says. "When did this happen? The last time we had dinner with them, they barely even looked at one another. They were just... *friends*, from all I could tell."

"Yeah, they didn't even leave together," Anna says.

"Well, that night, he ended up at our place," Jen says. "I saw him leaving the next morning when Clara and I came home... and it was obvious he had been there all night. I mean, last time I asked, she insisted they were still just friends. But you know, they *did* spend Christmas night together at the Ritz Carlton... she wouldn't give me any details, but if a man took *me* to the Ritz Carlton, I know I'd—"

"I just think it's too soon," Chris interrupts. "And, I mean... today?"

"I don't think it's too soon," Jen argues. "But, yeah, I just don't know that today is the right day, you know?"

"Yeah," Chris says.

"But if they're really in love..." Anna says, relief washing over me as I hear someone on my side.

"I think they are," Jen says.

"But today's about Nate," Chris simply states. "It just seems like she's running to Jack to avoid this... *reality*... of what today is."

"Today is a new day," I cut in. "Every day of this year has been about Nate."

"Emi," Anna says, blushing, embarrassed to be caught discussing me. She's never one to talk about people behind their backs.

"Thank God Jack isn't with me," I tell them. "He's very private, and I'm sure he wouldn't like to hear my brother and sister discussing our sex life... it's none of your business."

"Emi, we're just worried," Jen says.

"About what? Worried I'll be happy, finally? Worried that I'll finally be able to put this year behind me?"

"Worried that you're doing this for the wrong reasons," my sister adds. I stand in the middle of the hallway with my arms crossed in front of my chest, my coat, scarf and gloves still on.

"Well, why don't you ask me my reasons... no, on second thought, I don't owe you reasons... all you really need to know is that I love him... and he loves me. In the end, that's all that matters."

"I just think you should allow yourself to mourn today, Emi, that's all," Chris says. "It's okay." He comes over and tries to put his arms around me, but I shrug away from him, taking two steps back.

"I know it's okay," I say, defiant. "But I don't want to remember the horrible things that happened a year ago. I don't want to remember our last night together. I don't want to remember the sounds of the crash, or the silence that followed. I don't want to see his stare piercing through me. I've lived it. Over and over and over and over again, I have relived those moments. I'm ready for them to be gone. I'm ready to make new memories. I'm ready to love someone else."

"But this is Nate's day," Chris says, closing the gap between us.

"No," I push him away. "It is *my* day. It is *your* day. It is *Jack's* day and *Anna's* day and *Jen's* day... but if it's anyone's day, it's *certainly* not Nate's!" I yell. "He isn't here. He's lived all of his days, remember? He doesn't get any more."

Jen and Anna leave the room, leaving this fight to my brother and I, Nate's two best friends, the two people who knew him best.

"He deserves our thoughts today, Emi. He deserves the memories we can share. We should remember him for who he was, today, Emi. That's what today is about."

"Maybe that's what it's about for you, but Chris, I've done that," I remind him. "Time and again, day after day, week after week, I did that. And he knows I've done that. Don't make me feel guilty about wanting to move on with my life."

"I'm not trying to make you feel guilty!" he yells. "I want you to face reality here, Emi. Stop running into the arms of some other man that you hardly

345

know–"

"Hardly know?" I ask him. "I know him far better than you think, Chris."

"How could you?" he asks. "He's my best friend, and he's said nothing about you. And you're my baby sister, who tells me everything, and you've said nothing about him... to me or to Anna, your best friend."

"We didn't want to say anything," I tell him. "We wanted to keep it to ourselves, to have something for ourselves. Everyone has known my damn business all fucking year, and I wanted to keep him, this one person that I've grown to care about more than anyone... I wanted him all to myself... and I wanted to be sure about my feelings before I committed to him. We were going to tell you three today. Hey, surprise, everyone!" I rant, yell loud enough for Anna and Jen to hear in the next room. "Jack and I are a couple now! And, hey, we're sleeping together! Is that okay? Should we take a vote? Is that okay with everyone?"

"Jack," Chris says, going to the front door and taking one of the bags of ice from him. *Fuck!*

"It's okay with me," Jack whispers as he walks past me to the kitchen, eyebrows raised, my face turning fifteen shades of purple, his only moderately pink.

I want to crawl into a hole.

I want to run to a bathroom or bedroom or someplace private to cry or scream, but I have no idea where any of those places would be since I've never been to this fucking house before. *God, seriously?* I am an idiot.

"Jack," Chris starts from the kitchen, "I really think–"

"Chris, if you'll excuse me, I need to speak with Emi," he states, doesn't ask. I can't even look him in the eye when he meets me in the hall. "Let me show you the upstairs," he offers, taking my elbow in his hand and leading me up the stairway. I feel bad, afraid he's angry with me... I wait for him to speak once we get to what I assume is a guest bedroom and he closes the door quietly.

He lifts my chin abruptly and kisses me, a little rough, takes my breath away. "It looked like you needed that," he says with a smile.

"You're not mad?" I ask.

"Are you kidding? I'm having a hard time keeping my laughter in, Emi. Only you..." He kisses me again, then hugs me tightly and opens the door.

"No, guys, we're not doing it right now, don't worry!" he yells.

"Jack!" I say, surprised, backhanding him lightly in his chest and laughing with him.

"I love you, Emi," he says. "I love it when you stand up for yourself... when you stand up for us. I... just... love you."

"Well... thank you. I love you, too."

"What did I miss?" he asks.

"Chris wants to focus on Nate today. And he thinks I'm escaping reality by being with you."

"And what do I need to do to patch this up?"

"I don't know," I tell him.

"Well, I think I know a good place to start," he says. "Come on."

I follow him back down the stairs. He takes off his coat and gloves and helps me with my winter gear. We drape them on the stair railing and find my siblings in the main living area. His fingers entwine with mine.

"I love your sister," Jack announces to the room. "I always have, I don't think that's a secret. We've spent a lot of time together over the past few months getting to know each other, as friends. I always knew what I wanted out of it, but above all, I needed her to love me back. And that's what I was waiting for."

"And I do," I add quickly, following his lead. "I'm in love with him, and I want to be with him. And I'm not ashamed or guilty or anything. And I'd really like you three to be supportive of this."

"Oh, I am," Anna exclaims, an easy sell, always a champion for love. She comes over to us and hugs us both, standing next to me, challenging Jen and Chris. "Be happy for them," she pleads.

"If you're happy," Jen says with a half-smile. I nod at her. "Okay, then," she concedes less enthusiastically than Anna. "I just don't want you to get hurt."

"Chris?" Anna asks. His expression is hurt, angry. He walks out onto a back patio area and closes the door, hard, behind him. Anna starts to follow him.

"Let me handle this, Anna," Jack says. My sister-in-law steps aside and lets him pass through.

The three of us stand around, looking back and forth, as we hear raised voices coming from the back yard. They're just loud enough that we can hear a heated discussion, but not loud enough for us to make out the actual words.

"Why don't you two help me in the kitchen," Anna says. "We have one hour to prep enough food for twenty," she says.

"I don't get this," I say to her, following her. "If he wanted to sit around and be sad all day, why did he agree to this house-warming party?"

"He didn't have a choice," Anna says. "I didn't want him to sit around and mourn all day... I twisted his arm. I pushed for today. I knew it would be good for him."

"He was one of his best friends," Jen defends him.

"I know, Jen," Anna pleads, never one to argue, "but Emi's right. We have spent an entire year trying to get over this. It's been hard. At some point we do need to move on. I don't think Nate would want us to be sad today," she says. "Do you?"

"Well, of course not," Jen says. "But if that's what Chris needs..."

"Then he can mourn among friends and family. He'll have his entire support system here. Nothing wrong with that." And this is why I love Anna... her perpetually good attitude conquers all.

The doorbell rings, an obnoxious buzz.

"You have to get that fixed," I cringe. Anna nods in agreement.

"I wonder who's here so soon," she says.

"I asked Brian to come early... I hope it's okay," Jen smiles, walking to the door.

"Have you met him?" I ask Anna.

"No, you?"

I shake my head, anxious to see who my sister has been seeing.

"Brian," she says, introducing a handsome man to us, "this is my sister, Emi, and my sister-in-law, Anna."

"Brian," Anna immediately greets him with a hug. "It's so nice to finally meet you." I feel obligated to do the same, so I hug him, too, saying hello.

"We were just about to get some food started," Jen explains. "My brother and Emi's... boyfriend..." she says with an awkward pause, "are in the back yard."

"We need to get Chris to fire up the grill," Anna says. "Brian, would you mind going out there and letting him know?" she asks, and Jen and I both glare at her, wondering why she's sending him into the apparent firestorm.

"Sure," he agrees with a laugh, unsure why we're worried.

"You should probably take these," I tell him, grabbing three beers from the refrigerator and handing them to him. "Do you drink?"

"Yes," he says. "Thank you."

"Anna," Jen whispers as Brian walks toward the patio.

"What?" she smiles. "They won't fight with a stranger around. Lord knows nothing we say is going to make them stop. It seems like the obvious choice to smooth things over."

"I guess," I shrug.

"I want to keep this one," Jen says. "Why do we have to introduce him to our crazy so soon in our relationship?" she whines.

"He has to love us for us," I smile sweetly. "This is your life. We are your family. Deal."

A few minutes later, Chris comes in, walks briskly through the kitchen and up the stairs. "I started the grill," he mumbles while he passes us.

I follow him up after about ten minutes. I knock on the closed door, eventually opening it slowly when he doesn't answer.

"What do you want, Emi?" he asks.

"I just want to talk to you," I tell him, sitting down on the bed next to him. "Tell me how you're feeling."

"I'm sad, Em," he spits out at me. "I miss my friend, and I don't understand why I'm the only one feeling this today."

"You're not," I assure him. "I miss him every day. And that's just it. I've allowed myself to miss him, every single day. If you haven't taken that time, then, yeah, today's probably going to hit you a little harder than it hits me. I'm used to him being gone. You've had the distraction of an engagement and a marriage and a beautiful wife this year. So many wonderful things have happened... you weren't faced with this every second you were alone... because you were never alone.

"He wouldn't want you to be sad. How many times have you told me that, Chris?" I smile. "At least fifty-seven," I joke. "I stopped counting at fifty-seven." He doesn't smile back.

"Are you sure you're ready for another relationship, Emi?"

"I'm sure, Chris," I tell him.

"I mean it, Emi, you have to be one-hundred-percent certain."

"I am."

"Not just about a relationship," he adds. "About Jack."

"I *am*."

"I don't think you understand how much he cares about you, Emi. It used to be that I had to worry about you all the time," he says. "But I can see that you don't need me to be that person for you anymore."

"No, I don't," I tell him. "He takes good care of me."

"He is so wrapped up in you, Emi," my brother says. "If it doesn't work out between you two, Em, it would be the end of our friendship," he says. "I know it sounds dumb, but I don't want to lose another friend," he admits.

"Is that what you're worried about?" I ask him.

"A little. I'd hate to see either of you get hurt. I couldn't bear to see you sad again. And I wouldn't want to be around him if you walked away from him for a third time. He is the strongest man I know, but fuck, Emi, if that happens... it will destroy him."

"It's not going to happen," I assure him.

"It's too soon for you to know," he argues.

"Listen to me, Chris. As much as you don't want to lose another friend, I don't want to lose another boyfriend. And we're not talking death here. I know we're talking break-up. Whatever way I could lose Jack, I don't want to. That's one reason that it took me so long to make this commitment. I was too afraid of that off-chance that he would be taken from me, like Nate was. And then I realized, in trying to avoid that loss, I was growing so close to him that being apart from him for whatever reason was a loss I wasn't willing to live through again.

"My commitment to him goes deeper than just dating, okay? This is much bigger to me; much more important. It has to be. I know loss, like I never want to know again. I intend to be with him... forever... if he wants me. And I think he does.

"We've spent so much time together, Chris, really getting to know one another. We're good for each other, and we're good together. We have the same wants in this life. We come from good families, and recognize how important our families are. He will be a great father someday. And I want to have children with him."

"I just think it's too soon, Emi. Let me talk," he says before I have a chance to interrupt. "Especially to hear you say 'forever...' with him... I mean, Emi, I don't ever want to see you hurt like you were over Nate. And honestly, Em, I don't think I could have made it through this year without his support, either. I don't ever want to have to choose sides..."

"I used to let my own fear keep me from getting what I wanted," I tell him. "There is no way I'm letting *your* fear hold me back. I can't. I won't. It's not fair."

"I know," he whispers. "I want you to be happy. Both of you."

"Thank you."

"Emi, just be sure," he advises. "I know you say you're ready, but really consider everything before..."

"I have," I tell him. "And it's done, already. I have made this commitment to him already, Chris. I have. Mentally and emotionally, I have," I add confidently.

"But, Emi–"

"But nothing, Chris... Except butt *out*, please," I tell him. "I'm fine. I'll be fine."

"Well, when you realize you're not," he says, presumptive, "I'll be here for you. We all will be."

"I'm a little offended by that."

"Don't be, Emi. I just think that it's impossible to put it all behind you, just like that. You'll still need us. And I just want you to know we'll be here."

I nod, still moderately frustrated but letting it go. "Where did you and Jack leave things?" I ask.

"Unfinished," he answers.

"Will you just let us handle this?"

"Do I have a choice?"

"No," I tell him. "You really don't."

"Then okay," he shrugs.

"Chris, I love you, and I really do appreciate your concern."

"I love you, too."

"And I'm sorry that you lost your friend," I tell him, feeling the need to acknowledge his real pain. "It's okay for you to be sad. I need to be happy, though. So please let me try."

"Okay."

"Come downstairs with me?" I ask.

"I don't trust Jack with the steaks," he mumbles. "And I don't know this Brian guy at all," he jokes.

Brian and Jack have joined Jen and Anna in the kitchen, and are all listening to an apparently funny story that Brian is telling. I gather after hearing a few seconds of it that it's something that happened one night on a date he and my sister went on.

Jack twists open a bottle of beer and picks up a freshly-poured glass of wine, and brings them both to me and Chris. He and my brother make eye contact. They both force smiles... it's a peace offering, but I can tell this isn't over yet.

The house begins to fill up quickly once the first guests arrive. I recognize many of them from their wedding, most of them co-workers of my brother and sister-in-law. I see a few decks of cards and some poker chips laying on the coffee table in the living area. Jack lets me know he's going back on the patio for round two with my brother, and I decide to check out my competition.

"It's Emi, right?" an attractive man says to me, standing up to shake my hand. "I'm Cory. We met at the wedding."

"Yes, hi, Cory, how are you?"

"I'm good, thank you."

"Are you having fun?"

"Sure, just watching the game. We were thinking about playing some poker. You any good?"

"I'm not too bad." I look at Anna, her eyes encouraging me to stay with the guests. "I'll play. Does anyone need any refills before we start?"

"I'll get them," Anna says, coming into the room to take orders. Four other guests join in the poker game, all guys. We all introduce ourselves, letting one another know how we know the hosts.

I fold the first two hands, trying to figure out the tells of my fellow players. Nate had taught me how to play poker a few years back before a trip to Vegas... he was quite good and had a lot of good tips for me.

By the third hand, I have a few decent cards and decide to play it through. At the end of the round, it's just down to me and Cory. I am holding a straight, and I feel pretty confident it's the winning hand. I raise one last time, and he calls the bet. We both flip over our cards. He has two pair.

"Was that bluffing?" I taunt him. "I knew you didn't have anything."

"I was hoping for the full house," he explains, pushing all the chips toward me. "I don't mind getting beat by the pretty woman, though." I blush and look away, shuffling the cards for the next hand. Everyone plays the next round, and one of the other guys wins the hand. Cory folds at the beginning of the next round.

"I'm thirsty. Emi, your glass is empty, do you want some more?"

"Sure," I say, handing Cory the glass as he stands up to go to the kitchen. I win that round and all the guys are starting to banter about the girl playing poker.

"I was taught by the best," I tell them, shrugging my shoulders. Taught by him, but I never could beat him. I remember that, when he was alive, I used to tease him about how lucky he was in life. I smile wistfully to myself.

"Here you go," Cory says as he sets the wine down in front of me. "To winning," he says, toasting me. I raise my glass and drink. He continues with his competitive teasing, and quickly, the other four players lose all their chips and are watching Cory and me battle it out. I can tell Cory is interested in me, his flirting obvious. I know I should probably stop him, or tell him I'm with Jack, but it's harmless fun... he probably knows that already, anyway. Maybe he's just naturally flirtatious... maybe I'm reading too much into it.

"Steaks are on!" Chris announces to the room, his jaw clenched and nostrils flaring. All the other guests get up to fix their plates. Cory's making modest bets, so I sense he doesn't have a good hand. Plus, he keeps taking sips of his beer, just small ones... I think that's his tell.

I look up into the kitchen and see Jack talking animatedly to Chris and Anna. He makes brief eye-contact with me but looks away quickly. They seem to be having a pretty intense conversation. Jack looks strained, upset, a way I've never really seen him before.

"All in," I announce to Cory, pushing all my chips in, my attention now diverted to the conversation in the next room. I want to know what's being said... what's going on. My competitor goes all in, too, and I end up winning the poker game. When I stand up, he does the same and pulls me into an awkward hug.

"Good game," he says. "I guess I'm the loser... help me turn my luck around and say you'll go out with me."

"Emi," Jack calls to me as he walks in the room. "I was going to go for a walk. Would you like to come?"

"Um, yes," I say, walking toward Jack and looking back at Cory. "I'm sorry, I'm flattered," I tell Cory. "But I'm with him." Jack takes my hand and helps me with my coat. The sun is out, so hopefully the snow is melting and the sidewalks aren't too slippery. As we walk out the door, he pulls my cap from his pocket and hands it to me. I put it on, adjusting my hair, and when I look up, I see a strange exchange between Chris and Jack.

We begin to walk up the block, Jack completely silent, looking forward, biting his lip, holding my gloved hand in his.

"What's going on?" I ask.

"Nothing," he says, smiling. "I just wanted to get outside for a bit. It seems to be warming up a little, don't you think?"

"Yes, let's talk about the weather some more," I chide. "What were you and my brother talking about?"

"Nothing," he repeats.

"Really? It looked like you were still arguing about something."

"Chris should mind his own business," he says tersely. People don't normally get to Jack like this... especially his best friend. He releases my hand to run his fingers through his hair.

"What did he say to you?" I question him.

"How are you, Emi?" he asks, seemingly changing the subject. I stop in the middle of the sidewalk.

"I'm good," I tell him before he realizes I'm not next to him anymore. "What did Chris say?" He turns around and comes back to me, taking my hand back.

"Walk with me," he says. "I'm trying to tell you."

"Okay."

"He's concerned about your state of mind," he admits.

"That's silly," I respond. "I'm fine. You know that."

"I think you're fine," he continues. "But he doesn't. He thinks this shouldn't be an easy day for you. He's not sure now's the time for you to be making sweeping declarations about us."

I drop his hand, angry, and begin stomping quickly back toward my brother's house, ready to confront him for continuing to attempt to ruin my day. I thought he and I had an understanding. I thought he was going to let Jack and I work this out on our own. *This has nothing to do with him!*

"Whoa, whoa, whoa," he says, picking me up easily and turning my body back in the other direction. "Calm down."

"No, I'm going to give him a piece of my mind," I struggle with him. He holds my shoulders, attempts to still me.

"You're no match for me," he teases. "I'll always win these," he adds, trying to be funny but unable to relate the humor to me.

"I don't like it when you hold me down like that," I say to him, mad and frustrated, remembering when Colin used to do that to me. I shrug free easily once he realizes he was asserting his power over me.

"I'm sorry, I was just playing," he says. "I didn't mean to be forceful with you. You're right to want to give him a piece of your mind, Em, but will you listen to me before you storm off? I want to talk, just me and you."

"Fine," I say, walking away from him, up the street. His long legs catch him up to me quickly.

"He was just reminding me how fragile you've been... and it's true, you have been."

"God, yes, it's been a tough year, so the fuck what? I'm putting it behind me, Jack. I don't want to look back. I just want to move forward. With you. That's all I want. Don't worry about me, please."

"I'm not, Emi, will you listen for a second?" he asks, stopping me again, squaring his shoulders off with mine. "I told him to back off," he tells me. "That if he ever valued our friendship, he'd let you and me figure this out.

"I know it's been hard. But I have also seen you grow out of this whole experience a whole other person. I just want to assure you that I will never do anything to hurt you. I will never leave you."

Don't fucking say that! He said that, too. You can't know. You can never know. I hold my composure, wanting to scream, to hit... to cry... *I am not that fragile! He is not right about me. I will not let my brother be right about me.* Now he's not only put doubt in Jack's head, but in mine, too.

"I know you can put on a brave face, Emi. I know that. I just want to know that you're not doing that right now. I want to know that you're really okay. That you trust me, that you are choosing me. That you love me."

"I do," I say, a little defiance coming out in my tone. "I am."

"If at any point, Emi, any point... you change your mind about *anything*... I want you to speak up and tell me. Period. You need to be ready."

"I *am* ready," I cry, tears and all. "I've been ready. I'm committed to you." I feel betrayed by my brother. "You don't believe me?" I ask, sad.

"Of course I believe you, Emi," he assures me. "Just know that I'm not going to take your decision and run with it. I'll be with you, every step along the way. If you say stop, we stop."

"I won't," I plead.

"Okay, then, we have nothing to worry about then. Now why are you crying, love?" He pulls my cap down tighter over my cold, red ears, kissing my cheek gently. His demeanor isn't soothing me like he clearly intends it to.

"I'm just so mad at him!" I say through gritted teeth.

"Let's make a pact, right here," he suggests. "We file his concerns away, and we don't let him get to us. We don't let him ruin our day. Period. And we both have conversations with him in the future, asking him to let us handle things on our own.

"I mean, let's face it. Aside from Anna, we're the two people closest to him. He feels entrenched in this. He feels like he has a lot at stake, too. But you and I know–" he pauses, "and what he *doesn't* know– is how we really feel about each other. That's going to take some time."

"I guess it's sort of our fault he doesn't know," I add. "But it's not any of his business," I continue stubbornly.

"It kind of is," Jack argues. "Or at least it has been up until now. He's taken care of you this year. He's been my most trusted friend since college. We just need to assure him that we can take it from here, and that whatever happens between us, it won't change our relationship with him."

I nod in agreement.

"But those conversations can come later. Let's drop it for today," he says. "And let's celebrate their new house, and give him the support he needs, and let's get to know your sister's new boyfriend. He's pretty funny."

"Good," I smile finally. "She needs someone to make her laugh. I hope she's finally past all the ones who have made her cry."

"He's made a good first impression," he tells me. "You ready to go back?"

"I guess so," I sigh, wiping the cold tears from my cheeks. He links his elbow in mine and leads me back toward their house. "I'm more ready to go home, though," I mumble.

"We will, soon enough. How late did you want to stay tonight? Did you want to ring in the New Year with everyone?"

"Honestly?" I ask, slowing my pace.

"Of course."

"I'd like it to just be the two of us. I want to kiss you at midnight, and I don't want anyone to take that away from me."

He stops short, taking my face in his warm hands, understanding my meaning. "Oh, Emi," he whispers, his voice thick with concern. "No one is going to take that away from you." *Again, the tears form. Nate didn't make it until midnight.* I sniffle quietly.

"I'm okay," I assure Jack.

"I know," he says confidently. I stand on my tiptoes, anticipating his willing lips on mine. *I love it when he kisses me like that.*

A few new faces greet us when we get back to Chris's house. Cory is gone, so no awkward conversation there. Sadly, Jen and Brian also left after eating lunch, opting to spend the afternoon with Clara. They were apparently planning to come back later tonight, once Clara was put to bed with the sitter.

I offer to fix Jack a plate of food and suggest he go into the living room to watch the hockey game on TV with the other guys.

"Everything okay?" Anna asks once I'm in the kitchen.

"It will be," I tell her, smiling. "We don't want to fight with Chris anymore today."

"He doesn't want to argue anymore, either," she confesses. "He just loves you both, you know."

"I know." I smile sincerely. "I love your house, by the way. I'll like it better when it's not filled with drama, but it's very cute."

"Thank you," she responds. "Did you like the guest bedroom? I decorated that with you in mind."

"I love it, but why me?"

"I don't know. If I had to pick someone to be our guest, it would always be you. Plus, I know you'll be hanging out here a lot."

"Why do you say that?"

"You didn't see the wine cellar in the basement," she teases, her eyes sparkling.

"No way. Really?"

"Stocked with your favorite and about a hundred bottles of other things for you to try."

"Okay, I'm going to take Jack his food, but then you're taking me down there. I have to see this."

After I deliver Jack his lunch, Anna leads the way down to the basement, where an entire wall is devoted to various wines.

"My god, where did you get all of this?"

"Shopping spree last week," she says. "It was in the designer's budget, by the way," she winks.

"Smart designer. Which one should we try?" I ask, excited.

"You can pick whichever one you'd like."

"No, let's find one together. We'll share the bottle to celebrate."

"Um, Emi?" she stalls.

"Yeah?" I pull bottles off the shelf, reading the labels, trying to find something with an intriguing name.

"Emi, can I tell you something?" she asks.

"Of course."

"You can't tell a soul. Not Chris, not Jen... not even Jack."

"Okay, of course." I put the bottles I was holding back, taking note of her serious tone.

"I'm pregnant," she tells me, a happy smile spreading across her face, her hands both covering her tiny stomach.

"What?" I ask, surprised and elated. "Really?"

"Really," she cries.

"How far along? Wait, Chris doesn't know?"

"Only two months," she explains. "I haven't told Chris yet. We decided to try right away. But miscarriages are common in my family, so I'm really afraid... I just want to wait a little longer before making it public, and getting his hopes up. But I had to tell someone."

"Anna, my god, congratulations," I embrace her, warmly. "I'm sure everything will be fine. I just feel it. You're going to be incredible parents."

"Still, promise you won't tell."

"Sweetie, of course I won't!"

"That's why we haven't decorated the second guest bedroom upstairs. Since we're theoretically 'trying,' we decided not to jinx things. I almost spilled it when we were debating what to do with it earlier this month."

"I am so happy for you." I hug her again. "How are you feeling? No morning sickness?"

"No."

"No cravings?"

"Not yet," she says.

"Is there anything I can do for you? I could go to your next doctor's appointment with you, if you want."

"Oh, Emi," she says. "I'm so happy you're excited about this. I was so worried it would make you... sad..."

"Don't be silly, Anna," I assure her. "I couldn't be happier! Please, don't give what happened to me a second thought. You just better let me spoil the baby as much as I want."

"You better!" she laughs. "That's what good aunts do!"

"You can ask Jen," I tell her. "Where do you think Clara got every last one of those princess dresses she won't stop wearing?"

"I don't know if I want a boy or a girl," she confesses. "I really think I'd be okay either way."

"Will you find out?"

"Find out what?" Chris says, descending down the stairs. Anna loses all the color in her face, afraid he's heard us talking.

I pull a bottle from the shelf and show it to him. "I was asking her to find out where we can get more of this one. I had it at a restaurant a few weeks ago, but can't find it anywhere in the city." He takes the bottle and looks at the label while I study his face. *He didn't hear.* I shake my head at Anna and smile.

"Of course, I'll find out," she stammers. "I think I kept all the receipts. I'll check them out later this week."

"Did you find one you want to try, Em?" he asks, his eyes softer now, probably a few beers helping to ease the tension a bit.

"Yeah, this one," I pull another off the shelf.

"Did you find one, hon?" he asks Anna.

"I've already got something started upstairs," she lies.

"Let's go back up," he says. "They're playing poker for real cash now. Should be good."

"Jack's in?" Anna asks.

"Yep," Chris smiles.

"Is that bad?" I ask, having never played with Jack before.

"It's good for everyone else," he says. "Jack doesn't have a good poker face. He's just too honest."

"Oh, crap," I say, following my brother and sister-in-law up the stairs. "I've got to see this."

"How much did you lose?" I ask him on the drive back to his house a few hours later.

"I'm not talking about it, Emi," he laughs. "Just a little pocket change."

"There were hundreds on that table," I argue. "I could have bought quite a few new pairs of shoes with that money."

"I'll buy you all the shoes you want," he concedes, "as long as you don't bring this up ever again."

"Well, then, my lips are sealed," I motion to him, zipping them shut. "I don't think you know what you're getting yourself into," I whisper through my tight lips, calculating in my mind the total cost of the four pairs of shoes I fell in love with, just this week.

"You know, Emi?" he asks rhetorically. "I don't think you know what *you're* getting yourself into." He smiles smugly. "Hey, by the way," he changes the subject. "My friend Rick called earlier and asked us to come out to his restaurant for a drink and dessert before midnight. I told him we would... is that okay?"

"Where is it?"

"Just a couple blocks away. We can walk."

"I guess," I force a smile, shrugging. "But midnight, it's just us, right?"

"We'll be home well before then," he promises. I can't help but worry, though. The thought of being out there, our lives in the hands of others, at the mercy of strangers...

"Okay..."

When we get to his house, I unpack my duffel bag, laying out the two outfits I had stuffed inside, debating on what to wear tonight. I take a deep breath, resigned to go along with Jack's plan despite the nagging feeling in the pit of my stomach. "What's this restaurant like?" I ask.

"Casual. It's more like a bar with really good food."

"Okay... do you have an iron?" I look around his bedroom, having decided on the wool skirt and button down shirt that is very wrinkled after a day folded up in the bag.

"Yes, in the basement... in the pink room."

"You mean the *girl's* room. Lame place for an iron," I roll my eyes at him in jest, lightening the mood. "Bring 'em up right."

"Hey," he laughs. "I iron my own clothes. I can just see the television better from that room."

"Whatever," I laugh, bringing the blouse to the basement with me. Taking his suggestion, I figure out his remotes and somehow manage to turn the huge TV on. I look through his vast DVD collection and pick out a romantic comedy that I like. I sit on the couch while the iron heats up, watching the first few minutes of the movie.

The steam on the iron reminds me that I came down here for an actual task. My eyes glued to the TV, I mindlessly iron my favorite shirt, coming dangerously close to burning it or my hand a few times, distracted. I hang it on the door knob and head to one of the reclining chairs to watch some more of the movie.

"What are you doing?" he asks. I smile, happy that he joined me.

"Watching a movie," I say coyly, a part of me hoping he will settle in next to me and stay beside me all night. "This is a good part, come sit down." He mockingly sighs and takes the seat next to me, reclining it at the same angle mine is positioned.

I curl up in the crook of his arm, my leg draped over his hips. His hand strokes it lightly as we watch the movie together.

When we emerge from the basement after the movie is over, I'm surprised to see how quickly the afternoon has turned into evening. Jack starts to get ready as I fix him a drink downstairs. Admittedly, I have other things in mind, though, and start putting my plan into action. I doubt it will take much to sway him. I set the drink down on a coaster on his dresser and help him loosen his tie for a little more casual look.

"You look gorgeous," I say to him, unbuttoning his top button.

"Thanks... and for the drink, too. Are you trying to get me drunk, Emi?" he asks.

"I don't know what you're talking about," I smile as I walk toward the bathroom to change my clothes.

"I don't believe you, but thank you, anyway."

I get dressed and touch up my make-up, smiling at my reflection before heading into the bedroom. Knee-high boots, check. Thigh-high hose, check. Flirty wool skirt pulled up a little higher than it's intended, check. Crisp, black, button down shirt, strategically fastened, check. Hair looking oh-so-troublesome in pig-tails, check. Red lipstick, check. Perfume, check.

He laughs when I emerge.

"Amazing," he says, a look of confusion on his face, "but I think your buttons are a little askew."

"Are they?" I ask innocently. "I can't tell... can you fix them?"

"My pleasure," he says, using my hair to pull me closer into his body. He kisses my neck gently as he unbuttons my shirt to correct my purposeful error.

I inhale sharply as I feel his icy thumbs venture just beneath my dark lace bra. "Is that cold?" he asks, removing his thumbs and placing his hands lightly on top of the bra.

"Just a little," I lie. "I'll be warm in no time."

"This is nice," he comments, tracing the outline of the undergarment.

"Is it?" I ask. "I was just hoping it matches..."

"Matches... what?" he asks, his hand traveling to the hem of my skirt. I slap it playfully.

"Jack, what on earth do you think you're doing?"

"Oh, you are *not* playing fair again," he says. "I see how this is going to be." He slowly buttons up my shirt correctly as he kisses my lips. I unbutton the top one to show a little more cleavage. He pulls the shirt aside just a tad to kiss the top of my breast, then looks at me with a warning glance and re-buttons it seconds later. "That one's mine," he whispers.

I go back into the bathroom and touch up my make-up once more, stalling. It's already past eleven. "So you're set on going out?" I ask Jack, slightly disappointed.

"One drink," he says, checking his watch, amused by my impatience. "I told Rick we would stop by. We just need to make an appearance. He wants to meet you."

"Alright, then... let's go." He leads me downstairs and out the front door, and as I proceed down the steps, he locks the door behind us. When he catches up with me, he takes my hand and stops my forward motion.

"Forgot something," he says, leaning in for a kiss. I playfully push him away.

"Okay, if you can't follow through with this, you can't do this until we get back. I can't take your teasing me any longer."

"*I'm* teasing *you*?" he asks, disbelieving.

"What are you implying?" I ask, completely innocent.

"Withholding kisses from me, huh? Is that how we're going to do this?"

"We could go back inside... right now..." my thoughts linger, my hopes and intentions obvious, as I attempt to pull him back toward the house. He stops and looks at me, smiling.

"You're adorable," he says. "Completely adorable." He sighs. "Please, kiss me, Em." I can't deny him any longer– I want to kiss him just as badly. After his lips have left my muscles weak, he picks me up and carries me back toward the house. "You win."

A triumphant "Yea!" escapes my mouth, followed by a relieved sigh. He continues to laugh as we kiss more, all the way up the stairs and into the foyer, continuing on into his bedroom.

I look up at him, curious, breathless... *ready*... All of a sudden, his phone rings. He checks to see who is calling, and then looks at me, hopeful, apologizing.

"It's my father," he says. "I'm sure it will just be a second."

I nod and smile, taking a seat on his bed, listening to the one-sided conversation.

"Well, are you at the computer right now?" Jack asks. "Well go turn it on. I'll log in and see if I can take a look... okay, Dad, hold on." He covers the mic on the phone and apologizes quietly to me. "Computer crisis," he laughs. "It's always the end of the world with him if something doesn't work like it should. I'll be back in a few minutes... make yourself at home. Do you want a drink?"

"I'm fine, I'll get something," I whisper, encouraging him to tend to his phone call. I follow him downstairs, veering off into the kitchen as he makes his way into the office and boots up his computer. I find an open bottle of wine and pour a glass, taking it back upstairs with me. Here's my time to mentally prepare. I know I'm making the right decision. I love him, I do. But as the night wears on and the hour gets closer to midnight, I can't help but think back to last year, to the engagement party... to the night that Nate died. Is it wrong to want to be with Jack tonight?

Is Chris right? Should I give this day to Nate, to honor him? Haven't I done that all year? He's had practically every day, some more fully than others, but every day I've mourned him. Can't I put it behind me? Can I move forward? Isn't it time for me to start a new life with someone else? After all, today is just a day, another date on the calendar, and time passes so quickly... and I don't want to go another day without Jack. I glance up at the clock. Eleven-thirty. *Eleven-thirty.*

"Eleven-thirty," I hear his distant voice in my head. "We should be able to make it back to the room by midnight."

Eleven-thirty. We didn't make it back by midnight. Only one of us made it back at all. He was gone so quickly. It was all over so fast.

As if in real time, I recount the events. I offer him candy... he suggests I open the other bag... the small giraffe... the red light... his velvety voice, declaring his love... I cry, pulling the string again... I kiss him... green light... acceleration... bright light... screeching tires... the young boy's frightened face... Nate's peaceful smile, unaware... my scream... the impact... the smells and the quiet... his moans barely audible above the silence, and how odd it seemed to me at the time...

Love ya, Em, he had said his final words to me in the car... or was it in his bed amidst the blinding sunlight the following morning? I remember the cruel dream that had me believing everything was fine... the one I lived blissfully with for three days while I fought with the reality, my consciousness.

The clock shows eleven-thirty-three. His eyes haunt me. I try to blink the image away, close my eyes tightly, the tears still finding their way out. I lie down on the bed facing the window, away from the doorway. A deluge of past conversations rush in and out violently. Pillow talk to fights to just boring, run-of-the-mill discussions. How he loved me. How he thought I should change an illustration. How he liked his latte. How he hated to drive. How he wanted me to be happy.

How he wanted me to be happy...

I want that, too. I can have that. Jack *is* my happiness. I breathe in and out deeply, trying to compose myself, knowing he'll walk through that door any minute. He'll know that I've been crying. I just want him to hold me, love me, take care of me. I want that now more than ever.

"They were supposed to do the webcam thing with Kelly's kids at midnight, and it wasn't working," he says as he enters the bedroom, his voice trailing off as he takes in the sight of me. "Emi? Are you okay?"

I don't look back, instead waiting for him to come to me. He kneels down in front of me. Desperately, I pull myself up to meet him, attack his lips with mine. He grabs me firmly by the shoulders and holds me back. "Are you okay?" he repeats.

"Yes," I tell him. "Jack, I love you."

"I love you, too, Emi."

"I want you." After I unbutton his shirt, he helps to remove his arms from the sleeves. I take his undershirt off and run my fingers over his chest. I then remove my own shirt and sit in front of him, watching him intensely. He hesitates as I wait for him to unfasten my bra. The concern in his eyes makes mine begin to water again. I know he cares so deeply about me, wants me to be better, be okay, be happy. I will be happy with him. I can be and will be. I will leave this sorrow behind me. Jack can help me put the pieces of my life back together again. I try to stave off my cries, but I succumb to the lump in my throat and quietly weep. I cry with sadness for all I have lost, but am overwhelmed by the feeling that it will all be okay soon.

"Emi, please don't cry."

"Jack, I need you," I choke out as the tears flow. "I love you and I need you. Please, I need you." He takes me in his arms, kisses me deeper and picks me up off the bed, pulling the sheets back and laying me down again, my head resting on the pillows.

"I know, Emi. I need you, too." He lies down beside me, touching me, finally removing my bra and kissing my breasts. I lift his head so his eyes meet mine, pull his body onto me. His strong, warm embrace comforts me, his fingers awaken sensations on every patch of skin they touch.

I just want to be happy again.

Feeling broken for the better part of a year, I finally begin to feel whole again.

On the brink of slumber, I close my eyes, the vision of Jack's bedroom dissolving into the night. Shrouded in the darkness of his loft, softly lit only by the moon, I see Nate one last time standing in front of the door. My stomach jumps a bit, fearing the loneliness that usually follows this particular dream, but the warmth of strong arms around me lets me know that I am not alone this time.

As if he senses my fear, Jack pulls me closer to him as he sleeps. His hands clasp mine, and in that moment, the ending of the poem is finally clear.

One transcendent kiss,

that later makes lovers take

soft breaths, holding hands.

I swear I can hear Nate whisper the words to me from across the room, as if he's handing them over to me as a gift. He's smiling at me.

Longing for something, *someone*, I nestle deeper into Jack's embrace, and as the bright light from the hallway floods the loft, I can see Nate clearly now, see his warm eyes and friendly grin. He nods slowly a few times.

"Thank you," I say, sorrow stealing my voice. I struggle to smile back at Nate while a tear drops from my eye before he breathes one simple word to me.

Goodbye.

He turns slowly, walking into the luminous corridor, the door shutting behind him. My heart aches. It hurts more than it should.

"Nate," I plead to him, willing him back, whispering louder than I intend to. Jack stops breathing, and his muscles tense around me. I hear him swallow quietly.

"What is it, Emi?" he finally asks after a few moments of silence. He lets go of my hand, pulling my hair over my shoulder and out of my face. I close my eyes naturally, and concentrate hard to steady my breathing. He shifts behind me, and I feel him leaning over me, looking at me. "Em?"

I lie still, hoping he believes I'm asleep... *praying* he didn't hear me. One more tear betrays me, falling onto my cheek, and I can't help but think that it's really betraying *him*; that *I'm* betraying Jack. I *can't* hurt him. I *do* love him. *I do.*

He sighs heavily, and I barely feel his finger wipe the moisture away. He lies back down and holds my hand again.

A strange emptiness settles over me as I feel Nate's absence around me. I swallow back more tears that threaten to come, but I fight them with all of my strength. They're simply not welcome here anymore.

Goodbye, Nate.

Unsure I'll ever be able to completely move forward– beyond the sadness that continues to plague me– I repeat one request in my head over and over again as I try to sleep.

Let me go.

WORKS BY LORI L. OTTO

Not Today, But Someday (prequel to Emi Lost & Found)
Lost and Found (Emi Lost & Found book one)
Time Stands Still (Emi Lost & Found book two)
Never Look Back (Emi Lost & Found book three)

Number Seven (prequel to Steven War & Peace)

Contessa (Choisie book one)
Olivia (Choisie book two)
Dear Jon(Choisie book three)
Livvy (Choisie book four)

Emi Lost & Found and Choisie series Extras

Crossroads (prequel to Love Will)
Love Like We Do (Side A)
Love Like We Do (Side B)
Love Will

SPECIAL THANKS TO

John T. Perry
Shirley Otto
Clarinda Alcalen

Christi Allen Curtis
Katrina Boone
Alex Wheelus

Angela Meyer
Nikki Haw

Melissa Dean, Annie Walsh, Audrey Kay, Casey Corn, Cheryl Dent, Christen Fiermonti, Courtney Smith, Diana Arnau, Erin Spencer, Jamie Taliaferro, Jo Ann Stevens, Kelli Spear, Lea Burn, Michelle Ochoa, Stacy Bundy, Stephanie Cobb, and Tiffany DeBlois

17759060R00217

Printed in Poland
by Amazon Fulfillment
Poland Sp. z o.o., Wrocław